The Saltwater Ponygirl

On a tiny island called Chincoteague,

Big dreams are about to come true...

For a girl named Minnow,

and her pony Marshy.

A Novel by

Starlight Lilly Cherrix

Dedication

This one's for the man who raised me with can-do and to always follow your dreams. I love you Papa...

Also, to those with dreams – follow them! Listen to your heart – and enjoy the adventure!

Chapter One

The bonnie-lasses. In the pirate world, there was just cutthroat. Maybe Minnow's strategy was all wrong?

She growled grumbled-sighed and kept pushing the lawnmower forward, harder. She could mow her heart out, but still, girls aren't permitted to ride in the pony penning roundup – because it's tradition?

Minnow knows there's nothing mean intended. Yet, she contests. Girls. Still. Aren't. Permitted.

Maybe she was right to start with, a second ago. Mutiny may be her answer.

But that was still against the law nowadays.

There was no specific roleplay to speak of in piracy. The *pirates* were advanced in that singular sense. Skill prevailed, and barbary ruled – ok, so Minnow didn't care for the barbary bit.

Minnow's sister Windy could help with that mutiny on her mind. She's been fascinated with piracy and ships since she was a little squirt knee-high to a peg-leg, watching and reading everything about them she could get her doubloon dreaming hands on.

Today she is still thirsty explorer to her pirate archive on her side of the room, a daily visual proof to anyone in doubt! Which once anyone meets Windy, there isn't really a tingle of question to rub away.

The shark tooth she found and strung into a necklace at the young pirating age of five, never removing unless badly sunburned, is another indicator to one who is new to Windy. The pirate talk and mischief that is shortly revealed – explains enough said as much as it raises eyebrows.

Whenever they played pretend, which wasn't so much anymore – lots more of mowing, Minnow thought sarcastically. Not that she didn't enjoy mowing. On the contrary, she preferred mowing to many other chores – mostly those that took her indoors instead of outdoors.

Just then her blade, the shell of which Windy had painted teethe and eyes on and named Mako a long time ago, hit a thick cohabitation of tall-weedyness, forcing her to force the mower back and forth over the same spot multiple times. Between its stubbornness and hers, it's thickness and her minnow everything, Minnow battled nature with the one big gift she'd been born with – lots of heart!

"Eat the grass!" Minnow shouted. Normally she didn't shout at Mako, normally Mako ate everything in its path just like the ocean goat its named after that'll try anything once or twice – or three times.

Anyway, Mako was half her age, so maybe in machinery years he was getting cranky – or just feeding off Minnow's frustration today.

If that's so, goodness knows how Mako would behave for her little sister if Pirate Briny Wind was mowing. There'd not only be no safe blade of grass with her pirate mentality, and Mako her crewmate – insects, small reptilians, and dandelion would do wise to scatter! Before she, before Mako, defined another meaning of scatter.

Windy' play name was Captain Windy Brine, or Pirate Briny Wind. She had one good eye and one sea air dried and working peg-leg, courtesy of the fifteen-foot shark that'd tangled with the wrong pirate. She skinned the chomper, had a pirate buffet as any decent pirate should do, used the course hide as a cape, and then at nine years old switched to telling everyone it was for boot and arm chaps, which doubled as a blade sharpener And, thus her reputation as the young pirate girl who had cut her teeth pirating on a shark and sharpened her blade on the same shark, rang through every pirate and ship portal Pirate Briny Wind could think up.

But the scar down *Captain Windy Brine's* cheek harkened from the pirate who had stolen her heart, and then her ship; based of course on her younger sister's ex-boyfriends, as they happened. Best not to go into that.

But her yarns and close calls as Captain Windy Brine and Pirate Briny Wind grew, and still grow, more fantastical, and even plain (always stowaway when they were pretending) Minnow would join their family's uproarious laughter that doubled their tummies until they hurt!

Windy and Summer had the water baby genes. Three sisters were never so different and yet never more similar, nor closer. Well, with Summer. Windy and Minnow didn't get along very well, as they always did with Summer.

As Minnow had mentioned, they were all so different and yet never more similar.

For example, while Minnow enjoyed kayaking and helped out in their family business *We Are Adventure Excursions*, which had been affectionally named since forever by the girls as simply just the kayak shop, Summer's dream was to one day run the kayak shop.

The kayak shop faced Assateague, old and vibrant with life and color Minnow's family brought to it. Bright orange with electric lime trimming, and poison ivy draping both sides and curling along the back in the summer; it was storybook, treehouse, outpost, oasis, discovery, and home.

Display kayaks that were no longer of use on the water stood like entrance pillars, strapped upright to pilings Dad sunk himself when she was still learning to walk. The sign Mom painted to display We Are Adventure Excursions, Tours, Kayak Rentals, Decoys, and with the aids of cousins helped Dad mount on the front lower center of the roof, was chipped and weathered, and the more attractive for it.

The Kayak Stonehenge arrayed the lawn next to the straight-in clamshell parking that crossed the T clamshell gravel drive parallel to the front of the kayak shop. The awning offered shade and the decking less than six or so inches off the ground stayed cool.

The deck was so long that Mom had installed one set of wooden rails stretching out from the shop towards the marsh to hold kayaks up, and offer kayak storage underneath. Either side afforded a fleet of kayaks the sisters slid easily out for loading the truck and back in for the meantime between uses. The hose wound on the large hook screwed to the wall under the plastic brochure rack and Mom's colorful hand painted sign displaying am and pm tour times, rentals, and prices per hour per single or tandem.

It was Minnow's home. Summer's dream. And Windy' too.

Windy pictured herself as being Summer's top guide, and one day she would be – if she slacked off on the whole *walk the plank, Polly want a cracker, hang him by the yardarm*, side of piracy thing in front of the customers.

Blond hair the colors of amber and yellow honey blended together, Summer's hair was three hands longer than Minnow's hair, which came down to her shoulders. She always wore it in a ponytail threaded through the hole in her ballcap when she was in the kayak shop or on the water. Ever the true kayaker. Let down at the end of the day, Summer's hair rippled silky and wavy on its own without any brushing or special shampooing, until the salt wind got a hold of it and then like the water ripples, became tangled waves splashing into each other.

Windy' hair, gold brown, was almost dark with a red tint, and she wore it to the middle of her back. Unlike Minnow's, her hair had a natural straightness and the wind had to work twice as hard with hers to mess it up.

Minnow's hair was a type of blond she'd never seen with anyone else before. Coffee brown with lighter streaks of blond from being in the sun all day every day. There was no one spared from the salt wind drying or tangling their hair, but Minnow didn't mind.

Summer was the taller among them and the most responsible and athletic. Being the second oldest, and just by nature, Minnow came in second towing the extra ropes of being responsible and being expected to set an example.

Summer was more natural kayaking and working in the shop than Minnow. Sure, it was home, and she enjoyed it most of the time. But her dream was different from Summer and Windy. And it called to her the way the marsh whispering with the breeze at night tugged on her heart and felt like it was calling her name.

For while growing up clutching a paddle in one hand, she clutched a horse brush in the other. She daydreamed of horses. Night and day. In school, she's sketching in the corners of her notebook while she's supposed to be jotting notes Mrs. Simpson's explaining from the whiteboard.

Summer is like a kayak. Stable.

Windy, as Minnow established, is the heart-wide-open one – for all her flaws and what make her rare.

Minnow is squished somewhere in the middle – for while Windy still has a lot to learn, she, including Summer, are living their dream.

Minnow knew what her big dream was – just within reach but out of her touch.

Yet sometimes Minnow's biggest test was when she dealt with Windy, and being that bigger sister when she could muster herself up for it. It didn't help that they were just two years apart. Most of the time Minnow felt rivaled in mustering patience for Windy only by the endurance of "no's", summers past.

Their tempers ranged from hot, warm, to lukewarm. But if pressed, at the right time Summer could be hotter. Mostly in a protective predicament. She rarely had the blow up or lack of control over her intensity that the girls had. Windy was too unpredictable and chili pepper spontaneous to temper herself to a certain degree at any time except instant hot. Which made her the biggest teacher of them all, in a lemon cookie twist of irony; she was the continuous example of what not to say or do or how to do or put things and what happened when you did.

Minnow had sort of had the advantage in that respect. She's averted serious uh oh' just by watching Windy.

So, in a small two story tan house on the east side of the island, with a kayak shop to explore the outside world in from meeting customers who were people from all over the world, and with that adventure that came from being on the water, feeding their curiosities and imaginations – and for Minnow, there was of course Marshy – laughter, tempers, rambunctiousness and love filled the house they called home. The home with the front door that read *Our Happy Happy Happy!* in fun, loopy script faded by the sun, which they all took turns repainting every changeup season.

Minnow was a water baby like her sisters – but somehow Minnow was born with horse genes nobody else had. With the name like Minnow, the irony didn't escape her. But she was named after being born so small and underweight, not from any expectations that she'd be a water baby. But Minnow does love water; the saltwater, the ocean, and the horses born from it. Like their ancestors were reborn from it when their Spanish Galleon shipwrecked on the shoals in the middle of a nor'easter.

And now today, just like she was, they're born to it.

Minnow was a saltwater ponygirl. Through and through. But there was a minnow-little of the pirate, or being Windy' sister, a *tad* of her sister's piracy, flowing in her veins yet.

Minnow had decided and she was determined that this summer she was going to ride in the pony penning roundup. She just didn't yet know how she was going make that dream come true.

Minnow chewed on this thought, and dilemma, as she mowed. Figuring she'd still be hatching the decipher to her antique yet ever young and present code box when she hauled her sore bony bod into the shower, sticky, sweaty, stuck and matted with the sweet but itching grass bits and a nurtured does of irritation. The deciphering to this relic dilemma that is the key to unlocking what is the next step in her lifelong quest, halted by this code box and struggle to open it, is something she could scribble maps about or mostly tomes on otherwise how "Not" to succeed. Eventually if she doesn't hit on the answer right away, she'll know "*an archive roomful*" of avenues and lost tunnels and where the booby traps are, which ways not to go, that won't yield a drop of mercy or clue dials to turn on the code box that don't fail; set off other booby traps or situations that aren't a pleasure to get through and wind her back up where she started. Deciphering the code box. Hatching a plan that works.

Minnow had widely considered with dedication to minuscule detail, and dotingly pursued, every polite option to the point of strategy in her performance of pursuit in the questing. She'd gone to the fire department every year with the same question. They expected her. It'd become a tradition. And as so, a watered-down tactic that'd lost its potential and rung with little to zero effect.

Please and it's my dream? No.

Please and brownies? No.

Please and I'll do anything? No.

No, no, no, no. Nope.

Okay, so not as cut and dry as that. But reliving her past disappointments on top of her most recent one – tiring and discouraging.

Now that Minnow was going on sixteen and with this age as with every next age growing up more day by day, and in her mind, being big sister to a little pirate, exceeding with more capabilities to shoulder more and more responsibility, not to mention being a size up in coffee consumption allowance and saddle-wear than most of the young saltwater ponyboys in their britches half her age – Minnow didn't even have cute going for her!

She begged. *Begged!*

But there wasn't a whisper in the marsh grass of a chance.

It was just tradition.

That's why Windy piracy appealed to Minnow, and *was*, more and more by the second as she mowed. For it was seeming like her last chance, and her only answer now. But she didn't want to ask anyone for help, especially not Windy. She wanted to do this on her own. It was clear from the "no's", of summers past, "no" meant "never", and so Minnow would have to take her dream into her own hands.

Just on the how, Minnow chewed up the lawn with Mower Mako as she chewed on thoughts, searching for the right answer.

When there were no wild patches of grass to chew over, Minnow released the lever on the mower handle. Bird twitters every now and then filled the sudden silence. Minnow's body vibrated from the obnoxious lawnmower, but it was a sensation she braced up to.

Marshy' squeaky whinny drew her attention to her stocky little pony with big knees and spiky black mane and bushy black tail. She hung her chin on the top most rail, giving her a wide-eyed look from the side.

She'd watched her with interest as she chewed clover and grass, and grew anxious for Minnow's attention the longer and harder she mowed.

Minnow smiled through the stickiness and itchiness from bits of grass plastering themselves to her sweaty arms and face, peppering her damp sleeveless shirt. She'd worn jeans to protect her legs and sunglasses to protect her eyes. As she approached Marshy she tipped her sunglass back over her sweat matted hair she'd had the forethought to wind into a bun before getting started.

On her way, Minnow stopped by the veggie garden, a small bed of fresh soil boasting basil, mint, chocolate mint, leeks, onions, tomato, and Marshy' favorite, carrots. Marshy knew just what the tops of them looked like, smelled them through the dirt, and often stepped over the curl of chicken wire fencing and plowed at the carrot section. Sometimes she could even pull it up by the leafy top with only her teeth!

Minnow was partially to blame for her getting into the veggie garden more times than she should. When Marshy was a foal she'd been curious about what the veggie garden was, but her nose was so small and her sense of smell brand-new, that the colliding scents of mint and tomatoes and basil and carrot blended together in one strange new smell. Then she'd seen Minnow pull up long orange sticks by green hair and when she tasted it, she was in love!

As a result, whenever Marshy was out of her paddock and free in the yard with Minnow, Minnow had to watch her closely to make sure she didn't take all of the carrots at once!

But while Mom wasn't looking she let Marshy sniff one or two out and plow and pluck for them herself!

Marshy' paddock sat at the very back end of the wide yet tucked-in yard, set off the tangle of woods and thicket and vine and wild bushes behind their property. Minnow's chore was to keep it trimmed back so that Marshy didn't nibble on something that would harm her or hurt her tummy. But when it came to branches or tree limbs, her woodcarver Mom had to lend a hand. Just recently she'd trusted Minnow to use the chain saw, and for beginners Minnow had gotten to saw some tiny limbs!

She was finally old enough, as well as strong enough to bear the metal weight and hold the chainsaw correctly. She'd been watching Mom use the chainsaw all of her life, so even without Mom's final demonstrations before she handed the machine shark miniature to her, Minnow thought she would've been able to handle it. Still, she'd listened acutely and willingly and absorbed every word of her mother's cautionary instructions and rules. Number one as always, safety first.

Minnow had mowed the ten-foot clearing between the paddock fence and the ornery woods today already, which she diligently kept up on.

Marshy wasn't tall and not very big so she didn't need as much space between the woods as there was to prevent her from sticking her head between the railings and nibbling on trouble, but Minnow didn't take any chances. Marshy was a curious one, and while she'd never escaped her paddock like a horse she knew named Olive did regularly, and when she was free to roam in the yard hardly ever went near the road, Minnow knew it would be only a matter of time before her curiosity got the better of her and she found a way. So, Minnow made sure that didn't happen.

Again, Marshy wasn't a tall pony. Stocky and short and spunky was what she was. As so, her tiny run-in shelter, divided into a stall on one side and a shady hang-out space on the other half, was much more a palace for her than cramped quarters. That was the nice thing about being small, felt Minnow. Everything might be bigger than them, but a world being bigger had more to discover, and fitting into tighter or smaller places left more to explore and have fun with. They didn't need much space to live in; except for the openness of the day, to do all their adventuring in. And living on an island that was a good mentality to have; probably hereditary too. Yet even the island was bigger than small to Minnow and Marshy.

Minnow scratched under Marshy' chin, and she flared her nostrils several times with satisfaction; her eyes still wide with anticipation, as Marshy was always curious about what was around her and interested in anything Minnow was doing.

"We'll think of something girl," Minnow promised, stroking her cheek. Marshy pressed her forelock to Minnow in reply, rubbing up and down and making her laugh. Minnow was the most ticklish person anyone had ever heard of. If a breeze blew slightly that caressed her arms or the hair on the back of her neck, or when

Marshy blew breath on her cheeks as she gave her a kiss, just the whisper of movement or touch and sometimes even sound, and Minnow got tickled.

"Come girl," Minnow insisted to Marshy, her chuckles tempered and subsiding. "I've go to shower; as much as I love grass too, this is really itchy."

Marshy licked her shirt regardless, then the bits of grass on her arms. She cried out in distress and protest for Minnow to come back when she pulled away and backed up after she'd kissed her.

"I'll be back later," she promised Marshy, who continued to carry on even when Minnow was still peeling off her damp and itchy clothes. She climbed onto the washing machine long enough to look out the narrow, stubby window and see that Marshy was pacing the fence, throwing her chin in the air and squeaky crying out for her to come back.

Marshy had lifted Minnow's spirit but the aggravating itchiness of the grass was starting to take a toll again.

Chapter Two

Sad as it was to lose the sweet smell of grass, Minnow scrubbed and rubbed her arms and head ferociously. Scrubbing the grass and with it the sweet summer smell out of her hair to rid herself of this blatant attack of itchiness was something she wouldn't tear up over.

The itchiness had been ferocious and Minnow matched its irritations with ferocity of her own and the squirted attack of citrusy shampoo.

Thanks to the citrusy bubbles and scrubbing, the ferocious itching was thankfully starting to abate.

Bubbles and suds mixed with grassiness and dirt rinsed with the shower water streaming down Minnow, mostly from her hair down her raised arms as she scratched her scalp, feeling like she stepped out of the pages of a book and was becoming human again, where she'd felt like some grass-land creature from a story where trees talk and plants get dressed and stroll.

That's around when she thought she'd sensed motion and felt a draft as if the door was open, and, "Guess what happened today!" blared in her ear.

"I'm in the shower!" Minnow yelled angry and surprised, and not the good kind or sweet side of surprised, tugging the curtain back closed again!

Adding fuel to the words already flying out of Minnow's mouth when Windy huffed out a bored sigh, Minnow shouted, "What if I'd still had shampoo in my hair or on my face!" She emphasized, "It could have gone in my eyes when you scared me!"

"Fine, sorry," Windy apologized with a wince, because Minnow saw her face as she was sliding open the curtain.

"Hey, privacy!" Minnow spun her hip and covered one boob then jerked the curtain closed a second time.

"Oh, come on, I'm your sister," she said a little flatly and a tad annoyed.

Good.

But that stomping response with statement of satisfaction over Windy' tad of annoyance in Minnow's mind, was fleeting. Filled with the compulsion to justify and defend her flustered and angered right to privacy, she replied, "I still *deserve* and I still *want* my Privacy!"

It irritated Minnow that Windy ignored this simple, every person's right concept as much as it seemed to elude her by nature. Minnow could, or has, forgiven Windy' thoughtlessness on account of her carefree way and mostly stubbornness, with an older sister's affection, responsibility, and equal parts reluctant, trying, and give in understanding.

But there was a side of Windy that deliberately ignored and did what she wanted because she just wanted to do what she wanted, and *didn't want* anyone telling her what to do or how to do something, or to that point, what and how not to do something or behave. Especially Minnow. Which suited Minnow fine, but Minnow wasn't going to swim into that minnow trap of feeling bad for standing up for *herself!*

Minnow had the right to her ways too, that Windy trampled or discarded when she felt like it. She also had the right to her privacy and her own feelings, just as Windy.

"I've seen you before; a lot – remember? We're sisters," she said.

"That's not the point! I still have a right to my privacy, and I'd appreciate it if you'd respect that and my privacy when I feel like it!" Minnow stated a little defensively, then in a spurt of anger unhooked the showerhead and sprayed Windy just for a second. She knew what she was doing was wrong but she couldn't stop herself. From inside the shower Minnow heard Windy gasp and continue gasping with utter, initial shock, to anger mixed in as she grappled with that Minnow had actually "sprayed *her*" and she was soaking sopping wet in patches from Minnow's outburst.

Minnow crossed her arms in a stormy huff of satisfaction. That should water down her smugness!

"You got the floor wet!" Now Windy was shouting, and deflecting the root of her anger in a lay of blame rather than give in to acknowledging the actual reason for her spiked emotions and dripping wetness, which was because she'd provoked Minnow by crossing the line on her right to her privacy – for the twenty-thousandth time, Minnow might add!

Like Windy hadn't been the provoker, just a sitting duck!

Typical Windy.

Minnow opened her mouth to respond but Windy added first, "I'm going to tell Mom! Someone could slip, I could've slipped!"

"Then we're even! While you're at it, tell her that you invaded my personal privacy *and* scared me while I was *washing* my hair! Besides, it's my shower, and I got the floor wet, so I'll clean it up!" Minnow shouted, but knew it was half and half with who had the higher ground, as Minnow had lost a huge chunk of her ire's justifiablility the second she lashed out the way she did, and one wrong never equaled a right. Especially not, when the deed invited danger into a situation; what was then unintentional or

22

what was actually intended doesn't cut it, with their parents, and as a fact.

Even though Windy had started it, Minnow had gotten pulled into the gravitational slurp of Windy' world of, *I do what I want regardless of what anyone thinks or cares*, and somehow wound up to blame?

How was this fair!

Minnow knew why, begrudgingly. Because while Minnow shared the blame, it always got back to experience rendered, who was the oldest. It stopped with who was setting the example, or *should* be setting the example. Windy rode that wave of being the younger one, and Minnow wished she'd start showing more, any, meager crumbs of consideration and maturity for once, because at this point Minnow felt up to her neck with the lack. With Windy' attitude and the idea that she could get away with anything!

Minnow should've just stayed mad and not lashed out. She let the situation, and *Windy*, get the better of her.

If she hadn't swum into that minnow trap and done that, then when Windy told Mom Minnow shouted at her or Minnow beat her to it and told Mom in her own words from her side of the upset, why she had shouted at her sister, Windy would get the lecture and a lesson in just this, consideration and maturity. But instead of this lecture in "stop it", and "behave", or "no more", there would be the other point of focus in Mom's lecture, and that zoom-in on person was Minnow.

So, Minnow veered into another tactic with the quick-thinking from years of a sister's experience that might spare her from getting in trouble; harnessing her galloping frustrations and emotion like she's wrestled with them on account of Windy all of her life, which is harder than wrestling the reins atop Marshy. The sweetest pony in the whole wide world except when she catches a whiff of Mom's homemade waffles crisping golden and fluffy delicious in the iron. Minnow might be bony and thin but her will makes up for the small bulges she proudly hails as muscle with a proud smooch planted on each. All her life, to keep up and because she wanted to have some form of tone, Minnow had to develop strength in her arms and what she lacked in muscle mass she made up for in other ways; like speed, being able to squeeze through tinier spaces others couldn't but that smaller people can! She did have resilience, kayaking and climbing everything in sight with her best friend in the whole wide world Matt. But building muscle or growing taller seemed like her patience with Windy; it hasn't come easily or arrived entirely, and there is the gnawing question of, will it ever?

"You're a pirate anyway, you love water!" Minnow tried, even though trying to gain control of this runaway horse, Minnow was grasping at mosquitoes and no-see-ems, hoping she'd open her hands and have caught some. But like she couldn't take back spraying Windy, not even the soft serenity of seedling puffs showering the ease of summer air from the abundant bulrushes, speckled her sweaty grasp.

Up until verbalizing again what was quickly sinking into a pointless effort, Minnow gave the effort her best to be less aggressive in her remark as she attempted to gain control of the outcome of this galloping horse, or the galloping horse inside *her*. But on the cusp of speaking, her galloping feelings bombed, and Minnow faltered. "Tell Mom!" she challenged her little sister. "Tell her you barged in without asking first and how you keep refusing to respect my privacy!" she pushed, piggybacking to add, "Mom and Dad said we have to respect each other's privacy now that we're getting older!"

It was easier to have patience on waiting for a bumblebee that landed on her bare arm to fly away, than it was for Minnow in most ways to have patience with Windy when she did things on purpose for attention or because she could. With that said, it was easier for Windy to respect Marshy' space while she wasn't even eating a stack of waffles than it was for her to see this kind of respect or smart consideration through for her own sister!

Minnow sprung with the image of her privacy invasion being like an oyster or clam or even a crab's space as an example. Windy will dig them out of the mud or surf and boil them without a sign it was at least a little hard. *In those moments, Minnow did wonder if she should check her sister's temperature.* Sometimes Minnow can feel like those mollusks and shellfish, in Windy' grasp.

It was easier respecting Summer, their older sister and her privacy. With Minnow and Windy, there'd always been waves, but whitecaps since Minnow turned fifteen. All those changes had started for her in the fall, very appropriate for changes, and with Windy the opposite happened. Early for her age, she looked more like a young woman practically overnight than Minnow did in almost a year, being the Minnow that she was in every part of her except her personality and heart. Windy just went all out in everything she did, and it showed in every way. They said you are what you eat and so Minnow guessed it also applied to personality, you are who you are – wait – you look like who you are? Oh well, she gave up trying to piece together a mixed-up philosophy. Besides, when she considered the analogy there were instant flaws, because Minnow practically lived on whole milk mixed-berry smoothies from her blender and Mom's homemade waffles and she was still minnow tiny!

And if her personality was so huge, then why was she still so small?

Part of it was being a Chincoteaguer. Her great grandmother had only been four feet tall! The stairs in their home were original to when it was moved over from Assateague by way of the gut just across from the kayak shop. They were shorter than anyone's feet in the house by a half inch, other than Minnow.

If only Windy' maturity had counted in sensibleness as well.

Their emotions, amplified by these changes, were raging stars, out of sight, and within sight, and Minnow knew that had a lot to do with their antagonism, and the worse sides of their worsened attitudes towards each other, but that still didn't negate Windy' breezy, sometimes blatant meanness, or lessen the aggravation any less when she acted out.

Nor when they both went volcanic.

Minnow had never felt sorrier for herself.

Tempers up and down, took to heart too much, and needless to say they took everything out on each other anyway. Since both started this tumultuous odyssey, and were going through this nor'easter time in their lives at the same time, Mom and Dad had been counseling them on three points; personal privacy; respecting each other's privacy; and stressing the importance of having patience and understanding with one another.

Could Minnow blame them for this monstrous situation, and the rest of them? wondered Minnow, as she did a lot. What about for adding to the turmoil by stressing? Trying to instill the value of personal privacy?

They knew Windy rebelled against anything told not to do or to do, when it concerned Minnow! Yet, did they really? Could parents ever understand the antagonism between the middle sisters, the irritation they could cause, or how annoying the younger sister could be?

Minnow didn't think "not really", she knew "not really".

So, were they to blame?

She cut them slack with a flat no. There was nothing that could've been added or removed from this fire, to save or spare the kettle from boiling, or every hour of every day or every other day, boiling *over*!

It'd be nice to have someone or something to blame besides herself or growing up! There – mother nature was to blame.

Being five years older than Minnow, seven than Windy, it feels like Summer has always been a young woman. She's the responsible one, the one they look up to, and to whom even spoiled Windy listens. The older sister is normally always the second mom, and with Summer, Windy and Minnow were born having struck gold.

As the two youngest, Windy and Minnow have always shared a room, and so respecting one another's privacy has never been easy or an issue, yet was it ever in the cards?

Lucky Summer. She's never had the problem with privacy Minnow has. Not that Summer ever minds certain things as much as Minnow, but then she's not Minnow, and Windy crystalizes this clarity of difference with her own behavior around Summer and misbehavior around Minnow. For Windy never pushes the boundaries with Summer the way she hassles Minnow.

From an empathetic point of view Minnow and Windy were having a tough time with so many changes at once; and Minnow was losing her temper on tiny annoyances, like every second

Windy belched loudly or used her teeth on a spoon of ice cream, and it was only Windy, who Minnow minded, yet they had shared rooms since always. And Windy was having a harder time with respecting or acknowledging these new boundaries that existed almost overnight between her and Minnow.

But Minnow didn't feel like having empathy this minute!

Past the boiling point, and too hot with irritation and antagonism to let it go, Windy said sternly, "I'm still telling Mom!" and Minnow strained to hear a tremor or sign in her tone she was just leading her on to make her think so out of anger and spite, like they tend to do in the heat of the moment. While no one wanted to get in trouble, neither one wanted to lose the argument and give in either!

Banking on Windy not wanting to get into trouble but also wanting to win so badly, Minnow was hoping from where she stood in the shower thankfully concealed in the stall, arms crossed and in a frozen-still closely-listening state, that Windy was just being the usual ant or mosquito about the whole thing.

Minnow hoped her detection was spot on; she knew her sister so well she was predictable, but she didn't see the toilet flush coming on the squeaky heels of Windy' sharp and deliberate exit until she heard it happening. Windy slammed the door as a fused wall of cold water slammed into Minnow so cold it didn't feel anything like a shower!

Yelping, she did a hopscotch zig zag, first to get out of range of the worst, which was virtually unattainable, then zagged to curve around the wall of ice cold as much and as best as was possible, grabbing the showerhead and facing it toward the cracked subway tile, away from her!

The cool water had felt soothing and refreshing, but ice COLD water just hurt her sunburn, and now made her fume even more.

Chapter Three

It was a tight bathroom, altogether about as big as a normal size horse stall. Minnow was glad because there wasn't much floor to sop up. Although she did have to bend down low and press her cheek to the white and blue tiled floor to check to see if water had leaked underneath the washing machine.

Nope.

Minnow exhaled in relief – not because it would've been disastrous for the machine – she was relieved that she didn't have move it out. Which if it was wet under there that's what she would've had to do. As heavy and tightly fitted into its corner as the obnoxiously loud when on washing machine was, Minnow would've had to enlist Mom's help.

She wouldn't have looked forward to explaining why it was wet underneath the washing machine.

But she may have to answer that anyway.

Minnow mopped up the floor with an extra towel, all the while ears sharpened to hear Windy' rail, and Mom's soft but solid work-boot footsteps approaching the bathroom from coming inside from the workshop. But in the minutes, that had dragged by since Windy stormed out and Minnow shut the shower valve off in a huff, neither had happened.

With those uneventfully dragged minutes, the pulse in Minnow's neck and forehead that always thickened under her skin when she was upset or frustrated in some way, throbbed less.

In the combination, after she'd hung up the wet towel and began combing the shampoo smoothed tangles out of her hair, Minnow started thinking about her wrong and behavior, as her argument with Windy replayed in her mind with a flower wind-vane's rhythm and speed it picks up when the sea air blows a little stronger than a normal summer day's gustiness tends to.

When Minnow exited the bathroom to find the house quiet, empty, she peeked around the corner and surveyed from the safety of this spot. When Mom's humming drum sander suddenly screamed in the distance as it met in contact with the rough edges of a blocky duck shape in her woodwork shop portion of the kayak shop, in the background to the house's stillness except of course for the cool light summer breeze bringing summer warmth and grassiness in the house, it was clear to Minnow that Windy didn't tell Mom. Just not yet? Or had she changed her mind? More likely she was stalling telling Mom to have it out with Minnow after she'd showed her face first.

Minnow stared at the ceiling fan in exasperation. She'd reached the end of her tether today. The childish absurdity on Windy' part, and that the two pulled each other into these emotional minnow traps still, was awful, and just the plight of sisters she reckoned.

However, Minnow also felt glad. Glad that Windy had chickened out.

But now Minnow was in the minnow trap for losing *her* temper, with Windy holding her up to her huge face by the trap's rope. It was a guilt thing and an emotional tag they'd pulled since always, back when Windy was teeny tiny too.

Wow, she'd been a baby once!

Yet still, there was reason to be glad. For the fortune of this rigmarole was that there were openings, signs when they wanted reconciliation instead of argument or as last resorts, bringing their parents aboard the ever-turning carrousel.

Giving in without giving in by giving in on the appearance of not giving in. Which happen to be today not going to Mom, willing to test the outcome on each other first. Thereby leaving the choice up to Minnow. Don't hold the grudge or drag out the argument? Either move Minnow was the bad guy, because in this rigmarole there was a sense of fairness and Minnow had offended too and hurt last.

So even in a surrender and make-up, Windy still got to be the one who wasn't really to blame, because she's not apologizing first. Which the slightest give, can be taken as an admission, and it's not promised that Windy will be fair and fess up to her own mistakes. Unless her sense of fairness was stronger today than her ego or pride.

Though she did leave the opening there by not boohooing to Mom, who'd have no squeams or stutters or *throat choking with reluctance and stubbornness* to point out the faults with either one of them. So, Minnow took this opening as a tender admission there was an acknowledgement of shared blame and a seed of guilt, that Windy had been wrong. First? Or just wrong *also* – that was right now Windy' own personal inner struggle, and unclear to Minnow.

It was a frustrating, almost delicate, while also a straightforward sense of emotional blackmail, freeze-tag, and king of the castle mixed in.

Windy didn't want to get into trouble, that was clear, but Minnow was pretty sure she knew her chickening out was because she didn't really want to fight today, which when Minnow thought about it made sense. She'd barged into the shower wanting to tell her something exciting that'd happened.

And instead of being excited too and eager to hear it, Minnow had yelled at her.

Windy hadn't been prepared. So, she chickened out of her promise to tell Mom on her because in her heart she really wanted to make up, but at the same time Minnow had stoked the volcano and the stubborn bubbly glob wouldn't let her come to reunion easily. It was hard to want to make up when at the same time, you're upset and don't want to feel like you're the one who gave in, or for Minnow and Windy, who said sorry first. How had their small room contained the two for so long? For there is nothing minnow with Windy but Minnow, and everything Minnow about Minnow that aside from her size isn't minnow at all!

Well it hadn't busted wide open yet, so Minnow guessed that until it had, they'd continue this until it did!

Oh, the carrousel of not wanting to get in trouble and also wanting to be the one who was right, because they each think that they were right. Truthfully, they'd have to admit if they were being honest about it with each other, that they'd both been right, *and* wrong!

But who was wrong first and who was wrong most?

These were the things these sisters considered and argued over, in entanglements that could fill tomes but somehow fit into their small, shared room, in their small two story house, on an island she could traverse on bicycle from one end to the other in a matter of hours.

How then, is there any resolve for sisters who don't want to be the first one to let go, and say, "I'm sorry"?

Well, it's not easy at all. First. It's like an emotional game of tag with flames and different various speeds, that often involves other players – Summer, Mom, Dad, and sometimes all three at once.

Sometimes one does something and then the other to the other one until the carrousel is spinning so fast that no one's right as far as they were concerned, but the circles could wipe them out before either one admitted first that they were the one who was wrong. So, one threatens to tell, the other threatens to tell, and when neither one does, (which is more typical than one might think) whoever did the worst thing last is the "tag, you're it", while the one who may have been the one to start it can get on scot-free, because you're tagged.

By spraying Windy and her not telling, Minnow is "It" this time, even though Windy obviously started it. Minnow has to be the one to eat humble pie and apologize first. Unless she feels like arguing more. Which she doesn't. It's been a very hot, very tough, and very stressful day for Minnow. But she was wrong and she knows it. It's hard to admit that she's justifiably "It", even if it's unfair because she was sucked in, she let herself be sucked in. And as reluctant as they each are to blame themselves, it's about honesty too; and Minnow might argue with selfish, irresponsible, immature Windy, but her sense of fairness and honesty make her fess up to her blame in the rigmarole and share

36

of being "It" in their emotional tag more times than Windy. Even when Minnow wasn't really "It", because of unexplainable reasons, when Windy lowers her defenses it brings out her responsible nature and big sister mode. She'll find a way to smooth out the scuffles in the sand, and let Windy slide by making up with her when she turns pitiful and vulnerable. Minnow guessed in "those" pitfalls, when Windy acted human instead of pirate, it brought out the big sister and human in her, and she rewarded Windy' no walls with love.

Sometimes Minnow felt like she was the shark skin Pirate Briny Wind sharpened her cutlass on.

Sometimes it was a bummer to be the responsible one. Even though the one wronged first and pulled in, annoyed by this carouselling between sisters, or at least them two, Minnow was It again. Although this time it is saving her, because Windy didn't tell Mom. Besides, though Minnow was still simmering, while having this private, honest, me-moment with herself, she admitted she was primed for a fight when Windy burst in because she'd been frustrated all day.

The fire department said no again; and she'd been trying all afternoon to think of a plan, taking her frustration and aggression out on the grass. Even though Minnow stormed the yard and spent a lot of her frustration, it'd seemed to also bulk up her sore feelings and the cut deep down hurt in her heart, that's been there since the first "No". But this "no" and last summer's "no", has hit her the hardest. Because Minnow knows she's old enough and experienced enough; and still. The tradition takes precedence over her longtime dream.

Not that it's anyone's to worry about making true except Minnow. It's just like a sore bruise that can't or won't clear up, and gets sorer with every "no". Making her dream come true of riding in the pony swim among the saltwater ponyboys and pony descendants of her island, is the only way to make that bruise lift in a smile and turn to clear skin happiness.

So, if Windy wants to act like the sitting duck, so be it. *This* time, Minnow deserves to be olive branch bearer and as the older one, set the example. Man, being the older one is the hardest sometimes.

Anyway, this is better to sort out between themselves than getting into trouble with Mom, and that alone somehow opens the door or leaves it unlocked to the side of them with forgiving hearts. And mistakes or wrongs or who did or said what, or did or said what first, get acknowledged at last, and while other times battled out, in the end, either route, however eruptively come to, the volcanoes in them have been fed; whether that stomach growling hunger was simply sisterly antagonism or on top of something else bothering them, like Minnow's "no" today, to riding in the swim.

So, volcanoes fed, Minnow's ready to cap it and feel pleased with the fullness of their supper of getting everything off her chest.

So, Minnow took a big sigh, because she was going to be the big sister here – and a little selfish by cooling the remainder of this lava flow before the lava went airborne and did reach the foot of Mom's workshop.

She'd share the blame too, even though Windy had started the whole thing by barging in, because Minnow knew losing her temper the way she did and spraying Windy was the wrong move; either she could have slipped lashing out, or Windy, but regardless of who had started it.

Minnow heard Mom's logic even without a refresher course.

Who started it wouldn't mean anything when one of them was receiving stitches or worse from a slip that split something open or cracked a bone the wrong way. That's why Mom and Dad were always telling them it was bad to lose their tempers. And they had to be told daily. Especially now, with everything they were going through. They were going to say and do things they didn't mean, and it wasn't like losing their temper was avoidable or not healthy now and then, because it was, and sibs were going to no matter what, always. But doing something that could result in getting hurt, out of that anger or clawing frustration where she and Windy were grappling to tow the line? Big no-no all the way around.

It was just so hard when Windy got under her skin because she knew she could, not to react strongly.

Which made moments like these for Minnow rare, when Windy opened the window on her own. It told Minnow that she still had a bigger sister's small tether of influence, as much as two so close in age and tempers as they, could maintain.

Well what Minnow had done hadn't been mean, but it'd not been responsible either.

Now after starting it, Windy hadn't told Mom on her, and thus Minnow had been turned into the one on the hook for losing her temper that way. Though a big slice of humble pie was better than facing a lecture from Mom, or from Dad, who was on the evening tour with Summer. If Minnow didn't know it was her primed mood that'd made her erupt, she'd extend this and make Windy the one to come to the table, even if it meant spiking Windy' mood more and getting told on.

"Thanks for choosing the middle of summer for all these phases and life changes," muttered Minnow with clenched jaw.

Despite who was to blame first, or that if Windy had told then Minnow would have to confess her share of blame, that Windy hadn't told softened Minnow some, with a sense of relief, and probably against her will and better judgement, stirred her sisterly sense of closeness in their hot and cold and warm in-between bond.

As Minnow entered their shared room where she had a feeling she'd find her sister pouting, waiting, reluctant, volcanoes bloated and steaming, Minnow had an image of holding Windy as a baby and felt a wave of big sister flood her smoothly, along with a nibbling twinge of guilt or regret, the two were so similar she couldn't tell which. Maybe the twinge was a blend of both. For her own behavior. After all, Windy' attributes were bright also, not all spoiled. Vivacious, confident, unthinking sometimes but loving, and all pettiness aside, loyal to the bone when it got to the bone. Also, they *were* both going through a lot. Minnow didn't include that lightly either. They didn't mean everything they said, and respecting Minnow's privacy had been a pulling teeth transition for Windy.

In an altogether different sense, Minnow felt that pain too – when Windy acted out from it the way she did that made Minnow want to grind her teeth.

Giving space didn't come easily to ones as close as they all were, even when it's out of respect.

Windy sat on her bed with back against her headboard, legs up and arms draped atop her knees as she stared a little pouty and somberly at the open pirate book in her hands. Minnow could tell she wasn't really reading it now, and probably hadn't been more than a perusal before she walked in, because her eyes were fixed on one spot, staring, without the slight motion of roving swarthy sentences with intent fixation of being swept up in imagination drawing her in as they swordfight off the pages.

She looked in the mood Minnow figured she'd be in, pouty, steamy, at the same time somber, and knew she'd been replaying their argument in her mind like Minnow had, with wind-vane speed and continuance. As such, Minnow figured Windy had considered her side of things, like Minnow did, and Minnow suddenly just felt like being the big sister.

Minnow closed their door and on bare-feet still cool but not COLD from her shower, crossed to Windy' side of the room, sitting on the edge of her bed.

"I'm sorry I sprayed you," Minnow said first, her tone low.

"Sorry I didn't respect your privacy, and startled you while you were wet and soapy," Windy replied slowly, and Minnow knew because she took the time to say it in two parts, that she meant it. Which opened Minnow's heart to real, full, big sister mode and forgiveness.

"It's ok," Minnow replied, but going sincere with a soft word of strong advice, explained, "I just need my space when I want it." Minnow hoped Windy understood her side of things a little better. "I don't think I'd have minded you coming in if you'd knocked and asked first."

With that, Windy looked at her with full on focus for the first time since she'd come in, and the vulnerability there told Minnow much of what she herself hadn't really paid attention too. In-depth, or with perspective, Windy' side of things. Windy was rebelling this way more because she was feeling like she was losing her bond with Minnow.

So wrapped up in herself, her own raging emotions and side of the tantrums, not to mention in the mounted irritation of being

42

excluded from the swim once again, Minnow didn't realize until just this moment when she looked into Windy' open-book eyes, that Windy was feeling excluded too.

Hungry, for their sisterly closeness and bond, and time with her that'd been short this winter and summer, and shorter than short this last week before the swim.

Short on temper, and also affection, her time absorbed with helping in the kayak shop and not really getting to spend quality time with just the two of them, doing sibling stuff and summer stuff.

Now that they're older too, their kayak responsibilities have doubled this year.

Her vivacious and spunky little sister, looked at her hungry with hope and at the same time like someone who'd been left behind. So, Minnow kept explaining, and then knew what she was going to be adding shortly next, having decided to be open and honest with Windy. After all, Minnow had kept this battle bottled up inside her long enough; maybe she should talk to Windy more.

"But sometimes I just need my space," Minnow stressed softly, first off.

"Okay," Windy replied, like that was doable and wasn't much to ask in exchange for their bond not slenderizing, and for more time together.

"I'm still your sister Windy," Minnow said, and wrapped one sturdy hand around her ankle. "That's never going to change. Just how much you see me naked will," she said smiling, with a scuffle in her throat at the start as she tried not to laugh.

Windy' pitiful look vanished with the dawn-break of her beaming smile that lit every part of her up, thankfully so to Minnow, and she tore a pillow propping her back and whammed it into Minnow.

Minnow hung on expecting more of a fight but Windy had released it and was sitting back in revelry.

"Besides, it wasn't all your fault, why I got so upset," Minnow confided, which brought Windy' eyebrows together perplexed and concerned but with curious interest.

"I was primed, for an explosion, a fight," she said, letting Windy dig it out of her and ask, "Why?" before going on.

One of those things where she wants to tell and intends to, but as proof Windy was interested and really wanting to know, which either made telling better or just more meaningful, it was just one of those things siblings do, wanting them to and making the other dig it out of them.

"I rode my bike by the old fire station before lunch, and they said I still can't ride in the pony swim," she said.

Windy got heated. "You're twice as good as some of those boys our age who ride in the swim. Cousin Freddy is in the swim, and if *he* can be in the swim, golly, I could be in the swim; and I don't even fancy horses. Pirating's more my thing anyway."

"It's not about that," Minnow told her, "it's about tradition. There's never been a saltwater ponygirl who's ridden in the swim. Some of the old-timers still won't have it."

"You know though Windy," Minnow started, about to say something she'd never felt until this afternoon when she was told no-can-do again. "I've always dreamed of being the first saltwater ponygirl in the swim. But I'd be happy just riding in the swim now. I don't care about being first. I just want so badly to be there," she expressed with genuineness. "I belong there."

"You will be." Windy had bolted forward and clasped one warm and tight hand over Minnow's that wrapped her ankle, squeezing. "We'll think of a way."

"Mutiny?" Minnow said with lifted brows, knowing the pirate aficionado and natural pirate all Windy, was hoisting her flag.

"Somehow," said Windy as she focused in mulling thought on their wall with a rustling shadow.

Minnow shouldn't and didn't want to encourage this. "I wouldn't put it past you," Minnow admonished. Then, "I would've put it past me though; until today. I'm open," said Minnow.

To hear Minnow say that she was aboard for one of Windy' wild, rascally ideas brought a genuine smile to her sun-kissed face, tawny in the evening sunset washing everything in their white wall room in an earthy golden orange glow with form and figure. That Minnow had brought her astride this ride with her, even though she doesn't really like horses, wasn't a first, but it was rare. And Minnow bringing Windy into her confidence was something Minnow was happy, and a little surprised to say, that Windy took to heart.

"Leave it to me," replied Windy.

"Don't make me regret telling you," Minnow warned carefully but seriously.

Windy didn't have a gold tooth, so how was it that one in her bright smile twinkled at her?

At that moment, the sound of a horn blared in the evening dusk. Dad and Summer just pulled in the dock with the evening tour.

"We'll plan on the way and think while we work," Windy promised as she leapt off the bed.

Minnow had just taken a shower but rinsing life-jackets and paddles was a clean chore. The cool hose spray on her legs and feet, misting the air with its freshness; wet, rough deck her toes and splinter-experienced feet and hands know well. She looked forward to stepping on the squishy marsh mud globs from when customers stuck their paddles too far in the mud getting through a shallow part of creek. The black gooey slime she and Windy and Summer squished for fun or were splattered with when they were careless or in a hurry, propelled a smile to Minnow's lips. They'd been rinsing life-jackets, paddles, and boats since they were little, and could easily get through half a day or the task at hand without undo messiness. But where was the fun in that? Unless they were busy or in a hurry, or a perfectionistic mood while washing them! Which had been known to happen.

Rinsing paddles and boats was playing in water, and playing with water.

Minnow loved the water. Needless to say, Summer and Windy loved the water also; the saltwater best. Water was water, but saltwater smelled rejuvenatingly fresh, salty tangy, and was revitalizing to them; enlivening. It swept through the marsh, filled the piney forests, breathed in their hair and filled their lungs, greeted them on the gust of a light marshy breeze, welcomed them home on the causeway. Saltwater taste, smell, feel, was family and home.

"Nothing too extreme," Minnow was warning in answer to Windy' remark, following her out the door as another familiar sound dissipated in the distance.

Trained to the familiar blare of Dad's conk shell horn, and probably keeping an eye on the time, which when focused in carving and lost in the process as artists get, it was impressive but not surprising that Mom had heard, and the sound dissipating was her switching the sander off.

47

"I know, don't worry," Windy was replying as they clopped downstairs and raced to the door they crammed in together, causing a nudging and elbowing fight, that tickled to squeeze through together. Both kept some form of grip on the other so no one was really first. Minnow swears, Mom was lucky they weren't twins!

They cut through the slender wall of bulky bushes intermixed with seas of bulrushes and trees, assorted with rosemary, bayberry, maple, elm, poplar, briers, draped with vine and the budding of honeysuckle. It was a slender wall of woods that the girls knew by heart, with deer trails and trails of their own widening and frequent travels. It extended to the backyard where it not only cupped the paddock but deepened into woods the girls had played in since they were old enough to sneak out of the house and behind the house. Mom and Dad kept talking about trimming the slender border of woods mixed with all kinds of island plant and bush and tree, but all three sisters pled every time the subject was raised, to keep it. They compromised on topping the tallest trees for the time being, and in the meantime between not talking about it and talking about it again, their trees and bulrushes and bayberries and rosemary were safe.

Minnow and Windy crossed the wide-open kayak shop yard, rounding the north side of the shop with the old dilapidating mechanic's garage so they swung by the back way to run into Mom. They bounded onto the low square of decking and stuck their heads in the woodshop to let Mom know they were rounding the kayak shop to wait for Dad so they could help clean up the boats and gear. They'd travel through the woodshop that connected to the kayak shop via the gallery room, but at the moment the narrow way was blocked by Mom's unfinished egret. They could maneuver and duck under or crawl, but Mom was particular about roughhousing in the shop, and Minnow didn't trust herself or Windy not to elbow each other or disrupt something out of place, even though they'd just made up.

Minnow and Windy were competitive in their own ways, on top of being annoying and antagonistic to each other.

Pleased, Mom replied ok, putting aside tools and turning off machinery for the night. Lastly, she would dust herself off outside and peel off her sweaty and sawdust powered clothes and relatively wash up before starting dinner. Minnow surmised this all in her head because they see her doing it nearly every day. Not to mention she'd been doing this since they were born. The sisters could count Mom's steps or every move once inside the house, even though they were already running around the kayak shop to the front, hugging the side of the building on the narrow patch of un-mowed and leg-tickly grass before it meets road, as they run. For they sit on the corner of the lane and even at dusk cars zoom around the side all the time.

Windy throws out some suggestions – pleading with the mayor?

Pleading didn't get Minnow anywhere, with anyone. But she'd tried this already.

Radio?

Yes, if Minnow planned to antagonize every local!

Lay down in the middle of the road and pretend the heartbreak of having her dream crushed made her faint?

Too far! No drastic sympathy moves! That'd get her pancaked and in trouble with their parents at the same time!

With only two actual suggestions, they're tank of imagination seemed to bottom. Windy now met with the same wave Minnow was struggling to break over, when they heard the distant sound of Dad's truck leaving the dock in the quiet quarter mile down the road. Standing under the roof on the inch-from-the-gravel deck, they couldn't see him heading up the road as they would have, were they across the rough paved road with its unchanging tilts.

The one-eyed beacon of so much hope beamed across from them, and when the eighty-three hand-painted blue Chevy kayak truck came into view just before Clarence's motorboat repair shop, with Summer seated as usual atop the truck-bed side with a life's long kayak grip hooking her to the solid wooden rack Mom and Dad designed and built for Dad's kayaks, they jumped up and down waving.

Despite Windy and Minnow's argument earlier, or that Minnow's heart was still feeling bruised-bruised and silently heavy over another "no", it turned into a wonderful evening filled with laughter and plenty of giggling, starting when Dad shocked them by joining in their spray match that at some point everyone ruled and was continually overthrown seconds later. Once the kayaks and gear were rinsed off, the paddles shoved at an angle in their corner behind the thrice bolted three-inch-thick front door, and life-jackets hung on the eyehook threaded rope-line of two hoisted paddles with their partners to dry, they walked the one minute walk home together.

Dad, Minnow, Summer, and Windy were already rinsed off of course – they were soaking wet! And changed before a hamburger din-din rigmarole where Mom, Summer, Dad, Windy and Minnow shared how their day went. Minnow mentioned the recent "no" from the fire department; and there was understanding and encouragement before Summer changed the subject before Minnow got too down. But what Minnow didn't mention, and Windy of course would never give a skullduggery plan or chance at mutiny away, was that she was going to find a way to ride in the swim this summer. How? That was the hard part that needed sweat-worthy thinking.

Helping Summer and Windy mop up the front room, turned grass bit and puddle floor room, after they'd stripped to their skivvies behind a towel the others held up for each other on the skinny back porch – and taken turns filing carefully up to their rooms to change, had reminded Minnow of earlier. She traded looks with Windy, who must have been thinking the same thing.

"What?" Summer asked smiling, wanting to be in on whatever silly thing they were chuckling at.

"Nothing," Minnow started first and Windy finished first, adding to another round of laughter that crippled them flat on their hunches and arms.

Chapter Four

Minnow was the quickest to brush her teeth and so while everyone was busy brushing their teeth for bed at the kitchen sink, as they kept their toothbrushes and toothpaste in individual cups in the side shelf of the refrigerator to avoid brushing their teeth with ants, Minnow zipped upstairs to her room for a minute or two or whatever she could grab of alone time.

She stopped in front of Windy' library of pirate volumes, DVDs, and otherwise pirate paraphernalia, and stared. Half in thought, grabbing for ideas, feeling like there had to be a plan to get into the pony swim this time, and knowing she had to hit on it before Saturday. It was going to have to be something totally different. Something she'd never thought of; and yet how could she convince those who'd repeated the number of "no's" in summers past to her, to let her ride in the swim? How could she convince them that that's where she belonged?

Briny Bonnie Lasses and Lads, Pirate Short Stories, caught her strayed-in-thought perusal like someone sticking a pin in her arm. She'd been contemplating this title in her argument with herself while she was mowing the stubborn lawn with a plucky mower that didn't want to pluck or shave or "eat" the feisty clumps of grass. What was its reason for existence if it didn't do what it was invented for? she thought grumbly to herself. The aggravation was fleeting though and she sighed as she once again immersed herself in thoughts of the pony swim. She plucked the slender hardcover and turned the volume over in her hand in front of her. What would it offer? Maybe nothing. What could it suggest? Maybe everything. She'd cling to even a minnow of *something*.

She dared hoping for sparks of inspiration, but would settle for just a vague bit of friendship to give her courage and keep her company through the weeks long agony, to bring some green back into her slender hope for future summers. Or dare she say, this pony penning week?

If she thought of a plan this weekend, it might happen. She'd make her dream come true! If not, she'd face the disappointment with courage, and not lose hope; taking example from these stories about circumstances she shared with these real girls and boys all the way back when.

She flicked off the light-switch and pulled on her lamp string with a pony charm that she'd painted to look like Marshy, dangling at the bottom.

Minnow curled on the side of her bed with the strongest patch of light from her bedside dresser lamp, that seemed to take on an ambient illumination as she entered the world of pirates, cutlass, and ships on the high seas. The lighthouse further added to the air of suspense, flashing in and out of her room through the window aimed at the middle wall, as it does every night. But tonight, right now, it took on new life.

Minnow started reading from the middle of the book. It wasn't her horse adventure books Minnow normally and regularly devoured, but she was quickly enthralled. Wow! No wonder Windy stayed amped. How could she contain herself from doing nefarious or more skullduggery things with this much excitement coursing through her veins?

She guessed her excitement atop a horse, riding Marshy around the backyard or galloping along surf in totally freedom, was Windy' equivalent to a pirate's life, and immersing herself in their world, the way Minnow immersed herself in her world of horses. Still, Minnow was gaining great insight into her sister's tendencies here.

Giant blue sparkling endlessness and creaking bows of ships with full, pluming sail, pirate colors, red, blue, gold ships, and a pirate her age standing on the deck thrusting cutlass into the sea air, filled Minnow's imagination. So she was surprised when she bolted awake and discovered that halfway through the third tale on page one hundred and fifteen or something close, she'd fallen asleep. Not to mention drooled on her pillow.

She gave herself a break though, and wiped her mouth with the inside of her shirt, because yesterday had been a big, disappointing, emotional day, with a happy ending that had its draining power as well.

But a plan had struck her! THE plan!

It'd been nagging at the back of her mind all this time, and yet Minnow couldn't say precisely how long *all this time* was. Had it been formulating since a month ago, or more, last summer? Or just as newly since she mowed the yard in a state of hot and sticky frustration?

The answer had been staring her squarely in the face all along, in plain sight but she hadn't noticed it for what it was.

Until now.

Mom, Dad, Summer, Windy? Through her excitement, Minnow paused, and softly smiled, because one of them had tucked her in with her sheet. Minnow threw the sheet off and grabbed her cell from its spot on her bedside dresser, then with expert sleuthing feet that'd had a lifetime of practice, quietly snuck downstairs where she lifted the small rectangular window in the bathroom and fed herself out like the person getting too big that she was. Now days when she used her old escape hatch, as she called it, she felt more and more like an octopus squeezing itself through a hole. The front door was too squeaky for a secret nightly escapade, and Mom and Dad's room hemmed the living room, and with three still growing little girls they were very light sleepers, so the sliding doors, which weren't softer sounding than the front screen door, might unduly wake them. So, Minnow chose the unscreened bathroom window that she and Windy and Summer had used since childhood for fun and games. Summer was way too big now, and Windy was filling out more than Minnow thought she ever might, which suited her fine. She could run and ride and squeeze through slenderer holes like their window much better than if she filled out in the noticeable spots like Windy was, or Summer had, though Summer's predicament for being too large for their favorite window was more due to the broadness of her athletic build, unlike Windy' goddess shapeliness. All three sisters were rather stocky and short, though Minnow believed she would ever be the minnow of the family, which included to her younger sister. And that's alright, she thought as she steadied herself on the narrow porch railing that prickled her feet with tiny rough specks of wood.

Because while Windy would continue embracing her own growing up and brag about being taller if she shot up another six inches that would dwarf Minnow into looking like the younger sister altogether, including vaunting her curvy shapes as Minnow imagined she would do when she got around to it during the times when her spoiled side emerged, Minnow truly didn't give a holler.

She didn't want to change that much more. Running, riding, swimming, and squeezing came much easier to her as it naturally did to minnows, and those were all the things that Minnow cared about and was glad they weren't going to change. The single desire she would work towards achieving was more muscle. If a Minnow like her could.

Soft and padded spongy summer grass made spongier from the layer of shaven surface, also known as grass-hay, it felt as deliriously sweet to Minnow as it smelled, as she ran up the yard to the back section enclosed by fencing and suited with Marshy' run-in-barn shelter to the far most left corner, picking her way carefully to avoid roots where she knew they stuck up from being the one who mowed the yard the most.

Mowing helped Minnow to think and untangle knots in her stomach when she was upset or antsy.

Under the diamond stars and clear silver beaming moon, blasting through soft night air cool on her skin, spiced with the walls of trees and bushes and vines and briers that encompassed this back portion of their yard, kept in part for privacy, Minnow was glad she'd had a reason to bring her into this night.

The ocean was hyperactive, to be heard in the distance as she was hearing it, muffled though it was through the trees. She looked over her shoulder for a brief moment. It felt as though the ocean in the distance was applauding her.

Minnow smiled, sprinting up to the sturdy three railing fencing. Rough-hewn, it resembled most Chincoteague fencing for penning ponies or sectioning the yard from a neighbor's. The salt air dried everything out on the island, including certain trees and bushes, and most especially cut wood. But one didn't need much to pen a small pony, especially one as sweet tempered as Marshy.

Marshy heard Minnow coming as soon as she was squeezing out her escape hatch, and had swiveled her ears. Animals heard so much more than most humans or at least before most humans. But Marshy was simply keyed into Minnow's every move.

Marshy trotted over to the fence greeting Minnow with happy grunting and squeaky noises in reply to her unexpected visit, and Minnow's double rubbing both of her cheeks with each hand at the same time.

Minnow pressed her forehead to Marshy' face and drank in her horsy smell. Minnow could listen to Marshy' squeaky whinnies and noises all day – or night-long. She'd never outgrown the noises even as an eight-year-old mare. Mom and Dad still thought there was something amiss with her vocal development, but Minnow knew it was Marshy' sweet nature and childlike heart that harkened her cute whinnies and squeaks.

Marshy was a dark chocolate brown, almost mud brown in the bright sun, with ink black hair as thick and unwieldly as beach grass. Minnow only ever untangled it completely, twice, in her whole life, when she gave Marshy a big hose-bath and used up a bottle of Summer's special detangling shampoo! Which they kept on hand for those windy days.

But Marshy didn't seem to mind the tangles, and Minnow loved them, and this carefree part about her. A lot like Minnow and her sisters, bouncing out of bed and skipping the comb and brush routine; eager to greet the day, to get to what they're after or find that next or new something to chase, in the new day bringing it onward, or continuing from yesterday.

Marshy had just been a lanky little foal, with knobby knees and an unspectacular coloration that made her unappealing to buyers at the pony auction. As though she smelled like the marsh on its worst day, the crowd fell silent but for one or two unenthusiastic hands. Minnow had shot hers straight up, winning the bidding in the slack tide race with fifteen seconds of debate back and forth.

Minnow felt an instant kindship with the underweight foal, as the minnow baby she had been once. Her plain brown coat and then spiky dark black hair had made the skinny filly thrill-less to look at. White markings and pintos or palomino colored ones, foggy white or solid black, were more charming and attractive and exciting, than an underweight, big knee filly that looked like marsh mud, and whose spiky hair also made her look like a spiked sea anemone that'd crawled out of the ocean and been rounded up by the ponyboys. That was why Minnow named her Marshy. Perky and dark brown with springing spiky hair, she looked like she'd climbed straight out of the marsh with the fiddler crabs at low tide! A marsh dwelling creature rather than an Assateague pony that munches marsh grass but keeps to the tree-lines. Marshy' coat and personality was everything Minnow loved about her, and that had set her apart from the others. For without those looks, she would never have been able to bid on her and they wouldn't have each other now.

Even if Marshy had smelled like the marsh on its worst day, which was like rotten eggs, Minnow would have loved her still, and more, and bid on her regardless.

Marshy feels likewise, and couldn't be happier than where she was, or who she's with.

Minnow often sneaks outside at night to spend special time with Marshy. Things are different at night, and to know that you're awake while everyone else is asleep, is adventurous as well as thought provoking for Minnow.

But tonight, she and Marshy aren't sneaking off for a midnight ride down the lane or to the dock; nor did she come only to say hello. Though both are sorely overdue. Chores, kayak guiding, and fully days in the July busy shop scheduling tours, helping run boats back and forth to the dock, then rinsing them, and repeating, keep Minnow glued to her bed most nights now until the alarm or someone else shakes her awake.

Oh, to have a full night's sleep and wake up, unshaken awake, with birdsong and feeling a cool breeze on her face, before the wafting warmth of another hot summer day starts, as the sweet, tangy, moist piney smells of summer permeate her room and whisper to her skin that it's going to be an exciting new day and to get up and join. By knowing these whispers or gusts all of her life, Minnow's skin and sense of smell can detect a hot or mild day in the making. By the clear night that it is, Minnow guesses it will be a cloudless barnburner tomorrow.

"We'll go on a midnight ride soon baby," Minnow told her, pulling back a few steps to look in her eyes while they spoke. "We might be doing a lot of riding in the next two days."

Marshy squealed softly in question.

"Hold that thought," Minnow said to her, whipping out her cell from where she stashed it between her underwear and her hip.

Her phone glowed one side of her face, making her own pony do a doubletake. Smells like Minnow, mostly looks like Minnow. Not an alien?

Minnow noticed Marshy' confusion. She'd show her it really was her. "Yes, it's me sweet girl," Minnow told her, "not an alien." The sound of her voice and scrubbing her dark brown forelock center settled the matter. But she was going to have a harder time recognizing Minnow Saturday.

"What," a groggy, sleep-tired voice grumbled over the phone, with the hint of pitiful.

"Matt," Minnow said. "Best friend from the spit of island to the wide, wide world," she greeted him.

She could practically hear him perk up with interest and see him sit up wide awake. "What are you up to?"

"I knew you hadn't been sleeping!" she broke off to tag him.

"How's that possible? You got some all-seeing eye that's microscopic and can see through phones," Matt replied blandly, but she heard the grin in his tone.

Minnow smiled flatly, and she kept her voice mild so it wouldn't travel too far across the yard in the night. "You get off the carnival at midnight, and I know you can't go to sleep right away after you've gorged on carnival food. That stuff jacks you up tighter than a quahog guarding a pearl. More than me, and that's sayen something."

"Only amateurs gorge. I swallow whole," Matt said, but by the time Minnow rolled her eyes before intending to reply, he was talking again. "Want to meet on the roof?"

"I can't," Minnow said with regret, because it was a bug-free night with a cool breeze and a little while on the roof would've been really nice. "I've got to help on a big tour in the morning. You'll have to talk the junk food and sugar high out of your system with yourself," she almost chuckled.

"What kind of a best friend from the spit of an island to the wide, wide world, calls their best friend from the spit of an island to the wide, wide world, and says they can't talk the carnival sugar out of them."

Right! Minnow slapped a hand on top of her head. "The kind who wants to include their best friend from the spit of an island to the wide, wide world, on an adventure," she said collectively, crossing her one free arm around her torso.

"You're talking softly, like you're outside," Matt noted.

How could he not just ask her outright what the adventure was! Minnow thought frustratingly. He knew he drove her nuts when he teased her this way.

Then, at last. Matt couldn't take his own tease anymore.

"Whenever you start out with "best friend" in that tone where I can hear your smile, I don't know if I should worry or put my ballcap on."

"Put your ballcap on saltwater ponyboy," Minnow said, and indeed, she was smiling as she spoke. She sighed to release the tension of anticipation that'd built in her chest. "I need your help."

Chapter Five

Matt Evers?

Not a Chincoteague name, but that's because Matt moved to the shore from Rhode Island as a shy infant in the car seat. Some of their classmates don't let Matt forget long enough for a foal to sniff out the apple concealed in a pocket, that he' a "come-here" either. Not that anyone ever "really" let's that slide longer than it takes for her to fill herself a cup of coffee, or for her water shoes with water getting in her kayak.

But apart from the weekly Beacon that will point it out in your bio when you graduate or like the time when Matt won the best citizen volunteer award – to go with all of the other awards he wins yearly, in article trophies or invisible kindnesses. Or what an old-timer jokes, or a Teaguer mentions in general.

Once you're a part of Teaguers, of the island, you're a "come-here", but you're "their" "come-here". Joking was in good-nature and good humor, and Minnow and Matt had fun with the Teaguer and "come-here" labels.

That was how it was for Matt, if they didn't count the classmates who used Matt's come-here status as brier thwacks. The jokes and prods done with intent to bruise instead of tickle always riled Minnow up, but Matt was a duck when it came to such things, letting it roll off his unruffled feathers like water, and he wound up picking her up kicking and grabbing after one of the gnats instead of her protecting him!

Matt's unstaggered confidence and unruffled easiness wasn't good enough for Minnow, and Matt had rescued her from getting into trouble more times than she could count.

All she wanted to do was put the fake bullfrog sitting on science teacher Mrs. Jon's desk in Klepto Kevin's backpack, or get the last word with exacting Emily Brice. Which she couldn't always, but she couldn't help giving it her best shot. Her blood flowed hot with a Chincoteaguer's quick temper in tandem, especially when it came to the people she cared about.

Minnow became like a kid, without tethers of responsibilities to keep her on track. Wanting to put the favorite fake bullfrog in Klepto Kevin's backpack with only Matt's foot tripping her on the start up there from her desk, and his persistent *don't even think about it* stare to stave her, wasn't exactly reflective of the model big sister she was expected to be, and tried to emulate. If *anything*, what stopped her in time after Matt's *do you really want to go down that road* looks, and before foot-in-her-mouth moments, was so that she didn't give Windy an excuse to feel like she could do the same thing or act out.

As a result, away from her sisters Minnow couldn't say if she faced herself in a mirror and was asked, that she'd answer she'd been the best example she could be or she should be in general and in conduct for them, or for her parents. Well she could, but she didn't always like her answer, and she and her honesty often came to quarrels over this.

What was it about being away from her sisters that made it so easy to think exceptions applied, vanishing her normal tracking of her actions? Without her family as an anchor beside her?

Minnow wasn't a troublemaker, but she certainly had a knack for swimming into minnow traps.

Yet in a catch the breeze twist, something about teaming up with Matt also gave her a freedom that allowed her to be more of herself, and more of her age that she couldn't around Windy, when she was always being the big sister. She could make mistakes, because she wasn't constantly setting or striving to set an example, she was just being a kid. She could always be herself, a kid, and more around Matt.

"Jerks are always going to be jerks," is what Matt said when those mosquitoes who'd followed them all through elementary and middle to high, teased him in school. Which infuriated

Minnow and made her admire her best friend and his cool more, and she would add, with chagrin for herself.

Being more easygoing ducklike and tending to employ humor in a situation, where Minnow's first impulse was to fill her bilge-pump and pump every drop in one huge gush on the trio of two-legged mosquitoes.

Though she needn't. The jokes remained more of an irritant to Minnow than something Matt took to heart anymore. Horses had helped to bring out Matt's confidence in those under ten days of their lives, although with Matt's natural ducklike abilities he really didn't need Minnow as a bulldog even then. She still sent them glaring looks hot enough to flare their pants on fire.

Matt and Minnow had been best friends, each other's wingman, and partners in crime since they were guppies. It would be a disastrous wonder to picture all the ways of how they could not get along without the other.

The way beach has ocean, marsh has grass, Minnow loves wild horses, and Matt is part of that scenery, lodged in her heart and on this island.

When one thought of ice cream with whipped cream and a cherry, and then that ice cream smashed onto someone's face; there was Matt and Minnow. That pretty much summed up their friendship.

Matt was just as Teaguer as Minnow, if not more. Because Matt was a saltwater ponyboy, and "he" rode in the pony swim,

Minnow was suddenly reminded in her train of thought, causing her to bristle all over from her hair to her toes like she'd just swallowed something spicy.

Prior to Minnow bicycling her heart up into a frisky autumn ocean pounding, Minnow had helped on the morning tour then gotten snagged into the post behind the counter answering the phone, helping customers, and scheduling tours. She was there as evening drew on and as it got closer and closer to when she didn't have to be there, Windy sprung into the kayak shop and hopped up to the counter.

"Hey, I didn't get to tell you what I did yesterday, yesterday," she said, breathing as eagerly as she looked. She'd just rode back from the dock with Summer while Dad was up at the house taking a nap before the evening tour. She held dripping wet life-vests in each hand because she'd just rinsed them off, and the sound of static outside was Summer rinsing the tandem they'd retrieved.

Minnow was confused by what Windy said at first. "Tell me what when?" she asked.

"When I barged into the bathroom? I had something to tell you before you got all bent out of shape," Windy explained a little aggressively because she was overexcited.

"Oh yep, I remember – well you'd know wouldn't you, because you pulled back the curtain on me," Minnow growled through her teeth, moving forward toward Windy. She might have shoved her if the island-map-taped counter weren't acting buffer.

"Do you want to hear it or not?" said Windy, and then not taking the chance for Minnow to say no because she was still a little ticked at invading her shower, she added, "it's really good!"

Minnow couldn't help it. She really wanted to know. "Okay, what," she said quickly and in a direct, deep tone with a look that didn't give her anticipation away.

"I was kayaking yesterday with Freddy, Nola and Julie and guess who we bumped into along Assateague?" Windy said.

"Who," Minnow responded instantly just so Windy wouldn't prolong suspense.

In the mood Windy was in, there was fat chance of that however. Practically bursting at the seams, it was clearly making her breathing tremble as she spoke to keep herself from talking too loudly that Summer heard through the screen portion of the door.

"Tarantella Girl was kayaking with Izzy and Tizzy," revealed Windy. "Apparently, she was jarring spiders she was hunting up in the marsh."

"So?" asked Minnow. It was interesting that her sister bumped into them on the water but not earth shattering.

Isabella and Cecilia – Izzy and CC – pronounced Sissy, who Minnow and her sisters had nicknamed Tizzy – were twins.

70

Tizzy's chagrin for the outdoors extended to gaining written permission from her parents to be excluded from their Ecology class's fieldtrips to Assateague. Coming from a city, one would think fresh air and dirt and trees and birds would excite someone?

Tizzy saw it differently. Fresh air smelled like marsh mud, dirt meant filthy, trees produced pollen which swelled her eyes in the changeup seasons, and birds could leave presents in her hair.

Izzy didn't really see much at all. Her eyes were half closed in boredom most of the time.

Since the twins' parents first relocated the family from a city in Maryland to Chincoteague Island they've been trying to accomplish two phenomena's. Social engagement – or any kind of people engagement, with Izzy, and a cure for Tizzy's apprehensions about being in nature. They feel responsible for raising their daughters in a place that required air purifiers, little amusement, and too much careful but not enough play or attention.

"You know how Tizzy's always had a thing for Coby?" Windy said.

That grabbed Minnow's full attention. "Yep," she said nodding, engrossed now and *needing* to hear what happened.

There was one important factor that played into what Windy just revealed to Minnow. Guys didn't really go for the twins. Tizzy, because she was worrisome about the outdoors and on an island, everyone does everything outside – and Izzy because she looked so bored all the time and could care less what day it was, let alone if a guy thought her bland outlook on the world was cute.

Minnow had gone deep – but now she must go further back. Not to the bronze age, but to a particular point in time that felt as far back to Minnow, with as many entanglements as it brought with it.

Back to before Mr. and Mrs. Plenty bought used kayaks from Dad in the offseason – back when the Plenty family rented kayaks from Dad – back to the first tour they ever went on to try to spark interest for the outside world in Izzy and at the same time cure Tizzy of her chagrin for the outdoors, a real fear which went deeper than most would think.

It was then, that she'd developed a Velcro crush for Coby. He was one of Dad's guides on the tour that morning, and Coby tried to help her feel at ease on the water – with the mosquitoes, gnats, murky, seaweed water. Tizzy couldn't appreciate the snowy white egrets, dancing damselflies, or dewdrops shimmering silver and then golden with the sun rising.

When Windy started splashing with Minnow at the dock as they were putting in, Tizzy shrank in on herself, cringing in horror.

Coby paddled his kayak between them, even though the girls had stopped once they realized that they'd upset Tizzy. Once again, unknowingly endearing himself to the twin.

Coby had been kind and understanding to worrisome Tizzy, and she'd had a crush on him ever since.

There was only one little catch. Coby had a girlfriend; and in a few years, he was engaged to his fiancé Summer, Minnow's big sister.

For years whenever Minnow and her sisters would see Izzy and Tizzy, they'd try to befriend them and ask if they wanted to play. Tizzy was unsure about adventure though. It came with uncertain factors, like cuts that could invite infection, touching something that might be dirty or grosser – alive!

Izzy never really answered other than with nothing to say.

It was nearly impossible to be friends with either one, even if the twins had befriended Minnow, Windy, Summer and Matt.

Plus, she hung out with Tarantella Girl, whose snobbery and fixation with arachnids didn't win any friends.

The three of them sort of blended together and fell into an inexplicable friendship. Their inexplicableness' what made their friendship and cahooting so binding.

Now the three of them made up an inseparable trio, like Minnow and her sisters, Coby and Matt made up their kayak shop band with a special bond.

That's just how it was.

Also, Tizzy's jealousy of Summer quickly became a friction between all of them, and ultimately, they gave up on befriending the twins.

So when Windy just mentioned Tizzy and Coby in the same sentence, Minnow could only imagine what came next!

"The general mood was, hi, can't stand your guts, go away," Windy summed, acting out the general civility and mood of everyone and the atmosphere with looks and moving her arm in a gentle wave current. Just like that she snapped back with her large eyes and intent look, leaning forward. "Tizzy asked how Coby was? So I said fine. Then she replied, "When he discovers real love, then he'll be fine". I was about to snap back when I realized something."

"What?" asked Minnow.

"Remember Coby's life-vest that went missing last year? Tizzy was wearing it!" Windy revealed.

Minnow gaped.

"I thought Klepto Kevin nabbed it! He's the only one with a blue spiky topknot!" insisted Minnow.

Windy laid it out in short like a true detective. "Summer saw him riding his bike down the road the day it went missing, and Dad went to his house and Kleptomaniac's parents searched his room and never found it – because *she* had him steal it for her!"

Minnow was blown away and still processing. But it got better.

"I couldn't help myself. I said, "Nice life-vest Tizzy", and she blushed as red as a beet! Then," Windy began, sense of suspense anew. "Tarantella Girl cut in and said, "Picking up your sister? Or trading her in?" The way she said it with such entitlement!" insisted Windy. "Like nobody could touch her or put a hair out of place!"

Tarantella Girl and Minnow not liking each other was a whole other tale. Even though it sounded like the arachnid enthusiast was sticking up for her friend in her remark to needle Windy through Minnow, Minnow knew there was also snarky there to be found in the opportunity of the moment.

"Careful – likes to jump into boats; and she can bite," I said to Carly. They didn't like my joke – actually Izzy might not have really heard me – she was staring in the water – so maybe she did? Anyway, Tizzy was red and actually glancing around as though you were really swimming in the water and might jump in her boat! And Tarantella Girl glared at me," Windy explained. "So, I said "it's a good thing you have Coby's life-jacket on, with my sister on the loose". And Tizzy spoke up again, defending herself. "I found it last fall when we were hunting up spiders", and I said, that's not true," Windy relayed, playing out her flat, blunt response as well as Tizzy's attitude as she retold the story. "We went back and forth – it is, it isn't, it is, it isn't. She said I don't mind outside as much anymore. And so, then as we paddled by, I filled my bilge-pump up and gushed it on her!"

"And it got on Izzy and Tarantella Girl because they were flanking so close!" Windy added.

"You did!" Minnow sucked in air so sharply she made a loud choking sound!

Windy nodded, squeezing her eyes closed as she said with contained but utter delight, "I did, I did, I did!"

"I missed it!" Minnow complained with envy and unwavering amazement.

"I know, but watch her face next time we see her," Windy said, "I bet she does beelines in the store or something because she doesn't know what we'll do next! Tizzy was in such a Tizzy-fit that she swore payback – but she said, that stuff didn't really bother her anymore," said Windy with a shrug that stayed still in explanation for a second, before leaving her ears. "I'd worry about Carly anyway. We got into a splashing fight that worsened things. Tizzy's too – Tizzy – to get her hands messy in payback."

"Do you realize how major it is that Tizzy wore something someone else had worn and sweated in?" Minnow remarked.

"She probably soaked it in bleach," Windy replied.

76

At that point Summer was coming in and Windy scurried over to the wall facing east in the deeper part of the front room to hang the life-vests up.

She could've let them dry outside but she'd been too anxious to tell Minnow before she busted wide open. Besides, it was so warm they'd dry shortly.

The wet vests and Windy' sudden scramble didn't escape Summer though, and she looked at Minnow for the truth, as she always did and expected. Minnow couldn't hold the important stuff back from her, and as the second oldest, there was this innate and unspoken code of big sisters and principles between them.

"What's up?" Summer asked, holding back the quantity of her suspicion from showing. But Minnow saw it as up close as the beads of hard-work glistening her face and arms.

"Nothing," Minnow said shrugging, putting on her plain face.

"Nothing!" Windy chimed in, which it would've been more convincing if she hadn't.

Summer eyed Minnow, and Minnow smiled unassumingly.

She grunted, tugging her ballcap on lower as she took a chilled bottle of water from the old cola fridge and went back into the hot air and glaring sun to guzzle her ice-cold water and get back to work.

Minnow and Windy checked each other's thoughts with a look, both sensing Summer knew something was up but wasn't pressing it. For now.

If she wanted to she could. Maybe she planned on letting them come forward first, or pressing later.

In a way, Minnow felt sorry for Tizzy. Even with the friction between her and Minnow with her sisters because of her crush on Coby, plus the fact that she was BFF with Tarantella Girl.

But there were people around her, teachers, acquaintances, and her own family, who understood her proclivities and sensitivities, and tried to help her. Her sister was too bored with life to really put effort into helping Tizzy not be so Tizzy. However, there was no excuse for her meanness to Summer.

Dislike because she was marrying the guy she had a crush on? Understandable.

Getting their high school kleptomaniac to steal Coby's life-vest? *Hilarious!* And rather groundbreaking for the girl who avoided walking on grass barefoot.

But picking at her sisters wasn't nice. Windy had stuck up for Summer and Minnow, and while she'd let things escalate to an uncalled for extreme, Minnow confessed she'd have probably been tempted to do the same thing. She'd pictured doing it to Klepto Kevin and Tarantella Girl for years!

Besides, it was just water. Minnow pictured Tizzy throwing a tizzy-fit and insisting to her parents that she was running a fever this week from some sort of pollution in the water, but maybe getting doused with the good old outdoors and surviving it was just what she needed to put her on the path to less outdoor apprehension? Maybe not cure her of her conceived phobias entirely, but in the least, make her think about being nicer.

Minnow was stilling kicking herself. Tarantella Girl doused, and Izzy and Tizzy splashed! She couldn't believe she'd missed it!

Tizzy had sworn payback, but Minnow wasn't worried for Windy from a girl who didn't even sniff flowers. Besides, Windy was a pirate. After Tizzy's experience, Minnow thought the tizzy-fit twin was just blowing off steam.

Minnow helped up until Dad walked in wearing the relaxed look of waking up from a pleasant slumber.

She hugged him see you later and waved to her sisters, Windy waving like she wanted to go with her, wherever that was, and yet her legs were glued to standing in the shop because she was excited about going on another tour.

She'd managed to wiggle out of the evening tour by helping all day while Dad rested up for the tour, and now at last hopped on her bike with the sole purpose in mind to convince Matt to help her, and if unsuccessful, throwing him into the bay. But she had to convince him; she just had too.

Minnow said hello to Marshy before disembarking. "He'll say yes, you'll see sweet girl," she said, kissing Marshy' nose as she squeak-neighed. Minnow pushed and mounted her bike before meeting the road. "Wish me luck!" she called to Marshy, who wished her luck but wished more that she was coming with her!

How did Minnow expect to get away with mutiny? Well, it wasn't really mutiny. It wasn't really wrong either. And she'd played the stowaway with Summer and Windy in pretend, all of her life. As though she were practicing for this moment forever, and never knew she was, until now.

But none of this would work, without Matt.

Chapter Six

"Your idea's amateur," Matt was going on, filing the remainder of marquee letters in the recycled carboard box, bloated already with this past week's movie title; reminding Minnow of the tummies of how the wild ponies got from drinking saltwater in their main and coarse diet.

Matt always volunteered as marquee man when the movie changed. He volunteered at the carnival, rode in every pony swim, and in general anywhere else events asked him.

He should convince the theatre to recycle a bigger box, Minnow was thinking with light sarcasm, *that* would be helpful, but whatever, and shook her head.

"No, it's not – it's brilliant! It's been working for thousands of years!" Minnow said with a tone, because they'd been going in circles since she called last night and to pull it off, to make her dream come true, she needed Matt. He was her only in; maybe ever. Or this summer at least. And Minnow was determined that this summer was going to be the summer that changed her life.

"Besides, I'm not breaking any laws, just a tradition," she added in hopes it'd boost her side of the argument.

Did the thought of doing something new and similar to their scampers as kids tickle his interest? Well normal rule breaking wasn't something that appealed to either one of them, unless it was a silly rule to begin with. They'd broken plenty of rules on accident growing up. But by far, Matt's enthusiasm for adventure had always been a ready one. In recent years however, his time had been absorbed being a volunteer at the carnival, a fulltime saltwater ponyboy with dreams of one day soon starting a horse riding lessons stable with trail guiding from horseback, as well as absorbed in doing ordinary helpful things, like changing the marquee for the theatre because they often ran short of muscle. He'd had less and less time to do the things with Minnow that they used to do.

While Minnow hadn't had this problem of pocketing or losing her spontaneity at all, keeping the easily curious and interested-in-everything, childlike streak in her. Minnow couldn't help all of her flaws – she had a sister who considered herself a pirate!

It's remarkable in that sense that Minnow had managed to save or enrich any sense of ordinary or right and wrong, with a sister bordering on the spoiled, who constantly broke the rules and yet Minnow had to admit, even Windy possessed limits. She wouldn't cross Mom or Dad on purpose; if she could help it.

Minnow halted – she wasn't giving herself enough credit. Yes, growing up in a close family with two distinctive sisters, they faced their fair shares of mistakes and lessons learned the hard way, but they were also the glue that held each one of them together, and to task. Just the thought of doing something questionable, rousted Mom or Dad's voice, or a time between Windy and Summer or Minnow and one of them, that staved a reaction or uh oh with unintended consequences attached, or boosted courage. Families who love one another are like that. The voice in that back of your head or sprung up in your heart that cautions "not a good idea," or answers "what are you waiting for?"

Those voices inside of her were all of them. But her own little voice within it all, spoke to her the loudest yesterday, and right now. *What are you waiting for?*

Matt did not have to be a renegade, or the pirate that her sister was, or contain any streak of *childlike up for adventure even if it's a little bit of a big no-no* in his blood, to help Minnow out.

Which she was confident despite his bouts of unspontaneity in recent months, was still there. She sensed it, the way she called the weather based on what she smelled or how the wind blew in the marsh, how it sounded in the trees, and felt on her skin. Or if there was no wind, just stillness.

Glimpsing rustled interest in the look of listening in Matt's features, she knew she'd tickled the part of Matt who was always up for adventure. The very part she was sure she could tickle forever and forever since he was the most impossible to tickle anywhere else, being a smidgeon sensitive on "one" of his feet and on his right side.

Matt didn't have to be anything he wasn't. He just had to be her friend. And that, Matt and Minnow were; like grass is green and sky is blue, and marshmallows are roasted and pizza eaten best when you're doing it with someone you love.

So why was Matt not agreeing through the caution of his first instincts?

Minnow tried another approach. "It'll be fun! An adventure no one would ever know about but the two of us? We've had those all of our lives," she said. "Those are our adventures. What's so different about this time?"

Matt stared at Minnow for a long moment. She stared back, hopeful, not too much, and smiling.

"I'm already considered a come-here, and you propose a grand scheme that will have "every" Teaguer sour-eye me?" Matt remarked, half smiling. "I could be shunned from the swim, exiled from volunteering at the carnival and the oyster festival, or booted off the island with my hat in my hand and a see you never wave."

Minnow rolled her eyes because she didn't miss a beat in the humor part of his word choice, replying, "That's an exaggeration."

Matt eyed her.

Squinting.

Minnow held his stare because if she won then she could win his help, if she could just make her point understandable. Staring contests were a game between them, some with serious tones like now, when something precious or as stubborn as one's point of view was on the line. Minnow and Matt could stare unblinkingly for up to forty-three seconds. But this time Minnow's edge was too hot to control. It felt like Matt was holding an invisible bike pump at her toes with his look, puffing her up with the truth of his statement until her denial with more denial attached inflated her to the point of popping and she had to let it come out or explode.

"Alright, it's not an exaggeration," she burst, then squeezed her hands on her hips like she did when she upset or serious.

Had he been practicing or something? Since when did Matt win stare-offs because he was right?

Or looked straight through her doing it?

Fess up Minnow, she told herself. Plenty of times. But she was stronger than this.

So much was at stake. Minnow was having trouble focusing. Being ticklish every and anywhere unlike Matt's singularities, Matt normally tickled her without blinking to win the stare-off.

"I'm not a come-here; my roots grow up from this island three hundred plus years back; through time, tears, toil, and joy," Minnow began softly. She said, "It's my tradition to shatter more than most anyone or anything," Minnow said.

For a hold your breath moment Matt had the look of someone who understood, and Minnow felt like he was on the verge of nodding. So, Minnow's mouth gaped when he shook his head instead and on the tail of, "No can do," turned with the box of letters he now picked up to go inside the theatre.

But there was something in all she'd expressed and poured her heart out with that she wasn't saying.

"Alright, I'll do it!" she burst and tripped forward in her launch to clutch his arm. Matt nearly spilled the letters but she helped him to hold the pile bloating out of the box in his arms.

Standing there, she huffed and said, "I'll help you get back with Tarantella Girl."

"Got to be on a tour in the morning?" Matt asked smiling.

"No," she said between her teeth.

"See you in front of the kayak shop 5:30 on the nose," Matt said, and this time she let him leave. But not without a fire-breathing stare she hoped scalded his sunburn back.

Would he have still helped her if she'd punched him in the arm for that smile?

She should've let the marquee letters clatter.

Chapter Seven

Minnow didn't require an iota of motherly coaxing or extra incentive to bolt out of bed at 5:30, which was still cricket chirping time in the summer.

Mom was already in the workshop painting recently shaped ducks, and taking a small break from sanding others. Minnow knew one quick check outside Windy' window facing the kayak shop would reveal the lights on through the sawdusty windows because she smelled coffee and heard no sizzling from the skillet pan. Whenever there was a tour nobody ate breakfast except for coffee, and being an artist Mom drank coffee for breakfast nearly every morning, except when there was no morning tour and then everyone sat down for family breakfast and actually ate.

Dad and Summer were up at five to drink a stand-up-strong cup and transport the first load of boats down to the dock where they'd be set off to the side, out of the way of ramp users until they were ready with their group to launch.

Minnow heard the half ton truck she knew in every creak and sound and by speed and degree who was driving, returning to the shop, crunching easily or bumpily over the clamshells and gravel mixed drive alongside in front.

She rarely mixed Dad, Summer or Mom up with each other, though it'd been known to happen.

Windy was lagging a half hour behind when Minnow bolted out of bed to jump into her cut shorts and clean top.

She didn't care if Windy saw her naked this morning, but she did warn her with a quick, "Shut your eyes, a sec."

To which Windy sighed with a hint of catching her breath, "Seriously, now?" But she did it anyway.

They were both awake and pumping adrenaline and yet still plagued by sleepy led weights in the oddest places in their bodies – their calves, a thigh, noodle arms, and sleepy crusty eyes.

Bumbling to fit into her sleeve cut top, Windy looked like she was doing a belly dance very poorly and Minnow kept bumping into her within the small space in the middle of their room between their beds, like a newborn foal finding her legs.

Windy' ire stoked and flared warm the fourth-time Minnow's rump rammed her when she swung around, sending her groggy pirate sister sailing onto the edge of her tangled-up bed.

Leaving her straw saltwater ponygirl hat on her bedpost, Minnow dashed out of the house just as the truck pulled away from the kayak shop.

She waved to Dad and Summer, who hung onto the side of the truck with a big smile. She clamped it shut to keep out a mouthful of mosquitoes as Minnow hopped by the workshop with a kiss for Mom's cheek and let her know she was headed out to help Matt do volunteer work here and there with the hope of getting to help in the carnival, like she'd told everyone she was doing today at din-din last night.

Congratulations and applause had then erupted around the dinner table from her family, as Minnow had resisted volunteering outside of the actual pony swim in the stubborn hope that standing her ground may show her dedication and up her chances of being accepted at last. One will try anything even if it sounds harebrained, or is illogical, when you've pinned your dreams to something dear to you.

"Put sunscreen on throughout the day," Mom ordered as a tender but *I mean it* reminder, and Minnow promised. Then she left the workshop and darted to the edge of the marsh across from the kayak shop to wait for Matt.

She heard clatter noise coming from the front section inside the shop and figured it was Windy counting out how many paddles they needed. She hadn't seen her cross the yard, and the image of her sailing and crashing onto her bed resurfaced and made Minnow want to laugh.

And today, she'd need her sense of humor if she wanted to get through helping Matt without wimping out or gagging.

If she wanted Matt's help, she had to do this. Minnow crossed her arms, telling herself that she could. It wasn't like she hadn't done it time over before.

Helping Matt and Carly get back together felt as ritual as the tradition of pony swim sometimes, although it was unfair to compare that special event with tarantella girl and the monarch butterfly wearing her web even when she cut him loose.

There was no mistaking the sound of Matt's Dad's old truck with a bad muffler and tricky sparkplugs, or that the rusty teal blue square dot approaching her from the left was him. Matt was early. He rolled to a slow stop in front of her, looking too pleased and chipper about getting back with his ex, Tarantella Girl, for Minnow this early, and on an empty stomach.

Minnow yanked on the salt cranky, ancient and whiny door and once in, pulled it closed hard and stuffed a foot on the dashboard that cracked a little more every time she did it, though the contact is normally less aggravated, crossing her arms as Matt built easy, mild speed down the quiet east side road.

Matt's favorite old ballcap that he'd had since they were seven told the tale of their childhood. Minnow could identify certain how this grass stain got there, or why a smudge of black near the back wouldn't come out. Adventuring, spelunking, games of freeze tag, contests, and general roughhousing were the tips of the iceberg.

He never went anywhere without it, and while he'd given up one of his favorite longtime sweatshirt hoody' to Carly as a symbol of his affection for her, it gave Minnow some comfort to know there were some things he'd never part with for Tarantella Girl, or anyone else. Like Minnow.

Carly couldn't understand, or rather was annoyed that Matt was best friends with Minnow. Minnow felt likewise about how Matt could date a girl like Carly. How had they ever gotten off on the wrong foot?

Minnow doesn't think there had ever been a right foot in all of this, concerning Minnow and Carly, the spider fixated, slightly gothic girl. They were too different; Carly was a science, arachnid, and biology nerd, with an icy cold tendency and mean streak that came from her practical mind and having wealthy parents who probably weren't affectionate and nosey with her like Minnow and her family. Which was the hugest gap of difference by far.

Minnow was a nerd too, but with horses. She could be stubborn and get her dander up quickly, which were things that got her into many minnow traps. Her family was close; so close that her little sister Windy didn't understand the meaning of the word personal privacy yet!

They had family night two nights every week; there were no scheduled tours for Monday night or Saturday night, no exceptions. They laughed openly, joked together, and were so attune to each other's ways and hearts, Minnow couldn't imagine life as a family not being like this the way she couldn't imagine life with no thumbs or life without ponies.

Minnow combed her hair when she got out of the shower, but she woke up in the morning and greeted the day with jeans and if yesterday's shirt still smelled clean, then wha-la.

Carly's slightly gothic and organized lifestyle couldn't withstand one week, let alone one night, in Minnow's colorful and rambunctious and loud household.

Was there any circumstance where Minnow could see them being friends?

How could someone be a friend to someone who looked at them like they studied their spiders – collectively and methodically?

Yet if Matt weren't a football both of them wanted for themselves, would their differences really count for not being at least nice to each other?

Would Carly ever have a breakthrough moment? wondered Minnow, as she did now and then.

Fat chance, she told herself.

Tarantella Girl got her nickname from Minnow, not only because she owns an entire aquarium of hairy critters.

Carly mimics her pets in eerie, and to Minnow, deliberate ways. Carly's sophisticated, mostly absent mother and businessman father raise her, and yet similar to Mowgli with the wolves from the Jungle Book, she took example from her pet tarantellas and applied spider phycology to life in general.

It was well established in and outside of school that she considered herself a forward thinker in the evolution of things. With the goal of earning a scholarship to a university of science in North Carolina where apparently, they have a renowned course in arachnology, which of course is the study of spiders – Carly worked tirelessly producing theories and essays out of her critiquing studies of her spiders, as well as of the spiders on the island that she captures regularly in jars. Stuffed with natural habit for their species from where she found them, so that they felt at home, guessed Minnow.

It is the height of boredom for Minnow, and she can't get away from her in class, when Tarantella Girl announces regularly how that she's going to be an arachnologist, but one the world has never seen before. One who studies spiders and discovers extinct species or behaviors. Would that make her an arachnid phycologist?

Minnow would immerse herself in horse sketching and try to drown out Tarantella Girl's bragging to a group of Richardson's Landing kids; her pencil broke most of the time because she tried too hard.

Because Minnow was an honest person, she gave Carly credit for loving spiders as much as Minnow loved horses. That's all she was giving her credit for other than being mean and snobby. So maybe, there's a slim glimmer of hope for Tarantella Girl to have humanness? Her spiders could show her the way – if she stopped studying them long enough to let herself see the nice parts they possess too. Even Minnow could see on tours how much fun the baby spiders had swinging on their webs and flying through the air on the end of their string like a kid whose kite had gotten away from them and taken them along.

But Carly wasn't fascinated by most everyone's idea or sense of fun – she's obsessed with studying spiders. Namely, tarantellas. Not in wondering if they were having fun *being* spiders.

Minnow wondered if she should rethink her nickname for Carly. Black widow might be more appropriate. She also sucks the fun out of life and the life out of her mate and goes on to another. It just so happens that Matt never learns.

But she's been Tarantella Girl for too long to change it up now, which was Minnow's conclusion every time she considered the option.

The two have been breaking up and getting back together since middle school, over one thing or another, and yet to Minnow also over nothingness. As though breaking up and getting back together is everything that makes their relationship work. And doomed.

Poor Matt, Minnow empathized, but she was still ticked at him.

He's doomed.

She keeps telling him Carly's a spider that only looks like a person but he won't be convinced.

As any best friend, Minnow cares about Matt and she loves him. Minnow can only protect him so much though. Against the bully twits who call him a come-here to sting, was one thing doable. But the heart is another scope of the matter altogether. And his heart refused to shut out Tarantella Girl.

Minnow guesses he hasn't been main course enough times.

When on earth will it be one too many? she asked, exasperated and annoyed.

Minnow heard the echo of Dad's horn through the muffling forest as they were rounding the curve that opened up the road and a clean shot to the beach with the slight curve at the inlet crossing. The indicator that the morning tour had started and they were heading up Sheepshead Creek.

Minnow was heading up a creek. One with worse than having no paddle – having no point of return except completing the circle.

What had Minnow gotten herself into this time? The truth was she hardly knew herself. But it wasn't going to be like anything she'd ever swam into.

Enjoying the drive and the quiet start to the morning, Minnow almost let herself forget why they were going to the beach. Not happening. Because she was also stewing.

Thrilled Matt was going to help her?

Thrilled was getting on a roller-coaster for the first time. Seeing fireworks in-person. Yep. Minnow was thrilled indeed.

Grudgeful that her end of the bargain was reuniting him with his arachnid-obsessed ex?

"Muffins?" offered Matt.

Minnow slid a glance at the yellow paper bag sitting between them, crinkly rolled to seal out bugs. If only she, or even better, Matt! could seal out spider-girl the way he did other annoying and nuisance insects.

She knew by the smell they were last of his mother's batch of blueberry muffins she'd baked before she and Mr. Evers went on their road-trip to Athens Tennessee. According to Mrs. Evers, while she was loading up Minnow with a half a dozen that morning when she'd swung by to wish them bon voyage, it was the first pony penning, since three years after first moving to Chincoteague, that they were leaving the island on vacation.

Minnow could tell how much it meant for them to leave the hectic pony craziness, as involved as they were with having a saltwater ponyboy as a son.

They helped Matt through the long week every time; only this summer, for pony penning week, he was on his own. Matt felt excited, really excited. This pony week was his chance as well to shine, and prove to his parents that he could handle all of the responsibilities, as well as the independence they were leaving him with. Not that they needed convincing. Matt was a very responsible person. Still, this was one of the hugest, "I trust you," times in both their lives.

Matt knew how much she loved berries.

The warm tangy smell of microwave warm muffins wafted through the bag and permeated the inside of the truck, tickling Minnow's nose, tickling her appetite; her tummy made a whiny small growl.

He wasn't bribing her with *this* though. She told herself firmly that she could not be wavered.

She'd had her fill of bribery this weekend anyway.

"For the umpteenth time, no," Minnow stated simply. She acted indifferent but her manner and sarcasm was revealing her irritation underneath.

He'd been offering her blueberry muffins every two minutes. "I don't want to eat. I'm irritated at you that you've still after eight years got this obsession with Carly, that you've plagued us all with by the way since knee high to a glasswort reed and I want to stay irritated. Eating might soothe me," Minnow stated staring out the windshield.

"Want my eyeteeth instead?" Matt asked.

It was a ploy to bait her into talking and Minnow swam right into it, but she couldn't help it. "Yes. I could wear them around my neck, the way Tarantella Girl wears your dignity like a school ring."

That made him smile, which made Minnow roll her eyes. Matt was in a chipper mood.

Good for Matt.

Minnow's smiling sarcasm spread from her inner thoughts to her face, but she faced the shrub and tree scenery coasting by her. Yielding into marsh, the beach roared ahead of them, and Minnow straightened a little in her seat in anticipation of feeling herself splashing into the cool and rushing ocean, known to her as pure freedom. She vaguely sensed Matt's glance her way, knowing how she reacted around water or the beach as well as sensing the sudden alertness in her slight movement and trained focus.

The blue and foamy white waves arose and crashed, pounding into Minnow's heart through the sea breeze.

"Careful; you look like you might be starting to smile," said Matt, adding, "don't forget that you're irritated at me."

Minnow eyed him with a stinging upward look.

He lifted up the bag. "Muffin?"

Minnow growled, unable to hold back the tide of her frustration any longer. "You're too nice for her!" burst Minnow with insistence, startling Matt into a yelp and dropping the muffins bag, which startled her into yelping too. "Yep, scary right!" she said, playing off the opportunity in the moment. "She eats nice for fun – just like one of her spiders!"

"Right now, you're scary," Matt replied, petering into sounds of relief, though he still looked a little tensed.

"Bless your heart," she said, stretching and hitting his hat brim down.

Chapter Eight

Minnow ran the last few yards and splashed into the briny coolness of a swelling wave.

If anything could soothe her irritation, and if she *let* anything soothe her, it was the beach, and the ocean. She'd refuse blueberry muffins, her favorite smoothie, mixed berry, and ice cream for dinner if it was offered to her when she was angry or irritated. But Minnow was hard-pressed to refuse this, and facing the peak of sunrise let herself smile freely.

The one thing besides Marshy and horses, period, that alleviated Minnow when her dander was up, or soothed her irritation over Matt's Tarantella Girl complex, was the rusty under her feet and the briny coolness swallowing up her legs.

Wide, expansive, crashing blue.

Morning cool beach sand called to her from behind her to build a sandcastle, and she was tempted but not enough yet to leave the ocean. As cool as the shade under a tree, it was keeping the breeze from the ocean cool as it blew. The horizon glowed, yet daybreak. Minnow had time before the sand became too hot to play in.

Ocean tied in her ears with this cool sea wind kissing her face with greeting, and lifted blond brown waves of her hair. Minnow filled her lungs with salty tinged sea air – all her troubles and frustrations started allaying themselves. What was the big deal anyway?

Minnow had lowered her hopes and expectations that Matt would ever learn from Tarantella-Girl-breakups past. Minnow now deduced that Matt had to get plum-tired of Tarantella Girl's oscillating sincerity, of her playing this game with his heart. His susceptibleness to her spider-like precisions of seduction was shiver-worthy, but clearly only she felt that way. To Minnow, a relationship like there's meant either two things. Either they were very serious and this was real – which meant doom and yuck came to mind when she pictured Matt wrapped in her tarantella webby arms. Or Matt, and obviously, Tarantella Girl, hadn't a clue what real love was.

Did Minnow?

Minnow's dating record wasn't vast either, but not because she'd been breaking up and getting back with the same person for eight years. Minnow didn't really have any aspirations to date. She dated three times, Jamie for a month, Kyle for one day, and Pete less than a week. She simply wasn't interested. There were so many more important and interesting things she was doing in life and thought about. Summer and Windy could have the trouble. Although Summer was pretty sure, and so were the rest of them, that she'd found her one true love. She'd dated her fiancé Coby for two and a half years now.

Windy however had the most trouble with dating a boy for an extended time. Either she was bored by them or they couldn't handle her little sister's intensity, or attention grabbing trait. Whereas Minnow lacked the inclination altogether.

Minnow didn't want Matt getting hurt again – which was why she always tried to convince him that Tarantella Girl didn't deserve him. Minnow saw her using him like a specimen she studied in her tank collection. Dangling him on a spider string. But who knows – maybe they'll live happily ever after!

At this point, Minnow didn't care – she cared about Matt – but she was fed up with his dating routine. She'd go along with this next scheme but that didn't mean she was going to stop teasing and prodding him over Tarantella Girl.

Pretending to be moody Minnow trudged out of the deep part of the surge and faced Matt. "So, where's snuggle-bug?" Minnow remarked with arms folded as she scanned the beach. Fully prepared for and unruffled when she turned her head and met Matt's gaze with a flattened stare.

Not a humorous bone out of joint from the jab in her bruising remark or blue eyes, Matt smiled. Up till now he'd suppressed his happier than a clam on a beach extinct of seagulls, on Minnow's behalf. But saltwater ponyboys don't skip, or if they did Minnow wanted to see Matt do it.

Just not if Tarantella Girl put that skip in his step.

"Patience Minnow," answered Matt. "I did the legwork. She's jogging."

"Okay Detective Noir," replied Minnow as she checked the horizon. The summer sun was peeking at her in a ring of yellow, making her think back to her analogy about starting up a creek with no turning back. She had to complete the circle. She was going up that creek now.

Soon the current would be too strong to turn back. But if she wanted to ride in the swim, wasn't it already too strong for turning back around?

Yep.

She'd trapped herself into helping Matt get back with the girl she loathed, for the chance of making a once in a lifetime dream come true. Seemed fair; even though this part of the bargain would be a struggle.

The sunlight looked such a friendly shade of yellow, that Minnow wondered on the cuff if she could stare it back down behind the far and wide water with her inner irritation and infuriation that could keep her mowing grass for a week. Even if her stare-offs weren't what they normally were, lately.

Oh well, sighed Minnow, who looked up and down the beach without any effort to squint in the distance. But she saw three dots on her right, south, coming from the old coastguard station many joggers used as a distance marker.

One staggered, another grimaced, and the middle one held her composure.

Fifteen minutes, figured Minnow at this easy distance.

Matt must have noticed the glare return to her blue eyes because he noticed them as well. She watched as his chest filled with sea air, and something else that made Minnow turn her head and quickly speak just to take his attention off Tarantella Girl.

"So, what's your plan, this time?" Minnow challenged. "You wanna hear mine first?" Minnow didn't wait. "We, meaning I, stuff a crab or a mud snail down her tank and you come to the rescue–

"Not happening," Matt interrupted coolly.

"Really? It's brilliant. She loathes me and can't get why I'm your best friend, so if you yell at me and I pretend I'm crushed," Minnow said, pretending to tear up and overdue it on the sniffing, "it'd be dramatic and heroic, she'd glue herself to you on the spot," Minnow said.

"I've got something better," replied Matt.

"What?" asked Minnow.

"You're bait," revealed Matt.

"I'm BAIT!" she stated in disbelief, confused as to what exactly that would entail. She pictured herself as a tiny minnow stuck on a large web in the woods along her yard, wiggling her little body back and forth. Matt was the green cricket perched on a nearby twig holding a valentine in his hand – and Carly was the spider returning to her web to dress minnow up like a crispy spring roll for dinner. How exactly did Matt get Carly back by sticking Minnow out on his ex's clothesline? And how did this all turn out in the end for Minnow?

"What kind of a statement is that? I'm not going to be spider bait for your arachnid girl," Minnow said, crossing her arms. "How would I even do that? Her web is so big I don't know if I'd even show up," muttered Minnow on the last part.

"Trust me – you'll show up. But I can't tell you – I have to show you," Matt replied, but there was something in his eyes that to Minnow resembled hesitance, even though they gleamed with certainty. Like when she watched Matt taste grass on a dare game when they were five.

"Alright, so show me," Minnow said, now unafraid and more curious with remembering this dare game memory. "How would I be bait? Are you going to throw me in the ocean? Pretend to be guilting me over something like driving Carly away and tell me I'm not your friend? Kind of like my plan but I just don't get to do the mud snail thing?"

Her guess erased the hesitance in Matt's features and brown eyes. Matt's easy and endearing smile Minnow knew by heart told her she'd made his heart laugh, and that at least was something Tarantella Girl could never do or recognize in her oldest, most, best friend when it happened.

With a knowing look, hintingly daring Minnow Matt stepped forward and she didn't think twice about the closeness, other than tensing in case he tried to grab her and use her as bait by flinging her into the ocean or something without warning her first. He had that look that they both got when they were daring each other or about to pull something.

Minnow bet Matt's plan was to wrestle but look like they were fighting, or argue so that Carly thought there was bad blood?

Whatever the grand scheme or move was, was it really too difficult for his brain to translate verbally? Maybe Tarantella Girl had wound him up so tightly in her web this time he couldn't speak.

Matt anticipated her reaction because right after he said in reply to her question in one more attempt to use the mud snail, "This plan is better than mud-snails," Matt looped his arm around her waist and swept her up to him with a steady and kind hand on the small of her back propping her there on her toes.

Minnow hadn't known that was possible to do with someone except in the movies. The surprise and puzzlement delayed Minnow connecting the dots or inquiring how holding her close was supposed to work, or in thinking they were going to wrestle thought three moves ahead to wiggling free or throwing him over her shoulder like they have since those little grass-burn days. *Yep, grass can burn.* If Minnow could even do that flip nowadays since Matt had sprouted a head taller than her last summer. The muscles didn't really count. Minnow was willful and resilient; she'd never yield or quit.

It happened so quickly Minnow inhaled Matt when he kissed her.

Chapter Nine

Minnow startled from being kissed by Matt, and her startle from being kissed at all paired with the depth and yet lightness in which her best friend kissed her made her need more air and she couldn't breathe through her mouth so she breathed in his mouth and kissing.

Matt pulled back wearing one of his smiles through the frame of his grimaced features shaded by the brim of his grass, dirt stained and fraying ballcap. "Good idea, right?" he said.

Minnow pushed off of him and then pushed him and then stubbornly put her hands on her hips. "That's your bright idea? Now who's amateur!"

"Come on Mighty Minnow," Matt beseeched earnestly, and she pressed her lips in a firm line because he used her nickname since kids, hoping to win her over.

"Oh, using my nickname is not a good idea right now," she told him. Her muscles were already feeling mighty in her minnow arms and she was just north of wrestling him into the ocean!

"This is the only thing that will snap her out of her Harry trance," Matt explained. "If she thinks we're a couple, she'll climb the walls."

"Yep, she's Tarantella Girl," Minnow retorted. Couldn't they just wrestle and pretend to argue for Carly's attention instead of this whole couple, with kissing thing?

"What about my idea with the mud snail," she started with high hopes, adding, "can't we just pretend to argue instead of this whole couple, kissing thing? Besides, it'd be good, I wouldn't be pretending right now!"

But Matt cut her off with an imploring look and said, "At any other time with any other guy it'd be genius, but it's not strong enough to break this trance she has with Harry. He's a science nerd too, he speaks her language," insisted Matt. "The only thing that's goanna jolt her is if she thinks we're a couple. It gets under her skin just because we're friends."

"Of course, it does, she's jealous of anyone who's your friend because it takes attention away from her! That's why she's always breaking up with you! It makes you crawl to her and she feels like the center of your attention! This would make her super jealous," Minnow admitted, with a "but" coming. "But, so would a mud snail – or," Minnow stopped and her eyes grew big. "I could pretend to step on a spider! I could get a fake one, and insert it with ketchup!" Minnow was on a new roll. "You could come along and save a real one, one we took from her tanks, and be the hero – or even better!" Minnow couldn't believe her own genius sometimes! "We could kidnap one of her spiders and you could find it and be the hero! After that..."

Minnow wasn't finished but Matt interrupted.

"I want to win her back not scar her for life! She's my girlfriend. No fake stepping on spider or ketchup or arachnid-napping, and no mud snail."

"What am I, chopped liver?" Great, that was the definition of what he wanted her to pretend to be. Nice defense Minnow. Matt caught it too, and she talked to cut his chuckles off before they became audible. Minnow told him, "Fine, definition of bait, but I'm not doing it, I won't be your chum!"

"Please Minnow?" asked Matt. "I know it's a lot to ask. But you're the only one who can make her blood boil so hot she'll see what a mistake she's making being with Harry."

Minnow clammed up straight; she wanted to answer but she was fighting back flares, and tingles. She didn't know where to start first?

With the fury and disbelief at his obnoxious plan? They'd done a lot of jokes, and tons of tricks to get them back together when Matt and Carly went through their routine split-ups and make-ups.

However, this wasn't one of their normal jokes. Thinking up love notes to win Carly's heart, which Minnow had a lot of fun with and Matt edited a lot with the red pen he kept on hand because he knew her tendencies. Helping him shop for a present that would win her heart back? Stomping on a fake spider filled with ketchup or, as Matt put it arachnid-napping one of her spiders, had everything Minnow would enjoy!

This wasn't even considered a spelunker! Sneaking down the lane with flashlights at night or in the small patches of wood in the neighborhood, climbing the kayak shop roof and meeting on the peek at night? That was her idea of a spelunker. What Matt was asking wasn't even going to be have her kind of adventure or fun.

In the middle of all of this, her yearning to play something actually fun on Tarantella Girl, and the disappointment of having her ideas shot down, an obscure yet bothering part of this entire rigmarole creeped curiously in. Realizing an acknowledging fact, that she didn't feel like grabbing for mouthwash after Matt kissed her?

Minnow tingled from it and fought back feeling awkward. Not just awkwardness and embarrassment because her best friend had just kissed her and out of reaction she'd wound up kissing him back!

She fought back the awkwardness of how nice it had felt, and the tingles it had tickled. Minnow hadn't known she could be ticklish on the inside from a kiss!

Minnow didn't understand this, and she was mad at Matt for causing something when he apparently didn't even catch on to it.

Or notice and try to make her feel better about it!

A quick check up the beach revealed how quickly time had passed.

"It's a perfect plan," Matt tried again to convince her before Tarantella Girl and her two besties got within earshot.

"Nothing will make her turn greener with envy more, or drop Harry like a bottle of pesticides than if thinks we're a couple," he added in almost an urging whisper. He was feeling Tarantella Girl getting closer.

Minnow was forced to admit to herself that the truth in Matt's grand plan *was* genius. To think that she and Matt were a couple would make Tarantella Girl so mad she could get a job as a barbecue lighter at a food truck because one look would fire the grill.

Minnow growled aloud and shoved Matt's chest hard, causing her to trip over the wet clumps of disturbed sand when Matt didn't move, his solidness or her lack of muscle springing her backwards.

She spun over in a scramble to get up, a move basically shoveling sand down her pants. Matt was too concerned about Carly to laugh as he helped her up and she shook the sand out of her shorts.

"Why couldn't you tell me first!" demanded Minnow.

"I didn't know how to," Matt persisted.

"How about, Minnow my grand plan is to pretend we're dating!" Minnow interrupted, shaking her booty a little more and brushing her hands over and down to help the rest shake loose.

"I thought it'd make us feel awkward."

"Oh, some reason. Hey Minnow, best friend, let's kiss and oh by the way I'm not going to tell you, not awkward at all," Minnow rambled.

Matt rubbed his neck. "Point taken. Sorry." A seagull flew over with his merry band laughing at both of them. Matt waited another moment before softly asking, "Are you in?"

"How is it that you lose all track of things normal when it comes to Tarantella Girl," Minnow basically begged him to tell but at the same time felt defeated. She was way too itchy now, and it was taking her aggravation and focus off Matt.

"This coming from the person who's breaking all molds of normal to ride in the swim?" Matt asked.

Minnow blushed with feeling cornered by her own self.

"You've got things you want so much you'd do almost anything to make them happen," Matt said. "You've done it," he pointed out to her, then listed, with a sense of admiration in his examples that made Minnow blush and feel hard-pressed to keep up her dander.

"You saved up for Marshy for a whole year at just eight years old. You jogged on the beach every morning to run track when they told you that you were too small to qualify. And remember that time in sixth grade when you studied harder than anyone in geography to win us a place in that school fieldtrip selected by the county schoolboard, to visit Jamestown?" asked Matt. "And, now, you're risking the wrath of Khan, well, Chincoteaguers, to ride in the swim. I love her Minnow," said Matt, the whole essence of his speech, at the last.

He had to say *I love her.* Minnow reacted and felt like she'd been fed something sour or spicy. And another thing, Minnow couldn't stand it when he drooped. Even slightly. Why was she such a ball of dough when it came to her best friend?

Minnow sighed, positioned a look at Matt, and put her hands on her hips. She was in no way forgiving him for kissing her without first telling her, *warning* her he was going to, or for dragging her into his grand scheme without so much as a *here's the plan partner.* But she had promised to help him out if he helped her; and Minnow and Matt didn't break their promises – when they could help it. Could she help it, this time? she wondered in a small way, fleetingly. Because regardless of what the course of the plan was, and that she couldn't stand Tarantella Girl, or that it was her unwavering, impenetrable, convinced opinion that Matt and Tarantella Girl were all wrong for each other; who was she to stand in the way of love, or tell someone their hearts were wrong about, and wrong for, each other?

She was bait. That's what she was.

And she'd promised.

"Is kissing me in that category of doing almost anything?" Minnow replied. How could she offer up a joke? she asked herself at the same time, and yet when it was Matt, she couldn't stay angry at him for very long. Just sore. But very long was still a ways away.

"Please Minnow – I promise – I'll never ask you to help me get back together with Tarantella Girl ever again after this," said Matt. Even though the brim of his hat partially hid his forehead, Minnow could tell he'd lifted his eyebrows in hope and with earnest question lines.

That grabbed Minnow's attention.

Minnow looked at Matt and she was hard-pressed trying to look away. His face drew her in, and with this, she was sucked into his wild plan to win Carly McPherson back. But she wouldn't let it appear like she gave in just then.

"Really," Minnow inquired. "You'll never ask me to help you get back with Tarantella Girl when you guys split up next time, ever, again?

"My name's Evers for a reason I guess," Matt said smiling. "And us Evers mean what we say. And do," he added in as an afterthought. "I give you my word, Minnow."

Wow. This was big. Man to mars big. Wheel invented, man make fire big.

Minnow wanted to be skeptical, but she could tell by Matt's features that he was serious.

And when they promised something, they meant it; and unless moral prevented keeping it, which it was then understandable why they had to break their promise, then they stuck to it.

"Before I agree, I have to know one thing first," Minnow said, and Matt waited for her question. Minnow sighed aloud with exertion, and asked the plaguing question, "I mean I know she's hot and super smart, but really. What else is there to her besides a dubious arachnologist's obsession with creepy crawlies?"

"There's more to her than you give her credit for Minnow," said Matt. "She's kind, sweet, honest – a little gothic, and too practical sometimes," he said tipping his hand in rudimentary measurement. "But she's not as bad as you think. Honestly; I don't get what made you two get on off on the wrong foot," he said.

Minnow felt like telling him there'd never been a right one, but kept her mouth clammed.

"Her obsession with spiders is like your obsession with horses," Matt said in pointing out, which made Minnow clench her fists a little to be compared to Tarantella Girl and have her humanized by Matt to this extent. "In her own way, sometimes even funny," Matt went on, smiling.

This was getting to be too much for Minnow. The smiling was pushing the limits of her stomach contents to remain in her stomach.

That's how he smiled when he thought something or someone was cute.

"Just because she's more serious than us doesn't mean she hasn't got *some* sense of humor. Yes, she's a snob, but she doesn't try to hide it. We've all got faults. Even you; and me," Matt reminded Minnow.

Right now, Minnow's only fault was agreeing to something without knowing what it was first. Sure, it'd been the key to unlocking the code box to make her dream come true. But she promised herself never to go headfirst into something before she knew what it was.

Unless of course it was anything that excluded Tarantella Girl. Because Minnow loved adventure, and she was a spelunker, spontaneous, greet and embrace the day and new things kind of person.

How was it Matt could always win her over, in anything and everything he put out there?

Not this way. She couldn't take hearing one nicer thing about spider-girl.

"Alright! Fine. I'll do it," Minnow cut him off. "Just please stop telling me how nice she is even though she's a snob," implored Minnow with enough.

She growled when Matt swallowed her up in a genuine hug. "Thank you, Minnow."

Minnow patted his damp shoulder blade. "Yeah, Yeah," she grumbled.

The way silvery dewy grass turns golden yellow and shimmers when sunrise thrones Assateague, in his teasing way that he has Matt added, "Best friend from the spit of island to the wide, wide world." Taking her back to the night before last when she called him and it was one of the first thing she'd said to pull him into *her* grand conspiracy.

She backed up. "Just so you know, I'm going to give this my all," Minnow said, "and enjoy every millisecond making Tarantella Girl turn every shade of green known to man – and insect."

"Bless your heart," Matt replied.

Minnow would indeed relish with gusto seeing Tarantella Girl squirm. But she agreed to help her best friend, who she couldn't say no to that much often and mean it, or follow through with it at least, as she had just demonstrated now – ever the Minnow with the most difficult part being Minnow, being avoiding the minnow traps of her making, and cupcake center; even minnow traps sucking her in by the ones she loves and cares about.

Chapter Ten

"She's coming, quick!" Minnow prompted.

Minnow seized Matt's hand as he shot a glance up the dawn orange beach and pulled him into the next foamy surge that splashed into them with full force and traveled up Minnow as though she were a cliff, making her squeal in delight and surprise for the crispness of its temperature.

Without the intense beam of the summer sun to make her skin spew tears of sweat as it cried out for saltwater waves and coolness, it was a shock. Kind of like being kissed by Matt was a shock. Only she didn't fight back with the ocean.

In her rush as Minnow turned around in the racing wave, she lost her balance. Matt caught Minnow's waist when the splashing wave slipped under her feet and bent her knees forward at the same time pulling her backward to sit down in the playful hopes of floating her up the shore. Matt was her mooring however and caught her steadily. Minnow grabbed his shoulders and gripped tightly and held closely until the loll befell the swell.

"I was looking forward to that swim," Minnow told him in joking, because in her mind she knew it would've been freezing!

"You can swim away soon enough," Matt joked back.

"Look tenderly into my eyes," Minnow told him with humor, batting her eyes, to which he snorted back muffled laughter.

Her sides suddenly felt unanchored with absence, and drip dropping ocean fell like rain from Matt's hands near her face but only his thumbs touched her cheeks and one or so fingertips her neck. What sweet gentle sea air tossed her uncombed hair and stuck to his wet wrist and hands that the wave had splashed, Matt smoothed all out of her face as his eyes ticked to her eyes again.

His splashed hands were so close to her nose she could smell the saltwater on them.

Minnow felt like Matt was her a bulwark and mooring as the surge receded out to sea with a force trying to pull her away from Matt as though Tarantella Girl were the ocean itself. And trust Minnow when she called her a force – like a volcano forcing itself out of the ocean to make a new island, force.

But Matt and Minnow were too good of friends for this danger to disarray their friendship. Minnow just had to share Matt a little; it wasn't that she minded sharing Matt. Just with Tarantella Girl; she played too many head games.

Minnow only glimpsed Carly's expression when she halted. Sheen with exertion and panting, her face scrunched in abhorrence and disbelief next to her equally amazed friends when they recognized the two of them up this close.

Wasn't Matt supposed to kiss her?

"Is she looking," Matt whispered without moving. He'd frozen. But before Minnow could respond or even peer around his arm, they got their answer.

" *What*, is going on?" Carly's punctuating voice sliced through the beach splendor, demanding. "Matt, is that you?"

Matt drew a breath, bringing his easy smile within reason and turned around sliding his hand into Minnow's, which she gripped back and made sure she clung to the muscliest part of his arm too as they walked up the surf to the shoreline.

"Carly," Matt was greeting nicely and normally in his steady going manner. "Nice to see you. How's it been going?"

Panting from the jog, and the jolt, Carly was too bewildered to answer quite yet.

Breathless, her blond ponytail limp, Izzy had collapsed on the sand and leaned on one hand to stay upright. Jogging pushed the boundaries of reasonableness for the younger twin, like doing something active that made her sweat outside of her purified house pushed the limits with Tizzy. But Tizzy would have to faint before she touched the ground with anything other than her jogging sneakers. Unlike her sister, who wore whatever she touched first and pulled out from her drawer, which had been gym shorts and a loose grey with bland emoji sleeveless tee, Tizzy dressed particularly in her favorite color clean white; white yoga jeggings and a white active-wear tank top. She could see any specks of filth or otherwise on white.

Carly was their friend, so they lived on the edge, and teetered, when their friend went spider hunting in the woods or jogged. Two of Tarantella Girl's obsessions. Minnow had to hand it to them for their bond of friendship. Even though they were an oddball group of meanies.

Well; Izzy was really just there more than anything else.

Casual, Minnow waved. "Hi twins."

"Hunting for sea spiders Carly?" Minnow added smiling sweetly, but not too sweetly. She figured the best way Carly would buy their pretend was if she acted like herself to Carly. Besides, she'd told Matt she was going to enjoy this part of making Carly turn all shades of green, and that's exactly what she intended doing.

Carly eyed Minnow with narrowed glossy black spider eyes and a forced smile in her sparkly sheen face. Even sweaty and agitated as she was, even without her reading glasses she wore mostly in school that sharpened her keen looks, she still looked as cute as a button. Her short silky straight black hair was damp against her head and underneath the matting headband keeping her hair out of her face while she jogged. Minnow thought her black jogging jeggings were appropriate, as were all of her clothes that detailed spiders or spider accents. Her black sleeveless tee cropped above her bellybutton read in white block letters with shimmering web accents, *Do I Arachnid You?* And the black cord necklace with a spider medallion Matt had given her for a present three years ago gleamed in the sunlight.

Not to mention her pants. Spider webs with smiley spiders swinging from them like monkeys on vines imprinted her pants, only Minnow thought those happy-faced big-eyed spiders suddenly looked red-eyed with steam pumping out of their ears. If spiders had ears that is.

Addressing Matt, Carly noted, "My, how the mighty fall."

"At least there was someone there to break his fall," replied Minnow.

"Where'd you pick her up then? The Op shop?" chimed Tizzy, the youngest twin by thirty seconds, sizing Minnow up. They knew Tizzy loathed the Op Shop. Second-hand clothing, furniture, blankets, spoons and coffee mugs would send Tizzy hyperventilating and fleeing if she found herself there for more than fifteen seconds.

Her remark was meant to puncture Minnow, but it didn't faze her at all. She remembered Windy' story and pictured Tizzy's tizzy-fit when Windy pushed down on the pump handle to her bilge-pump that they'd used to chase and spray each other all their lives.

Also, Matt's plan was working. Carly was jealous, and her friends were rallying around her. They'd recovered from the stark surprise and fallen for their act like the toads in the toad hole all the time, even if they were having to convince themselves of what their eyes were seeing. There seemed to be this sense of scramble in the air and Minnow wondered if Matt could feel this tension and scrambling or if it was just a girl thing he couldn't pick up on unless she pointed it out to him?

Regardless of the ins and outs, she knew that he clearly picked up on Tarantella Girl's obvious loathing, thinly masked by an uptight effort to remain calm while boiling.

Her pin-sharp eyes gave her away.

That, and the expression shift in the spiders on her black pants.

Even Izzy had emerged from her normally bored state and showed eyes wider than Minnow was pretty sure no one had ever seen before. They looked actually open!

"All sorts of hidden treasures there," Matt responded in answer to Tizzy's remark, giving Minnow a look that she felt the friendship through.

126

Carly must have seen more than friendship, and for her point of view, affection was just what they were aiming to portray for her. "Well, we'll see," Carly said, picking up her feet but staying in the same spot, warming herself up for the last stretch to her car. Back to her bored self, Izzy dragged herself to her feet and slowly followed. Keyed, Tizzy instantly copied.

Or as Minnow liked to call them, sleepy-Izzy and Tizzy-fit. It wasn't Tizzy's nature to be quiet; she must still have a sore throat from her last longwinded conversation.

Or from swallowing a bilge-pump of saltwater.

Minnow bit her lower lip.

"How's Harry by the way," Minnow asked openly and keeping it casual, raising her voice a tad over the gentle roar of another crashing wave that raced up the shoreline and circled Matt and Minnow's ankles, sounding to Minnow like the soft wind in the trees outside her window, as well as from Marshy' paddock.

Harry was the science nerd who moved to Chincoteague last autumn. Minnow didn't have any classes with him yet but she'd seen him in the lunchroom and hallways. Minnow admitted candidly to herself that he was handsome, and very fit for someone whose favorite pass time was looking through a microscope. Fit, handsome, smart? No wonder Carly had fallen for him. But this wasn't Minnow's first choice. Minnow would have to have someone who loved horses, being outside, joking, and whose idea of a date was laying in the backyard counting fireflies or doing chores together like mowing, raking leaves, gathering firewood in winter, cleaning the barn, feeding Marshy, and shoveling her stall and paddock.

Mostly he'd just have to be a good guy. One who could make her heart sing like the chickadees in morning time when a new day threw them into anticipation and in evening time when evening orange excited them so. One who could also make her heart pound like the ocean and race as though thousands of unstoppable galloping horses were charging. He'd have to be someone she woke up restless to see and spend time with.

Someone like Matt, she thought, but not Matt. He was her best friend; and though he wasn't for Minnow, in light of Tarantella Girl's choice, like all of her other guy choices, it just told Minnow once again how much Matt wasn't for Carly.

She deserved Harry; after all, they spoke each other's language. And Matt deserved a girl who liked the things he did, loved horses, which Carly didn't, and would rather make his heart smile than ache or break.

At the mention of her new boyfriend's name, Harry, Carly's features sharpened at the same time her eyes widened a scope. "Mighty. Very mighty," she replied, and with that, started jogging again, Izzy and Tizzy on her either side. "See you at the birthday party Izzy and Tizzy's parents are throwing. Maybe," she added over her small and toned shoulder, Minnow knew mostly to Matt. Although she could be also telling Minnow how invisible she was.

That's okay. Minnow relished the squirm and struggle it would be for Tarantella Girl to block out the image of her and Matt standing close, nearly nose to nose, gazing tenderly into one another eyes.

When Minnow thought back on that moment, she became aware that she hadn't been pretending. But she cared about Matt; that look with her eyes and affection in Matt's touch was friendship.

Minnow shook her head and shook it again. She wasn't the one who was supposed to shake it out of her mind, Carly was!

Grrrr! Was nothing ever simple or doable or anything she could be liberated of when Carly was in the equation?

There was one bright side, and when Matt squeezed Minnow's hand it brought her the rest of the way back into focus.

"We did it," Matt elated in an underscoring tone.

The hook was in. Minnow knew it, and so did Matt by the way he squeezed her hand tighter. Minnow felt the same excitement too. Ironic, mused Minnow, that the girl who studied spiders and wove webs for others to be snagged by, would be snagged in the web she and Matt had just spun. Not that a minnow and say a grass cricket were much of a match for a spider, which made it all the more silly and ironic that the expert in webs would be foiled by a couple of amateurs. Though Minnow guessed when one was in love, or simply possessive of something or someone else, they could be convinced of nearly anything.

So now, all that was left was for her hopeless friend to reel in Tarantella Girl. Looked like Minnow wouldn't have to play chum much longer. Good. Because she wasn't looking forward to being a crispy minnow spring roll for spider girl; and too much more of their encounters while pretending to date Matt would intensify Tarantella Girl's hunger!

Since Tarantella Girl and the twins were far enough away to talk openly, Minnow let herself burst, "I've never seen her that boiled!"

Matt was grinning too and said, "It's working! I told you!"

"Good, that means I won't be playing bait much longer. Come on, let's get some shells and shark tooth hunt before the tide starts coming in. Windy' still bragging about the last one she found in June and made an earring out of. The rest of us never find any and she's getting so smug that I want to bite her with one. Besides you owe me for embarrassing myself, and kissing you," Minnow said, pulling her hand away and moving up the beach.

"Admit it Mighty Minnow; I'm not that bad," he said.

"Because *Tarantella Girl* says you aren't?" Minnow teased him.

Matt's face actually blushed through his sunburn, granting Minnow more than she could have asked for!

Worst still, he knew it, and Minnow burst into laughter. "You're hopeless!" she told him. "One day Tarantella Girl is going to swallow you whole after she rolls you into a spider spring roll, and then you'll be asking yourself, why didn't I listen to my oldest best friend from the spit of island to the wide, wide world when she told me Tarantella Girl was too shallow and snobby and cold for me?"

Scooping a heap of ocean with both hands, Minnow shoveled it at him.

Matt stuffed his ballcap in the big pocket of his tan cargo shorts, bolting into the ocean instead of shying away, just like he ran through the hose spray and tackled her if they didn't trip on the wet grass first, or would chase her when she threw down the hose to outrun him! Matt bolted into everything in life, and they splashed like they have since guppies until their arms started hurting. Which then yielded to their unspoken splashing contest by rule. Who would give up first?

The ocean tugs and pushes though, way different from a pool, and they were down to the pitifullest slapping of splashes within minutes, and yet still going on.

Gulps of saltwater down the pipe from big splashes, Minnow tasted the yummy, too salty water in her mouth and on her lips, and from swallowing some huge splashes, belched!

A seagull screamed in reply and a small flock of shore birds raced and flew away.

Matt followed suit, and Minnow smacked the water onto his face in response and for his belch being a tiny tad louder and longer!

Chapter Eleven

Minnow and Matt conspired on the drive back to the house. Tarantella Girl had made the remark of seeing him at the birthday party the twins' parents were throwing. "Maybe."

The twins' parents were always throwing big parties for their two daughters. They had been since Minnow was eight. Everyone was invited – classmates, their classmates' parents, even grandparents! As part of their hopes for social connection for one daughter and their desire for their other daughter to learn to enjoy being outside, and since their birthday occurred in the summer, the beach was the perfect place. So perfect in fact, that when Tarantella Girl mentioned the twins' birthday party, she didn't need to specify for Matt to know where. Although the parties were so big even if it wasn't taking place on the beach, they wouldn't be hard-pressed to discover where it would be instead.

Mr. and Mrs. Plenty's aspirations for their daughters was a fulltime job, trying to bring one daughter out of her shell, and finding a way to cure the fear of the outdoors in the other. As a result, Minnow sometimes wondered if their parents, while loving and attentive, were being too pushy? Without meaning to be, it could sometimes happen. Because in eight years the twins hadn't improved. Not worsened – just sort of stayed frozen in their peculiar ways.

Matt and Minnow decided they would go to the beach that day after the first roundup. Minnow got happy chills just thinking about it. The roundup that is, not helping Tarantella Girl and Matt get back together. Although, she admitted, the turning Carly green and making her squirm like a spider that just got stunned with a flyswatter, was growing on her.

Yes, thought Minnow to herself, folding her arms with inner satisfaction and nodding softly. This squirming aspect was quickly growing on her like moss on fast-forward.

By the beach party, thanks to Tizzy who could never keep her mouth shut unless her throat was raw or it was pollen season, in which case she *was* genuinely allergic and wore a nurse mask to catch the bus, rumor would be circling and when she and Matt stepped onto the beach together everyone would be talking! A circulating the rumor that would intensify the image of Minnow and Matt and then Minnow clinging to his arm in the ocean this morning, which was already emblazoned in Tarantella Girl's mind's eye.

It was late afternoon and Matt was due at the carnival for setup that night, and at Minnow's house it was family night.

But in the meantime, Matt and Minnow went to say hello to Marshy.

Standing inside the fence grooming one half of Marshy, while Minnow brushed her other side, Matt asked over her marsh brown back, "Are you up for going undercover tomorrow morning, saltwater ponygirl?"

Minnow replied instantly, "I've been waiting for this all my life." She smiled wide and with a sureness and a hint of challenge said, "Are you?"

Matt chuckled, a noise she hadn't heard come this easily in two days, and against her grudge right now, eased those crinkly feelings a tad. It was nice just to hear her old friend laugh and see him like the Matt she knew, instead of the Matt who misplaced himself when Tarantella Girl split up with him or looked at another guy the way she looked at him and he felt her slipping off of his arm.

"Yep," Matt told her. Then after a minute, said, "You know, it's a gigantic risk?"

"I know. And I promise Matt, I'll do everything right so I don't give us away," Minnow assured him. "The last thing I want is for you to be socially exiled for helping me."

Matt stopped brushing Marshy while he said, "I'm not talking about me; I meant you."

His reply made Minnow's hand slow and stop brushing too. "What about me?" she asked.

Marshy snorted, and they started back up again, smiling at her need for attention and craving for being brushed with the firm bristles.

Then Matt continued. "Say your parents get wind of it; or the saltwater ponyboys pick up on you being a girl?" he said. "What do you have in mind for disguising yourself?"

"Trust me," Minnow answered with assuredness, "They'll never recognize me."

"What," scoffed Matt, with a glean in his eyes as he said, "Does it involve a beard?"

Minnow kicked her loosely tied and stinky old sneaker off in the space under Marshy' belly and watched Matt sidestep but not soon enough. Though like it really hurt!

"Crossed my mind," she said seriously, with rising enthusiasm in her heart. She'd thought of everything and anything far and between gluing a beard on her face, as far as having saved up clippings from Mom and her sister's hair when they trimmed them every four months. But she had something better than that.

"I'm serious!" Matt insisted. "Don't leave me hanging."

"You'll see," said Minnow, sticking to keeping him in suspense. Half of her wondered if he'd approve or think she couldn't pull it off, so she didn't want to tell him yet.

"What about Marshy?" he asked. "I still think it's a bad idea to ride her in the swim. You'd blend in more with one of my horses."

"Marshy has to come," insisted Minnow. "She wants to come."

Matt lifted one brow. "She's a gummy worm. She's as sweet as summer grass."

"You seemed to get a kick out of that sweetness when we were five," she said with a giggle on the tail of her voice, "so Marshy should be just fine."

"You dared me to that," he said, "and if I recall correctly you wimped out when it came your turn."

Minnow's mouth gaped. "I did not! I just spit mine out sooner than you! You *tried* to swallow your taste!" Minnow pointed out.

Matt seemed amused and proud of himself in the retrospect, and then returned to the subject at hand by saying, "Anyway, you get my point. Marshy is as sweet as summer grass *smells*." The distinction was not lost on Minnow, who eyed him flatly while trying not to laugh or smile one hint.

"Those wild horses will smell her good nature and nip at her the whole trip," Matt went on. "Besides – how are you going to explain to your parents why Marshy' not in her paddock?"

Minnow drew her eyebrows together, exhaling through her nose. She gazed into Marshy' half closed brown golden eyes, contented from them grooming her sunny warm hide, and undoubtedly the direct and easy warm summer sun in the blue sky was making her feel extra lazy.

"I don't want her to feel left out. This is something we were always going to do together. I know she could handle it Matt. She still remembers what it was like to be free. To live among the wild herd. Before me, and you, and my sisters, they were her family."

"Are you sure?" said Matt flatly, referring to Marshy with a nudging look sideways.

Minnow looked at Marshy, eyes closed, lower lip slouching in contentment, her round stocky body weight shifted towards Minnow.

"Yep. I'm sure," Minnow said, but she didn't muster a very convincing look.

"Olive's experienced in the roundup," Matt said.

Olive was a black tall horse with stocky shoulders and flanks and slender legs. She'd obey Matt and Minnow's every request and behaved like a really lady. But she had one trait of mischief.

One that Minnow could understand. Olive was an escape artist. She loved to go spelunking!

Only in April had she nudged down a section of fencing by plowing at the ground and nudging the pole, having smelled the rotting from this spring's drenching showers. The ground had been mush for weeks on the island after the rain had finally stopped.

Matt had gotten a call from one of the firemen spotting the herds in preparation for the spring roundup in which they all got checked by the vet.

Olive had escaped and swum to Assateague!

Minnow had helped Matt all week install new fence posts, which they did the smelly gritty job of cementing in the holes.

"But I know Marshy can do it," insisted Minnow.

Matt shook his head. "I'm sorry Minnow. If you're going to take this job seriously, I'm putting an experienced horse under you. It's not an option," said Matt. "Take it or leave it. You're choice."

The ultimatum grated Minnow, but she saw the commonsense even though she couldn't stand it. She was a kayak guide and she'd never put a novice in a streamlined single unless she's was taking them out for a one on one tour. And out there in the roundup she and Matt wouldn't be one on one. They'd be part of a group of saltwater ponyboys, experienced pony penning riders like she was an experienced guide, and even though Minnow knew how to ride, she'd only ever played pretend roundup with Marshy. There were wild horses in this version, bigger than her, bigger than Marshy. She had to trust Matt, and listen to him. He was the guide out there. She knew it; and she didn't want to put Marshy in danger. And Matt would know, just as well as Minnow does. He was a horseman, a horse whisperer really. He didn't even use a bit when he rode.

Minnow turned a relinquishing gaze to Matt. "Fine. But for the record I still think Marshy could handle it; but I respect your call. If I were in a kayak I'd make a similar decision with a novice who wanted to rent a kayak before they went on a tour and learned the how to'," she said.

Matt seemed to be letting her absorb her own words.

"But if we get through this swim undiscovered – will you help me teach Marshy how to roundup?" asked Minnow.

Matt nodded once sturdily. "It's a deal," he said.

"Thanks," Minnow answered, and she meant everything in that thanks, and he knew she did.

"Yeah, Yeah, Yeah," he droned on, replaying her answer back to her when she agreed to his plan on the beach. It made her smile, and then think back on that kiss. But she didn't want to ponder that right now. Matt, her friend was right here with her, brushing Marshy like he'd helped and spent time with her doing hundreds of times. She wanted to relish this moment, in the comfortability of their friendship, where they stood in happy silence in the company of one another as well as in their own thoughts, brushing a horse. A very *contented* one.

Chapter Twelve

It was 3:00a.m., and the stressed white plank bathroom door sealed off the light Minnow switched on. Not even Dad or Summer was up yet. But they arose early to prepare for the a.m. tours. So, she had one hour minimum to do what it was she was pumped up for and skedaddle to meet Matt before her family knew she was up and vamoosed. Once they were up and saw her in disguise she'd never slip away.

Minnow snipped intrepidly. She'd waited too long for this very morning all of her life to wimp out or second-guess herself now when the hour was upon her. Next, she plugged in the cord and switched on Dad's buzzer. She'd clipped her long thick soft wavy hair down to where she had hair shorter than Matt's thick black hair that always fell forward and towards his eyes like it was wet. Until he'd been outside long enough for the salt breeze to ruffle it up like it dried out and tangled the girls' hair constantly. Although Matt wore his favorite ballcap so much his hair was mostly *matted* all the time. Minnow muffled her chuckle for her own pun. Matt's *matted* hair.

Short enough to use the buzzer, Minnow ran it over her head in slow and gentle strokes, wearing a smile. The vibration tickled her scalp and oddly enough she felt sensations down on the bottoms of her feet.

Grinning all while completing her disguise, once through and buzzer switched off she studied her new look and ran her hands over her peach fuzzy head. She still saw her; smiling, inquiring, lively blue eyes that sparkled like the water still – her smile, the shape of her face – but the entire picture taken in at once was clearly different. Her buzz cut accentuated the contours of her face, exposing her small "minnow" ears and giving rounder shape to her head.

Making haste Minnow swept her hair remnants with the broom and dustpan she conveniently left ahead of time in the bathroom last night and wiped the fine buzzed hair off the sink using a wet clothe she promptly discarded into the washer. Minnow giggled at the strange new feeling of showering with fuzzy short hair as close shaven as her freshly mowed yard she sweltered shortening the day before yesterday.

Water didn't trickle it *ran* down her face, freer than it did when her long hair was there to soak it up. She instantly found that she enjoyed the freedom and the unbridled flow of water over her face and cascading her body. But she cut her enjoyment short once she'd rinsed herself clean of tiny hairs. Dry, she wasted no time in layering her identity with the disguise of boyfriend jeans to obscure the contours of her slender hips. Adding a red plaid with the sleeves cut off autumns ago, over the strapless sports bra mashing her boobs in place. As long as no one suggested she take her shirt off to cool down during the roundup because the sun was roasting, her disguise was completely passable.

For final effect Minnow tugged on one of Dad's old, old ballcaps, and grabbing her water thermos with clinking ice cubes and the dustpan of hair, snuck out of the house through the escape hatch in the bathroom. She couldn't risk Mom or Dad or Summer or WINDY catching sight of it in the waste basket and wondering what on earth was going on?

Outside she rubbed her hands in some mulch and dirt and grass hay from in the veggie garden and then scrubbed her face to roughen her feminine features and lend the appearance that she was a typical boy.

Jogging around the side of the house Minnow donated her hair to birds for nesting.

"Where are you goen?" Windy called down hoarsely from Minnow's window.

Minnow stopped cold but didn't have to dig deep to find the ire to reply, "Get off my bed!"

"What are you doing?" Windy demanded after she moved aside, which the gesture, and knowing where she was bound, made Minnow smile and answer.

"Turning Pirate!" she whispered loudly. "Cover for me?"

"Aye, Captain!" Windy agreed readily and saluted without even knowing the reason.

In that moment, Minnow felt the strength and meaningfulness in their bond and that they were really sisters.

Minnow started sprinting.

"Can I come?" Windy asked.

Minnow halted so fast she dug into the ground with her boots and tripped forward. She whirled around long enough to tell her, "No! Cover for me." Then ran and didn't stop to look back.

Chapter Thirteen

"I pull off this reunion with you and Tarantella Girl, and you keep me in the best you can," Minnow was reminding Matt.

"When have I ever let you down?" asked Matt with his usual easy manner, smiling.

"Does that time my hand slipped out of yours when we were climbing your tree in the Tall Grass and I fell on an ant bed, count?" said Minnow with eyebrows pinched in thought as though giving consideration to the matter.

· "No – besides, even if we were you missed the tangle of burrs right next to where you flattened those poor little bugs," he said while shaking his head, adding with a tone of slight pity for effect, "they saw what was coming alright. You aint no minnow to insects," Matt told her for a fact.

Minnow smacked his bear arm hard but she was smiling, especially when it made him suck air through his teeth from the sting.

"They've got your sweaty hands to thank for my rear-end dropping in," she muttered through her teeth.

They'd crossed the bridge thirty-seconds of birdsong and banter earlier, and were coming up on the straight shot to the beach. Matt had spent the noir of morning with Minnow acquainting her with Olive as rider in the roundup on the sixteen-hand mare with round black eyes glistening sweetness and intelligence.

Minnow had ridden Olive a handful of times, but not enough to consider herself completely in-tune with her desires and bad habits, the dos and don'ts when she was on her back; not in the pony swim at least.

But she did know Olive enough from seeing her since she was five and brushing her and feeding Olive her sweet favorite alfalfa treats, to notice that she was looking a little on the pudgy side.

"Matt, has Olive gained weight?" asked Minnow, squinting at her black belly pooching a little more than usual.

"She hasn't been exercised enough since Ish came; and Coby you know how doesn't come by for riding that much in the summer because he's so busy at the kayak shop," Matt explained, testing that cinch was secure but not too tight. He patted her thick neck heartily so she felt it and stepped back for Minnow to grab the horn and mount.

"She's not overweight in terms of horse obesity though. She can still have her alfalfa treats," Matt told her smiling, with full knowledge of Minnow's and Olive's special bonding in giving and receiving the treats. Minnow enjoyed Olive's delight, and Olive of course loved Minnow the more for delighting her!

Minnow returned it but didn't say anything. She looked at the stirrup, grabbed the saddle horn, and stepped on the tree stump to mount Olive.

Matt knew better than to ask if she needed a hand. He got the same answer when he asked her such things. A stern, "No! Do I look like I need help?" in typical Chincoteaguer temper. It wasn't that she got super angry with Matt. She, like most of her family, had what they called flares. Islanders were fiercely independent even though their natures were helpful and humorous at the same time.

Matt enjoyed prodding at her though so that she flared, and it'd become a game between them. So he threw himself into the briar patch and said, "Need a hand?"

And through a smile she was fighting she replied sternly over her shoulder, "No! Do I look like I do?!"

Matt choked back a soft chuckle. "Bless your heart," he replied, another Teaguer thing they had fun with every chance they had. Bless your heart or lands sake were two phrases the islanders said all of the time, being appropriate for any occasion.

Once astride Olive – without anyone's help getting there – Minnow took in the view, though it was still dark and everything seemed like tones of dark and lighter shadows. She'd forgotten how it felt to ride a tall horse, as well as what the world looked like from someone's shoulders.

Two times taller than Marshy and Minnow, Olive's sweet disposition contrasted to her imposing height without trying. Olive was so sweet that little Minnow could handle her from the saddle, though if she had the mind to bolt it wouldn't be much of a contest as to who would win. Olive's shoulders and bulky belly were brute strength, while Minnow just had brute will.

She smiled. Maybe it would be a real contest?

However, Olive was too sweet and gentle a giant for that. As if confirming this, Olive sighed heavily and bobbed her head twice when Minnow patted her neck and rubbed the spot thoroughly so the big gal felt it, and didn't mistake her hand for an annoying greenhead fly.

It'd been sometime since Minnow had ridden anyone but Marshy, and while she'd dreamed of the roundup, practiced and played pretend with Marshy in the backyard or on the beach, and studiously watched every horse movie and documentary known to girl and horse yet, Matt was doing just what she would do at the start of a tour.

Minnow had given paddling instructions to adults and kids her own age since she was eight.

So, Minnow appreciated Matt's advice and instruction as he walked her through simple moves and demonstrated astride his loyal friend, Ish. Short for Ishmael.

Minnow started to tell herself that she couldn't believe she'd never asked for this mentoring from Matt before – but she stopped herself because it became clear in two blinks. She liked to do things on her own first.

But today, this week, there was no room for error. Plus.

Guiding was one thing she wouldn't scoff or challenge anyone on, unless of course as a guide herself she discerned someone giving advice or instruction who wasn't a real guide. Minnow had seen them come and aptly go. Fly-by-nighters whose irresponsibleness and simple dollar greed put safety, quality, and general commonsense anywhere but on the water, where in a kayak business was precisely where in needed to be.

So, Minnow listened acutely to Matt's advice and memorized the moves he showed her. She did not flare or huff either when he corrected her move. She listened willingly, and with patience and self-correction keenly tried again.

Olive was one of those horses who was responsive to touch – lay the rein to the cheek of her neck and lean her body right and she would veer right – lay the rein to the cheek of her neck on the right side and lean her body left and she would turn left.

Matt's instructions weren't anything new, and yet they were. More sensitive than Marshy, Minnow would have to be thoughtful of her movements and what exactly she was asking Olive to perform. Minnow harkened to paddling instructions – if you want to turn right put your paddle behind you in the water on the right and push out – if you want to go left put your paddle behind you on the left and push out – basic, simple, but important.

Although Olive was more sensitive than even the water, on which paddling worked better when one was gentle. So, Minnow would just have to be extra, *extra* gentle.

Matt told her what to do if a stallion or mamma mare charged. "Yell and swing Olive around me," he said, "I've got a whip I can crack and scare him off."

Matt told her next as he repositioned Ish, "Don't tell Olive anything, just hold on to her mane and move with her." Minnow grabbed handfuls of black thick mane and when she nodded Matt began herding her the way she'd herded kayakers straying into the middle of the channel. Matt flanked her, easing closer, and softly nosing her in the front at a guiding distance.

When they'd done a wide circle and returned to the other side of the truck, Matt grinned and patted her on the back, then bent low and stroked Olive's thick neck. "Good girls," he said. Then he let Minnow try.

Minnow calmed her heartbeat, sliding into the water shoes of a kayak guide and yet into the boots of the saltwater ponygirl she always was in her heart, and was born to be.

She touched Olive's rein to her neck on the left side, and walked with her around Ish and Matt, pressing sideways gently, which was all the signal Ish needed to obey Olive and flow with Minnow and Olive together in the steered direction of the paddock.

Aware that wild ponies would test her and Olive, unlike Ish, Minnow made a mental note, but was still excited for she and Olive's harmony and correct movements.

Minnow saw the tight squeeze and contact with the paddock and Ish's belly coming and once that was closed she wouldn't be able to steer him smoothly towards her destination.

Minnow tapped Olive's tummy, prompting her to trot forward and trod between the space, veering Ish and Matt away from the paddock. Minnow then allowed space between them and kept her eye on Ish, thinking three steps ahead to if Ish stepped out of boundary, stopped, and to when and how they would moor. She guided Ish by the indication of Olive's nearness and pace, and when they reached the back end of the trailer Minnow smoothly delivered them too as a symbol of she and Olive's graduation as partners together, tied the bow by sealing off the path beyond the back end of the trailer in front of Ish.

Minnow reward Olive and thanked her by patting her neck and rubbing hardily. Smiling, Minnow looked at Matt and leaned forward on her saddle horn. "Well, do we pass?" she asked, already knowing the answer.

Matt clapped softly. "With honors. You must have had the world's best mentor," he noted.

"Well, he did have the world's best pupils," she played along in reply.

Now they were in the truck cab, *which Minnow climbed through the passenger window to be in since the door was sticking and she didn't feel like fighting it;* surrounded by other trucks and trailers with their riders unloading or saddling their mounts. This was it. She was here. The saltwater ponyboys conversed and joked just outside of Matt's Dad's old teal with white trim 67 truck.

But Minnow wasn't in yet.

"Okay, one last check – am I dirty enough to look like a boy?" asked Minnow, facing Matt in her seat.

"You always look dirty enough to be boy," joked Matt.

"Yep, but this counts more," Minnow said.

"You'll notice I smell and look fresh out of the shower," replied Matt smugly.

Minnow shrugged one shoulder. "Some boys then. Can you tell I'm me?"

Matt studied her face, and pinned a gaze in her eyes. "Even with your sisters' hair glued onto your face for beard effect, I'd recognize you," he told her, and while Minnow took that as a compliment, he didn't answer her question.

"What about Sailor Man Sharp and Bumble? Am I disguised good enough that they won't give me a second look?" asked Minnow.

As usual, endearing Matt to Minnow by being herself, and finding amusement in her dare like he did with her reactions, flares, and otherwise original only and simply Minnow quirks, her question revisited his attention to her new look.

The length she had gone to by shortening one of her features, actually buzzing all of her hair, made him smile and want to laugh.

"You were right about your disguise. If I didn't know you so well, I'd be hard-pressed to place you," said Matt in answer. "Lands, Minnow," he said with admiration. "I never doubted that you'd find a way – but I gotta say I'm impressed at how."

"Thanks. I surprised myself," said Minnow honestly, wishing she could run her hand along her fuzzy head again. "I look like just one of the guys, right?" Minnow was looking at Matt with a smile. She tried to read his thoughts past his features and the gaze of friendship in his sharpened eyes.

The longer he went without answering, wonder started to creep into Minnow's mind. Please tell her he didn't think she couldn't pull this off? She knew her face smeared with dirt may have been overdoing it, and buzzing all of her hair when she'd only ever trimmed it to her shoulders before *was* bold! But this was her only chance. Her one shot. Would she get another? Not as good as this one. Once the jig was up, if it got to that she was discovered for the boy fraud she was, she assumed she had a good chance of being sour-eyed as Matt had said he would be, by half of the island, and hailed as some heroine for her dare by another small portion. But Minnow didn't want either of that; the alienation or philosophical triumph in failure. She just wanted to ride in the pony swim. She belonged here. She knew she could be the best saltwater ponygirl, ponyboy, that'd ever matched up with or ridden alongside these islanders. She'd ride as long and work just as hard as them; she was ready for this, and she wanted this.

Minnow was entering a very rare band of people, fellow islanders, who were also everyday people just like her. Islanders. Saltwater ponyboys. Did they consider their part in this tradition sacred, as Minnow did?

Minnow knew they must. They were islanders, just like her. These were their roots; including hers. The island; the saltwater – and the ponies. How Chincoteaguers pull together, without fail, every time there is hard pressure or need, is the whole reason the pony swim started, and why there is a pony swim to this day. Some people are defined by the island. Some people define it. In their own similar sense, they are both. They are island. Island, is them.

"You always were one of the guys," answered Matt. At the same time his words warmed Minnow's heart, she still needed encouragement to smote the last of her inner nervousness that'd crept up on her.

"Know me that well do you best friend," said Minnow, prepared to stay confident whatever his answer.

"I know you," Matt said first. "You deserve to be here Minnow," he told her, which reinforced her confidence to hear it said and know her friend stood beside her. "So. You up for doen what every girl and boy from far and wide dream of doen when they hear pony swim?"

Minnow knew Matt already knew the answer to that.

"Never been more ready," Minnow said, feeling tall and stocky for once in her skin and bones, happy, with decision. She tugged her ballcap brim to snug it on her head, and both she and Matt yanked on their uncooperative door handles at the same time.

Chapter Fourteen

Matt threw up his hand in greeting to the group as they rounded the back of the trailer. Minnow did likewise, thankful that Matt had thought to park with the rear facing away from the others.

There were about two dozen saltwater ponyboys saddling up in the sea breezy, seagull yacking, blue ocean roaring morning. Minnow inhaled thoroughly until her lungs couldn't take it, smelling tangy salt air and horses. Two of her most favorite smells in the world.

Along with freshly cut grass of course. Which included being accompanied by the smell of horse.

"By the way, don't forget about the twins' beach party tomorrow afternoon. Love of my life will be there," Matt was saying as he eased the trailer tail down with Minnow's help. It was heavy, but she was pleased with how well she struggled through helping set it down without dropping it too hard.

"I can't believe you!" Minnow whispered loudly, not attempting an iota to hide her tone or feelings of disgust to Matt. "She's broken your heart so many times I'm surprised to find a thump," she said, pressing her ear to his chest. "Wait, it was there two roasting' ago," she said with fake confusion. She lowered her ear to the right lower chest where it realistically didn't exist, then his tum, tum. "Did it shatter and fall all the way in your gut this time?"

Matt shoved her away, which was easily done because of her slenderness. Used to her strong dislike of his school sweetheart on again off again girlfriend since middle school, while he defended her in effigy against Minnow's barbs, there was a sense of humor that Matt always found and a cuteness he enjoyed in Minnow's antagonism, and moreover enjoyed elbowing at to get her to flare.

"You're swimming towards a minnow trap," he said, well aware of those in Minnow's life. Elbowing her, he added, "Still want to proceed?"

Minnow should still be cranky at Matt for bribing her, or blackmailing her might be a more accurate description, into once again another scheme to win back Tarantella Girl. But she was too happy and excited to be entering the tribe of saltwater ponyboys that her mouth sprung its own smile on both herself and Matt and she felt it morphing throughout her whole being with the shape of those happy feelings as though her entire body was smiling, and she elbowed him back.

Matt introduced Minnow to the group saddling up next to their respective trailers as his cousin from Rhode Island, visiting for the summer. She secretly needed no introductions, acquaintance or friend of the family as they were, save to three new riders, De Juan from Florida, Carlos from Arizona, and toothy thirteen-year-old Miles, Cheddar's grandson, who Minnow hadn't seen in a few months and was no longer wearing his braces. She wanted to clap for him, knowing how much those toothy mechanics had bothered him, but she wasn't supposed to know who he was. Who any of them were.

Others Minnow had grown up seeing around the island or who knew her family, made her adrenaline pump with a smidgeon of nervousness. Would they see through her disguise?

Bumble – nicknamed because he's big for his size and seems lazy, but he knows what he's doing and exactly what to do when it needs doing, and is good at it.

Calculative AJ. Thin, aging, precise, and on point – he's sort of the all-around organizer who does a lot of the talking that needs to be said even though everyone knows by rote and by heart what roundup tasks need doing and whose best there or going where. He's the prompter.

Hammer – tough as the million nails he pounds in a summer, he got his nickname without much need for explanation. A roofer on every other day of the year except for pony penning, he implements his talent for straightness, getting it done right the first time, by singling people out the way he shingles roofs, hammering off directions mid task or post and pre. He's always got something to holler, criticize, and tough-talk over. He's the group's natural foreman.

It's a feat to tell if he's truly fed-up or only testing you. It's just his roughhewn personality and bluntness that comes with the territory of roofing. Everyone's used to it. He and AJ clash like waves and sand regularly, AJ being an organized person by nature, which makes him a good accountant, and Hammer, for his strictness and code of accuracy in the dangerousness of roofing, making them lock horns inside and outside of pony penning. Similar men but different power points. AJ fine-tipped, and Hammer blunt.

Thus, it's generally known that they pointedly ride with different groups, for though being short in height they are never short on opposite and heated opinions.

Then there's cheerful Cheddar, with a belly like a round cheese block and a pleasant, satisfied disposition as though he's always just eaten a block of yummy cheese. He is a man who wins smiles on a grey day. Needless to say, Cheddar gets along with everyone.

Sailor Man Sharp – nicknamed for his nautical wits, people smarts, and innate instinct for weather changes, he is a person set in his ways, who aint changing likely, but an all-around likeable, commonsense, reasonable fellow, he doesn't lock horns without good reason, which Minnow has always admired. It reminds her of her mother and father and Summer. As a close family, and each of them being kayak guides, Minnow appreciates this responsible and reasonable sense of leadership when she sees it. He was their bellwether.

Sailor Man Sharp was a man who's been old forever and since Minnow was little, so he didn't look too much different to her now, if maybe moving with a little favor in one knee. But atop his tan latte pale, off-white pinto mare Loran, named for a ship's position finder, he was able and spry in movement as he was sharp as a fishhook. With pickle-like features and weathered tan skin he looked as much of a sailor man and fisherman as would come from a child's imagination. He'd always been a good friend to Minnow's family, since the girls were tiny, often mooring his skiff to the small docking in the gut and traversing up the skinny clamshell pathway splitting the marsh grass and sprouting tiny hairs of it, to talk with her Dad, both being waterman.

He taught Minnow and Windy how to bait their hooks, watch the tides for fishing, the nautical structure and standards of his skiff, and setting "minnow" traps.

Instead of bounding up to greet him like she and Windy do though, and asking if he'd go fishing off the dock in the gut with them, she'd have to steer clear of him for this week. As Sailor Man Sharp's the one person who was likely to pick up on something familiar about her or recognize Minnow outright, even with his weathered squint acquired over a lifetime of searching blue skies for signs of storms and with signs of storms, or crinkled against the blinding shimmer of dazzling sun glaring the ocean expanse and sparkling the waterways.

Minnow finds him squinting with such focus while Matt introduces her. Minnow cautions herself to stay *sharp* and to keep her talking to a minimum, or even better to one word responses. Reaffirming to herself that even in a pinch she must bring her inquiries to Matt, or figure it out on her own.

The saltwater ponyboys are anyone and everyone on Chincoteague who can ride a horse; volunteers, fishermen, boaters, accountants, roofers, plumbers, high school boys grown up with their dads or uncles and grandfathers with ponies and around the swim. They're everyday ordinary Chincoteaguers, pulling together and carrying on a tradition that predates talkies. Keeping alive a part of their heritage that intertwines with the wild ponies, shipwrecked long ago on the island. Little did either the Teaguers or the shipwrecked ponies know then, how their lives would intersect, and one day rescue one another. For the island rescued the ponies – and the ponies rescued the Chincoteaguers from out of a scorched plight.

The fire of the nineteen-twenties that consumed most of downtown had been devastating for everyone. Thanks to the wild pony roundup and auction, the fire department was able to update their equipment to better retaliate against future fires, and ever since then the fire department, islanders, and volunteers, known as saltwater ponyboys have been rounding up the wild ponies.

Not just anyone was allowed to ride in the swim. One had to be a fair rider, and if one was that and a family member to one of the saltwater ponyboys, like Miles or Spencer and her cousin Freddy – who was the ruddy faced blond haired boy with his ballcap swung backwards – then it was time to saddle up.

After all – who wouldn't want to share this with someone they loved?

But Minnow wasn't just strolling in unannounced. Everyone in the group was expecting her. Or that is – Matt's cousin.

Matt had had to gain permission for Minnow – that is, Mitch, as she'd decided calling herself – to ride with them.

According to Matt earlier, Matt encountered a few tough questions from Russ and Chowder, but all in all no objections.

Minnow felt so lightweight with amazement and excitement a sneeze could push her back. For all of her life she'd only ever gotten "no" for an answer, and even though she always hoped in her heart for "yes" when next summer rolled around, Minnow expected another "no" in the back of her mind.

Since Matt agreed to help her, Minnow knew all along that Matt would pull it off. To everyone he met Matt was the prince of the volunteers, and a prince among Teagure princes. He'd always been a helpful person and his good nature and quick, playful sense of humor drew good people to him. He was a person without guile or envy. He was more Chincoteaguer than some Chincoteaguers.

That's why she couldn't sneeze wrong or talk in a lilt. If she had to she wouldn't burp, she'd belch – but she did that anyway, so she was set there. Since she and her sisters, and Matt, were little, they'd held burping contests. And for the minnow that she was, Minnow was pretty good at waking up the neighborhood from their afternoon naps.

She couldn't mess this up and let anyone discover she was really a girl. Minnow. At this moment, she truly realized what all Matt was risking to help her as his friend. Everything.

She wouldn't let him down.

But did he really have to take this in-disguise thing to this next level?

Knowing Matt, why was she surprised? It's not like she wouldn't try it with him. But really? Really?!

Best *friend!*

Minnow was introduced as his cousin from Rhode Island, a fair rider – he was doing great, and Minnow felt like puffing out her chest in the glow of his compliments, which she caught herself from doing, just in case. Did he have to throw in there that she was just recovered from a bruised tailbone?

"Riding in the roundup has always been a dream for Maximus," said Matt.

Matt clapped her on the back and she was so fuming inside she kept both feet firmly flat on the ground. "Yep, it has. Thanks for having me. Nice to meet you all," Minnow replied plainly, trying to allow her genuine smile sunshine without beaming. She thought a dose of frankness would add believable effect.

She was so glad for her wear of sunglasses and hat, which were her two main disguises, right at this moment. Although Minnow's fairly certain the ire in her private glare at Matt melted those twinkles girls have in their eyes, like the ones she noticed still speckled hers in the mirror this morning as she observed her new look. She remembered them rehearsing her cover story, but that hadn't included mentioning any bruised tailbone!

From behind her sunglasses she slid a scathing glance Matt's way, while managing a pleasant face.

"Had one of them," Bumble related, nodding. "Aint for sissies."

Minnow shook hands with Bumble first, nodding in frankness at his relatability. She had a feeling Maximus and Bumble would get along just fine.

Take that Matt, thought Minnow. *Bruised tailbone aint for sissies.*

She also shook hands with a few ponyboys nearby who put out a friendly effort, and smiled and nodded to those who threw up a hand or greeting, undisrupted in their work.

Minnow shook the hands of second and third generation saltwater ponyboy and older timers she'd known all her life slapped her on the back in welcome as they walked their horses past, or gave her a second's dry, quick nod, seeing to their horses.

She was just one of the boys. And it felt great!

Russ was one who lent a dry, quick nod. His eyesight wasn't what it used to be, but that wasn't why he didn't pay her too much mind. He had a job to do, and was of the type to "just get to it".

His oldest friend however, Chowder, a hardware clerk and a clamming captain, had plenty to announce, stepping forward with an incredulous tone of voice.

"Maximus?" he declared. "You need anchors for feet or sand in your boots son," he referred and advised. "I could blow you over with one sneeze! I reckon your parents had higher hopes," Chowder predicted in gesture to her small muscled arms and general frame.

Minnow wanted so badly to kick Matt in the shins. How on earth was he keeping a straight face? She hoped he was struggling, *struggling* not to laugh as hard as she was trying not to injure him in the open.

"I reckon," was her flat response.

"Bless your heart," said Chowder.

Chowder clapped her on the shoulder with an iron grip hard enough to force her a step forward as he said, "You'll fit right in here; Teaguers fill out more but they don't tend to sprout taller than a decent tump. Matt, feed your cousin right while he's here," he announced, to which Matt nodded largely, in concur.

"He aint got no hope up, but with luck after three days of clam and potatoes at least he won't be blown off his horse."

"Welcome aboard," the clamming captain stated with a wide yellow tooth and friendliest ever grin.

It was that grin, and that hardy inclusion that erased almost the entirety of her deep embarrassment.

Introductions over, Minnow and Matt returned to the tail end of the trailer to unload Ish, the foamy white grey gelding, and Olive. Her sable solid black with one white caterpillar marking off-center on her muzzle gleamed in morning yellow sunshine.

Once at the trailer and then two horse's tails, they were out of earshot enough to safely whisper hoarsely.

Minnow remarked to Matt, who was ripe with unshed laughter, "I thought of a sure way to win Carly back."

That snagged his attention.

Minnow played thoughtful and casual. "I think I work it so we're alone together long enough to mention how you were a basket case and blubbered yourself to sleep every night since you two broke up. That's when I swooped in and made you forget about her and her webs."

"Whatever wins her back," Matt said in answer, which disgusted Minnow and made her want to *puke*. She wasn't going to go through the terrible feeling of throwing up on account of Tarantella Girl, if she could help it. It wasn't like Matt was in "dire" need of help, even if Minnow argued that Tarantella Girl was leeching off of him. Still, it hadn't reached critical mass yet. She'd throw up for him then.

His doom for this feme fetal was dire and clear to Minnow, but Matt didn't see it that way, and certainly not her expressing her disgust with them as a couple by losing her breakfast was going to break the spell she had over him. Intrigue, tricks, two people obviously not made for each other but hooked on their history and reeled back in through it, splitting up and making up? It made Minnow dizzier than the rides at the carnival! The only tingle of delight strong enough to stanch her gag reflex was when Matt saw her expression and stopped grinning. "You're joking, right?"

Now it was Minnow's turn to smile and bloom with unshed laughter. She grabbed Olive's reins from him and said with a one shoulder shrug, "Whatever wins her back, right?"

"You would, wouldn't you," Matt said, one eyebrow arching his wary look.

Minnow shrugged again, casual. "Is *anything, else, bruised?*"

"Pride? Ego? Sense of humor?" Matt listed off.

"That one's still throbbing," she answered sweetly through her teeth.

"Nothing else I can think of," Matt replied decidedly.

Minnow turned away with a smile for herself.

Chapter Fifteen

"What'd you do to your cousin Matt, run over him in the driveway?" asked De Juan, referring to the newbie's dirt smudges.

Minnow spoke up but in a low voice and before Matt could embarrass her again.

Sporting her best boy tone, practiced enough from the plays she and her sisters had put on and still did on occasion, Minnow replied, "Naw. Was up a three helpen Matt dig up his old rain ditch before he got tied up with the swim. That thunderstorm' expected to move in sometime in the next day or two."

Minnow knew this of course from the kayak shop where growing up with the weather channel on and as a kayak guide herself she was keyed into the weather on a day to day basis because that hour could matter the most, meaning the difference between canceling a tour or gauging the wind on your face and smelling the air to make the call.

Plus, the fact that it'd been relentlessly hot for almost a week and a half straight with no break in the heat. Minnow watched the weather channel as a double-checker for Summer and Dad, but also preferred and relied on her own instinctual barometer before, and sometimes after checking. She tested herself, sharpening her instincts.

The people on Chincoteague were up at such 4:00am mornings, way before the crack of dawn, so Bumble and Hammer didn't think twice about her dirt cover story.

Bumble nodded his agreement to get that done ahead of time, and Hammer grunted approval, being the man of strict work ethic that he was.

Teaguers were as tough as the island but to survive the four seasons on her, they had to be smart too. As a matter of living on an island all Teaguers worked around *and* with the weather. With a lot of "against" that had to be, in there too.

Three hundred years among these pines, on these waterways, and amidst nor'easters and knifing winter winds with bone breaking cold that turned the bay and channels and creeks into chunky layers of tundra – sizzling, mosquito doted heatwaves, one took what came and made the best out of it. One toughed it out and made it work.

So, Minnow felt she was safe with this believable cover story of digging a ditch at night before the real day's work began. She counted herself mostly right in thinking she was safe, because she mostly was, until AJ made mention of her dialogue and adeptness of island weather.

"You talk like you're a real Teague," observed AJ.

Minnow kept a pleasant enough expression but swallowed a tiny lump of fear. She'd just talked the lingo and weather like she knew it as well as she knew she knew it. "Hangen around Matt enough hearing about Chincoteague will do that to a fella," she covered plainly with a smile, earning grunts and some chuckles from the group.

Whew. Less talking Minnow, she told herself in her mind.

This was Minnow's first roundup, but it wasn't for the wild ponies. Russ, flanked by Chowder, announced the game plan to the group, chopping them into groups of five and seven with directions west, north, and south. He and his marsh-posse were scoping east.

Minnow was roundup partners with Matt, Bumble, Carlos, De Juan, and Hammer. Bumble and Hammer leading, Matt sticking with Minnow bringing up the rear, or she should rephrase, the *Maximus*, and De Juan and Carlos flanking the middle until they reached the woods, and then they spread out. Within the first fifteen minutes, they came upon their first small

herd nibbling. They had a pickle of rounding up the dozen and
three ponies with their foals.

Through tickly and pokey enclosed woods in the rising heat
and in and out bright sun, Minnow didn't think she'd ever sweat
this much, and longed to be able to wear her bikini top so she
could take her shirt off. But to the others she was Maximus – or
Max.

Her ballcap was damp with swelter like the rest of her, and in
all her summers and guiding with Dad and Summer and Windy
on the water, she'd never felt this claustrophobic with heat, or
again sweated puddles to this extent. At least it was too hot for
mosquitos. But she'd have ticks for sure when she got home
tonight. Having short hair was a plus for her in this regard.

Was it crazy to say, even with the ticks probably already
feasting somewhere, despite the tickles of sweat drizzling down
her face and neck into her shirt, making her keep lifting her arm
to wipe her neck on her shoulder and her face on the other,
overwhelming heat, and being called Maximus, she was having
the time of her life?

She caught Matt shake his head at her more than once, but
she couldn't help it. She smiled the entire time, panting to
breathe when she cued Olive into cutting off a mare and her foal
that broke away, or spotting one cued her to head them off and
steer them into Matt or Carlos's pocket.

Rounding up horses for real was a lot like kayak guiding. She stayed on the outside, adjusting herself in her kayak to round another kayak in the group from veering into the wider water, when they were supposed to be in single file.

But Minnow only had to cue Olive in and move with her like an extension of her, being the pro that Olive was, having done this roundup half a dozen times.

Minnow wasn't only natural and confident from riding Marshy, fluid and yet holding on firmly to the reins with hands stuffed in her mane, but that's how she was smoothie smooth in her kayak. They were each an extension of herself. Kayak, horse, her, paddle, reins, and mane, Marshy and Minnow. Minnow and Olive. She allowed Olive to do what she did best, and she supported her by holding on and letting her.

At a point in midday, Minnow, Matt, and their group of ponies with Carlos and De Juan flanking the other back and Bumble and Hammer the front quarter, met up with most of the old-timers, Russ, Gilbert, Chowder, and Pots. As well as Cheddar, Spencer, and Miles, with a handful of others.

They merged the testy herd of twenty-plus and drove them down the fenced, slightly windy and hilly pathway to the corral, about a football field away. There, Russ and Chowder oversaw. Minnow and her partners were directed by AJ and the older conferring old timer saltwater ponyboy Pots, to hunt up stragglers.

Cheddar joined De Juan, Hammer, Bumble, Minnow and Matt while Carlos stayed and helped the others. They rode across an open field of grass and sand mud dirt, spent some time plodding through the forest with their mouths clammed shut to listen for activity. Twigs snapping. A snort. A whinny.

They broke for a small break on the loop to rest their horses and once more rehydrate from the thermoses of ice cold water in their saddlebags every single one of them chugged down thirstily.

Minnow did so quickly, trickles spilled from her mouth down her neck. Instantly refreshed, Minnow tucked her thermos back in the galloping horse printed satchel in her saddlebag and wiped her foggy sunglasses using a clean place on her shirt, with new energy. She stroked Olive as the mare inhaled water, reminding her of how she'd inhaled Matt yesterday. Minnow couldn't explain to Olive why she felt the need to chuckle, but she promised herself she would explain sometime.

Bumble and the others exchanged looks from where they sat on the sliced log bench, like they took her mood as a sign rehydration came in the nick of time, which made Minnow want to laugh more, but was also what helped her to button it for now.

She still had much riding to do, and she couldn't have her partners thinking that she wasn't up to it or was lagging in any way.

Minnow shared half of her blueberry muffin with Olive. She liked them dry and cold as well as steamy and moist. Who wouldn't? It's like summer and winter – she enjoyed both!

Matt had stuffed two in a paper-bag for them both this morning. Minnow could believe whole heartedly in why she'd left home without thinking of lunch. It was as though Matt knew she'd do it too. She'd been too excited.

On a pony swim tour Summer and Windy always made the run to the grocery store and stockpiled all flavors of granola bars and cases of water in the fridge, which they sealed up in plastic sealing bags and tucked in their kayak cockpits for themselves and the customers in case someone got hungry or thirsty while they waited for the ponies to swim.

Sometimes they could be waiting for hours, but they left early to secure prime spots for watching the breathtaking moment when they herded them up the hyper green marsh and splashed into the slack blue water.

Minnow told herself, tonight she would plan for a lunch tomorrow, and bit back her giggles as Olive's lips nibbled through the muffin and tickled her fingers.

They came up zip on stragglers, but found a driving breeze from the ocean that the shady forest made cooler. Audible, sore and dry moans of relief soared from all six partners' throats as refreshing salt air puffed over their sticky sunburn skin and sweat soaked shirts. A band of Cruso' gazing upon rescue with the relief aloe brings to sunburn. Without exaggeration, the feeling of exiting the tight pine forest equated feeling like Minnow had been splashed with a bucket of ice cold water after stepping out of a suffocating pillow on fire. They drank their fill until the cooler air started to feel chilly to their sunburn and because of their soaking wet shirts. They all shared a smile, even Hammer a dry plain one, which coming from him meant a lot, and cued their horses to circle back to the corral, by way of the rescuer beach.

During the whole day, Minnow's energy rode an unstoppable train. Through her tired and the misery of being sweat-tickled and hot like she'd never been before, her excitement remained invincible, with new exhilarations popping up to introduce themselves to her around every tree and on every soft and surprising gust of air that relieved for just a second. She couldn't have been happier. And it was just the first day.

Chapter Sixteen

Okay, Minnow remembered what she told Matt about his crack concerning her tailbone, but when Minnow flopped onto her bed, *every* part of her was sore!

She didn't mind one bit either. Well, it hurt, but she embraced it, and smiled in her pillow. She'd ridden for hours and rubbed down Olive after it'd been a long day for the both of them. Matt had insisted he'd rub her down for her this time, saying, "You're going to be feeling it soon," but she brushed his offer aside, certain she could handle it, as she'd handled tougher days than today, besides the doubled effort and energy she'd put in her mountain-climb job today, wanting to prove that she wasn't a sissy, that she was useful, and not just in the swim for the experience or a ride. Which the last one sort of sounded like an oxymoron, but nonetheless, Minnow was serious. She'd ridden

Olive, and she would unsaddle her, remove her halter, putting the tack away properly, and feed and water and give Olive the queen of rubdowns that she deserved. Which she stayed and was proud to say she did.

Minnow started transforming into a sloth as the next two hours wore on and she stood behind the counter. Stillness allowing the day's activities and exhaustion to sneak up on her and plant tiny anchors in different parts of her body. Her arms, legs, head, eyelids.

Halfway slogging through rinsing off a kayak, Dad happened by the door and noticed her stiffness and sluggishness. Under the impression that she was helping with carnival preparations and repair to the fairground pony accommodations, he thought she was sore from all that labor. Dad had no idea that she'd been rounding up the guests for said accommodations.

Smiling his warm Dad smile that put Minnow's world to rights even when it wasn't off kilter, Dad took the hose out of her hand, which in her sluggish state confused her at first. He told her to go home and rest. "I don't know what they've got you cleaning or how many acres of fairground you've mowed over there, but you're spent. Looks like you got loads of sun too."

At the mention, Minnow was reminded why her skin felt tight and spilled coffee hot. She'd gotten a little sunburn today. Staying mostly in the trees helped with that gladdening word "little", in aspect.

Looking at Dad's tanner-than-anyone's arms from being in the sun the most or longest on top of having the superhuman ability to tan better than most period, Minnow wondered why Summer was the only one to inherit good tanning molecules. She looked red right now, but in the morning, she'd be blotchy, which was annoyingly itchy, but happily be adding to her disguise.

"Head on home and crash," Dad told her. "Rest."

Rest. Crash. Minnow couldn't believe how good those violent words sounded.

"Okay," she answered sleepily with a weak smile. She obeyed with her lost person smile, and hugged kayak-broad Dad slowly, before maneuvering herself like a drunken person up the road, staying on the grass.

"Careful!" Dad's voice boomed caution. It woke her up some and Minnow replied, "Yep, okay," over her shoulder, making a point of walking sturdier even though it made her footsteps slower. At least she was barefoot, she thought, counting herself lucky in that respect too. This was a new sore unrelated to rinsing off kayaks and paddles when Dad and Windy returned with them from the dock where the renters had left them to the side just as they were supposed to and Dad told them. She'd been knocked to the ground, wrestling, spun off of Marshy in the early days when she didn't expect her to swing to the side, not to count how many bikes she'd crashed.

Minnow crashed herself onto her very soft, so inviting bed, imagining herself as a castaway washed up onshore the most beautiful patch of dry ground since forever. Her pounding heart beat into her soft mattress as her breathing started to even, and slowly grew content and deep the longer she laid there, the more she gave into her laziness. With the cool breeze puffing through her windows kissing her burning cheek and arms, with a single bird throttling tender and sharp melodies, Minnow drifted off to sleep within moments.

Minnow awoke to the westerly sky glowing bright orange and gilding her room tawny. She'd drooled on her mattress instead of her pillow this time, and as she wiped her mouth she was reminded of how Dad's jaw had dropped when she entered the kayak shop. He'd stood behind the counter going over this week's tour-log, and the bright day along with her ballcap had at first blinded him to her full view when she walked in, as well as from noticing that her hair was as short as his. She'd slowly rounded the counter as she explained to Dad it was on account of ticks at the carnival, and that she'd donated her hair to charity – she left out that it was bird nest charity. "Are you mad?" she'd asked.

He'd swiped off her hat and scrutinized the top and then the contours of her head, turned her chin side to side, sighed loudly, and then told her in no minced words, "I guess it's acceptable."

As she'd pressed herself to his damp shirted chest in a hug, smiling because of Dad's humor and approval, he'd added, "No ticks either," and she'd giggled.

The bigger surprise came at dinner. Minnow smelled the delivery pizza the instant she stepped towards her door, feeling heavy with being fully rested.

She slowly walked down the light blue carpeted stairs and peered into the kitchen where Windy and Summer were setting the table as Dad entered from washing his hands up to his elbows. Mom had been painting today, and had clearly washed as much from her face and hands and up to her elbows as would come off without a long and very soapy shower over a two-day period. She was presently opening a two liter of ginger ale.

Sensing her lingering presence or maybe it was also the creak in the stairs her barefoot lightly released as she stepped down another carpeted hardwood step slowly, everyone moved their attention to her.

Dad must have prepared them but Mom's shocked, jaw-dropping expression was as rewarding as the gapes and cheers from her sisters, prompting her to trot the rest of the way downstairs and present herself with hands lifted.

"You really did it!" Windy exclaimed, and instantly Minnow felt like they'd been drawn together in a stronger bond through her buzzing her hair somehow. She also felt like Windy looked at her with a blend of longing, respect, and admiration – three emotions never seen at once, and each emotion practically pulled to the surface like teeth that don't want to come in, when she did get to feeling some of one or the other.

"Oh my," Summer's voice breezed out of her mouth, like everything she did emulated with purpose or breezy. Surprised, her hand partly covered her open mouth while her stunned eyes were glued to the new look of her little sister.

Minnow felt swollen with their attention and was loving every second of their thrill and surprise and shock. Yes, indeed it had been bold of her, very out of character for her to do something so drastic and make such a big change without talking to one of them first; asking their opinion, advice, or Mom or Dad's permission.

Dad reintegrated her excuse for doing it just as Mom found her voice and legs again and came up to Minnow to touch her fuzz hair and caress her head without actually touching until she reached her face, and then cupped her cheeks.

Her expression, both of surprise and sadness, along with her approach and closeness tapped the brakes on Minnow's glee and happy absorption of attention. She could tell Mom missed her longish, wavy hair, making Minnow realize just how big of a shock this was for her. What a big change from someone, her daughter, who'd always looked one way. Kind of how Dad grew his beard in winter and shaved clean in summer. It took getting used to, but even that routine was something the girls and Mom were accustom to since infant days. Could Mom see that it was still Minnow?

Maybe those twinkles in her eyes hadn't been completely obliterated by her buzz and pretending to be a boy, or when she got her dander up at Matt over the bruised tailbone remark?

Maybe her twinkles were still there, in her blue eyes?

She was hoping Mom would approve by the end of her perusal. And it seemed she acclimated to it affectionately, sweetly smiling at Minnow's twinkle blue eyes and then rubbing her fuzzy head for real instead of like she was a globe of glass. "There you are my love," she said, having found Minnow, and accepted her new look. "You look beautiful my dear," Mom told her, bringing Minnow's cupped face to her lips where she planted a swift, strong kiss on her forehead that'd been spared sunburn thanks to her ballcap, and wrapped Minnow to her in a tight, swift hug.

Minnow wore her bright smile as her arms shot up to encircle Mom. Summer and Windy cheered and applauded along with Dad, whose clapping was always loudest, and the one person other than Mom, or Summer, who Windy didn't feel competitive with to try outperforming.

Chapter Seventeen

It hadn't been until Minnow and Mom had joined everyone at the table, where Dad held open the lid of the first pizza box for everyone to grab their two slices, that the question came up. "Tell us about your duties at the carnival," said Mom.

"Huh?" is all Minnow could produce, one chomp away from her first bite of deliciousness. In spite of her sunburn arms, or maybe because of them too, she froze, goosebumps shielding her from Mom's first question.

"Dad said you were helping the volunteers do things such as cleaning, mowing," Mom added with a smile, and at that everyone agreed with smiles and nods and noises with what Mom meant in her tone. Minnow enjoyed mowing grass; it was kind of an odd hobby, but Minnow really and truly did enjoy mowing grass. The sweet smell of freshly cut grass, the sound of a mower, getting to push one, which she'd always been excited for; the energy it takes, and the weird feeling of vibrating afterwards like she's still pushing the mower, along with the sweat dripping from her face and dampening her shirt, felt and smelled like summer to her. And Minnow loved her summers. Her sister Summer, and the island summers.

And yet Minnow just didn't simply "mow" grass. She crossed deserts, climbed cliffs; maybe the fate of the world relied upon her completing the task of mowing; if she gave up or braked or broke early, maybe Pirate Briny Wind slipped out of her grasp on the storm-tossed sea aboard her sister's pirate ship, or Matt won the next time the raced?

It was all an adventure. Mowing the lawn was an adventure!

And Minnow's enjoyment for mowing grass was the volleyball of good natured and continuous humor in the house. But right now, the joke was on her. What could she tell them?

This wasn't an adventure she'd ever played out before – and it wasn't pretend either.

"I, mow grass," confirmed Minnow slowly and while grinning, perking up so she sat straighter. *I'm not lying, it will be true, just as soon as I run upstairs after din-din and SOS Matt.* "We've been prepping stands too; I'm wherever they need me. Kind of the handyman or handywoman's handy assistant."

Everyone made noises of impressed because their mouths were full.

Windy spoke through her mouthful, which afterwards earned her the light spanking on her leg from Mom, who she sat next to across from Minnow. "Which stand are you working at night?"

"You're working a stand at night?" asked Summer next to her with pleasant surprise.

Leave it to the pirate, thought Minnow with grim sarcasm. "I don't think I will be working a stand at night," answered Minnow.

"What? They're fine letting you sweat and burn in the hot sun so they can clean up after a long carnival night, and more over repair what needs tinkering during the day, but you can't volunteer at one of their stands during open hours yet?" Mom said with shocked disappointment in her tone.

"No, Mom," Minnow tried.

"I'm going to speak to the chief," said Mom, squaring off a bite of pizza.

"Do you get free tickets for rides?" asked Summer, who stood with two fresh slices and rounded the table to the microwave.

"What about free tickets for family members?" asked Windy with bright eyes and excitement.

The microwave dinged, punctuating every nerve already on end in Minnow which she tried to keep undercover.

"Maybe," she told Windy to shut her up, "I'll ask Matt, I might be able to swing it."

Windy ate another bite with a gleeful squeal.

"Calm down honey or you'll choke," Dad warned. Windy was so happy she actually turned a tad serious and nodded, obeying. Summer was sitting back down next to Minnow when Mom stood up to warm her next slices up as well. Minnow raised her voice a little to be heard in the musical chair and microwave ceremony. "Mom, please don't talk to the chief, I finally got into the carnival and I don't want to blow it."

"It's not right honey," Mom turned around and said. Her pizza dinged and Dad took over. "She's right sweetie; it's only fair you get to do the fun stuff at night after helping them with the hard work. The carnival will be over soon, too," Dad also pointed out in thinking of her feelings.

Oh, she had to fix this now. "Matt's helping me," Minnow said, smiling with the hope that this made the difference. "They've just got so much help it's sometimes hard to put extra volunteers somewhere. Especially someone who's not done this kind of thing before."

"You're a kayak guide," Dad said with incredulity.

Oops. Bad approach.

"He's right," Summer piped up in agreement.

Her whole family was coming to her defense, and yet she knew they didn't need too. She loved them for it, but she had to end their disgruntlement and possible interference before this went further beyond what she could handle.

Minnow opened her mouth but Dad started speaking up again the instant he'd just said something.

"I've seen you handle thirty people with your sisters, and plenty of situations on the water on your own. Situations *I will add*, that full-grown men wouldn't know where to start with if they were in your water shoes." Dad's tone was no nonsense, calm, sturdy, encouraging without confetti. "You handle people from all walks of life and you're not even an adult. You can swing a hammer and throw out the garbage or shove a lawnmower in ninety degrees but they won't let you ride in the swim because it's tradition. You, and you're three sisters," said Dad, using his pizza as a pointer around the table, "are three – two and a half," he added towards Windy to get her attention, which was delayed, but a glance once at everyone told her he meant her – to which tickled laughter and smiles from everyone, as he'd intended, to break up the serious turn in tone of their dinner talk. Everyone knew Windy had a lot to learn, being prone to untactful acts of behavior, as well as mischievous tendencies. "Are two and a half of the most capable people I know, and that I've known, in all my life. Including your mother," Dad said, bringing shared moment and warm smiles between them.

Windy and Summer and Minnow all three, shared smiling looks.

Dad wasn't finished though, and continued with saying, "Mom and I will sort this out tomorrow."

"No wait, please, the thing is Matt's trying to get me a spot at the cotton candy stand and hopefully Pony Fries. I know it's unfair, you're right, but I've finally decided to volunteer and I don't want to cause a ruckus," she said begging. "I should know what stand I'm in tomorrow – please wait till then?"

Minnow had just put a time crunch on Matt, but it was the only way to allay their dander and belay her parents confronting the chief, which would mean jig up for her.

Mom and Dad shared the question with one of their Mom and Dad look conferences, and made a mutual consensus. "Very well," agree Mom properly. "But I'll have no one treating either one of my daughters unfairly," she remarked. "As soon as you know either way, you let me and Dad know."

"Yes," Minnow agreed, and then Minnow sighed quietly. To which Windy squinted at her a little for. How did she do that? Sense things Minnow was hiding? *When anybody was hiding them.* Minnow was sure she'd seen that suspicion in her eyes earlier too. She had a pirate's mind anyway to go with her pirate smile, and Minnow had the sinking feeling from past experiences she wasn't likely to get by with her thin reasons with sharp, suspicious Windy.

She'd caught her sneaking off anyway at 4:00am before anyone else was up. She'd seen her toss something across the yard, and by now she knew it was her hair. Something was afoot, and Windy had a vivacious hunger and desperate need to know and to be included in everything. Exclusion had been her Achilles tendon since birth. Trust her, being the middle child, Minnow knew her since day one. She often wondered why she didn't demand Mom go into labor early because she was missing all the fun with everyone staying in her tummy.

"That was very thoughtful and sweet of you to donate your hair to charity," Mom said approvingly to Minnow.

Minnow choked on her ginger ale mid-gulp. She coughed, and Summer automatically slapped her back without a pause in eating.

Sisterly love.

Windy said, "Better slow down; you don't want to choke."

It was Minnow's turn to narrow her eyes on Windy. Yes; sisterly love; so much second nature and first, automatic reflex with Summer. So very complicated and rivalrous with Windy and Minnow.

Minnow had once again, swum into another minnow trap. This time two at once.

Chapter Eighteen

"It's not funny," Minnow was scolding Matt through her cell phone. "You've got to get me into the cotton candy stand, and or the Pony Fries stand by tomorrow night, as me, Minnow, not saltwater *Maximus*," she added, still edgy about his changing her pretend name around to sweeten his joke, "or the jig is up for both of us," she hissed so no one would hear her downstairs.

"You bet it's not funny," Matt retorted, although he'd just been laughing. "Alright, stay cool, I'm on it."

Minnow exhaled, shutting her eyes. "Thank you. Txt me when you know," she said. It wasn't a sure "we're in the clear" but it was close.

"Alright," Matt said, a break in tone that brought up images in Minnow's mind of fault lines in the earth opening wider. She rolled her eyes and pushed the end conversation button before he laughed outright and irked her.

As hot as it had been today Minnow expected the sun to be melting in the western sky, regardless of the flaw in her analogy because the sun was made of fire. As it was the sun had dipped behind the treetops but the orange blue sky hadn't faded quite yet. So, when Windy entered their room, shutting the door quietly behind her and looking intense and tawny, Minnow noticed the light glint off her tooth – but she didn't have a golden tooth?

The reoccurring idea threw Minnow merely a split second. "What's really going on?" Windy demanded in a low but urgent tone. "This morning you left before anyone was up and you said that you were turning pirate. *And* you buzzed your hair! What was that for?"

In Minnow's excitement, she'd accidently clued Windy in to her mutiny plan, even though Windy didn't know exactly what she was up to. She was smart enough to have it put together on her own before the week was up. Since she didn't want Windy resorting to following, which the last thing she needed while pretending to be a boy to ride in the swim was a tail, she had no choice but to bring Windy into her confidence.

She grabbed her wrist tightly and Windy pulled back but Minnow had already yanked her to sitting on her bed with her and now gripped both of her wrists and hands with hers. She started sternly, "You've got to promise that you won't tell anyone. Mom and Dad wouldn't approve because it's not strictly honest, but not bad dishonest," she said with wincing.

"What is it?" Windy was bursting at the seams with seriousness and eagerness blended to know.

"I buzzed my hair because I'm pretending to be a boy so I can ride in the pony swim," Minnow revealed bluntly.

Windy' blue green eyes popped and she instantly gripped Minnows hands back. "You did it! You did it!"

"SHHHHHHHHH!" warned Minnow, but she was smiling. Minnow tried not to topple off the bed when Windy crushed her in her embrace. She kissed her neck and Minnow winced softly, but she'd accept it this time. "I'm so proud of you," Windy said meaningfully, and as she pulled back she made a point of stretching on her knee and kissing Minnow on the very top of her fuzzy head in honor of her bold move in the form of buzzed hair.

Minnow broke into a partial laugh and smile at Windy' funny gesture as she plopped back down looking at her intently. "Tell me everything that happened today, from the start," Windy wanted to know.

Rare is the time, that Minnow had half or all of Windy' attention span, let alone her rapt attention, and this did not slip past Minnow's awareness. She enjoyed the feeling actually, of being the center of Windy' attention and rapture instead of the competitor Windy saw her as sometimes because she was hot tempered and a little selfish.

Who could have guessed it would happen that Minnow would, one, be riding in the pony swim at long last, or two, that the "one" and "only" person she was telling, and "trusting" with her secret, outside of Matt, was her little sister who she'd had and has more thunder-bumpers with than she could count?

There was a strengthening and a closer-ness she felt blooming within their turbulent yet loving bond, that she only felt on occasions like these when they decided to be closer and were behaving more like sisters than mosquitoes. But this was more. A blooming like a new tether winding itself around their already ball of tethers that bind them together – love, DNA, their family, their dislikes and their likes, their similarities and broad differences even. One of those rare and golden ones that leaves a mark and traces backwards and forwards every time you think about it, or wherever and however you go on from here. This moment of real sisterly love, without squabble – well, that won't last, but neither will squabbling – made today one of the best days ever, for Minnow, and for Windy. For little to rare also were the times Minnow confided in Windy, outside of their cease fires in deciding to be closer. Minnow often didn't treat Windy worthy or capable of her confidence, and the tricky part was Windy often didn't act responsible or considerate and caring enough to hold her confidences, which altered Minnow's opinion of her and staunched her willingness to confide her secrets. Windy still had a lot to learn, but Minnow learned just now, or rather was reminded, how trustworthy Windy really was and can be, and in this Minnow learned another lesson too; and from now on she would give Windy more credit. Because she deserved it. Maybe by not giving her enough credit for things, for herself, she'd hindered Windy in ways, and contributed to her rebellious attitudes and rivalrous tendencies. The way if one talks baby talk to a baby forever they'll never learn how to converse properly.

Although, Windy would always be a bit of all this. She's her pirate sister after all.

Chapter Nineteen

Minnow sat very still while the vibration from the hair buzzer tickled her neck as Mom brought her skill in shaping to her fuzz at the base of her head. She felt Mom's cool and lightly calloused hand gently sweep over the place on her neck and head she shaped with the buzzer, visualizing through her touch the duck tail shape of her hair perimeter. She was enjoying this, as well as the nightfall's approach breezing through and cooling her, when the Mosquito Man started buzzing up the road.

Summer and Windy had been watching, each one betting the last of the chocolate chip ice cream on if Minnow could contain her laughter or would the buzzer be too much for her overly ticklishness? However they were prompted into a hustle to close the windows before he drove down their lane, starting with the kitchen window over the sink that Minnow had been drinking the cool stirring through.

"Don't laugh!" Windy shouted as she bolted loudly upstairs.

"Slow!" Mom warned without breaking her focus, her touch remaining gentle, as always.

"Laugh! Feel free!" Summer told her from the living room as she slid closed the big bay windows. "I've known her since she was a baby!" she hollered deliberately so Windy could hear her, crossing through the kitchen to the bathroom just as Windy' thunder feet stomped and stormed into Summer's room to shut her three windows.

"She can't hold it in that long!" she yelled as the Mosquito Man buzzed shrilly down the road.

It was said that the spray the town truck emitted now days wasn't harmful, but her parents wouldn't take the risk, even all these years later. Needless to say, the girls felt the same. They still screamed and ran and hollered, "Mosquito Man!" when they were caught outdoors and had to hightail it in to the house.

Minnow felt her pocket buzz. It broke her concentration and she giggled. Just as she was fixing to swipe it from her pocket Mom patted her back that she was done and to hop up. "There, better," she said, admiring Minnow's new hair along with the results of her sculpting skills.

"Thanks Mom." Minnow hugged her and trotted to the bathroom that Summer was leaving, to check out her new and improved haircut.

"She couldn't hold it in; Minnow giggled!" Mom called to be heard in general.

"Told you!" Summer shouted so Windy could hear her, and then everything became muffled to Minnow. Looking in the mirror Minnow felt of her head and tilted her profile side to side wearing a big grin. She looked more like a girl with a pixie than a baby fluff animal. Her pocket buzzed again and she swiped her phone out this time, having completely forgotten about the first txt in that short second span.

In ten? Read the txt message. She clicked up to the first one.

Got news. Secret spot?

Matt was asking to meet in their special spot, the kayak shop roof.

A new one dinged before her thumbs could tap a reply.

After the Mosquito Man's gone.

Ok, she punched and sent with a smile.

Minnow snuck away, visiting Marshy with a very quick hello and hastily plucked carrot from the veggie garden, and then climbed the roof using the blocks of wood next to the back of the shop which was the entrance to Mom's woodshop. That got her to the woodshop roof, which she crossed the narrow side of pitch carefully, hopping to the steep incline of the lengthwise kayak shop portion, and cresting the pitch, sat down.

Absorbed in her thoughts on the last few days, Minnow's gaze was glued on Assateague's dark evergreen pines gradually silhouetting against the nightfall sky, as the mesmerizing lighthouse beam spanned in glass encased orbit.

She heard jogging crunch and saw Matt's form with ballcap climbing onto the side and then roof of Dad's truck. She lent her hand when he neared close and pulled him next to her.

"Is it good news?" Minnow asked.

Matt didn't belabor suspense. "You're in," he panted.

"Thanks Matt, whew," Minnow said in relief. "That was close."

Matt squinted through the dim light. "Did you cut your hair again?"

"Mom styled it for me," said Minnow. "Better?" She presented the back and side tilt of her head.

"Yep," Matt agreed. "It looks real nice."

"I think so," Minnow said, feeling her head again.

"So why do we call this our secret spot when we're in full view for anyone to see?" asked Matt, scanning their surroundings.

"Because that's what it's always been," she told him in reply, and smiled with the memories he'd stirred. "We pretended it was secret, and for a while when we were little it felt like it," she reminded him. "Hardly anyone ever catches us. Mom and Dad wouldn't like me being up here at night either," she said, lowering her voice and glancing at her house across the yard. The bushes and trees obscured Mom and Dad's downstairs bedroom window view facing the kayak shop, but if they looked longer than a swift glance they'd discern two dark figures sitting on Dad's roof, from between the foliage.

"Yep," Matt replied, smiling in response with the same memories. "Best spot on the island."

Gazing over the marsh on a nightfall Assateague, crickets chirping, from the roof of the kayak shop, with Matt beside her, and minimal bugs endangering their nostrils and eyes, Minnow couldn't agree more heartily.

"It's the northern herd roundup tomorrow, right?" asked Minnow after a moment of companionable silence admiring their view. Minnow knew the answer but felt safer it was true hearing it from Matt's lips. This was actually happening. She was a rider in the pony swim.

"Yep. You know that," Matt answered, giving her a look.

"Yep, but it all still feels like a dream," Minnow replied, shivering once with tingles of delight. "Just checking," she said softly.

Matt smiled in kind. "Well, some dreams do come true," he said.

Minnow looked at Matt. "Thanks helping mine come true."

Matt replied, "Well, you're earning it. Cause after the roundup you get to put your Minnow hat back on and spend a few hours in sun and surf with yours truly."

"You just had to ruin the moment!" Minnow pressed, but she was smiling, and didn't shove multiple times too hard, although tomorrow when she was pretending to be his date in front of Tarantella Girl she may wish she had.

Matt just grinned and absorbed her abuse.

When Minnow gazed at him with question for further details and turned out her palm upright, Matt was ready with response. "Carly's going to be at Tizzy and Izzy's birthday party remember," he said.

Minnow laughed. "I'm glad you still call her Tizzy, like me," she said.

"I think everyone will always call her that," Matt said in reply. "Even her."

"But we thought of it first," Minnow reminded him, feeling a sense of ownership for the nickname they'd given the talkative and worrisome twin.

"Till she heard about it and adopted it as her idea," Matt pointed out with frankness.

"So remind me, what makes Harry Macroscope so irresistible for Tarantella Girl," remarked Minnow a little jokingly, but half meaning it.

Matt caught the nickname original Minnow had just made up based on Carly's own description of her new boyfriend, Mr. Mighty. With a science twist, he'd probably appreciate.

"A brain that thinks in terms like hers; he speaks science," said Matt. "He's just a faze; she gets those and grows out of them."

"Yep, but you don't have that problem," Minnow pointed out.

"That's because I'm me," Matt answered.

"Still; you go through this at least twice a year. When is twice a year goanna be twice a year enough for you?" Minnow pressed mildly, feeling like someone prying open a clam that refused to acknowledge it was in a spot. Close to a pot.

"My point is, she doesn't mean it," Matt responded. "She has a hard time refusing head-smart guys."

"You're smart," Minnow said confused.

"Brainiac smart," said Matt.

"If she splits up with you she aint so smart to me," replied Minnow, "and if you keep getting back with her every time she gets bored with the brain boys, you aint so smart either."

"That whole logic smarted," Matt replied, faking *head hurt*, with a slight grimace.

"Yep," Minnow said, gently whacking said head. Maybe it'd knock some sense loose for use.

"The point is she always comes back; they're a month's fancy, a faze. She'll grow out of it one day, and we'll never split up again," he said.

"Harry's a four month faze," Minnow mentioned with a furrowed thoughtful look too, as she was correcting Matt's explanation.

He lifted his eyebrows in acknowledgement without redirecting his gaze of focus from the marsh. "Yep; now you see why I had to reach out; and dig deep for a behemoth and idiot-proof stroke of genius plan."

Minnow growled in frustration, she couldn't help it. "You are such a butterfly in her web! What do you see in her?" She looked at Matt. "No, honestly, I want to know, make this bargain less painful and tell me what you actually see in Tarantella Girl that makes her the girl for you."

"I told you on the beach," said Matt.

"Yep, but I don't think I really heard you," said Minnow.

"She's kind. Honest. Enthusiastic about spiders. She loves them," Matt listed. How could he be so lukewarm when Minnow was boiling inside?

"She's a snob," Minnow stated flatly.

"Like I told you before, there's more to her than you know Minnow," Matt replied. "You know, you both might actually get along if you both stopped despising each other's guts for one day."

"No thank you," Minnow answered, twisting back around on her seagull's perch and facing the view. She hadn't realized that she'd twisted sideways in the culmination of her frustration and annoyance. "I see a girl who's shallow, self-centered, and a snob. She teases you, and I don't have any desire to befriend her because of that alone."

"Look at it this way; you get to take delight in making her jealous this week," said Matt.

"Trust me, that I will," responded Minnow.

"I thought you'd appreciate that," said Matt.

Minnow eyed him out of the corner of her eye, and when Matt caught her staring with one of his own looks, she jerked her glare straightforward. "Okay," Minnow surrendered. "I'll changed into my me clothes once we're in the clear after the roundup."

That had Matt smiling like himself again.

"Don't smile," said Minnow.

"Why?"

"Because I'm annoyed at you," she explained.

He scooted an inch closer. "A manuscript walks into a yarn shop," Matt started, followed by a pause.

Minnow flattened her focus, caging her throat closed against talking.

"He sits down next to a basket of string," Matt went on.

Minnow studied the moon, trying to lose herself in its silver glow and discern shapes from its greyer markings. Were there any horses?

"And the string said, you know this is a yarn shop? and the manuscript nodded and replied, I'm here to spin my yarn too."

"Shut it!" Minnow blurted, biting her lower lip and cringing with frustration and to contain the impulse to laugh. She really didn't want to give in! "We'd better get some sleep."

"No counting fireflies? They'll be out soon," Matt said, but he was moving to catch up to Minnow, who was already in careful crab motion, scooting her seat along the seagull's perch so that she sat above Dad's truck.

"No," Minnow answered. "Only in my head as I try to fall asleep."

"Yep," agreed Matt, and they slowly but with feet of memory inched down the steep incline and helped each other steady in the transference from roof ledge to the first belly up kayak strapped to Dad's truck rack.

"Hey," said Matt, and Minnow slowly spun around with her head tilted to the side, wearing a look. He tugged on her arm and pulled her into a hug, and she embraced him back, closing her eyes. She'd had it up to her eyeballs with Tarantella Girl, and she didn't want Matt to get hurt.

"Still my wingman?" asked Matt, his voice a little muffled in their embrace.

Minnow rolled her eyes, unable to help the soft smile that came for a brief second. "I'm always your wingman. Idiot."

Minnow and Matt parted ways with this tender hug and a shove to part them, for they were friends even though they disagreed on Carly.

Minnow knew she had to rise before the rooster, but she'd not paid enough attention to Marshy in the last few days. Marshy wasn't in the swim either, which Minnow knew must bother her. And so, once everyone was fast asleep, she bridled Marshy, hoisting herself astride bareback with the bottom fence rail for a leg up, and ventured into the night down the road for a midnight ride. Marshy hadn't stretched her legs beyond the medium size paddock and she felt her pent-up energy begging for the rein. Minnow gave it to her and they cantered on the grassy side of the deserted road all the way to piney island. Tarantella Girl lived in one of the huge yet tucked houses on the creek. There were no lights on as she and Marshy went by.

Minnow couldn't help wondering about Tarantella Girl and Matt's relationship. She'd already told herself that she wasn't going to interfere, even though she still gave him a hard time, because there was nothing she could say that she hadn't already said that was going to convince him how shallow Tarantella Girl was. But for some reason she kept picturing them arm in arm, the way Matt had held her on the beach. She didn't know why that it was nagging at her like the faintest of side aches. She usually felt a cross to sick or bland when she saw them being close and sweet. Maybe it had something to do with her being on the receiving end instead of Carly, giving her insight into what transpired between them, that made her unable to stop putting herself in Carly's shoes – or rather, reliving standing in Matt's touch. Because he was her best friend. There was no way it could be anything else, other than her empathy and infinity of affection for her best friend Matt.

Chapter Twenty

Minnow was glad she'd confided to her little sister before she'd crashed early last night, because Windy was rustling her on her shoulder while it was still night.

Her afternoon nap evidently hadn't refilled her tank nearly enough because she'd just slept through her wristwatch alarm. Thankfully Windy hadn't.

Minnow leapt out of bed, dressed in loose boyfriend jeans, one of Dad's old shirts with tiny holes and no sleeves, tugged her ballcap on, and shared a smile and genuine hug with Windy, who was just as excited for Minnow and to be helping her as Minnow was excited for this morning's northern herd roundup that awaited her in the starry predawn night.

And while Minnow and Windy were being close and trusting with each other, Minnow admitted to herself, that she was glad Windy was a part of her charade, or mutiny, or whatever they wanted to call this. To Minnow, it was her dream coming true – every morning she woke up – every time she climbed in Matt's truck through his window because the door was sticking and they were in a hurry, or when she mounted Olive among the saltwater ponyboys, on Assateague – with each new facet of the roundup, it was like the crickets chirped splendid tunes every morning as she ventured out into the dark and sweet grassy night air.

In this way, Windy and Minnow were just alike. Windy craved inclusion and reveled in it that way Minnow had thirsted for inclusion into the pony swim and was thrilled and tickled each morning to belong to it, to be part of what she'd always felt like she belonged with and to be in.

So, her new partner in mutiny acted as lookout while Minnow plundered the fridge. The light bathed Minnow as she quietly filled her arms with the charcoal gray porcelain bowls containing tangy raspberries, sweet blueberries, sour blackberries, and the saranwrap plate of Mom's homemade strawberry waffle leftovers. Windy saw the armful when she glanced over her shoulder and helped Minnow disassemble the balanced fruit bowls from her tiny arms onto the counter with minimum clatter and tinkling when they grazed or touched each other. Minnow went back in the cool and humming fridge for the maple syrup.

Minnow constructed herself a mixed berry filled waffle sandwich, oozing maple syrup and wrapped it in saranwrap. She grabbed her thermos she'd filled before hitting the hay and slipped her lunch into the burlap satchel imprinted with a galloping horse on each side. Mom had made it for her for her last birthday. At Matt's, she hid it inside her saddlebag where no one else looked.

Minnow closed the fridge and tiptoed into the bathroom, Windy checking the house for creaks and noises that someone was getting out of bed as she followed.

Minnow shimmied through the bathroom window and Windy handed her the satchel through the opening.

On the washing machine, Windy stuck her head through the window, which was all she could fit since she'd filled out and forward. It was almost amazing to think back to just a year ago, when Windy was as thin as Minnow and used to climb through the rectangular opening all the time.

"Good luck ponygirl," Windy whispered hoarsely.

"Thanks pirate," Minnow replied back in the same hoarse voice, and set out.

With the silver, dewy bejeweled grasses and whispering marsh grass swaying beside her and joining the crickets in their harmony, Minnow watched out for headlights with glances over her shoulder, treading up the road feeling wide awake and fresh despite having the capacity to sleep through her alarm. She probably would've slept straight through sunup if Windy hadn't been there to pull her from the soft anchorage of her pillows. Lightning bugs put on a light show for her as she walked, enhancing her good feeling about this morning.

Headlights caught her attention however, but she didn't stand on alert, ready to drop her chin and tug her ballcap lower and keep trudging, because the familiar sounding truck blinked its headlights at her and she knew right at once who it was.

Once inside Matt's truck, which met her several houses down the road, she was still smiling. She couldn't help it.

"Goanna bring up the rear again today, Maximus?" asked Matt with playful, easy humor.

Feeling playful as well, Minnow stretched to tickled him on his right side which had him gluing himself to the truck door to escape her squid hands! She chuckled at his joke now instead of getting her dander all the way up. "You will pay for that somehow if *you* keep bringing it up!" she warned him. "Somehow, I will make you suffer!"

She didn't feel like wrecking the truck so she resorted to another form of torture.

Matt bulked up against her arm smacks and fists that were pitiful in comparison to a real punch, Minnow's small fists barely making bruises until several times! How had she ever thrown him over her shoulder or won a wrestling match? Oh, for the days when he was as scrawny as she'd stayed, when she could make a point with her punch instead of make him smile from trying. But at the same time, she got to beat on him even more than in those days because he was harder to dent, and while he was bulked up like a shield she pounded and shoved him until the laughter crippled them both.

Rounding up the herd came more easily to Minnow the second time. She knew what to expect and what to look out for more than she did the first time, and worked with Olive rather than let Olive lead her as much. Although she still gave Olive her rein when she asked for it, Minnow felt more confident in the saddle and kept her seat through Olive's twists and halts and rounding foals and their mothers, anticipating her moves.

The exhausted and loud mares and foals and stallions were penned and grazing on fresh hay with muzzles deep in troughs sparkling freshwater, amidst their fans huddled outside the newly constructed fencing. It was time to call it a day, at least for Minnow and Matt.

"Like it back here Maximus," asked Bumble with observation, who'd dropped back beside Minnow for a how ya doen.

The small hint of humor in Bumble's word choice was not lost to Minnow.

"I do," Minnow answered. *Keep it short and to the point,* she said to remind herself, in her mind.

"Careful with those two words – they'll get you in trouble one of these days," Bumble remarked with a belly-jiggling bellow of laughter afterwards.

Minnow snorted. She didn't mean to, but the laughter just burst forth without warning. That was a line Matt and her family played on each other every chance they got. Bumble had learned that line from family dinners at her house!

"Not much of a talker, are ya," Bumble noted.

"Way I am I guess," Minnow answered frankly.

"Couldn't help but notice how you sounded earlier when you and Matt were bouncen directions back and forth to head that young colt off. Got a frog in your throat?" asked Bumble. He hedged. "Maybe it's the bulrush seeds floaten out here, or the sweetness of the pine shats – tickles mine sometimes."

"Take my coffee strong," she replied back as Maximus.

"It's okay son, no need to fear it, happened to us all," said Bumble plainly back with a supportive nod.

Minnow tried to keep the question accentuated with a deliberate underscore out of her expression but it must have showed some, or Bumble always intended to add, "Another year roundabouts, it'll clear up. No more frogs or girly squeaks. That coffee will go down however you want it then."

As Bumble moved up to round a mare and their foal from deviating it dawned on Minnow what he was talking about!

Voice changes!

Incredibly funny, and the perfect cover! Minnow felt her cheeks turn searing red under her sunburn while she was muffling her laughter, at the same time beaming with delight! It was a good thing she was bringing up the rear of the herd, or the *maximus* as she and Matt were calling it now. And obviously Bumble.

Minnow realized –

Now she could talk!

Chapter Twenty-one

Minnow and Marshy practiced rounding up a pretend herd once the flock of mallards finally flew away, after every effort not to spread their wings failed and they still weren't quick enough to evade the nomadic barrier of Marshy' stomping and trotting hooves.

Marshy wasn't as sensitive to touch with commands as Olive, so she required more time to figure out what Minnow meant and remember it. But she was a curious little pony, interested in everything movement and Minnow, and after about an hour and a half, with small breaks for water out of the hose and a carrot that they shared for their hard efforts, Marshy was starting to get the hang of what Minnow meant by leaning way left and way right. The light touch of the reins wasn't helpful for Marshy, her mane so wavy springing thick and her neck too stocky to really make any rhyme or reason out of the signal.

Minnow didn't want their fun practicing to end, but she felt the slant of the sun nearing the middle of the afternoon. Which meant she was supposed to meet Matt down the lane at his house to drive back out to the beach and give Tarantella Girl a green blush of envy.

When she meandered up to Matt's house, she rounded the side into the backyard. His backyard layout was similar to hers. Both their paddocks were in the very back of their yards, close to the woods and thickets that were of course trimmed back.

As many times, as Olive escaped, it was a wonder she'd only ever had an upset tummy where they had to call the vet three times. When she escaped, she explored wherever the wind took her. The woods, a neighbor's yard, downtown, Assateague! She'd even turned up many mornings outside of Marshy' paddock, like two lifelong friends and neighbors yacking it up. Minnow's been eating dinner and glanced up and spotted her *twice inside* Marshy' paddock!

In an hour and a half Matt had given Olive and Ish a rubdown, extra oats and fresh water, hung laundry on the line – Mrs. Evers would blush and gush with pride! And from the strain of a valve and gurgling piping with cranky reach in the house he'd just turned off the shower. Like her house, Matt's family's home was an older Chincoteague cottage style home, with two bedrooms, unlike her two and a half. *That half in a growing and noisy family*

217

of five made a lot of difference. A small kitchen with table, medium living room with fireplace, and a shared bathroom, rounded the Evers's charmed and charming abode. For it was they who completed it.

Minnow's house wasn't chipping paint or rotting wood as badly as Matt's eggshell white with peeling green trim. But his house was like her second home. His mother's rosemary that Minnow's mother had gifted to her from their yard flanked either side of the front of the house, making his home when coupled with the smell of horses, smell almost exactly like hers too. Where her mother was always cooking waffles, Mrs. Evers baked muffins.

Mr. Evers, as a high school teacher, wasn't much of a handyman, but with Matt's help they found projects to work on. Part of their quality time together, Matt and his father had slowly cleaned the chimney one year, tore out the rotting front steps and nailed down a brand new one, which Mrs. Evers blushed over as well, so proud of her men and her new porch steps. The windows, Minnow knew were original to the house and Matt and Mr. Evers restored them into shiny glass with fresh paint – now if they could only get them to stop sticking –

Minnow's house had the same trouble; it was never going to reverse. Besides, it was kind of fun for Minnow to struggle with the window. It'd be rather boring if it just slid open like it was supposed to.

Those were just a few things about the Evers's home. The bright orange and yellow spear flowers with elephant leaves encompassed the circumference of the house, attracting bumble, wasp, and humming bird alike to their nectar.

It was nice in the summertime just to sit at a window and watch.

Minnow was striding with a happy swagger in her step, entertained by her own thoughts, when the clothesline fluttering laundry dry since midmorning caught her eye and an idea struck her.

Minnow glanced at the house and then raced to the clothesline. She saw plaid blue and plucked it, two clothespins clipping as they popped and boinged in the air. She checked the windows and raced to the truck, stuffing it in the saddlebag she'd left in the front seat on her side.

Whistling a Celtic tune she'd heard recently from Summer in the kayak shop, Minnow skipped up to the barn and retrieved alfalfa treats from their plastic container. Matt wouldn't be much longer but there was time for indulging two of her favorite friends. Olive and Ish had notice her arrival but in watching her skip to the barn could sense what she would bring back with her. They were already crowding up to the fence and pressing their chests against the wood, nudging their heads up and down and stretching their necks, Olive with lips curling upward.

Minnow fed Ish some too so he didn't feel left out. As Olive and Ish's lips tickled and drooled on her hands, she studied

Olive. She shook her head. "Maybe I've been feeding you too much of these over the years," Minnow thought aloud to her. "Or maybe it's also like Matt said; Coby's been engaged elsewhere."

Minnow laughed at her own unintended pun!

"Which would make him engaged everywhere he goes," she joked. Olive sweetly blinked her eyes in a soft bashfulness, while Ish whinnied for more alfalfa treats!

Minnow had heard a noise behind her and guessed she figured Matt was coming, yet she was so involved in studying Olive and feeling her tickly lips that Matt snuck up on her.

"Ready to go?" he asked.

Minnow turned her attention to Matt, just as a gust blew a whiff of him her way. She expected shampoo, soap, that clean fresh out of the cool shower smell. Was that musk?

"I thought you showered," Minnow said.

"Really Minnow," Matt said in undramatic but pretend offense. He took his weight off one leg and leaned forward on the railing, grazing Ish with his touch when Ish came around to greet him and inspect him too. "This coming from the girl who smeared dirt on her face because she was under the impression boys were filthy. A shower," he said in a lower softly derisive tone, as if showers were man to mars. "Did you expect renaissance overnight?"

Minnow gave him a flat, upward, unimpressed look. Even though his humor was tickling her giggle buttons. "You smell like my Dad or Coby when they've been working – musky. I was expecting soap – you still smell good. I just never thought of you smelling like that."

"Like what? A man?" Matt asked, lifting one quizzing eyebrow.

"Yes, Peter P," Minnow answered smiling.

Matt's layer of annoyance came through underneath, which she hadn't known he'd been masking. He grumbled. "The shower came on for a second but then cut out. I guess it's the ocean for me today."

Minnow didn't think that was second best. She could understand how it might seem inconvenient after a long sweaty hard day in the saddle and under the heat of the sun, and you'd give up pizza for an entire week, just for half an hour of cool refreshing shower and soap.

"What happened to your shower?" asked Minnow, feeding Olive the last of her alfalfa treats in her pocket. Which it wasn't a good idea to store them there. She'd smell like treats in her pockets until she washed her shorts, and that invited nippers. Even created nippers in horses as well-behaved and sweet as Olive. So, Minnow hoped Matt didn't catch her unintentional no-no.

"The piping again – I can fix it. But tonight," he said in reply. From Matt's expression, partly tired, partly resigned, he wasn't looking forward to it. Minnow felt his plight. He had a lot on his plate; a shower when you're working hard and long all day is as crucial as that big din-din you've been slowly going caveman or cavewoman over all day looking forward to it, growing hungrier and hungrier. Minnow knew this from experience. She'd worked in the kayak shop long days and weeks in the summer before and felt like a new person after real food and a shower.

"Need help?" asked Minnow. They had the carnival tonight, but she could come by early and assist him. It didn't take long to fix Matt's piping, and she'd helped him before.

"Naw," Matt declined, starting to sound less annoyed and more like himself. "It's not a problem; just a pain right now."

"I didn't shower either; I've been practicing what you taught me bout rounding up, with Marshy in the backyard," said Minnow. "Do I smell good too?" She lifted her arm and in one hop was close enough that her armpit was near Matt's face. He closed his eyes to take in what she'd just done and possibly recover, although Minnow was tickled to find out which one more – from shoving her armpit close for him to catch a whiff, or the whiff itself. Minnow didn't test her armpit. She wanted to know Matt's reaction first.

"You do smell good," Matt replied.

"Thanks Matt," Minnow said brightly, knowing she really shouldn't believe a word of what he said, but too pleased with his response to be smart.

She'd just folded her arms together over the top trailing and being pleased with herself stood straight and pert when the spell was broken; no, the bubble burst.

"For a minnow," said Matt in addition.

The burst bubble though, was filled with giggles and laughter that exploded, and she was able to roust that smile back out of Matt by her joking and this laughter, bringing him back into the now, where he wasn't stuck in tonight, imagining himself up to his elbows in piping banging on pipes and listening for the water to shoot through cleanly and out into the bathtub, hoping he eventually hit the right spot and the right pipe; as well as hoping he didn't disturb the wrong one.

Chapter Twenty-two

"She's here," Matt said in a confidential aside to Minnow as he unhooked the bungee cord looped through the handle of the ocean kayak from the metal eyehook ruggedly installed on the top corner of the truck bed by the cab.

It was hard to miss the twins' two big ten by ten tent tops, north of where they found what had to be the very last squeezable parking space on the beach. There were two picnic tables in one, where classmates, some sort-of-friends, and their parents and a few grandparents ate and played cards with the deck held down by conk shell. While a picnic table topped with coolers of food and canned sodas filled the other tent.

Their parents were there socializing. Mrs. Plenty, the slender, tall woman in a white floral breezy dress was laughing alongside her husband, the suntan potbellied man telling a favorite story about when the twins were babies to two senior couples, who looked enchanted at the apparent adorableness of the tale. Unsociable Izzy sat at the picnic table with chin rested on her arms as she slowly ate a forkful of yellow white-icing cake.

It was always safe to assume wherever Izzy and Tizzy were, Tarantella Girl was around too.

"We'll walk through the center," suggested Minnow for a game-plan. Once their ocean kayaks were unloaded, Minnow and Matt preceded to drag them up the hot-hot sand, life-vests loosely clutched in their free grip.

The bright blue ocean was calm outside of the frothy white, perfect for ocean kayaking. Minnow had thought that a guise other than holding hands and looking cute together or kissing would strengthen the believability that they were now a couple. Couples would do fun, active things like ocean kayaking together. Especially Minnow. Matt kayaked for fun with them growing up and still does, but ocean kayaking has always held more appeal to Matt. Minnow is torn. She loves the calm of the creeks and there's so much wildlife and nature to see in the marsh. Yet the ocean is like paddling on a giant horse, and riding the waves in felt as though Minnow were galloping.

She often thought of the wild ponies when they'd wrecked and swum ashore, or when they were free to roam the beach before Assateague became more of a tourist spot. Having wild ponies stomping on a visitor's sunburn while they're napping wouldn't be good advertisement or policy!

Taking in the cool saltwater smell, the coasting breeze buffered part cool at first and more warm as it lessened; then Minnow looked forward to the next gust, and enjoyed it; looking forward to the next when it tapered off. She hadn't stripped to her bikini or dragged her ocean kayak very far up the sand and already the sun was radiating off her arms. It was a good thing she'd put on sunscreen like Mom always warned her to do before she went out. Minnow was better at keeping up on it than Windy. Everyone had those times where they got bad sunburn; but Windy' track record wasn't leading her anywhere pleasant.

The sight of sand and ocean blue and frothy crashing roaring waves, called Minnow, and she felt welcomed home and eager to join in with it like sometimes she just can't wait to crash into her bed or sit down with her family after the day took them in different directions and catch up.

Minnow was caught off-guard only for a second by Tizzy's voice and the singsong mutter under her breath.

"Boyfriend stealer."

Minnow halted and turned her attention on her left where Tizzy sat in the shade, large white rimmed sunglasses over her eyes. She wore a white self-cooling fabric long sleeve with tapered linen pants and her gorgeous blond hair hung loose and brushed. For a girl who had tizzy-fits over small things the human being encountered everyday – dirt, dust, pollen, pet hair, dandruff, she looked like a sports model who seemed as though she could never be ruffled – when a flying pollen particle wasn't threatening to drift up her nose.

"Guess it runs in the family," Tizzy added, with a sideways look and slight turn of her head that allowed Minnow to see her eyes behind her sunglasses.

Minnow worked up and put on a flat smile with her lips together. "Why Tizzy, sounds like you need to rinse your mouth out with saltwater," she said.

Tizzy tensed a little, obviously not expecting for Minnow to either know about that or bring it up.

"If you need help, I'll be down there, with Matt," said Minnow, leaning in until she touched Matt and then leaned back to straight standing again.

Matt was a little perplexed, so he remained quiet and observed, assured that Minnow would fill him in later, which she planned on.

Minnow took her first step forward, when she stopped, the slight twinge of disappointment in her chest a nudge she didn't like feeling or carrying. She'd looked straight down at the sand, the idea occurring to her as it happened, and picked up the white shell that matched Tizzy's white attire and sunglasses. White was her preference; it was clean and saw dirt.

"Happy birthday," Minnow said, smiling without the placation of before, but not quite fully smiling because after all, they weren't friends or really friendly.

Tizzy wasn't expecting this either – but to Minnow's inner bewilderment she took the shell softly, and didn't have a tizzy-fit at handling something from the outdoors.

Maybe because the ocean was clean, she presumed, as Minnow now noticed she was wearing white-strapped sandals.

Maybe she just needed a little more friendship instead of everyone always trying to cure her of her sensitivities?

Minnow hadn't figured it out; and now wasn't the time to start trying. As she picked her blue-white-swirl kayak nose up again by the handle and started pulling it up the beach, Matt alongside her, Matt inquired, "What was that all about."

"I'll explain later," Minnow said, because Matt wasn't going to want to hear her little sister's story now.

Minnow had spotted Carly quickly. She was in the surf, linked inside of Harry's very muscly arms, laughing skyward.

Minnow dropped her kayak handle and her kayak landed softly, barely a whisper on the sand. "For a guy who loves science stuff as much as her he's really built," Minnow remarked with some surprise. She'd never thought of the two crossing before. "Sure he's not a linebacker?"

"Yep," said Matt, dropping his orange and white kayak alongside hers with a stare. "Just a very, smart, built, science guy," he added.

"Right," said Minnow, slapping Matt on the back to buff him up into alertness. Right now, he was "alertly" staring and so she changed the subject a little so her friend would stop withering in front of her. "Then let's use what he aint got."

"Which is?" asked Matt, still looking like he was wondering how he was going to compete with this guy?

"Me. Bait," said Minnow simply and shortly. "Get ready, we're going in," she urged him hoarsely. "We'll test the water, so to speak. Don't want to get in our kayaks and then not be able to gloat or tease her."

Matt was normally taking up for Tarantella Girl, even though he let Minnow slide in her remarks and sometimes thought her antagonistic flares toward her were cute and amusing, which could also irk Minnow. But right now, Matt was reaching desperate measures to win her back, and Minnow knew gloating and teasing was in the armory and flat on the table.

Minnow couldn't wait to find out what next there was in the armory as well.

This might be more fun than she'd ordinarily thought!

She didn't have to prod Matt to hurry him along to remove his shirt after that remark, so they could sprint to the ocean and look like they were having one of the best days of their lives. *One of the best couple's time of their lives.*

Matt promptly tore his earthy red slim and worn shirt over his head while Minnow did the same, tossing her jean shorts next to her thin light blue tee.

"Wow," Matt said. "Minnow?"

"What?" said Minnow, irritated her bikini might be on crooked.

"What happened?" he said.

"What do you mean?" she said, scanning herself everywhere quickly. "Is my bikini on crooked?" Minnow asked, really hoping it wasn't.

"No," Matt answered to her immediate gladness. Still ripe with irritation though, because she'd thought something was out of place for the public to see, and she still had no clue what he was talking about. "But you look like a girl."

Minnow growled and rolled her eyes. She got enough from Windy when she whined about respecting Minnow's privacy. Why did so much attention revolve around this type of thing?

This mature thing was really starting to irritate her.

"Yep, I know, and I hear enough about it and all it comes with from Windy, so don't you start. Come on, Tarantella Girl' with the Harry Macroscope." Minnow shoved Matt to get him moving and their sprint to the ocean turned into an instant race to outrun each other.

Minnow was normally faster than Matt and splashed into the ocean easily but her impetus braking and the playful wave knocked her into the surge and she floated up to Matt's feet with exhilarating speed. Matt helped her up but she wanted to do that again.

First thing's first though. Matt and Minnow were near enough for when Carly turned around she would see them, but far enough for them to speak without being easily overheard above the roar of the crashing waves. The tide was coming in, deepening the swell with each wave.

Minnow crossed her arms around Matt's neck. "Get ready, she's about to turn around," Minnow clued Matt in.

Matt's attention was split between understanding what she said and being a tad nervous in the imminence of he and Carly's next encounter; where were the rest of his thoughts?

"Matt, where are you?" asked Minnow, continuing to shoot a look past his arm to keep a check on spider-girl and Harry (not really hairy) Macroscope guy, as she'd decided she was calling him now.

Then she stopped and just focused on her friend. It was when she did that the dawn broke. Minnow stepped back and lightly tickled the one place other than his right foot where he was ticklish, on his right side.

Matt bent and shot back, protecting his side. "What was that for?" he said through the dwindling chuckles.

"You're distracted; I did it to focus you," said Minnow, then she snorted a dose of pent-up laughter. "I distracted you," she said.

"No, you didn't. Maybe a tad. It's a lot to process," Matt replied mildly in his defense.

Minnow snorted-chuckled again. "Not according to Pirate Briny Windy."

Breaking into a grin, Matt came back in reply with, "Your nefarious sister has a lot she could still gain, in the mind; not anywhere else needs it more."

It was her sister Matt was reprimanding but Minnow laughed alongside his smiling criticism like only she could with him and no one else who had a severe, albeit a light severity, to say about her sister. No one criticized or yelled at her sisters except for her, but Matt was another member of the family almost; he had been since before she'd lost her first tooth or they'd all broken out with the chickenpox.

Suddenly Matt swooped her in pose and began smoothly and with that ease in his nature dancing with her as well as one could on the wet sand with the surf towing in and out, but he did it better than anyone Minnow hadn't ever danced with on the beach before. The fact Matt started dancing with Minnow made her want to laugh. "What are we doing," she asked, chuckles tickling in her voice.

Smiling, Matt shook his head with that ease and with recognition for the paradox in his expression and tone of voice, replying, "I haven't got a clue."

Which of course tickled her the more.

Minnow barely heard Carly's laughter anymore. Tarantella Girl had blended into the other voices nearby, and Minnow was just living in the moment with silliness, having fun with Matt. As so Minnow didn't distinguish the one who was laughing at whatever Harry had just said was Carly as she spun around holding his hand while Minnow was still turning in crab-walk circles with Matt, trying not to be a noodle in his arms. But the grip of silliness on them both was a bit intoxicating, like having eaten too much cake.

"Enjoying yourselves," a pert voice spoke up.

Minnow blew soft laughter between her lips when she and Matt both looked at the same time and saw it was Tarantella Girl, already. She looked like she was steaming next to the bulky arm she lightly clung too, which didn't have anything to do with how she looked in her black bikini.

"Yes," she and Matt answered in unplanned synchrony.

"So are we," Carly replied, seemingly recovered to her normal haughty self, as she attempted a loving and sweetheart gaze in Harry's eyes, but Minnow saw the phoniness a mile out to sea.

Matt however didn't stop dancing, and Minnow was glad because she didn't want to stop their crab-walk circles.

"How's it goen Harry," asked Matt.

Minnow took in Harry. He'd buffed up since last she'd glimpsed him in the hallway before school let out. She couldn't help comparing his smile to Matt's. Where Matt's smile was genuine, warm, and laughter all in one like some all-spice with different notes that she could always rely on, Harry had an unspoken confidence in how he smiled and stood that bordered cocky.

He wore yellow trunks and a smooth bare chest that bulged muscle that made Matt look minnow. Matt was strong, and resilient in other ways though, knew Minnow. Early mornings, long summer days, and hardworking chores and volunteer work gave Matt strength that could outlast gym strength, even if he couldn't overpower.

Matt's shoulders weren't broad like Harry's, but Matt also carried himself with an added self-confidence and easy manner that Harry didn't possess. Which Minnow just found more endearing and what should be attractive to a girl; regardless that someone might argue she was looking at this from a bias point of view. Cockiness just wasn't her thing, even if the guy was built like Achilles and as smart as Einstein.

If his brain was as massive as his muscles, Matt was in trouble. As far as Tarantella Girl was concerned, and winning her over.

"Couldn't be better," Harry said with a tender look at his sweet honey spider behavioral dissector, seemingly oblivious to the shades of thinly veiled envy emoting off Carly. Poor fellow. He'd flown into the web as well. Minnow sighed inwardly with pity on his behalf. She pictured him as large flying beetle. When Carly hitched a ride on his withers and yelled charge to the center of her web where Minnow was stuck, her spider hair on fire, Minnow stopped her wild imagination. Before she got too carried away – really carried away. This epic story needed a happy ending anyway. And the way things had been going in her head, it wasn't looking too good for bait girl.

"Carly would know," muttered Minnow after Harry's reply, which everyone picked up.

Then Carly looked directly at Matt. Her expression light and without scrutiny, Carly stated, "I found one of your sweatshirts when I was cleaning my room Matt. Since we're not a thing anymore, would you mind dropping by to pick it up?" she asked.

"My school sweatshirt?" asked Matt, openly surprised. His favorite hoody, Minnow remembered; he'd given it to Carly as a token of his love for her. After ruining it in the wash that took all the stains out, she'd worn it to school and out many times.

"That one," said Carly, the icy, heartless heart-stomper.

Minnow did her snorting-chuckle again – she couldn't help it! "Yep, together it got pretty spooky in the neighborhood. Matt's no longer a thing, just you. Thing. Wasn't there a horror novel about Things?" asked Minnow, in general and yet to herself. She looked to Matt for an answer as Carly's iciness blasted her from the side. "Isn't there like a How To manual for the average and innocent, on Thing survival?"

"No," stated Matt firmly in a mutter. Matt's arm around her waist tightened and he spun Minnow so that her back was to Carly and he faced her with an apologetic and frank smile. "She's been in the sun for a while."

"What, all her life?" asked Carly. Then Carly shrugged one shoulder lightly, nonchalant. Minnow knows because she craned her head backwards tilting to the side as much as she could and had a beginning view of her. Was Harry pressing his lips together in the name of composer, against losing laughter?

Minnow decided to be a nuisance and started tilting herself backwards as far as possible. Eventually, Matt started to show signs of soft strain to keep her any kind of upright.

"She doesn't look sunburned to me," answered Carly, "but then you never know. Some people are less tolerant than others."

Minnow kept tilting.

Carly put on a smile and finger fan waved. "See you later Matt," she said to him. Then waved her hand in a no hassle gesture. "Or, I could just throw it away if it's not important."

"No, it might be," Matt replied with a hint of strain in his tone. Of course it was important to him! But now that Carly had ruined the best part of it and it smelled like her perfume maybe it'd be better if Minnow got him a new one.

Minnow was now starting to strain against his hold and bare all her weight down.

"Then, see you later," Carly said again, smiling as she, and Harry who was marveling at the strangeness of Minnow between curiosity and amusement, continued strolling up the beach.

Minnow was smiling up at Matt, who spun his head back to her, one eyebrow lifted and lips pressed in a line of strength as he combated her brace.

"That went well."

"You're right," Matt agreed, and without warning pressed her into the swell of the incoming wave. Minnow surfaced gasping and grinning and tasting saltwater! She should be irked, but she had her old Matt back, even if Carly was getting her old section of him back as well.

Minnow splashed to her feet and tackled, holding on and yelping when Matt ran with her through the surf trying to sling her like a monkey from his back, which was no use even with the slipperiness of being wet!

Minnow wasn't sure of how much Tarantella Girl watched or saw with her beady dagger spider eyes. She only wondered a few times on the water. She was too distracted having fun talks with Matt about everything from the story about Windy bilge-pumping Tizzy into a tizzy-fit, the swim, why she still was disgraceful for not being a fan of peanut butter, to how his parents were enjoying their road-trip. Anything and everything in-between. She lost all consideration of being watched when Matt drove the first paddle-splash and started paddling backwards, daring Minnow to catch him and splash him.

Minnow might have tiny arms and tiny everything but she was strong and swift in a kayak like she was confident and at ease on Marshy bareback.

Besides, her namesake had to count for water in some way, and with the conveyance of a smooth hull without much current to thrive on as she did with a challenge to fight against, she held a smoother edge. Still!

And the splashing battle and ramming each other's kayak tasted salty and epic!

Chapter Twenty-three

Evening drew on in the kayak shop. More while she was feeding Marshy her din-din of hay and fresh water.

It got harder and harder to push Matt swinging by Carly's out of her mind. What could happen between them that hadn't happened before?

That seemed to be what nagged at her, and yet she couldn't pinpoint what the nuisance was that made her restless. She shouldn't let him do this by himself, she was thinking, for the thousandth time since this afternoon. "I shouldn't, should I Marshy?" she said to her friend who was chowing down on sweet hay. "Or should I?" she asked herself as well as Marshy. She rubbed her forelock absentmindedly. "It's in his ballpark now; but what if he needs backup?" Minnow suggested, thinking it possible – and likely. "She likes to use him. We want her begging Matt to take her back, not the other way around. Matt's a marshmallow – like the spider behavioral analyst she is, she'll wind him up in her web. We've got to be there to help him, just in case," Minnow said, and Marshy made a noise that suggested, What? In the middle if dinner?

Minnow tethered Marshy to the backyard patio near the gazebo where she was shielded by big, colorful hydrangea and neatly planted beach grass. Matt was already in her room – Minnow ducked more. Carly's balcony French doors were wide open, the cooler evening breeze fluttering her pristine veil white curtains.

"Stay here, girl – I'm just going to check it out," Minnow whispered to her. Minnow didn't know how much of this idea Marshy thought was a good idea, but she stayed quiet as Minnow snuck on sleuthing feet around the gazebo, tucking close to the bulrushes and flowers the way she hugs the marsh in her kayak. The current is always least strong hugging the marsh.

When Minnow reached the section of yard at the bottom of Carly's room it struck her that barefoot would help her best for stealth and grip. She removed her sneakers and socks, padded up to the pine tree, and started minnow-monkey climbing, finding footholds without difficulty. Not only did she climb trees for fun, she and her sisters and when she was with Matt, with Matt, climbed for the challenge and simple pleasure to see if they could, all the time.

She was confident and didn't think twice about the transference from tree limb to balcony ledge, as it was similar to the kayak shop roof and top of Dad's truck she'd transferred with Matt just the other night. And well, all of her life.

Minnow began hearing muffled voices softly floating on the air, though the circling air flow didn't aid much on its way back out, as the breeze coasted in, in just that lightness of stronger than when it circled outward.

Minnow swung one leg after the other over the railing, and hugging the wall in severe need of power-washing, tiptoed just far enough she could see past the fluttering curtains when they drifted in the breeze. It was too risky however, and so she pulled back, deciding to just listen.

"Thanks for not trashing it," Matt was saying, and Minnow glued herself to the slimy green stained wall, just as something else slimy made its presence audibly known.

"No problem," said Carly, making Minnow's nose wrinkle.

"Does she make you happier than I did?" said Carly, and at that Minnow's eyes popped and she stretched her neck out a little further, glimpsing spider-girl draped lightly on her bed, making a pyramid space between her hip and palm and armpit.

"Does Harry make you happier than I did?" Matt answered with a question.

A fair question, thought Minnow nodding her head in his defense.

"I'm starting to second-guess my choice, to be honest," replied Carly, and there was little pretend in her voice that made Minnow wonder. His plan was working, great, but why didn't it feel great?

She couldn't stand the heartstring yanker's guts for yanking on *her* best friend's heartstrings, right now *and* their entire middle-high school life!

But that didn't explain the spiky irritation or feeling of impulse to do something but she didn't know what, and yet it had driven her to stand where she was standing now. She didn't understand this drive – was it jealousy? *No*, she dismissed posh, *of course not*, nobody could ever come betwixt her and Matt. *Then seriously, but so what was it?* Minnow urged herself in thought. She didn't have time to unravel it, nor the focus needed either, and the conversation was getting worse.

"When Harry and I partnered on Mrs. Ion's science project in April it felt like he spoke my language," said Carly, and her honesty and excuse made Minnow mad because it sounded reasonable and understandable. Normal. Tarantella Girl had never been either of the kind, to Minnow.

"But when I saw you with Minnow," Carly trailed off, searching for the words, and sounding confused, "is this thing *real*? Are you doing this just to make me jealous?" asked Carly, rising with hope from her mattress and crossing her white flat carpeted floor to where Matt stood near the wall between the window and pretend dew shimmered and spider dotted curtains, across from Minnow. She tucked back but only slightly. And Carly stopped herself when it seemed like she'd just started. "Minnow? How can you date Minnow?" she said. "You can't be attracted to her – not – not..."

"Not when I've dated you, you mean?" asked Matt.

Minnow was a little surprised by Matt's tone. He was defending her in his own quiet, easygoing way, and yet there was something firm about him. Minnow's heart tugged with their bond of friendship, but wasn't he also playing hard to get?

Matt couldn't really mean one hundred percent of what his tone was leaning with. Couldn't he?

"Exactly," Carly answered with brightness, thinking Matt understood. "So, you're not really, are you?"

Matt didn't answer. He had ten seconds too but Carly decided to express herself first and crossed the room, throwing herself at his arms only she didn't land in his arms she smashed into the wall because Matt sidestepped. Carly looked shocked and worried when she spun around.

Matt said, backing up, "I'm not goanna kiss another guy's girl."

"Maybe I won't be another guy's girl very much longer," she replied a tad miff. "Then again, maybe I will."

"Maybe I won't be around when you maybe will or maybe won't," replied Matt. On that singular note, he left.

Minnow's mouth had fallen open, and she was so proud of Matt! He'd stood up for himself and Minnow was reveling with that when Carly snapped her back to the present, putting a halt to her celebration inside as she stomped over to her white computer desk and spider tanks. Whipping up her tablet, she focused on analyzing the moods and behaviors of the spiders.

Minnow thought she was also analyzing her own, along with Matt's, and could picture the Tarantella plotting her next web to weave. She decided to flee before she herself was snagged, and retraced her steps, picking up her sneakers along the way.

When she rejoined Marshy, Marshy was pawing on Mrs. McPherson's prized tulips! She was looking for carrots, the evidence flowers she yanked up with her teeth and discarded.

Minnow covered her mouth but in her heart, she was laughing. "Marshy, this isn't a vegetable garden!" she told her.

Marshy made a confused nickering sound as Minnow grabbed the reins under her chin and led her away before they were seen!

Minnow couldn't believe what she'd witnessed. But it wasn't Marshy plowing her hoof through Carly's mother's tulip bed in search of sweet juicy carrots. That had been hilarious!

What thrilled Minnow was seeing Matt sticking up for himself to Tarantella Girl. What she *couldn't believe* was that she'd watched Carly showing openness and honesty, up to the point of portraying her conceitedness when she more or less asked the question out loud, how Matt could find any other girl attractive after dating her?

One girl, actually, and that girl being Minnow.

It galled Minnow to admit it, and almost made her wish she hadn't seen it – but for once she'd experienced a glimpse of what attracted Matt to the arachnid-girl. Something he never could get through Minnow's dense skull when he listed the supposed virtues versus vices in Carly.

Even in her snobbery, she was honest.

Really though, guys found that trait combo cute?

She *was* intelligent and avid in her field of study, which came with its attractions as well, Minnow supposed. She found smart *guys* attractive, when they weren't snobbish as well!

Although Minnow couldn't see herself falling head over heels for a guy who obsessed about spiders the way Minnow did over horses, constantly talking about their behavior and anatomy. It'd be similar to Windy going into detail about how pirates tortured each other while she was trying to enjoy din-din.

She didn't have anything against spider or insect lovers! Minnow loved butterflies, honeybees, dragonflies, and moths!

But she was by golly squishing any mosquito that buzzed in her ear and if she couldn't catch that spider to release him into the wild out back she was going to get him with her shoe!

Minnow wasn't into bug-study, but she decided she might find his enthusiasm endearing, if she fell for someone who had a passion for insects.

Is that how Matt looked at Carly?

Was there no way to win with her own arguments? Grrr!

Why did a snob like Carly get to have a guy like Matt? And not just any Matt. Minnow's Matt.

Matt deserved someone wholesome, who didn't play those kinds of heartstring games with him, who either enjoyed talking about horses and being around them, or enjoyed his love for them. Someone like Minnow – but not Minnow. Someone better. More feminine, but who also didn't care about the grass stains. Matt never cared about the grass stains. In fact, growing up, grass stains were a badge of honor to them; they'd compare the grass stains and dirt on their jeans and elbows and all over to see who'd gotten more and whose act of acquiring them was better and ruggeder. Which made for a lot of rolling and running to slide in the grass to reach victory. Skidding crashing bikes on their side in the yard, falling out of trees, jumping off of boats!

Bottom line Matt deserved someone who appreciated him; and who loved him for who he was. Carly may care for Matt, but if she truly loved Matt she wouldn't string him along and weave webs every time he got out or she kicked him out of her web.

Yet Minnow just couldn't wrap her head around that when Carly wasn't carrying Matt in one of her tanks, she was fawning over him. Fawning! She didn't think Tarantella Girl ever fawned. Maybe she hadn't been jealous over any other girl like she was over Minnow. It wasn't that Minnow posed any real threat; but Tarantella Girl obviously didn't know that. It was nice to know someone could swim into minnow traps other than Minnow – or into Minnow and Matt traps.

Minnow pictured her scene before, and as a charging Carly spider with her hair on fire charged after Minnow, Matt jumped onto the web and whammed her with his violin! Carly was stunned with confusion, but Matt put his skinny legs on his hips and shook his head. Carly's hair smoldered and she turned away to relocate beetle boyfriend.

What was going to happen next?

Chapter Twenty-four

It was nighttime but in July and downtown, there was little sleeping to be desired when the carnival opened at 7:00pm. Which was where Minnow found herself bound, riding her faded orange bike that could use a new chain down the back roads to bypass the lines of traffic and crowds.

For the most part she succeeded until she turned off Church Street onto Willow, where she was met with the beginnings of what would shortly evolve into tentacles of traffic draping the roadways.

Instantly upon stepping up the two worn red concrete steps and pushing her bike with her, the first whiffs of food and the sweet and subtle pine wafted up her nose, just as the blare of the carnival surrounded her. People talking, excited, laughing, conversing all spun into noise. Lights blinked and rides with screaming occupants blended into one or several main colors. Everything had movements – the people, rides – everywhere there was different noises. Music blared from speakers mounted on different vendor buildings – to the right were pizza, hamburger, fried fritter lines. To her left was more food and then games as it curved inward. Big old fans on stands and small ones on the traditional white wooden counters made the air move in the kitchen and counter areas. Even though it was warm air, and the kitchen and fryers and food hot, to have the air move helped. Minnow thought of the fan in the kayak shop.

Every building was traditional carnival white, some sporting the American flag or banners advertising their group, cause, or wares. The signs presenting food lines like Pony Fries and Fritters looked just as they had when Minnow was a kid and rode in the twirling Teacups.

At first, entering the carnival was disorienting. The ground liked to dip and rise underneath her without warning, so she had to use her bike for support as she gripped her wits and found her bearings. But she was excited.

While a lot to take in at first, having not been to the carnival in what felt like ages, since she helped out in the kayak shop more now and pony penning was their busiest time of the year, Minnow felt the regeneration of old thrills and anticipation. She got a wholesome, fun, and ticklish vibe that drew her in and made her want to be part of the carnival more.

These were her fellow islanders, this was her heritage, and family and friends and islanders both from here or now a part of here, surrounded her like one big family, filling and warming her heart like she'd just walked into family night with everyone she knew or knew of and hadn't seen in a while or hadn't yet met. Which was all true in a way. Her extended family was here, friends of her family, classmates, and new people. It was like the world opening its living room and backyard to everyone, even though it was just the Chincoteague carnival gates. There was big to be said about small.

The excitable atmosphere prompted Minnow to hurry along and Minnow parked her bike roughly alongside the cotton candy booth entitled Caramelized Popcorn, Candy Apples, Cotton Candy, and hopped inside to learn her job from Matt, who was waiting for her.

Minnow learned with appetite, which she meant in its literal sense as well. Her first taste of her own spun cotton candy tickled her sweet tooth, and Matt rolled his eyes, probably counting the ways of how she's a hopeless cause and anticipating how unbearably giggly she was going to be for the whole night.

Minnow teased Matt about carnival food effecting his sleep? The joke was on her now. It'd been so long since she'd partaken of any that she felt a little delirious.

She'd swum into her own joke but she didn't care about this minnow trap. It was sweet and tickly!

250

Matt spent another two minutes with her to see her through the first one dozen bags of cotton candy, then made pony tracks to take his turn at the Carrousel.

Eatable magic did exist, and would be found at the carnival. The color of this magic was pink.

Minnow half expected little fairies to flutter over the counter and make their sugar delivery. This cotton candy surely had to come from somewhere magical.

But it was all bagged sugar and Minnow. And she wasn't half bad, if she did say so herself.

Minnow worked alongside Tonya, who candied applies on a pike. Next door, yet to be caramelized popcorn exploded in a small popcorn machine that had been in use since she was five. It was probably older than that.

As Minnow was mixing and spinning more and bagging it to toss into the big box in the center of the booth after Matt left her on her own, Minnow couldn't believe she had never done this before.

She had to stop eating before she got a sugar headache while she waited for customers to arrive, which they were steadily doing as the carnival tilted, wheeled, fried, and merrily went around the hour.

Taking pleasure in her customers' marvel as they watched her spin the sugary clouds of magic as well as their reactions when she handed it to them for eating, Minnow didn't notice who was next in line until she stepped up to the counter.

The balloon that popped was in the arcade across from Minnow on the left of the crescent flowing booths, but she was pretty sure it was masking her own popped balloon when she turned with a smile to the next customer and saw spider eyes smiling at her.

"Spiders and insects have more in common with humans than the majority of people think," Carly said.

Minnow could take that two ways. Oh, how did Tarantella Girl insult mankind while complimenting them, while showing off her intelligence as she was at it?

Of course, Minnow could be criticizing her a little harshly. She probably didn't intend to refer or indicate people don't mostly think. Minnow's own low opinion and skepticism of Carly led her to suspicious assumptions and conclusions.

"You and Matt think you have real feelings for each other? But he's just on the rebound. Besides," Tarantella Girl offered in a matter of fact way, with a spiced hint of placation or sarcasm thrown in her mannerisms. "Just like spiders and honey bees and butterflies can convince themselves its spring during an Indian summer," she said. "It happens."

Minnow's nostrils flared as she kept her inner flare reined in, but there was a part of her clear enough to wonder fleetingly, was that true about bugs?

She knew it was as soon as the thought occurred and forcefully tamped the truthful factoid down in the very, very back of her mind.

Appropriate. Bees, birds, butterflies, summer and spring. Drawing parallel and correlation to her opening analogy about spiders and certain bugs being more like humans than they give them credit for, in her conclusions.

Clever. Cute.

Saying she and Matt were confused like butterflies and other bugs in an Indian summer, Tarantella Girl was telling her that they wouldn't last. What happened to them when the changeup season turned true to itself and froze out the butterflies, fireflies, and ants; even the spiders.

Minnow had been confused about a lot of things in her life, and she would still get stumped down the road. But she'd figure it like she always did. She didn't need anyone, especially Tarantella Girl, to do the legwork for her.

Besides. Carly had no idea she and Matt were pretending. Why did it irk Minnow so, then? Because Carly assumed she had all the answers, that Matt would come crawling back up her web in tears. For the first-time Minnow realized she'd be the one dumped and Tarantella Girl would gloat and hold it over her head forever. All she'd have to do was give Minnow a look that told the tale of this summer. But Minnow had the last laugh; her and Matt both. The spider was caught in her own web and didn't even know it. So Minnow smiled brightly, tossed her a cotton candy bag, which Tarantella Girl caught, and said, "Two dollar-roonies."

"Two more," Carly said with a flat stone look.

Minnow tossed her two more and Carly flattened the last one on the counter to keep from falling on the ground. Tizzy would have a tizzy over that. Carly must have thought the same thing too, as well as not appreciating Minnow's cavalier, because she sent her a knowing glare.

Minnow smiled with her lips closed, hands on the counter, promptly waiting for six bucks.

Tarantella Girl forked it over from her black zip up money pouch with the sparkly and glistening orange slice shaped spider web on both sides.

She slapped it down on the counter and spun around. Minnow was glad she didn't stay a second longer to see the dollar bills pick up in the breeze and blow all over the dirt and wood platform patched ground of the booth. She scrambled every dollar up though.

Windy bounced up to the booth not too long after. "What are you doing here?" asked Minnow surprised.

"Mom and Dad are playing Bingo, they'll be over to say hello later. Can I help?" she asked, hanging over the counter by the support of her elbows and flattened tummy.

"Sure, but get out of the way, there's customers behind you," Minnow replied, waving her up. Windy sprung around the side of the open-front building so fast she almost tripped on the questionable ground through the open door.

Minnow instructed Windy on the art of cotton candy spinning, which she took to like it was a chest of gold doubloons; getting richer by the churn! Minnow had to quite agree for once with Windy – this treasure was something to melt in her mouth.

Minnow felt proud to be showing Windy how to do something and that Windy was actually willingly listening.

Chapter Twenty-five

Minnow bought the infinity of carnival ride tickets, a wristband for her and Windy and Summer. They were always color-coated for the night to avoid sneakers the next day. They rode the Tilt A World, Paratrooper, and every other ride, even the toddler ones they could barely squeeze into.

Her sisters and parents rode the Paratrooper and Scrambler and Farris Wheel together when they rejoined them after Bingo. They didn't win but they had a blast, and an even more fun time with their daughters. It was rise and shine early tomorrow however, as it rarely wasn't in the summer, and they hugged Minnow goodnight before disembarking the carnival, knowing she would be coming home late.

Literally high, from the top of the Ferris Wheel, to low, behind every booth counter, Minnow sought Matt. The last place she expected to find him was the one place she'd never have thought to look for him – a place where he wasn't volunteering. Wonders never cease, though was this an anomaly or the start of something new to be expected in the future? Matt Evers, actually off early for the night. Matt spun Carly in circles like Minnow had spun sugar into clouds around soft paper sticks all night.

It was half an hour to midnight, when the carnival closed, so Matt wasn't stepping too far out of his normal habits; but it irked Minnow that he'd done it for Carly.

Minnow watched from the carnival string-bulb twinkly shadows on the edge of the grassy dancefloor, a girl among the stars, and yet unseen. Only one person mattered to her, who was important enough in her heart for her to pine to be seen this much besides by her family, and only one person made her invisible to him.

The live group played from the skinny and just barely awninged stage, which was a plain white building with a porch; round green and spaced shrubs, along with gently tipping beach grass touched by the stir in the air, skirting the skinny stage.

Minnow picked up on movement in her peripheral and in her bland state looked over her shoulder, to see Harry Macroscope. He wore a yellow t-shirt that read in stencil lettering, *Are You My Eon?*

Minnow instantly thought of web-fingers over there on the grassy dancefloor. Wasn't Tarantella Girl Harry's eon?

Was she?

Then more seriously and cynically, Minnow wondered to herself, *Was She?*

A school friend had just spotted him and tackled him in a bear hug, momentarily waylaying his approach to the dancefloor. He must be arriving from the ticket booth, because he carried on him a second wristband color-coated for tonight, which also told Minnow that he might have just arrived to the carnival. How long had Carly and Matt been spending time together tonight?

Minnow could hash this new realization over later. Right now, she had to rescue Matt before Harry saw him and Carly together. Harry was an oblivious guy in many ways, but one look at ex-boyfriend and ex-girlfriend dancing and Matt might wind up with his sense of humor out of joint in several places.

Minnow untethered herself from the carnival stars among the shadows of Matt and Carly's outer space in her exile, and tapped Tarantella Girl on the shoulder. "Your boyfriend is on his way. Mind if I take mine back?"

"Are you sure you ever had him to begin with," said Carly in clear tone.

That's just what it took to erase the pinch that'd been gnawing in Minnow's stomach since she saw the two of them dancing and watched from the twinkly shadows. Minnow's light smile of confidence exuded her untroubled mind on the subject, and she replied, "Why do you think he wanted his sweatshirt back? Scoot – your next dinner is approaching."

Carly's surrender was ripe with poorly, thinly veiled reluctance, envy, and a particular *I'd squish you like a bug if I wasn't a bug-lover* look for Minnow, as she forcibly made herself sidestep a step back.

Minnow slid in Tarantella Girl's spot with the ease of a sea breeze, feeling like the girl with the butterfly net rescuing the blue monarch butterfly from a glistening diamond spun web. Although technically, didn't tarantellas make their homes in burrows in the ground? Made sense to Minnow that Carly would be a spider from a hole in the ground, and decided to work on her scenes in her imagination that equated to their real-life and continued saga being more accurate for spider-girl. That'll be a fun pastime on a day when it's too hot there's nothing really to do.

Minnow danced Matt in a quadruple circle away from Tarantella Girl's tender and annoyingly sticky tethers, a spin on spin on spin upon spin that provided Minnow with an unplanned view of Harry and Carly's affectionate reunion. Harry couldn't see the recovery or slight seething and disheveled Carly in her moderate breathlessness as he swept her up, unaware whose formerly affectionate arms she'd seconds earlier clung to, that the warmth of her cheeks was not solely from a day in the sun.

Minnow put most of that fury pink there, and Matt colored the deeper shades. Although she figured at this point fury towards Minnow claimed dominance over the memories and passion and affection being near Matt once again stirred in her.

Minnow relaxed, crossing her arms in a loose way behind Matt's sturdy and dirt speckled neck, giving up the lead. At that moment, the song ended, followed by brisk applause, and the chords of a slow island-Irish-string song began.

Swaying, Matt avoided gazing Carly's way at the same time stealing a single look.

Dancing closely with Harry, it looked as though she and Matt didn't exist. As though he'd never existed for her. Which was a lie. Because a moment ago, it was hard to tell them apart they danced so closely. But that was all Matt, wasn't it?

How can someone pretend affection with another guy, when your heart is truly calling to someone else?

"If" it's truly calling to someone else, Minnow corrected herself.

Minnow's chest tugged for Matt, and she put all joking and dislikes about Carly aside.

"A book walks into a café," Minnow started with.

Matt knew what she was doing, but too blue to appreciate her motives like she'd been too frustrated to fall into his joking and gesture last night on the roof, Matt avoided Minnow's gaze by looking at something else. Last night, for Minnow, it had been the moon and discerning shapes or sense out of its darker grey markings. For Matt, it was what Minnow had always called the carnival stars; *but they're bright, aren't they*, Minnow thought when Matt blinked and sought something else to train his focus on.

Minnow went on in a casual and story-like tone, nonetheless. "And the barista says, Black, with cream and sugar? And smiling, the book replied, You're a fast reader."

Matt tried not to smile by twisting his mouth and glaring down at her. Minnow could tell she was half way to breaking in his wall, and smiled a closed mouth smile up at him, looking up with only her eyes as she rested her forehead on his chin

Matt avoided her look and turned the next circle swiftly, releasing tension.

"Come on, I know that one was funny," she said to him, kicking him lightly in the shin.

"Yes, it was," Matt told her, smiling at last. "I can't really appreciate it right now though. You're not being fair you know."

"I know," Minnow drew out with satisfaction, "and neither were you last night."

"So, was that my payback you swore this morning that you'd reek on me?" he asked.

"Ha!" Minnow declared. "You wish."

That made Matt genuinely smile, and Minnow's heart warmed with that smile's arrival.

Without warning it started raining. Not a thunderclap, a flash of lighting, or really any overcast but some billowy cumulous nimbus. A sudden burst of soft downpour that scattered the grassy dancefloor's companions, as well as carnival goers around them and across the carnival grounds; families and friends and pairs searching out shelter in booths, under the friendly giant awning that shields the Scrambler and Carrousel, digging purse and pocket for the jingling clump of their keys, many sprinting for their cars. Including Harry and Carly. She made it before her hair soaked all the way through, which was more than poor Tizzy. Tizzy whined with lament at the wet soaking her hair and clothes and mudpuddles splashing over her white-sandaled feet and up her ankles.

Suddenly Klepto Kevin, who'd been volunteering in the Pony Fries stand, leapt over the counter and whisked her into his arms. This startled her but she only fought him for a second. Abhorred, disappointed, and then sad, she blubbered and held onto him tightly as he clutched her close and hurried carefully while leaving the rain as fast as he could, depositing Tizzy under the nearest awning, which was the Pony Fries food line.

"Klepto Kevin just nabbed Tizzy," Minnow laughed and still pointed out to Matt, even though he was already watching.

"I don't think she'll fit into his pocket," replied Matt.

262

Tizzy appeared not to be able to make her mind up – whether or not to accept the beach towel Kevin timidly offered – or to suffer with the rain and mud on her. In the end there was no telling where he got that towel, or from *whom* he'd gotten it, and just then a volunteer lady who'd rounded the counter some minutes before led her down the food line for somewhere dry and where she might sit.

Izzy took shelter in the Bingo area, crossing her arms, and shaking water droplets from her stringy soaked hair.

Matt was breaking into another smile however, at the same time Minnow was, and just like that they moved closer and swayed at natural ease with one another again. Just Matt and Minnow. No scheme. No show to make ex's or o's jealous. No saltwater ponyboys. No Maximus. No Harry Macroscope or Tarantella Girl.

Something else; goodness and joy. Simply more.

As the lyrical music song gave notes to the soft rain and its instant gush of fresh coolness it brought like the billowy air from a waterfall, Matt and Minnow shared their smiles with each other. It seemed like years since pony penning week started and they'd just let loose and been themselves, to everything around them, with themselves, and with each other.

Minnow plastered her cheek on Matt's rain soaked chest as they danced. They swayed and moved, he tickled her and she struggled back with defensive shoves!

Matt dipped Minnow lightly back, which made her think back to today in the ocean when she tilted all the way back to put strain on his hold around her, then he'd dunked her in the next swell. But there were no swells here, or puddles that deep, so Minnow felt safe enough.

Droplets sprayed in twists and drizzled onto her face in the moments when their smiling faces were nearest, turning into a splayed cascade on Minnow when Matt dipped her backward and he loomed deliberately holding her there long enough to drizzle her in the rain running off of his ballcap brim that tasted like his hat, sweaty salty horsy and grassy, making her shake her head and laugh. "Stop it!" she told him!

The five minute forever feeling song later ended on tender, joyful notes. They hadn't realized the carnival stragglers who'd stayed or the volunteers from their respected booths bulky with some visitors seeking dryness, had been gazing sweetly and quietly, watching. Until of course at this moment when mild and intermittent clapping filled the air from the sparse onlookers, and instead of the band taking a bow, they joined the applause as well.

As so, Minnow and Matt exchanged an in-sync impulse and bowed extravaganza and gratitude to their admirers.

Chapter Twenty-six

Dough kneaded, rolled out, and placed in a cool dry place to rise, Minnow drifted to sleep in her bed, smiling at the replay of her and Matt's dance in her mind. Her heart picked up pace a little as she relived the movement and feelings. Warm rain that had slowly drenched them. Minnow still smelled the rain on her skin. Her cheek plastered on Matt's soaked chest. Solid. Heartbeat thumping.

On Summer's say-so, Minnow had rubbed her head with a towel. Other days Minnow would've done so on her own without prompting, but to soak up all that good feeling and rain tap-tap off of her fuzzy head felt like asking her to close her ears to birdsong. Besides, without long hair one would think they didn't need to dry their head off, but Minnow guessed Dad did all the time, so it was still a good move to stave off a summer cold.

Minnow's thoughts absorbed her like the rain had her clothes and her clothes the carnival smells of fried goodies and sweet pine shats. The imprints of Matt's hands and arms and closeness had tattooed her through her clothes as well.

Minnow felt the grip and touch and solidness of her friend each day. She would feel it tomorrow. She tried to figure out what this meant to her – but she was dough tired, and drifted into dreamland faster than she anticipated.

Minnow woke up with a sense of lightness and shining outward. Her dough had risen fully, and she hadn't drooled on her pillow last night!

Tarantella Girl felt as small to her as an insignificant bug, bland, barely a puffy cloud in her blue sky, one she was hardly noticing.

Matt had to be starting to glimpse Carly's selfish and shallowness, Minnow told herself as she looked out her window to take in the and greet the morning.

For Matt had named the virtues that outweighed anything else concerning Carly, but last night was another side of Carly he'd never seen on the receiving end of. The snob, who acted like one didn't exist, or if she did deign recognition, one was less than bug, which was highly esteemed on her chart of importance. One was dirt. Plain dirt.

Matt had never been dirt – just tickly grass she'd get annoyed by or bored with but return to because – well? Who could resist soft, sweet grass?

Tizzy.

Last night on the grassy dancefloor had to be eye-opening for him. While it'd visibly stung, and frowned his heart, Matt had to be thinking about other fish in the sea. Right?

Minnow had uplifted Matt at the carnival, and she would continue to uplift and support her friend as he rediscovered life outside of Carly's observation tanks.

Minnow was feeling like she was getting her best friend back after having first started sharing him eight years ago with Tarantella Girl.

Minnow brushed her teeth with the confidence that Matt would bounce back. Minnow could and had always Matt smile and laugh. Whether on purpose or accident, by being irked or just her. They could always make each other smile, laugh, get back in a good mood, and feel uplifted.

This time wouldn't be any different, just bigger, because of the huge step it was for Matt in backing off of Carly and taking a walk on the normal side of life outside of her spider tanks. Minnow had a really good feeling about today. She had a good feeling about the rest of the summer.

Chapter Twenty-seven

The walk down the beach was something out of a dream. One of Minnow's dreams.

But with this, the ancestry of these ponies and this island struck Minnow with fresh perspective, the way raspberry smoothies were tangy and pert and made her eyes water with joy. And sitting atop Olive among the saltwater ponyboys had something to do with it.

A storm, the worst nor'easter she remembered having stayed up at night through, snuggled between Summer and the wall with Windy clutching Summer on Summer's other side, sprayed in comparison in Minnow's mind with the dark crashing waves and thrashing hooves and heads plowing the whitecapped ocean. She put herself in the ocean with the ponies. The groaning thrashed Spanish galleon sinking and then broken apart as it splayed on the stormy ocean bottom.

Were the frightened ponies, eyeless by the Spaniards for obedience in the mines, bound for the dark bottom as well?

Minnow would have been cold with fear. The will to survive however, is more powerful than fear. Even fear that strikes the way a smack of ice cold water does. Once solid land was beneath their hooves again, they were free.

The harsh life of the unfamiliar island must have tasted the sweetest. Minnow knows it would have for her. But sweet is often accompanied by bitter or sour too; and living on Assateague takes a special kind of breed and a stout heart, or at least having grown up with it. And these ponies, Teaguers, and come-here's, like Matt, were that in a pound of sterling silver and more.

Minnow looked up and across the grunting and plodding ponies at Matt, who didn't notice her staring immediately and so she watched him sitting at ease in the saddle, his confident gaze studying the herd but also on the lookout for a mischievous foal or overzealous tourist getting too close. He rode on the middle outside of the herd right in front of her on her left.

Minnow and the saltwater ponyboys created a netting, with them as the half circle in the rear, on the side, and in front. Aptly, the ocean completed the circle; as it is where the ponies came from.

The hum of conversation...the recoil of whips snapping salty air...tourists snapping photos...the sense of pure joy and enthrallment from the crowd at a safe distance from the pony walk...ocean roaring, racing up the sand and splashing brown, black and white, chestnut, pale tan and white pony legs...baby ones, old ones, restless ones.

Rangers rode beach ATV looking vehicles on the far outside, flanking in a straight line the curve of the half circle of saltwater ponyboys.

Seagulls joined the walk, circling and drifting playfully overhead.

Pony bellies brushed Minnow's leg every now and then, and as much as Minnow enjoyed the experience and the sensation, she touched her rein to Olive's neck. Olive had the same idea, and curved, pulling forward to widen the space between them.

Minnow didn't have to be expert to know that wild ponies could become aggressive suddenly or in being protective of their foals nip at the saltwater ponyboys or each other. She didn't need Matt telling her that on day one, two, or three, which he did to stamp it into her memory.

While this was Minnow's first roundup it was one of many for Olive, as she had demonstrated to Minnow their first day, which was why Matt selected her for Minnow's mount and protector. So she trusted Olive to guard this space to keep the nippers at bay long enough for her to look at Matt. She wanted him to see her.

Minnow admired Matt with respect she hadn't known quite well enough before, perceiving a depth and bond of friendship in Matt, as well as existing in life, that she hadn't perceived with such clarity in anyone else in all of her life, apart from maybe inklings of this when was little. In those days, she'd looked up to Summer for everything, almost more than Mom and Dad. She still looked up to Summer. Yet Minnow's feelings then, and so much more, while tangible and very important to her, in hindsight were feeling infant to her now, compared to this clarity of experiencing and recognizing this sterling quality in Matt that had been his trait all along. Nothing had ever meant so much to her than to ride in the pony swim. Who else would risk reputation, and their place in their hometown, to help make a friend's dream come true?

It took a true friend. A prince-of-a-friend.

Matt had always been her truest and best friend. His help shouldn't surprise her; and in a way, it didn't. Minnow was surprised by herself, that it took her pretending to be a boy to ride in the swim, as well as being his accomplice to win back Tarantella Girl *again*, to re-realize the depth of their friendship on this scale again.

Of course, everything one does feels like the biggest leap they've ever taken until the next leap. Minnow can't see right now how anything would top this leap either one of them had taken and day by day continue hopping up out of bed as though its waffles and mixed berries every morning, eager to greet – and eat!

But Minnow knew, as she always did, as close as she and her family and Matt were, that the difference wasn't the leap as much but who was there taking that leap with you. Minnow and Matt had always been each other's sidekick, wingman, partner in crime, confidant, and best and truest friends. If anyone would be the person to go on a journey with her, or that she would go and did go to for help, or want to go on any adventure with, it was Matt.

Now, while Minnow *was* scheming with Matt to reunite him with his ex-girlfriend Carly, in all honesty that had been a matter of coincidental timing. Matt would've helped her even without a bribe. And Minnow would have done the same. But never one to allow a humorous tease or play to slip by them, they'd bargained like sailors with each other.

In that sense, Minnow admitted to herself, it made this thrilling week twice as exhilarating and also interesting, even as irksome as the ploy looming over her was. As their leaps, always were, when they banded together.

Minnow smiled with this friendship warming up her blood like cinnamon spice, and at Matt's naturalness in the saddle. This was where he belonged too. She watched for a full moment, wanting to imprint this image of Matt in her memory for keepsake. She'd almost given up and told herself it was okay he didn't turn around, and was about to return her full attention to Olive and the herd alongside her, when Matt glanced over his shoulder and snagged her staring.

She mouthed the words, "Thank you." And he knew how much she meant it. From the bottom of her heart.

And "not" her bruised tailbone.

Chapter Twenty-eight

"Is that my shirt?"

Minnow was wondering when Matt would notice it. She turned a pleased smile his way and leaned against the patched-up door with her arm draped on the windowsill. "Maybe," she said.

"You took my shirt?" he said.

"I borrowed it," Minnow told him. She wore the blue plaid sleeveless she'd *borrowed* from Matt's clothesline yesterday. "I'd do the same for you," she said with reminder in her minor defense and innocent tone.

"Thanks, if I want to go for the skintight fitted look I'll take you up on that," Matt said.

"I was running out of clothes to borrow at home that looked like a boy's," explained Minnow in her defense. "I live in a house with one guy," she added a little dryly. "You likey?" she presented.

Matt looked. "I think it looks better on me. I fulfill its potential."

"How fashion forward of you," played along Minnow with a wry upward look.

"I kept telling myself I must not have washed it, or maybe it blew away, but it's not been real windy," said Matt.

Minnow chuckled.

By early evening Minnow had been knocked to ground and squished between a frightened, disgruntled foal and the fence.

She, Bumble, and young Spencer herded the brown and white filly towards the chute, where penned in, the vet vaccinated the foal, then freed her.

All afternoon she and the saltwater ponyboys played this game of *catch me if you can*, one Minnow was ready for. She'd played this game all of her life with Matt, her sisters, their school friends, and Marshy.

Guys astride, like Sailor Man Sharp, Russ, Chowder, Matt, and others, divided the mare from the wild herd and with sly and deft maneuvering divided the foal from his mother. It was harder with the littler ones because they traveled in their mother's shadow.

From there, boots on the ground like well-placed Hammer as leader, and helpers Bumble, young Spencer, AJ, cousin Freddy (who hadn't paid her any attention – typical brat), and others, hollered and yelped to herd the foal in the direction of the chute.

Everyone took breaks and turns being on foot except for Sharp, Russ, and Chowder, who were their champions in the saddle.

Of course, those on foot like Minnow didn't dare to herd a wild full grown pony with their body. Only the young foals. Minnow identified with the foals' fright. She didn't like the doctor's either, though oddly enough she'd never minded the dentist.

Once it was over, the foal whinnied in glee as he was released into the opposite portion of the penning with the rest of the herd that'd had their teeth looked at and rumps stabbed by a needle.

Much to the amusement and banter of the fellas, Minnow fell on her gluteus maximus so many times she lost count. But not how many jokes poured from every *wham!*

Minnow hadn't a bruised tailbone before – but she was pretty sure every part of her was bruised today.

Finally, they spared her last unbruised spot of epidermis when Hammer put her on duty opening and closing the chute beside Bumble and De Juan. The saltwater ponyboys took the opportunity to break from the saddle, and the fellas outside of the fence who'd finished lunch and were waiting, swung eagerly and gingerly onto their mounts.

Minnow was thankful for the new posting. She decided however that she wouldn't shoot like limping lightning to the new spot a good walk away even though she was eager for it. She'd given herself enough to live up to by putting herself in the swim among the champions, and Matt had given her enough to live down as well!

Minnow was surprised to spot Carly, peering persistently over someone's head to see better. Minnow knew she hadn't come to ooh and ah over the breathtaking wild ponies. Carly didn't even like touching horses. Or their smell. How could Matt date her when his whole life revolved around horses?

He was going to open a stable on the island one day that gave riding lessons, and taught you how to listen to and have a conversation with your horse. He was the best horse whisperer Minnow knew, and bet the best she would ever know.

Minnow huffed and wiped the sweat pouring from her dirt smudged face with the inside of her slightly oversized shirt. Dad wouldn't miss it right away. She planned to stick it in the wash before he could ask where it was or why it smelled like horses?

It was obvious.

Carly had come to watch Matt.

She stood at the fence observing with a hint of yearning and seduction in the expression of her gaze. How did she do that? Any girl? asked Minnow in her mind, perplexed and alert by the look.

Alongside her, Tizzy covered her nose as dirt and the smell of horse and pine were kicked up, mixed with men's musk and sweat and tourists covered in bug spray and suntan lotion.

Tizzy, for different reasons than her sister Izzy, wasn't an avid jogger like Carly. She just went along because they went. Like being here, now.

The act of sweating at all was a sign the sensitive-to-everything Tizzy had courage. She'd prefer to stay in the air conditioning of her hypoallergenic house, but she dared the outdoors and things like this for her friend. Minnow gave her credit for her loyalty to her friend. Maybe it just made her itchy all over to not be included in things, like it did Windy. The one thing Tizzy was sensitive too that squashed her other sensitivities like a fist landing on a bunch of blueberries.

Tizzy's personality and intention at the start of a new day evolved around not one hair out of place. Poor Tizzy. With a sister like Izzy, who wasn't sensitive to anything to the point of where kids in school, and Minnow at times, questioned if she was apathetic – and with a go getter for a friend like Carly, Tizzy seemed destined to be in a Tizzy for possibly forever.

Though some distance away and squished among the onlookers snapping pictures on phones, Minnow was still gladly relieved for the corner of obscurity.

She kept her hat brim low and focus forward on her responsibility and in the hustle and bustle involving the occasional kick or rear they ducked from, and tried not to lose her hat.

Chapter Twenty-nine

Minnow dragged a very large haybale out of Matt's feed room, that looked like a palace compared to her little alcove in her tiny shed barn. She knew this was for two big horses, but she was thinking there should be more haybales made for fun size people and ponies. Her and Marshy for example. Although Minnow wasn't easily daunted or deterred by a big challenge.

The sweet, sweet smelling haybale reminded her of a cube of sugar, yet this hairy prickly square wasn't anything close. Unless you were a horse. Big.

Sore and tired, it was a nuisance to tighten her arms around the bulky prickly haybale, but she did it. Then, energy drained, it took all of Minnow's strength in her sun-zapped body to heft the meal fit for queens and kings up into her arms.

Easing the pressure when she relaxed the bottom on the roughen edge of the middle fence railing, made from angle-cut wood, Minnow exhaled. Taking a deep breath, and grunting loudly she gave one big heft and shoved it over the top railing.

Panting, Minnow grinned through her exasperation. "Yay!" she panted, feeling victorious. "Triumph!" she said to Ish and Olive, who looked at her with curious question in their gazes and pricked ears. They were probably under the impression that their little friend had gotten too much sun.

It was quite possible. But oh well, thought Minnow. Up she went and *oof* she splat onto the other side of the paddock to cut the string for removal with her pocket knife. Ish and Olive had already meandered up to the haybale, and nibbled at Minnow's hat. They sprayed her with sweet horsy huffs and nudged her with velvet muzzles, all of which tickled and made Minnow giggle. They felt like she did too, even if they'd retained more of their faculties than sun-zapped Minnow.

Sluggish, hungry, thirsty, exhausted, Minnow seemed the only delirious one in the herd. Well; how did Matt feel? What was his opinion?

She got her answer as though he'd read her mind or been a part of her and Ish and Olive's silent conversation. "Feeling happy?" was the way Matt worded it.

He was a horse whisperer, and a natural born bellwether. Minnow knew Matt's gift counted with people too. Especially one he knew so well as he did Minnow.

Minnow reeled up the string around her hand, using the last bit to wind around the middle and stuffed it in the deepest bottom of her pocket so Olive and Ish wouldn't mistake it for food. Or a treat like they might if they spotted the tips of it peeking out from her pocket.

She then parsed out armfuls and transferred the hay to the dry trough that sat higher up from the ground than the water trough, until there was a nice feast of hay all plated for the two of her friends.

Minnow still worried a little that Olive had put on weight. She hoped there wasn't something wrong with her; yet maybe Matt was right. She just needed more exercise.

Olive hadn't been ridden much since Matt bought Ish two years ago. Coby often rode Olive when they all went riding on the beach or around East Side, but in the summer, he's as locked into the kayak shop as Dad and Summer were. They've got tours every night but family nights and its heavy duty in the day transporting to and from the dock, as well as rinsing the boats when they get back. Then turn around after a long day of that and take out an evening tour.

Whew!

Minnow knew from her experience, it took it out of a person by the end of the day. Who had enough energy to do anything in their slack time but nap in the sun or watch a movie on the couch?

During all this, Matt was filling their trough with fresh cool water, which upon taking the first prickly bite of hay that itched their throat, Olive and Ish decided to partake of.

Minnow giggled, tired, and happily so. "Very," she said in answer.

Matt then sprayed the horses, which was like turning on moaning and groaning machines. Ish swung his head and whinnied sharply in delight, and Olive turned herself like she was posing, until every spot on her sides were gleaming wet in the glare of late afternoon sun.

It was still hot, and Minnow felt the sun radiating off her arms, even her cheeks, and they were shaded by her ballcap brim.

"That looks refreshing," groaned Minnow, taking after Ish and Olive, yet with her own extreme yearning. "Spray me too."

Matt obliged, beginning with a light spray on her face but she walked further into it instead of backing away. Then they took turns holding the hose and rinsing off the layer of horse mustiness and dirt and sweat under the icy, cucumber cool spray in his sunny backyard.

"You should plant a tree back here," Minnow was saying as she held the hose for Matt. He was scrubbing up his arms and his tan bicep bulged and glistened water. Minnow blinked the mesmerized stare out of her eyes and continued before he had the chance to noticed she'd been staring. Why had she? was the fleeting thought that tucked itself into a hiding spot in her mind for now. "I like it open too; but it might be better for Ish and Olive," she said, referring with her chin in the direction of the paddock. "Especially when you open your stable."

Matt turned and looked with an overview of the large backyard. "I've been thinking about that too," he said.

Minnow's eyes felt a little heavy. Bulky biceps or not, she had to go home and take a nap. Wait, what had she just thought?

Ooooo, she definitely needed a nap.

Refreshed, and feeling lazy, she said, "I'd better head home. Mom and Dad might need my help with dinner."

"Right, it's family night," remembered Matt. "I've got my days mixed up."

"That aint all you've got mixed up," muttered Minnow on her way past, handing him the hose.

"Come again?" asked Matt as she felt him grab her wrist. Nervous excited fear jostled and tickled in her stomach like a two liter of soda shaken up and spewing in all directions. Smiling, hoping she could slip through his grasp because they were both wet, Minnow uttered, "The yard could use your fixing up."

Cover was no good, nor hiding cover. Minnow sensed his intention and bolted all the same. She slipped free in the nick of time before he sprayed the hose down the back of her shirt.

If she was going to be tickled he'd have to chase her down!

She was glad to make him fight for the chance, circling around and ducking under the clothesline that he whipped out of his way and got tangled up in by swooping his arms.

Minnow slipped on the grass and seeing an opportunity Matt dove for her ankle but she kicked out of his grasp and bolted again.

Olive and Ish munched on their hay, ears sticking straight up, enjoying their entertainment while dining.

Minnow was small but she was fast and she ran around the small two story house twice before ducking on all fours into the rosemary bushes. Matt darted past, thinking he was just on her heels. *He thought wrong.* Minnow gripped that satisfaction smiling, and crawled further under the bushes before breaking free and running up the short, stubby front deck through the front door. Half mad-dash through the kitchen to the living room Matt had headed her off through the screen-door, forcing her to think on a skid and backtrack to backdoor, bursting into daylight again!

Minnow thought she'd use the drainpipe since she was light and climb the barn but she barely made it to the paddock when Matt tackled her and tickled her. Knowing she was ticklish everywhere, Matt alternated. He tickled her tummy, as she panted and scream giggled, "Stop it," then her neck, which turned her laughter into a sound like frogs sucking breath through a sore throat, as tickling her on her neck always did! It made Matt break down and weaken in the joints and his grasp, like her ticklishness and tickled sounds always did him, and she tried to take advantage of it but he recovered and switched to her foot, clamping her leg between his side and the bicep she'd been, "slightly", admiring. In this position, she pushed on his back and tried to sit up and wiggled and tugged back on her prisoner leg but she could do it all day and never match up to his strength. "Okay, okay!" she said finally.

Matt tossed her leg aside and she relaxed into the grass for a few breaths before swaggering into a crawling position that circled her around next to Matt with space between them as she gauged whether or not he was sincere in accepting her yield.

"Give up?" he told her.

"I said I did," she told him, wary-eyed. She felt poised and ready like a cat, and wondered if this is what tigers feel like all the time. Alert and suspect, poised in readiness. "I'll get your right foot one day when you're not looking," she promised. "Who's only ticklish in the tummy and one foot anyway?"

Recovering from the winded chase and wrestling the speedy Minnow, Matt said in answer, "This, coming from someone who's ticklish everywhere."

Minnow smiled, and gently removed one hand, one leg, and then the other from supporting her on all fours until she'd laid herself gently on her tummy. "I don't want to get up," whined Minnow.

Smiling, tired, Matt held out a hand, still refilling his lungs at a steady pace.

Minnow summoned the strength and took his hand. She felt worn out and even more lazy from being tickled and laughter than from the hard day's work she'd put in.

Matt stood and gently yanked her up onto her toes. "You're only faster than me when you're barefoot," said Matt.

So she *had* made him fight for his chance to catch her.

That made Minnow smile wider. Breathing pretty normally compared to Matt, she replied, "I knew I'd made you fight for it."

Suddenly they were close......or Minnow had just realized the proximity they stood in front of each other. Matt seemed to realize as well. Neither one of them made an effort to back up. Drawn toe to toe, were they drawing closer?

Minnow's mind wasn't forming words, or really thoughts; she just knew Matt was about to kiss her, and that she was okay with it.

Instead though, his forehead crashed onto hers, closing her eyes like a light switch that'd been flipped. Inside, she felt the lightning bugs and saw them clearly in the dark with her eyes being closed.

Minnow couldn't explain the intensity she was feeling. Friendship and love? This was more than their normal bond. Those two things mixed up with lightning bugs into a feeling that made her nervous and curious to know the whereabouts and why-abouts but then maybe it had something to do with having just been outrunning Matt, why her heart was pounding like it was. Like the ocean belonged inside her and it had come home. Dozens of galloping horses' hooves.

She couldn't rely on perception right now, when her adrenaline was shooting out of control.

"See ya at the carnival," said Matt, lifting his forehead off hers with one of his gentle, easy smiles.

It was like there'd been no intensity. Someone looking like Matt had put his forehead on hers. And the Matt she always knew and relied on looked at her now.

Minnow felt a little jostled by this. Like someone had snapped her out of a dream. Had what she felt really happened? It had her scrambling inside, and she worked up a normal smile too and said, "See ya there," thinking to herself as she walked past him, the carnival had already started, and all the rides were on at once inside her.

Minnow was dripping wet as she walked down the lane. The baking sun was still so intense and had started drying her clothes. She walked in the shade or grass, the rutty road burning her feet. She was certain it would sizzle an egg if she cracked one open on it.

Did Minnow share a moment with Matt? An almost kiss? She was questioning herself all the way home, and yet asked solely, over and over, how could she let this happen?

She hadn't imagined those feelings, right? One-sided as they'd seemed, she'd felt them for sure; what was happening to her?

What *was going on*, the logical part of her started, was that she was juggling more balls than any juggler at the carnival. She wasn't particularly good at juggling on this scale anyway, and some balls had gotten mixed up.

That was it, she told herself. Right?

Chapter Thirty

"Sunscreen," was the first thing Minnow heard when she hopped up the sunbaked steps. It was Summer's voice, and she sounded in a good mood, but firm, like she meant what she'd said.

Fresh into the house Minnow saw that Summer and Windy were dressed for the beach and they encouraged Minnow to join them.

"What happened to you?" Summer asked of her wet puppy – minnow – appearance.

"Matt and I gave his horses baths, since it's so hot," replied Minnow, and it was true. She liked telling Summer something wholly true for once since this week started. It made her feel nervous and edgy, not being upfront with her family. She'd trimmed the truth in the past – Minnow could count times when

Summer and Windy each had too; it had to be this way for now for her plan to work. She was following her dream....and she couldn't stop now.

Windy however knew the backstory trimmed out of her answer, and her expression was flooded with curiosity she couldn't express or satisfy with digging answers out of Minnow about how her day went, yet.

Minnow wished she was feeling her normal antagonism to thoroughly enjoy Windy' squirming – but as it happened she was bursting at the seams to tell Windy everything she wanted to ask!

Minnow felt like Jack-in-the-box being wound, trying not to transmit more than was leaking from Windy' features, or Summer would surely pick up on there being a Jack in hiding.

Standing in the living room where her sisters were checking beach backpacks last minute, Minnow was surprised that she suddenly felt more tired than very sore. It must have been all that tickling and laughter had mended and soothed those sore muscles and achy joints.

"Come to the beach," Summer said in her usual bright and calm personality. "You weren't here earlier; Mom and Dad asked if it was alright if they had a dinner date out. We said it was alright with us. So, you'd be home all by yourself."

"*All by yourself*," Windy emphasized slowly and drew out deliberately.

The marvel of sisters – or only Windy. Minnow should probably stop trying to figure her out. She just wasn't normal.

With a flat-eyed look at Windy first, Minnow said to Summer, "Give me a second to grab my stuff," and returning to her flat expression pressed her hand on Windy' face and gave her a gentle shove hard enough to land her on her hinny on the sofa.

Windy didn't fight Minnow this time. Instead, she sailed with the gentle force of her shove, exuding a sense of drama and, élan!

Minnow hadn't needed one dewdrop of coaxing to agree to go with her sisters to the beach. Occupied with the pony roundup, Minnow hadn't spent much time with her sisters in these last few days, and with a good four or so hours until she was due at the carnival, Minnow jumped on the opportunity!

It was also family night, and Minnow was looking forward to relaxing, dropping the juggler balls into their basket for the rest of the day, and just being Minnow. Not Maximus. Not Matt's pretend girlfriend.

Summer gave a look of sweet exasperation, acceptance the number one rule of being the oldest – and surviving. Minnow agreed with a similar expression in return. Even though she sometimes fell into that category with Windy, that Windy' pulled her in even when Minnow knew it was a minnow trap. The gravitational slurp of her little sister's world was a strong one, that knew how to get Minnow's attention. Mostly by poking at her.

Minnow still felt sluggish when she darted upstairs to change into her bikini. She grabbed a simple short sleeve that was thin and felt a little flowy to wear on the drive.

It dawned on her that she'd left her Max clothes in Matt's truck! Oh well, she decided, relaxing her tensed-up muscles. It was just Matt's truck. Not like she forgot them where a saltwater ponyboy would notice or mention – even so, Maximus was Matt's cousin.

After all that work in the heat Minnow was tired from soaking up sun and from getting knocked around by wild, frightened foals. But Minnow had felt this way before – not sore when she should feel sore, which meant when she finally stopped to relax and her adrenaline cooled, the full force would hit her hard and at once.

She knew she was pushing it but she wanted to spend time with Summer and Windy. She'd crash hard when she gave in tonight, and pictured herself dragging her feet through the carnival grounds later. But it would be worth every stiff joint and aching muscle soon throbbing her whole body.

The nice part about vaccinating the herd was that she moved out and *in* shade, so she still had skin to spare for the sunburn awaiting her. That too, would be worth the special time with Summer and Windy.

Minnow got a thought, and stopped shy of the threshold. The family photos on her and Windy' wall drew her attention.

Marshy and Minnow when Marshy was a wobbly big knee baby foal.

Minnow and her sisters stuffed like birds in a pie in a pile of autumn leaves they'd scraped together and thrown at each other.

Matt and her sisters when they'd all rescued toads from their neighbor's toad hole – a hole in the ground outside her house that once was used for piping but was filled in up to sixteen inches shy of level earth. No matter how many times they placed something over the top to lid the hole, toads still found their way in there.

Then there was the selfy of her and Matt – and then she and Matt when they were about nine.

She swallowed, biting her bottom lip, and opened her phone.

She never pictured then, that she'd be curious about what it would be like to kiss Matt for real, let alone in pretend, and that she would want to try it for real again. That she could get tingles from this boy she'd grown up with, always seeing as her best friend.

Minnow didn't even enjoy dating, unlike people her age – and she was now tangled up through a bargain that had the feeling of blackmail to scheme him and Carly back together – *again!*

At least, that's what felt like the dilemma before. Now, Minnow found herself replaying her forehead and Matt's forehead pressed together.

That was the strongest moment, that had been a moment between them.

Moments as friends, sure, agreed Minnow. But this felt more than friends; yet this feeling was strengthened through the bond they shared to begin with.

The last few days hemmed this strong imprint inside Minnow, that'd happened a little while earlier in Matt's yard.

Looking at Matt with new perspective; were these even her eyes? How could they wander to Matt's solid shoulders and arms earlier, and make her wonder? She didn't really know about what. She just went blank and had to blink to break the spell. Tarantella Girl didn't know how the strength in his muscles got there – Minnow did – through volunteering, chores, and taking care of the horses. Did she even know that the strongest part of Matt was his indelible sense of humor and his good heart?

Watching him herd from the saddle as he worked in concert alongside of her to channel five mares and their foals through the pine trees as one group to meet up with De Juan and Bumble ahead? That's where Matt belonged. Leading by bringing up the rear with the slowest or most novice one – which this week was her. He would be a great trainer when he saved up enough to expand his parents' property and build a full-grown stable with extended paddock.

When Matt kissed her for the first time – no, zip that. Minnow shook her head, because that had been strange, and it still felt strange.

When they'd crab-danced on the beach though, that had felt like them, kindled with the friendship only they had.

Minnow needed to re-instill this. Remind both of them. They'd been playing pretend dating for so long it was starting to get to where they couldn't act or feel like them around each other. It was getting harder, complicated, and Minnow knew she needed to remind herself and Matt that they were good friends, best friends forever, and reconvince herself that this Carly scheme was just one of their schemes.

Because it was! Minnow still had Matt's back, and she wasn't going to let this scheme needle them when they were around each other in any way.

With a jolt of determination, Minnow inhaled, feeling on track for the first time in a while, and sent Matt a txt.

Mom and Dad having date dinner. Going to the beach with Summer and Windy. Wanna come?

Minnow was starting to think that Matt had crashed on the closest place that felt soft, for a nap like she'd planned on doing, and that he wasn't going to get her txt until later, when they were probably back home, when she received his reply in the truck as Summer was starting it up.

You're on.

Minnow thumb-punched, "*Need a lift?*" and sent it.

Matt replied.

That's ambitious of you. I'm not calling myself fat, just you skinny.

"Hey guys, do you mind if I invited Matt?" asked Minnow.

"No," they both said, shrugging their shoulders. "We haven't seen him in a *long* while, it'll be fun; does he want a ride?" asked Summer in her usual sunny, pleasant and cool calm delighted way.

"Yep," answered Minnow, and they turned down the lane to retrieve fatso with Dad's patched up half ton.

Chapter Thirty-one

Minnow and her sisters and Matt hunted shells and rocks until Windy asked if Summer had brought the sponge ball. Everyone's attention pricked forward like a bunch of ponies asking silent questions and all thinking the same thing.

Splattering each other playing sponge ball tag was one of their favorite games to play. They could throw something at each other and hit them, well try, and it wouldn't hurt or get them yelled at. They were having so much fun it felt like they'd been playing the whole day at the beach.

When they finally did sprawl out on their towels, Coby had joined them. Minnow was hard to outrun and catch, or hit for that matter, but Coby's floppy curve ball throw was difficult for even her to outmaneuver.

Every person trying to tag always chased after Minnow the hardest because she was the team's best asset. On the last game she got frozen and Coby was the tagger. Matt was frozen, and Windy and Summer were zigzagging – he could only choose one, and he chose to wall off Summer, who was gaming to unfreeze Minnow.

Little did Coby know, the pirate and her sister had worked out a plan seconds prior. Windy and Summer signaled through the slightest nod from eye-contact, and charged to unfreeze their teammates at the same time.

Summer lured Coby out from his proximity to Minnow by skidding in the sand as though to backtrack and he tackled her.

Meanwhile, Windy unfroze Matt.

"Get her!" Summer called, holding onto Coby's wrist as Matt and Windy were charging to unfreeze Minnow, who stretched out her arm, a sail catching wind though unable to weigh anchor from the sand her feet were swallowed up by!

How was Summer a match for one-hundred-seventy pounds of muscle Coby?

Summer's kayaking resilient and strong body, toned in the spirit as well as muscle from shepherding tours of strangers in their novice element, but her prime element; and paddling between ten and twelve miles every day but family nights, spring to late fall as weather allows and tour schedules promise – not to mention loading, unloading, and rinsing rentals during the day –

plus the kayaking up to before winter's tundra cold masked the island, and time she spends with Windy and Minnow playing – making her stronger in inner combs of her – had something to do with how Summer was able to hold onto Coby. But when it seemed he will slip loose and in trying to yank free he pulled her to her feet, she leapt like a marsh grass frog and encircled his waist, holding on like a human tutu as he spun her around and tried to tickle her off!

Summer's ticklishness wasn't as extreme as Minnow's – which Minnow's pretty sure counted for everyone on earth – and thus instead of kerplunking like Minnow, she struggled to hold on.

Matt and Windy both raced by her, bringing with them a rush of air, which when stirred behaved coolly, like stirring sugar into fresh squeezed lemonade. Unfrozen and with a burst of reinvigoration Minnow raced away with Matt and Windy before Summer releases Coby.

They'd run far when they realized nobody was chasing them and tentatively risked slowing down to glance back.

Summer had let go and was standing close to Coby; the way Minnow had stood close to Matt, twice. Once in the ocean, and earlier in the yard. But neither Minnow or Matt were thinking about that right now. He and Minnow smiled a little, and let them have their moment, Windy panting more breathlessly between them, for as in everything and anything she did Windy went all out, often putting more energy or force into something than required.

"I thought your sister was the pirate," Coby said, caressing the hair from her face the gentle beach wind blew, wanting her attention as much as Coby had it.

"This coming from the man who has stolen my heart," said Summer in a soft clear tone. She leaned on his chest and stood on her tiptoes just as Coby smiled, and they kissed each other.

Had it been anyone else displaying public affection of any sort, they would give Windy grumbling or spark her to roll her eyes, but not with Summer and Coby. They hadn't grown up with Coby, but he was the kind of person who felt like he'd always been a member of the family.

And he was Summer's true love; so, that alone made him their friend and family.

From the looks she exchanged with Matt and Windy, Minnow knew they felt the same as her.

Minnow didn't feel like sunning just yet. So she slipped on her thin wavy tee shirt. It defied logic to wear her shirt now when the sun was setting. But the cooler sea breeze gave her sunburn chills. She thought about wearing her hoody, but she wasn't ready to give into complete comfy yet. She'd gotten her second wind and wanted to walk some more down the beach. She also had another purpose.

Windy had found another shark tooth and Minnow was determined to find one as well.

Windy had a knack for finding some treasure no one else did, and it wasn't fair. Not to mention she'd brag about it until everyone's ears burned.

Seeming to have gained a second wind as well, Matt joined her.

"She always finds a tooth or something on the beach," Minnow was complaining. "I never do – neither does Summer! But does she brag to Summer, no, she gloats to *me*."

"It's just her nature," Matt reminded her, but Minnow was the last person on the planet, or this island – or the other one, anyway, who needed reminding. With this awareness clinging to her like wet sand, she straightened and stared at Matt.

"Trust me, I know," she said.

Minnow appreciated that Matt was trying not to smile, but she couldn't look at him trying not to any longer and went back to treasure hunting.

Minnow wasn't expecting to bump into Tarantella Girl. She'd wanted Matt to join her and her sisters because she was getting mixed up in pretend and real life – between being Maximus in the pony roundup and Matt's pretend date in front of buggy. Looking at the family pictures in her room made her aware of how much she was craving the old days and how much they all, she and Summer and Windy and Matt, just needed to be ordinary, themselves. Okay, Minnow admitted, so she needed it most of all.

Matt saw her at a distance before Minnow was even aware.

Sunset turned the pale beach sand orangey, and the ocean sky blue and sun glob orange. The surf that rinsed up the shore was speedy but gentle, the placid ocean gleaming sky blue and sun glob orange producing smaller and softer waves to pair with the soft faint breeze and cooling sand. Bubbles and white suds floated on top and inside the mild surges, so see-through clear Minnow spotted crabs, shells, and her own feet.

Minnow saw something glistening in the receding wave. Were her eyes playing tricks on her? Did she want one so badly she was seeing things that weren't really there?

She chased it, not realizing Matt was chasing her. Minnow thrust her hand into the water and feeling the razor-sharp edges poking her palm, knew she had caught it!

Minnow spun around, slinging saltwater with her. "Look! Matt, I think I found a shark tooth!"

The last thing she expected was for the suddenness of Matt cupping her face and tipping her head back in a kiss. Hands sun-warm from drinking up today and calloused from his good deeds.

On her toes and Minnow felt like she was falling, even with his other arm balancing her upright and close, and unable to fall free from his kiss, Minnow found herself kissing Matt back, and more, with response.

"What was that!" Minnow shouted, looking around. Had a rocket just gone off from Wallops Island?

Oh no, had her sisters seen?!

"What do you mean? Carly's here," Matt explained, but wound up, Minnow didn't really hear him or care that Carly was here!

All that happened inside her?

Minnow yelped and sidestepped the surf that snapped her out of her frenzy. It was the ocean she told herself, but it also wasn't the ocean.

"A crab bit me!" Minnow tried.

"I take insult to that," Matt teased, putting his hands on his hips, and stealing a quick glance over his shoulder towards the sand-dune crest.

She'd also felt the shark tooth pop out of her hand like a kernel of corn and softly but with pointedness in her ears, go *kerplunk!* in the swell.

"My toooooth," she said with sad longing. There went her bragging rights over gloating Windy. She'd probably never find another tooth! One thing was definite, Windy wouldn't be shutting up tonight, or any time soon.

She glared at Matt. "You're worse than a crab right now," Minnow stated, squeezing her hands on her hips and standing firmly as another wave rushed in and reached Matt's toes. It was clear that the tide was starting to come in but she'd still jumped pretty far.

"Why didn't you warn me first?" she demanded. "My sisters could've seen, and I lost my shark tooth!" She was really unhappiest about that part.

"There wasn't time, she could've looked this way," Matt answered, checking over his shoulder again. Then dawn sort of broke through his Carly obsessed one track mind. "Wait, you haven't told your sisters about this?"

Forget that she lost her bragging rights over Windy in all of this, growled Minnow sarcastically in her mind.

"No – I haven't had the chance – or – they wouldn't understand," Minnow fumbled and came clean at the same time. "Summer would think I was nuts and probably look at me with that disappointment that withers me where I stand; and Windy would laugh and tease me until the end of time!"

"You've got to tell them," Matt said, but his voice held back laughter. "You guys never keep anything from each other," he kept trying, and if he didn't stop, was going to royally fail.

"I can't tell them about riding in the swim," hissed Minnow in point. Then, "Actually, Windy caught me so I had to fess up to her, but she's into mutiny and piracy and all that good, or, bad stuff, so she's actually got my back with this."

Matt was somehow able to talk himself into being serious, and with a down to earthiness in his manner closed the gap a little as he spoke. "They're your sisters. But I've known them all my life too," Matt started. "I think it's kind of funny that you haven't told them yet. But do you want them to find out by word of mouth? Windy will never let you live it down if you don't get ahead of this with them first. And I know how close you and Summer are. To me, she's been like the big sister I never had. Trust me. Tell her. Or she'll put us both in timeout – and not the kind where we just go to our rooms."

Minnow understood Matt's meaning. She'd rather be sent to her room for reflection than to face the kind of exile or timeout that came with disappointing Summer.

Exclusion was Windy' fear, and qualm. Dishonesty and secrets were Summer's big qualms.

Minnow noticed how Matt seemed more at ease than previous times this week on their pretend dates – besides that crab dance in the surf when he'd been hard-pressed not to laugh outright at her odd behavior, as well as equally embarrassed, which had played a role in her motive. He must feel like Carly was closer to his arms than before.

"Fine. I know. I'm going too," Minnow admitted with agreement and stated. But. "You made me lose my shark tooth," she said through her teeth and punched him hard in the arm.

"No I didn't," Matt said confused. "You haven't found one yet. We're still looking."

"I'd just found it!" she insisted slowly. "But you kissed me off-guard, and then the crab bit me," she lied a little, "and the tooth popped out of my hand!"

Matt put the brakes on a bolt of laughter which ended up sounding like a snort.

Minnow eyed him flatly.

"A shark tooth that pops? It must have popped right out of his mouth," he teased with a mild string of chuckles.

Minnow stood straight and started stomping up the beach. He wasn't taking this seriously, and he'd just kissed her off-guard for the second time. Minnow was feeling so many mixed feelings right now, but stormy was the hot breeze on a hotter day blanketing the rest.

"I'm sorry, it just happened; I wasn't thinking," Matt explained, the tone of his voice genuinely apologetic. "Minnow, wait up, come on." He caught up to her speed walking. "I'm sorry."

Minnow believed Matt but she was in one of those moods where she wanted to be irksome and not soothed or happy just right now. At the same time, she was open if he would convince her that he really meant it.

Matt touched her arm and she halted promptly, spinning around to face him.

Her heart had to melt around the edges when she saw his expression, didn't it?

Matt did know how much that shark tooth meant to her. But what was he meaning sorry for? Losing her bragging rights to shut up Windy, or kissing her so well? Minnow didn't mean that, she meant kissing her *off-guard.*

Yes – as Matt said, something had just happened.

Minnow wanted to answer; she was breathing swiftly now, though not quite flames yet, but a minute ago, her heart pounded fury and excitement in her chest, and she was still fighting trembling from it. She didn't know where to start first?

With the confusion?

Once again, she didn't feel awkward after his kiss. The nervousness over awkward wasn't good. Not good.

He didn't feel that?

Lightening bugs?

What's there when you turn off the lights. And your perspective changes.

The moist wind in the ocean of trees with rain thick in the air and windiness?

Island.

Minnow didn't understand this, and she was mad at Matt for once again causing something and more when he apparently didn't even catch on to it or feel it either.

But she was like summer so hot when the clouds do burst with rain its torrential, gushing the air with coolness and sending off misty steam from the tall grass and moist ground.

Matt had convinced her, and he was the one person besides everyone in her family but Windy, who she couldn't stay upset with.

"It's ok," said Minnow in a milder tone, less edgy. "You just surprised me. I'm not used to this you and me being romantic side, even though it's obviously pretend."

"Yep; you're right," Matt admitted and reassured, which was the first-time Minnow had the firm impression he'd been going through any of the mixed emotions that she was. So she hadn't been imagining her own feelings, and what she'd wondered, and sensed or felt from him at times either?

Matt rubbed the back of his neck, and it was clear to Minnow that the explanation was obviously ending there. Which was fine with Minnow. Talking about how awkward it was, made it feel more awkward, and she was happy to can talking about how not used to kissing or acting like a couple with each other they were.

Minnow changed the subject, though this one too was important. "You owe me a shark tooth. Or a hunt until we find another one."

"Okay," agreed Matt.

Tarantella Girl had shrunken into a dot on a picnic table higher on the beach, wrapped in Harry's arm, watching sunset. She'd also shrank in Matt's mind too; for the time being. Minnow would accept all the time being with Matt as her old, unencumbered Matt that there was.

Minnow nodded, and then after a second's inner check with herself to see how she felt, continued down the beach looking closely at the sand through the liquid glass clear surf. Light was falling and the tide was rising. In minutes, she'd have to turn around and with Matt they'd head back up the beach and find her sisters and Coby. They'd get ready and head home before nightfall and no one knew if they were stepping onto sand or into some kid's ankle-twisting mote.

Returning to his normal self, without tension or apprehension in his brow, Matt spoke up. "Your turn; aren't you going to apologize to me?"

"What?" asked Minnow in a stunted tone. She straightened herself and gaped at him.

"You did call me a crab," he teased.

Minnow rolled her eyes. No, she wasn't calling him a crab, she was trying to hide that she'd felt a crate of fireworks go off inside her and thought it was really a rocket taking off from Wallops. But as long as he was thinking she'd insulted him, she wouldn't correct him.

Matt was still under that impression, wasn't he?

Minnow made a note to herself. She had to stop getting startled when Matt kissed her unexpectedly. Though this was the first time she'd been startled of herself when it happened.

"*Kissing* – is, just." Minnow paused to find the words, then stated, "*Like* getting bit by that crab. Surprising."

Despite her tone and vague sternness, they both chuckled over her joke.

"Maybe I should kiss you off-guard and show you what it's like," she said, serious.

"Just try to surprise me," challenged Matt.

Minnow narrowed her eyes. "You will rue those words," she told him confidently, but not overconfident.

"Thanks for the warning," Matt replied nodding.

"If you wouldn't be startled then why would you thank me for a warning?" asked Minnow, crossing her arms.

"Figure of speech," answered Matt.

"It's on," Minnow replied. "Better watch your mouth."

Minnow agreed to the challenge because she'd never turned down a challenge from Matt Evers, nor had he her.

And there was one more reason. That sensation still tingling up and down her arms, and deep down inside. Surprise like someone had thrown ice water on her and yet emotion stoked a forge inside that felt hotter than the most brash of summer days.

What was this?

She'd felt this the first time he'd kissed her, as unexpected and strange as it had been for the two best friends.

She should be used to Matt's kiss by now – but that's just it. Every time he kisses her, she feels something different. Something new. Something more. He's still Matt; but she finds herself asking, with these feelings who is she anymore?

And what is this side of Matt she is seeing up close for the first time?

Minnow had hoped to put these tingles and mixed up feelings behind her. But now that she had felt this – coupled with their strongest moment earlier today, wrapped up in some kind of sundrenched intensity, soaking wet from the hose, under the sunshine and blue sky of his un-mowed backyard, Minnow had to know what this meant or she'd never be able to look at Matt like she had her entire life. As her best friend. So she'd find out what this was, nip it in the bud, because it couldn't be more than some phase brought on by unorthodox circumstances, and then like cresting a wave she wasn't expecting, return to waters she could swim because of how familiar they were and thus how well she knew them. She had to see this curiosity through or she'd never understand it and she'd never be able to go forward or bring her best friend back into focus.

Minnow didn't have the chance to think deeper on it. They weren't even a seagull's lollygagging form of laughter from heading back to meet up with her sisters and Coby, when they spied Carly higher up on the sand. Harry, curiously enough, wasn't with her anymore.

Spurred, Minnow grunted, "She's coming."

"Hah," Matt said wryly. "Nice try."

She grabbed his hands and started leading him into the surf that was twice as chilly with sunburn than it was without. His expression changing along the way. "You're serious," he said.

"Yes, pumpkin sweet," Minnow couldn't help chirping, and smiling. She slid her arm around him as they reached the toes of the racing wave that splashed around her ankles and hastened up to the hem of her tee shirt.

"Just a friendly walk on the beach. She might not even see us," Minnow said, resting her head in the groove of his shoulder and collarbone.

She felt shielded close to Matt like this, with her cheek on his chest and her arms around his waist. Even though the cold ocean water and light wind caressing her sunburn made her tremble. Minnow fought back, sinking into the feel of Matt's arms around her holding her too. Holding her to him. This was where she belonged. Tarantella Girl had a chunk of Matt's heart he couldn't function with unless she held onto it. But right here, in this spot her cheek rested, in the groove of his shoulder and collarbone, with her arms around his waist; comfortable silence, piping plover to beach grass closeness, friends. Her friend. Carly wouldn't take this place; even when he held her close. She knew she'd never find this place; this place was where Minnow belonged. Where she dreamed, and had nightmares, breathed and loved and shoved at Matt and sometimes when they napped together, drooled.

"Harry's not with her anymore," she informed him as a note, one spy to another.

"Really," Matt said a little surprised, and she stopped him from glancing over his shoulder.

"She's on the hunt," Minnow told him. "Don't you believe otherwise. Let the huntress hunt you down. Play a little harder to get. You know you're a little predictable, and that's why she knows she can always have you back when she's done feeding on the other guy."

Matt grimaced a little. "Thanks for the graphic, and reducing me to dinner."

"Welcome to the club; I'm known in some circles these days as *bait*," Minnow enunciated.

Matt snorted a bolt of laughter, which despite everything, easily made Minnow smile. Matt tugged her closer.

It turns out that Carly was craftier than Minnow gave her credit for. She didn't hunt them down after all; instead she kept her distance, and at one point disappeared. So Minnow got her friend back after all. She still had a lot of mixed up lightning bug feelings and things to figure out; but she was glad to have found her friend through the muddle.

At this point, the day had been swept up into a fusion of colors and brushed over the horizon into the west like Mom's sawdust and wood shavings at the end of the day were swept up and out the door, and dusk was left.

Like the wood chips, and sawdust clouds fading fast on the air when Mom's broom brushed them outside, the clean sweep of dimming color as well settled down, now that its heavier woodchip, the sun, had sank into the sea of evergreen.

Chapter Thirty-two

Minnow and Matt were spent. She couldn't believe when she was laying on the beach after making it back to Summer, Windy, and Coby, how good the cool sea breeze felt to her throbbing body, even with the chills of her sunburn.

"Coby remembered his flashlight," Windy told them, "So we can stay out and roast marshmallows!"

"With a flashlight?" teased Minnow, just to play with her. She knew exactly what Windy meant. They could walk safely back to the truck without tripping and twisting their ankle in an unseen hole.

Coby was digging the fire pit and Matt helped him. The hole reminded Minnow of those that turtles build to lay their eggs.

She looked up and saw Summer trekking from the truck, marshmallow bags in both hands.

Minnow looked back at Windy with soft scrutiny. "How are you helping," she questioned, drawing out her words a little.

Windy held up a single match next to her face. "I'm lighting the fire," she said. There it was again – that twinkle bouncing off her eye tooth – but she didn't wear a gold cap!

Minnow's forehead fell flat and she monotoned her voice deep and softly dramatic, droning, "Oh sweet. You let her have a match," she said to Coby a little more normally with a glance around her arm.

Minnow glimpsed Coby's wide grin in reply, knowing her meaning, and looked back to Windy.

Her other hand lifted and a matchbox appeared close to her other cheek.

"Oh, alright, that's it!" Minnow said in open finality on the subject. "If she burns down Assateague it's on you dude." She inched on her knees to her backpack and unzipped the back layer as pleasant looking Summer plopped down in the sand on her knees.

Windy tiger crawled past Minnow looking transfixed and hungry on purpose. Minnow just stared unimpressed as she slunk by, giving the twilit sky with the first stars of the night an upward look when Windy kicked up sand by scurrying the last ten feet just after going past Minnow.

By the time Windy struck the match and dropped it into the woodpile, Minnow had pulled her shorts out of her backpack and cozied in her hoody. Matt had crawled over to where she sat zipping her backpack up and offered her a marshmallow. She said thanks but tucked it in her hoody pouch for later. She didn't feel like eating right now.

Was that the fifth match stroke? wondered Minnow, glancing up at her family aglow with firelight.

"Please, just five more?" begged Windy.

"Two more," Summer specified.

Struck down at the same time skyrocketed, Windy struck the next match rapidly, and then savored the very last one with precision that Minnow found pleasing to hear. The long, deliberate but smooth run of the matchhead along the rough side of the matchbox, with a quick smooth snap at the end, and the mini roar of flame.

Matt plopped on his back and looked at the stars with heavy eyelids. *Good idea*, thought Minnow. That's exactly what she had been headed for.

She settled in for twice as cozy with her face snuggled against Matt's chest. The smell of his skin, the outside air and sundried smell of his hoody from the clothesline, and the loll of the softly roaring and crashing waves, along with the good tired in her sore bones, lolled Minnow to sleep faster than most winter nights cozied with both of her sisters in bed. Or those summer days when she laid in the grass with her face pressed to Marshy' warm, velvet soft brown neck. This memory she relived in her mind carried with her to a pleasant dreamland, where she slept in gentle blackness.

Chapter Thirty-three

Minnow had only intended to lay down for a short while.

Telling herself maybe she'd just rest her eyes. Never thinking she would quickly drift off, yet she should have expected it. The sounds of soft ocean roar, seagulls, and her sisters laughing with each other as they roasted marshmallows.

She hadn't felt the full throttle of soreness up till now, only good tired, and since she'd laid down her body was telling her in great detail where every part of her was bruised and scratched and tuckered out.

She felt anchor heavy, beached whale immobility.

In the water, she was buoyant – but once she laid submerged on land, every part of her felt heavy and hard to move.

She was surprised to hear Summer honking what was the patched-up blue kayak truck and lifted her head up. The fire was smothered and the headlights blinked once at them. It'd felt like she'd just laid down a few minutes ago, not a half hour earlier.

"That went fast," Minnow groaned as she slowly picked herself up.

"Sleep well?" asked Matt.

"Yep, you?" asked Minnow. She should've picked up on that sound in his voice sooner.

Tugging his ballcap on even at nighttime, grinning sleepily but with clear-eyed keenness, Minnow saw the wet patch on his shoulder before he said, "I thought I had till you showed me up."

"You know I can't help it when I'm really tired," said Minnow, shrinking back a little as she started moving forward. Matt kept an eye on her, nodding his head softly, planting the fear in her that he was going to tickle her.

Matt started forward quickly and halted like she'd seen horse's start to run and pull back, making her scream and fear that he was going to tickle her, lightning streaking her. He let her slide though, and his smile told her he wouldn't tickle her. Not after the victory of today he was clearly still riding the wave of.

Matt and Minnow dragged themselves across the sluggish sand and crawled onto the bed of the truck with Windy. The metal felt hard and cold and severe to Minnow's knees and poor hands.

She anchored herself to a corner, feeling lazy and stiff and sore all over, but wearing a tired, smiling grimace. She'd enjoyed every minute of what'd turned her into lumps.

Matt was clearly sore as well. He moaned long and easily as he did likewise, anchoring himself in a corner. Windy sat between them, not wearing a hoody or shorts, which instantly drew Minnow's concern.

She squinted in the permeating truck-cab-light but she knew it before she saw. Windy' painful wasn't going to be as bearable as Matt and Minnow's. Her legs were hot but didn't look near as red as Windy did all over, telling Minnow if she looked this red an hour out of the sun, she was in for a painful night.

Minnow knew without asking that Windy had skipped a second and third time Summer had told her to reapply her sunscreen. She'd have to learn the hard way this time.

"Aren't you guys hot in those hoodies?" she asked.

"No," Minnow replied, shaking her head along with Matt. She couldn't help feeling sorry for Windy, and at the same time think to herself that this was a deserving lesson for her about what happens when she doesn't take the time to stay on top of her sunscreen. Five minutes with fun on pause. Five minutes!

Matt didn't say a word but she sensed similar readings in his expression. A grimace he bit back and yet furrowed his eyebrows in thinking on the hard, painful sleepless night ahead. That's where Minnow's concern had gone too. They'd all had sunburn, Matt and Minnow had some now. But the two of them knew how miserable and excruciating *this* time was going to be for Windy, who tolerated pain pretty well for someone who expressed every aspect of it, during it like someone who couldn't bear it.

"I'm craving ice cream after all that sun," groaned Matt after Summer pulled into the parking lot across from the carnival.

"Me too," said Minnow, groaning.

"I ate too many marshmallows; I can't stomach ice cream right now," said Windy, wearing a small grimace. She looked like she was focused on something she couldn't see, and Minnow knew she was processing the stinging and that her stomach must be turning a little.

Minnow squeezed her fingers through the small sliding window in the middle of the rear windshield and pulled one half towards her. "Hey Summer, I think Windy needs to get home. She's sunburn really bad," Minnow explained.

By the look in her eyes Minnow knew Summer wasn't happy. "You didn't reapply your sunscreen, did you Windy?" said Summer with pointedly forced pleasantry.

Windy sighed. "No," she admitted in a complaining tone.

"Alright, I'll drop you guys off and get her home," said Summer, the sarcasm drained from her voice. She picked up by her tone that Windy knew she'd been careless, and was learning her lesson for it, and as they all three knew when someone felt bad they needed to make that person feel better, not add to their misery. There would be time for scolding later.

"Poor Windy," Matt said as they waited their chance to cross the road.

"Summer will give her a shower and put aloe on her," said Minnow, but she felt bad for her little sister too. "Maybe she'll learn this time."

A nice man in a truck waved for them to go ahead, and they jogged sore and awkwardly across the road, probably giving pedestrians and other folks in cars a laugh.

Well the carnival didn't have any clowns, and Minnow was happy someone could get a laugh out of their soreness.

Stepping into the booth with ice cream, Minnow put herself in front of the big fan on a stand. Matt started for the ice cream and then joined her, before getting a better idea. He stuck his head with half of himself in a long floor freezer.

Once they retrieved their ice cream, a craving that coupled with their droopy shoulders and sunburn faces drew many smiles and laughs from the fellow volunteers, they parked themselves on the ground alongside the booth, backs leaning against the traditional white wall. There wasn't much leg room in the lumpy dirt alley with grass that made it strongly resemble a balding man's head, but it was a place to sit peacefully.

It was as though they hadn't done hard work before; roughhousing and playing around all day qualified for the amount of energy and labor they expended rounding up and dividing the foals and ponies for vaccinations. They were being a little bit of babies about their soreness and exhaustion, even as real and familiar as being spent felt.

"Forgot to ask – did you see Carly at the fence today?" asked Minnow, testing the water, and diving into her ice cream cone again. She didn't care if she got brain freeze.

That perked Matt up – slightly. He nodded heavily. "Yep," he said but he wasn't smiling that big, and slurped up another soft bite of chocolate.

"Aren't you happy?" asked Minnow, confused, but at the same time, cautiously glad. Was he getting tired of trying to win a girl who kept splitting up with him every time she went through a phase, or met a boy who spoke her language? Which was bug, brainy, and biology.

"Inside I am," answered Matt. "It's working its way to the surface."

Minnow meant to shove him but it flopped into a nudge, making him slide sideways down the wall and Minnow catch herself on the dirt with her elbow, holding her ice cream cone free of mayday like Liberty's torch. Grinning weakly, Minnow and Matt both put out the huge effort of righting themselves again.

It wasn't Minnow's blueberry, raspberry vanilla milkshake she made at home that always infused her with energy, but it was cold, refreshing, just what she craved. Ice cream, and Matt's company had added a skip in her step by the time she entered the cotton candy booth as herself. And feeling much more like herself.

Now, to see what the fairies had delivered?

Chapter Thirty-four

Minnow was allowed a complimentary bag of cotton candy, and as tempting as it was to devour on the spot, she made up her mind to bring it home for Windy. Maybe it would help her feel better on the inside and take her mind off the bad feeling on the outside. She'd save it for her if she was asleep when she went home.

Minnow searched for Matt, bumping into Bumble at the Carrousel, who pointed her in the direction of the corrals, where she had no choice but to smile brightly and greet Sailor Man Sharp on her way past.

She told herself not to feel self-conscious; after all, as Maximus she never went without her ballcap, and tonight she deliberately wore just her new haircut. Along with blue diamond earrings she borrowed from Windy the other morning, and distressed jeggings to keep out the mosquitoes and accentuate her narrow hips. Normally Minnow wore boyfriend jeans and a tee, but as long as she was moonlighting as herself, and by day pretending to be Maximus – would that be sun-shining as? Oh well, anyway, as long as she was pretending to be a boy, she needed to look as much like a girl as possible when she was herself. So, she went on telling herself, apart from sporting short hair for the first time in her life, she shouldn't look suspicious at all. So she acted confidently, normal, bluffing herself into make believe that she wasn't a rider in the pony swim.

Sailor Man Sharp greeted her back warmly but she felt his questioning gaze as she strode with purpose swiftly up the fencing.

Unable to yet bump into Matt, Minnow wove her way into the stall part of the area, doing a swift walk down the tiny dirt pathway under the stall stable awning.

"Enjoying the carnival?" asked someone in the shadows of a pine tree by the chute fencing.

Minnow swirled with a ready smile, recognizing Hammer's tone and making out it was him in the dim. "You know me," she answered. "I'm off shift and was looking for Matt – have you seen him?" asked Minnow. "Bumble said he was around here."

"Went chasing a pretty filly," answered Hammer in his usual gruff manner. "Of the two-legged kind."

328

Carly.

"Thanks, I'll catch up to him eventually I guess," said Minnow, and before she could take two steps Hammer's voice stopped her. "Glad to finally have you onboard kiddo," he said. "You're doen real well."

Minnow swallowed. "Yep, me too. Spinning cotton candy is more fun than I'd imagined. And it feels good to help out," she replied.

"Cotton candy," repeated Hammer plainly. "What dreams are made of at the carnival."

"The sweetest kinds," answered Minnow smiling. She tipped her head to Hammer, who tipped his carpenter company hat forward in response from where he leaned on the wooden slats of the corral-chute right before the kennel fencing started. The best with a hammer and nails, he'd been tasked with repairing an old railing and must have been taking a break when Minnow traipsed along, which would account for why she hadn't heard any noise indicating anyone was there in the shadows.

As she walked away from the penning and towards the Ferris Wheel, careful not to slip on the patches of carnival sweet pine shats, she had the strangest feeling that there was a double meaning in Hammer's tone.

But he couldn't know? She'd be kicked out this very minute if any of the saltwater ponyboys knew, even though they were fellas she'd known all of her life growing up. Fellas who respected her parents and watched she and her sisters grow from sproutlings into young girls. No girls permitted to ride in the pony swim was tradition. And it had never been broken. Until now – with Minnow.

But it was vital nobody find out. It had to remain a secret so that Minnow could ride in the rest of pony penning, and so that Matt didn't face exile.

Minnow had been riding the Ferris Wheel endlessly for half an hour. Walking through the carnival crowd, Matt spotted Minnow gazing in lost thought as the bucket wheel churned up and down like a windmill. He waited below for two more sets until her bucket was second to last on the entrance-exit platform. How long had she been riding? From her lazy yet serious state, a good while. When lost in thought, it's like a rainy day, and time evaporates. He was curious and concerned about what had smoothed the smile from her face and replaced it with such concentration. Matt planned to tickle the reason out of her if need be to replace her smile on the thrown of her cheeks, where it belonged like sunshine in the face of the sky.

Minnow was surprised when Matt plopped down beside her, the volunteer who secured everyone in their bucket securing the guardrail.

Before Minnow could squeak they'd moved up two spaces for the transference and exchange of riders in the bucket seats behind them.

"I thought you were snuggle-bug with Carly," said Minnow, with a half knowing half sly look.

"It was just getting snuggle-bug behind the Pony Fries when Harry chirped her phone," answered Matt.

The twinkly wheel was churning air and the delight as well as fright in some of their riders. Lights twinkled at them like oval stars or someone spinning a can poked with holes hugging a tender flame inside it.

That was apropos, because that was how Minnow was feeling right now. How Matt made her feel. She was mixed about these stirrings.

At the same time she wanted to know how and why and exactly "what" this was, she'd also fought it, battling with herself to push it to the back of her mind or the bottom of her stomach.

"What are you up to?" asked Matt. "From down there you looked like something was bothering you."

"Nothing," said Minnow, promising herself that as well as Matt knew her, he wasn't a mind reader. "I'm waiting for the fireworks. Weren't they supposed to start an hour ago?"

"You've been up here an hour?" asked Matt.

Minnow shrugged. "Weren't they?"

"That Front was coming through. It looks like it'll bypass us but to play it safe we delayed till eleven," he told her.

"Oh," she said, a little disappointed. Half an hour away. "I'd better get home then. We've got a big day tomorrow."

"Want a lift?" asked Matt. Their bucket had parked and Minnow hopped out first. "No thanks, Summer's letting me drive tonight," she said with a smile, slightly forced. She was trying to keep her edge out of her body language but she couldn't control it much longer.

"I'll let you drive," offered Matt. Great, he senses the reef she's constructed like a dedicated sea organism.

She grinned. "Yep, but that won't fly with Summer, or Mom and Dad. My foot can't reach your peddle that good. See ya tomorrow."

She waved and spun around walking through the carnival crowd and navigating the aromas normally delightful but right this minute burning her eyes, and turning her stomach.

Chapter Thirty-five

Minnow pulled open the cranky truck door and had to blink several times to adjust to what she saw staring at her inside.

Windy smiled at her from the middle of the seat as red as a beet. Minnow could tell her teeth were freshly brushed even more with her red face.

Summer peered around her from the passenger side. "She felt better after the shower and wanted to come," Summer told her, with explanation that resembled a hint of apology, understanding how overpowering Windy can seem. "Mom said it was okay."

Minnow hopped in and held up the cotton candy to Windy, who had already seen it.

"Keep calm," Summer ordered in a gentle tone when Windy gasped in delight, eyes widened.

"Okay," she whispered as she gently accepted the bag of fairy sweetened cloud from Minnow.

"This reminds me of something that happen the other night when we were at the carnival," Windy said, including them both in her jogged memory as Minnow found the peddles, adjusted to her shortness, and turned the key. The familiar sound of Mom's truck starting up soothed her some. As she pulled it in gear, she wished she'd been alone in the truck cab with Summer for two reasons.

Windy prattled – *prattled* – from start to finish with buildup about her friend throwing up after twelve rides on the Scrambler in a contest between them the other night to see who could hold their carnival food down longest.

Honestly, sometimes Minnow wondered and worried about her little sister. Minnow didn't want to see her sick, but *she* was getting sick of her incessant throw up tale!

Even Summer was struggling to hear the rest of it.

She wore an airy dress over her sunburn that Summer had applied multiple layers of aloe to already. How was she not feeling sick yet?

Minnow thought twice about that in view of Windy' story. Apparently, she had a pretty good gut – or her stubbornness about being first on what she wanted or not first on what she didn't want extended in ways and regions Minnow had never known about. Mind over matter, is powerful, she admitted. Then shook her head. She wasn't delving any deeper into Windy' gross story.

Minnow felt like confiding in Summer tonight. Telling her everything. From riding in the pony swim pretending to be a boy to pretending to date Matt so that Tarantella Girl would get jealous enough to dump Harry Macroscope and swing through the trees with her spider webbing to get back to Matt.

Summer was too disgusted with Windy' story and in the process of lecturing her on the five reasons why that was a terrible thing to challenge each other too, that she didn't pick up on Minnow's downtrodden mood, even while keeping one eye on the road as Minnow drove at a mud snail's pace. Besides, after halfway through Windy' tale Windy had drawn Minnow halfway out of her own shell of misery by the sheer sense of disgust that overpowered what was now not troubling her as much.

Minnow had fallen behind in learning how to drive for two reasons; one, most importantly, Minnow's feet couldn't reach the peddles that well, and two, practice during the summer was nearly mute because the kayak shop was busy twenty-four-seven.

She sat on two waterproof cushions normally used for kayaks just so she could see over the steering wheel.

Mom's red nineteen-thirty-six flatbed Ford had a long way to the wheels. She'd installed an adjuster though for when Minnow drove, which was a block of cotton wood strapped to the peddles.

Mom and Dad were fast asleep; they'd catch up on each other's days tomorrow. Minnow had smiled when she peeked in on them. What gold she and Summer and the pirate had struck when they got them for parents, thought Minnow warmly. They trusted the girls to be back at a proper hour. Or expected them to, and entrusted Summer to see to it. But that confidence spread to her and Windy as well.

But Minnow was lying to them.

Minnow had always been so small, she could squeak by or squeeze through anything. But this was one tight spot she didn't think she'd get through without getting stuck, and caught.

Minnow told Summer she was going to visit Marshy, and she did for a moment. But when she heard the first firework explode in the night sky, she had to climb the kayak shop roof and perch herself facing west with her back to Assateague.

Minnow was so focused on the sky she didn't see the tall sturdy shadow walking up the lane until she heard scraping. She brought her gaze from the burst of green and blue sparkles and saw Matt recovering from a minor slip as he made his way a little more cautiously up the rooftop where he perched himself next to her.

"Thought I'd find you here," said Matt.

"I was saying "night" to Marshy when I heard them go off," answered Minnow, gazing once again as several bursts of yellow and blue and orange flame exploded above the soft and fluffy pine tree tops. The breeze from the south east blew a few bugs their way, but so far this summer had been tolerable in the bug department. *If she didn't count Tarantella Girl of course.*

"Something's bothering you," he said softly.

Minnow couldn't hide it from Matt. She should've known better than to have tried.

"Talk to me Minnow," Matt said softly.

Minnow rested her head on his shoulder and tucked her hands forward between her knees.

Instead of mentioning the lightning bugs, Minnow confided in Matt something that had punched her in the gut just tonight.

"I just realized I've been lying to my parents," said Minnow, as Matt gently wrapped his arm around her like the gentle tether of a mooring to a fishing boat on a calm, lolling tide. "Not just keeping Summer out of the loop on everything. Windy can wait," she said, adding that last part a tad firmly. "I've just never done that before."

Matt waited a second before speaking. "Remember when we were five and eight and ten, and all those years in-between?" asked Matt, giving Minnow a feeling that this was just for

337

starters and he was leading up to something. "We weren't supposed to sneak into the thicket?"

They're thicket. Minnow and Matt and her sisters would sneak into the thicket pretending that they were explorers. They'd go in there at night with flashlights, and sneak into the neighbor's yard where there was a rope tied to a branch and swing from one junk pile to the next.

The hollow globe inside the towering patch of briers seemed as though it'd been hollowed out just for them. Of course, they thought up stories of how it got like that, played the same pretend stories out and added as time went on. Two dwarf cedar trees hid the entrance, and a short winding tunnel that orbed upward in a tiny and brief miniature of the first hollowed out and up portion led into the open Tall Grass, with trees on their far right, and denser thicket on their farthest left. Minnow was the best at navigating the thicket because she was always the smallest. But while Windy barged ahead and Summer cautioned that they shouldn't be in there, Matt and Minnow enjoyed the adventure. Matt never left Minnow behind and she never left him stuck in something, even when her parents were calling from Minnow's house or Matt's from down the lane.

"Of course, I do," answered Minnow. She'd almost gotten lost in memories.

"How about exploring the woods down the lane, behind Mrs. Camellia's and Mrs. Dee's with flashlights early in the morning?" he asked.

Minnow smiled. Those were some of her best childhood memories. Not that she's an adult. But that does feel like yesterday and yet a long time back. "What are you getting at?" asked Minnow.

"We weren't supposed to," said Matt. "But we did it anyway. Would you go back and change it?"

"Never," Minnow said, pulling her head from Matt's round shoulder and giving him a look. Why was he serious about asking her such a thing?

"If you could go back, would you change riding in the roundup?" Matt asked her seriously.

Understanding settled on Minnow. "No," she said plainly, and she knew it in her heart to be true.

"Do you want to back out of tomorrow?" Matt put it to her. He'd built up to the question in a way that she was forced to face herself and admit the truth.

"No," she said, and looked at him with confidence and earnest.

"You're following your dream, Minnow," Matt told her, cupping her shoulders caps and twisting her lightly and gently to face him on their delicate perch, but with firmness in his grip. Which was maybe also to keep her from falling. But to make his point, and Matt added, "If this is your dream, then chase it. You'd be dishonest to yourself unless you're true to yourself.

Dreams don't come true all on their own alone," he said. "You've got to chase a star if you want to ride it."

Matt pulled something from his back pocket and handed it to Minnow. Minnow's hands felt the shape but even in the dim lighting she knew it was her Dad's old, old ballcap she'd been wearing in the pony swim. She left it in Matt's truck today with her dirty clothes when she'd changed back into her Minnow clothes at his house.

Just like in the thicket when they were little, Matt was beside her and wouldn't let her down in a tight spot or leave her. She was in a tight spot again – but also within reach of her dream. She was living her dream this one week in summer. Which was all she'd ever wanted. She could not stop this far – she could not wither, or lose heart, this close to touching sky.

Minnow took Matt's words to heart. She knew he was right. And she knew she was right, and she knew she was also wrong. But Matt was right. She'd be dishonest to herself if she wasn't being true to herself. Riding in the swim was her dream. She'd chased it this far.

Minnow's heart pummeled in her chest with the thousands of sparkles exploding in the inky sky above the darkened green trees. Crickets chirped from the grass as though they were upset by the interruption of their melody, or were cheering on for *more, more fireworks!*

She could feel the singe of those sparkles like she felt the enthusiasm reignited in her blood.

She chose to believe the crickets were cheering on, *more fireworks.*

She got one shot at her dream. More than most will get in their life with trying. A fuse was lit. Just like the fireworks. Dreams never took flight without making some noise.

Chapter Thirty-six

There are days you look forward to for so long, you begin to wonder that they'll ever come. This morning, Minnow no longer had to wonder. She barely slept last night, as hard as she tried to go to sleep. She finally got up when her clock numbers were glowing 1:30am and gently shook Windy awake to ask something she hadn't asked since she was twelve.

"What," Windy mumble-whined.

"Can I sleep with you tonight?" Minnow whispered to her. "I'm can't sleep."

Windy didn't even open her eyes. Minnow saw her tired, happy smile in the silver moonlight as she lifted her arm with her light blanket like a wing that Minnow snuggled into. She snuggled herself in like piping plover in the beach grass, letting

Windy curl to her and wrap her arm with the blanket around her waist.

Minnow stroked her sister's long hair out of her face, Windy being one never to mind about her hair being in her face unless it was humid and sticky outside. But she shouldn't sleep with her hair in her face. Minnow has told her time and time again that it could wrap around her neck or work its way into her eyes.

But tonight, Minnow didn't chastise her sister. She simply stroked her hair away from her eyes and clear of her face, and then settled her arm around her.

Held close and snuggled to Windy, Minnow was able to drift off to sleep at last, until her watch alarm woke them both, and they scrambled out of bed, unclear right away as for which part of the pony roundup today was, but after the first three days of cruciality in getting up ahead of time, they found themselves scrambling out of habit.

"Ow, ow," whined Windy, taken by surprise though acutely aware her pain was from her sunburn.

Minnow had felt the heat of her sunburn radiating off of her last night. They'd gotten ahead of how worse it would have been using the aloe; but she's sure Windy didn't see it that way. Or she should say, feel it that way.

She moved stiffly and Minnow couldn't help but put herself in Windy' pirate boot shoes. She'd been in her condition of sunburned skin before, and being smaller and susceptible to things twice as much as others, Minnow empathized and sympathized with her sister. "You should've put sunscreen on again when Summer told you," Minnow scolded her softly and insistently.

"I know," Windy whined.

Minnow was torn only for a split second. "Here," she said to her, and with hands that barely touched her hot red arms gently guided her to a better sitting position on her bed.

Minnow grabbed up the bottle of aloe on the floor by Windy' pile of socks and sandals and a pair of her worn-out pirate boots she wore even in summer, and squirted a huge dollop in her palm, then slowly touched it to Windy' left arm.

"Take your shirt off," Minnow instructed Windy as though she were five again, when part of life was Minnow dressing and bathing her, or rather chasing her to change her clothes when she got dirty from playing outside. She'd been a very energetic, and slightly ferocious child.

Out of habit from those days, and being the big sister that she was, Minnow stepped easily into those shoes with second nature reflex and helped her little sister gently remove her thin and airy tee, glad for the cool breeze blowing through their windows. It would aid and hasten the effect of the aloe in relieving Windy' red jalapeno skin.

"I know what this is," Minnow said in an attempt to take Windy' mind off her burning skin.

She didn't fall into it immediately. "What are you talking about?" she said, tears glistening her eyes.

Her sister's discomfort and feeling bad made all of Minnow's edgy feelings towards her vanish as though they never existed and she was still just her baby sister.

"One of your skullduggery schemes? You figure getting sunburn will make me feel sorry for you and I'll forget about regulating our new privacy rules."

Windy appreciated that train of thought and smiled through the pain. "Sometimes my unconscious genius shocks me," she said thoughtfully but grimacing slightly.

Before she became too incorrigible Minnow snipped the subject in the bud and replied flatly, "Bless your heart."

She told her to turn around and grabbed up the bottle again, taking her time to squirt in zigzags across her back and spread it out and smooth the cool moister in with her gentlest touch.

"I think you've got sun poisoning. You need to stay inside today, and have Mom or Summer pick up more aloe and keep applying it – all day," she added the last part strictly, with pause in her efforts to peek around Windy' shoulder.

Once Windy nodded she continued, for the first time becoming aware of the burning on her own legs. She wouldn't let Windy know that part however; that she'd sunburned herself while treasure hunting in the sun with Matt. It could've been much worse for them both if it'd been during the pinnacle of the day.

Windy gasped, "Today's the swim!" She remembered for the first time since waking up and then being stricken by burning.

She'd slept so soundly with Minnow beside her that she hadn't felt her sunburn until she woke up. Which made Minnow's chest pull in with emotion.

She'd been tough on Windy lately, when all she wanted was her sister's closeness. Minnow needed to be more considerate of Windy. Again, Minnow was thinking that maybe the closer they were and the more time she spent with her would lessen her spoiled attitude and other self-centered tendencies; maybe she'd been using too much tough love, and letting her own temper get in the way of truly connecting with her little sister.

"I wanted to watch you drive the ponies across the water!" Windy said.

"Windy, you don't want to make yourself sick," Minnow ordered her just sternly enough. "You need to stay in bed."

Minnow pulled her legs forward so they stretched towards her, squirting dollops in Windy' hands so that she could dab her chest.

"What if I stay in the shade?" she suggested, grimacing.

"You know how sunburn is," Minnow reminded her, "once you've got it, especially when you've got it bad, the sun finds you even in the shade; it's like a magnet."

"What time's slack tide?" she asked in that case.

Minnow thought for a second. "Sunrise; around seven."

Just then they heard Dad and Summer loading boats into the truck for the pony swim.

"You can't go out in a kayak – that life vest will chafe..."

"I know," Windy interrupted, because the pain told her so. Just sitting here with a cool light breeze and cool moist aloe and she was on fire without a tight something hugging and chafing her body or the sun beating down over the trees on her red skin. "But I'm coming somehow," she told her more firmly, rubbing her chest with aloe gel a little more bravely.

There was no arguing with her. Arguing would only drive Windy to do something on her own, and that might not be a smart something she thought up. So, Minnow grasped the moment while Windy was still open to suggestions, and said, "Okay. Then have Mom drive you."

She seemed to like that idea. "Okay," Windy agreed, smiling through her furrowed face.

Her little sister was tough, Minnow thought proudly.

Mom would make sure she stayed in the shade too. Even if Windy was likely to get all the encouragement she needed from her own skin.

Minnow dressed in shorts and tee and stuffed her disguise clothes with ballcap in a small backpack to avoid Mom asking too many tiny questions that might add up big.

Stuffing her ballcap into the unzipped pouch, Minnow thought back to last night at their secret special meeting spot, and on what Matt had said. Thinking back on there last night made her smile, and she felt a surge of sturdiness, excitement, and the joy of and joy in embarking on an adventure, as well as joining in an adventure, grip her. Smiling twice as big in her heart, Minnow slid her backpack over one shoulder and quickly trotted downstairs.

Minnow retrieved Mom from the kitchen where she'd just poured a cup of steaming hot coffee. "Mom, I'm headed out; Windy wants to ask you something though. She's got a really bad sunburn," Minnow started, and Mom set her coffee cup down with a look that said she'd expected this to happen, not only this morning, but also sometime this summer.

"She's not going to like missing the pony swim tour," Mom made mention, and Minnow sensed a tender annoyance for Windy' carelessness.

"Maybe this will be just the thing to teach her to put her sunscreen on when she's supposed to," Mom commented, winding her hair into a neat bun.

For an artist, Mom had such silky hair. Not wild and thick like some artists Minnow had seen. Although raising three little girls, with one of them being Minnow and the other being Windy, it's impressive that she kept her neatness of hair, and neatness of everything else about her.

In the same way, Minnow was amazed by her mother's constant togetherness, she admired her for it too. She guessed there wasn't time for bad hair days or bad days or days off period when you were raising three young girls, or any children for that matter. It came naturally to Mom, the way her art did, the way kayaking did to Summer, Dad being Dad, Windy bringing back piracy, and Minnow loving horses and being around them.

"I just helped her put some aloe on."

Mom sighed, patting her arm in mother's well done and thanks. "I'll go take care of her; you have fun today, and don't work too hard down there at the carnival," she said smiling.

Mom's soft nature was endearing, and her protectiveness and fierceness underneath is where Minnow and Windy and Summer got a lot of their spunk, though Summer was more like Mom than either she or Windy.

Summer didn't get angry unless there was unfairness involved or the situation was serious, and even then, she had the captain's attitude to deal with the problem and solve it. Dad was the same way too; so Minnow and Windy seemed to be the only two volatile ones in the house, although Minnow wasn't volatile around anyone or anything more than she was Windy, who she loved just as deeply and deeper than the times of her most angry feelings towards her.

Minnow kissed Mom's cheek back and plodded out the door as she moved towards the staircase.

She'd been afraid before the week was over one of these morning's she would wake up too late and have to explain her early exit, or be forced to eat before she left, which would consequently make her late meeting Matt, and late to the next day of the roundup. But this morning she'd had to chance it for Windy, and because she'd stayed to help Windy in her distress, she'd fallen behind.

In the woods, Minnow rummaged her backpack and changed into jeans and another plaid, sleeves cut off tee. She'd left her boots in Matt's truck as well. Which worked out in her favor as it turned out, as sneakers were called sneakers for a reason.

She slapped her ballcap on and tugged it close, whisking through the Tall Grass and crawling through the thicket as a shortcut.

While falling behind had been her only concern, something else took its place with a thunderclap into her chest when Minnow reached Matt's house. Instead of risking being seen by someone down the lane leaving for work when they rousted, she jogged to Matt's through backyards and wooded areas she'd traipsed all her life. Minnow rounded the truck, fishing out her boots and stuffing her sneakers behind the seat. He had loaded Ish into the trailer and bolted it without Olive inside. "What's going on?" asked Minnow. "Where's Olive?"

Chapter Thirty-seven

"With foal," said Matt, looking a little disheveled. He'd obviously been trying to put together a plan B, and from his appearance and expression Minnow knew without asking, without success.

"How?" she asked, "They said Ish was a gelding when you bought him from the horse rescue sanctuary in Delaware, and in years nothing's happened."

"Remember when Olive pushed down the fence after all that rain in April?" Matt answered. "They found her on Assateague?"

"Oh," Minnow drew out with remembering. As sweet as the delicacy she was named after, Olive was one of the most mild-mannered horses one could come across. She was a lady, but very curious, and as so quite the escape artist. Minnow believed it had become a game for her after the first time. She escaped and they found her. Like Minnow played tag with Marshy, Olive was keen on hide and seek.

It made sense that as many pony penning roundups as she'd been on, she'd fallen in love with a stallion. Swimming the channel was a piece of cake for her – she crossed it every summer!

In spite of the situation Olive's romance had put Minnow in, amazement was blended in with her surprise and worry. "She's going to have a foal," said Minnow with gasping voice. She met Matt's eyes. "Matt, this is so cool! Olive's going to have a foal and the proud father is a stallion from Assateague!"

"Don't tell the whole neighborhood," Matt hushed her.

Then worry gripped Minnow. "Matt, wait – you're not going to tell the fire department, are you?" she said, trying to read his thoughts because she wasn't so sure about his expression. "You wouldn't turn over Olive's foal to the fire department, would you? It's Olive," she persisted.

"Of course, not," Matt argued, but was clearly conflicted even though he'd made up his mind. "I've broken one of the biggest rules of all anyway; what's one more," he said.

Even though Matt clearly didn't like the position it put him in, which was having to conceal something that technically didn't belong to him from who it technically did, Minnow knew the specialness couldn't be lost on him, and that he had to be excited deep down.

"That's the spirit," Minnow said, clapping him on the back like he'd done her on the beach her first morning as part of entering pony penning. "Besides, the foal has as much right to be yours as much as there's. Olive's the mother," she said, and leaned on the fencing with a gaze that took in Olive. Olive munched on another bale of hay, this one all for herself. She was eating for two after all.

Her pudgy belly made sense now. With seeing that, fear gripped Minnow. She was afraid to ask but forced herself to because she couldn't stand not knowing. "Did rounding up hurt her?"

"No," said Matt. "There are some mares we herded who are still pregnant on Assateague. But Olive's not a wild pony. Strong, with heart, yes, but she's goanna be taking it easy now, whether she likes it or not.

Minnow felt relieved, and wondered if this was how flowers felt when they were stepped on and then stepped off of. "I think she'll like it," replied Minnow.

Matt sighed heavily next to her and she knew his mind was still on his decision not to tell the fire department.

"You'll find a way to square it," Minnow assured him without doubt.

"Yep," Matt said, leaning next to her with a look like he had to hang out more laundry. "The fire department will receive a big donation at the end of the year, just as soon as I take a hammer to my piggybank."

"Oh Matt, this is going to be so much fun," Minnow said giving him a squeeze hug. "What will you name her or him? It'll be born in the winter. I guess you can think up some and when he or she's born whatever feels right, even if it's not one you had in mind," she rambled in excitement without realizing that she was.

"We're still in a pickle," he said, and it was then that Minnow remembered. The swim. No horse.

"What are we going to do?" asked Minnow, perking up straight. "Who do I ride?"

Matt lifted his ballcap and scrubbed his hand over his itchy head until his hair ruffled up but still no idea produced itself, and his expression said so. He hadn't shaved and the stubble made him look a little older than he was, and slightly harried, though it was evident they *were* in a spot.

Minnow also found herself forced to shake her head to stop herself from thinking the thoughts that sprung as stubbornly and surprisingly as crab grass; that stubble made Matt very attractive. *Very.*

First his arms. Then his stubble. She could growl. Minnow shouldn't think such thoughts. Matt was her best friend! Although he did get distracted by her in her bikini the other day;

355

so, she kind of owes him a payback. But not right now. They were in the middle of a crisis.

"There's not a rider-less horse on the island or off, pony week," replied Matt finally.

"Then what?" she said. Minnow started concentrating. There had to be an answer.

"Marshy," said Matt, "but she might give you away – even if she doesn't spook."

Matt would do this for her? Minnow was surprised, and touched, but only for a second.

"No, she won't, you'll see, I promise," Minnow said pointing and already backing up. "She's tougher than you think."

"Someone will recognize her – or you two together will jog their memories and the similarities could add up to who you really are," he pressed.

"No, it won't, I've got an idea," Minnow was saying, running. "Just be down the road in twenty minutes!" she hollered over her shoulder. She knew he understood by road she meant the road winding east side, because their word for the lane was the lane.

Minnow crept into the backyard along the side of her own house, and snuck back inside through the bathroom window. The humming told Minnow it was Windy in the shower and not Mom, which was a relief. The question running through her mind was, where was Mom?

On her way through, with a peek between the bayberry, Minnow had noticed Dad was back with the truck – Mom must be helping Dad and Summer and Coby prepare to receive customers already.

Mom would assume that Minnow was already bound for the carnival, as she'd told them she would be early most every morning to help clean up and do light preparation for the night, and she'd already seen her off minutes earlier. It wouldn't be good if Mom caught Minnow and asked a lot of questions like, what was she doing back? Wasn't her Minnow wearing shorts, sneakers, and a light blue t-shirt? Why bring Marshy to the carnival with her? Questions that could give her away in a heartbeat, because the answers would be very badly thought up fabrications.

Minnow wormed through the window onto the washing machine and eased herself onto the tiled floor. She could tell her sister was dancing by the tone of her voice and humming and pictured her using the showerhead as a microphone even before she saw her posing shadow. "Windy," whispered Minnow in a hoarse tone.

Windy screamed and sprayed Minnow from the shower!

Minnow scrambled behind the scratchy, three shades of blue tones towel hung along the rail to the bathroom door as she shouted out, "Stop it, it's me, Minnow!"

Gasping, Windy lowered the showerhead into the tub and covered her mouth as Minnow peeked out from behind the towel, water tickling her head as it dripped down her face.

"I'd appreciate it, if you'd respect my privacy," said Windy, forcing herself not to chuckle outright as she said it, which made her chin dimple and her pressed lips curl inward unusually with the amount of control it required.

Minnow bit the sourest words on her tongue. "At least I gave you fair warning before I sprayed you!"

"What do you want?" asked Windy, acting like the Windy she knew so well. Spoiled, self-centered, gloating. She felt more like herself in that cool shower Mom must have eased her downstairs for and helped her step into. Once she got out though and it wore off she'd be back to burning and feel bad and wanting affection and cuddles.

How had she looked to her for sisterly closeness last night to cling to and help her sleep? Minnow thought in a spurt of irritation. Next time, she told herself in her mind, she's going to Summer.

"I need your help, but if you don't want to help me," said Minnow, feeling like the one holding a showerhead nozzle now as she nonchalantly straightened and emerged from behind the towel. That shut down her gloating and suddenly nice little sister Windy was back, eager to help and play a part in Minnow's mutiny, which now sounded a little drastic to Minnow for what she was doing, even though it was probably an accurate description in the grand scheme of things, taking the whole picture into account. She was breaking all the rules, snapping in-two almost a hundred-year-old tradition, and bringing in her little sister as coconspirator. Yep, that sounded like mutiny.

"Don't slip!" Minnow scolded her sternly as Windy scrambled to get out of the shower and gently dabbed at herself to dry off.

Minnow threw the towel she'd hidden underneath onto the floor and moved it around with her foot to mop up the puddle, simultaneously ordering, "Where's your one-day hairspray?"

"In my treasure chest, why?" Windy said hurriedly.

"Get dressed, I need you to show me how to use it, I'll tell you on the way," Minnow said, leaving her sister in suspense to hunt up the hairspray. It would be good for Windy to experience a little patience, unpleasant as it was.

The house was so quiet that the crunch and idle of cars settling into gravel and clamshell driveway, and tires softly rolling over grass reached Minnow through the window screens. She paused to identify that it was the pony swim tour customers arriving, only for a second. East Side was normally quiet, apart from Mom's bandsaw, and except when a neighbor had family down. And so in the dark of night or dim predawn Minnow often laid in bed identifying the different sounds of nature. The wind blowing in the marsh grass. A house sparrow poking at a nook where the roof overhangs the house. Hoping to find a soft spot where he can hollow out a hole for his nest. Marshy munching on grass. Pacing anxiously up and down the fence, waiting for her to come and play or feed and brush her.

However, there was no time for those enjoyments this morning.

Windy hadn't even combed her hair, just dried off and dressed while Minnow hunted for the one-day hair-dye on Windy' half of the room where she said it would be.

Her treasure chest at the foot of her bed was crowded and overstuffed, and running slim on time Minnow just scooped everything out to filter through it on the open space of the floor.

Minnow lifted it up like lady liberty's torch!

"Short story, Olive's pregnant, so I'm riding Marshy," explained Minnow when she and Windy collided in the doorway.

"Ow," Windy winced, hobbling backwards.

"Sorry!" Minnow grimaced too, and she meant that sorry.

She didn't have time for an argument over respecting each other's personal things, so she shooed Windy forward, not too hard because of her sunburn but enough to make her want to back up out of reach and closed the door on Windy' rummaged treasure chest before she could see it.

Dressed in a light airy spaghetti strap beach dress the soft color of peaches that looked as though its color itself would sooth her sunburn, they galloped downstairs and raced across the back yard, her sister barefoot and Minnow wearing boots sweeping across the grass louder than Windy.

"Won't they recognize Marshy and put two and two together?" asked Windy. She gasped! "What if *Mom* recognizes her!"

"Not if we use this?" revealed Minnow smiling as she stopped at the paddock and held up the spray.

Why was Windy frowning? "Minnow this won't hold up to humidity," burst Windy, snatching the spray can from her.

Minnow frowned. "Why not?"

"It's temporary," she extrapolated, "that's the only reason why Mom and Dad let me use it for the opening of that movie last year," she exclaimed. "Once you hit water or sweat, it starts bleeding."

"Then, we'll just have to take a chance," answered Minnow, calm and assured. She climbed the fence next to Marshy, who had trotted over and tossed her head with anticipation. She knew when adventure was instore.

Windy followed right behind her.

"What'll you tell them if they ask?" said Windy sprinting next to Minnow who dashed to the tack room, hefting saddle from the horizontal pole, and unhooking halter from its flathead nail.

"What should I tell Mom?" she insisted in an urgent tone just shy of a loud whisper.

"The truth; Olive is pregnant," Minnow started, and as she went on, it made perfect sense. "Pony penning week there's no rider-less ponies on the island or off," she said, repeating Matt's information. "We'll say that Minnow, me, let Maximus ride Marshy, because Matt asked."

She'd smoothened Marshy' hide in preparation for placing the blanket and saddle on her back. Marshy knew that this meant going outside of the paddock, on a ride, and she stayed unwaveringly still.

"They all know me and Matt are best friends."

Minnow swung the lightweight western saddle with inside padding to add comfort for Marshy, over Marshy' blanketed back and let it rest snuggly.

"They'll never question it."

"Doesn't sound like the truth to me. You'd never let anyone ride Marshy. You won't even let me ride her sometimes, even though I'm not a horse person and haven't, or wouldn't really ask," replied Windy harmlessly, not being mean just making an observation that happen to be thoughtless. And right.

Minnow had just cinched the saddle and stood up straight, resting her hand on Marshy' withers. "Since when is your pirate chest chuck full of scruples?"

"I didn't mean anything like that," Windy hurried to say, but also defend herself with, "but I might like piracy, and I enjoy mutiny, but that doesn't mean I don't value the truth."

"Then don't say things like I'm being dishonest," replied Minnow.

"I'm sorry, it just slipped out," insisted Windy.

Calm, and unexplainably without irksome feelings or spikes, Minnow stopped what she was doing, which there was nothing more to do. Marshy was saddled, haltered, and eager to join her friend in this adventure.

"I'm doing what I was born to do. I'm being true to me; and living my dream," she said. "That's the truth that matters, right?"

Windy gripped her shoulder, looking directly into her eyes. "You don't need to convince me Minnow. Or yourself; now ride."

Minnow was grateful for her little sister's support, and hugged her gently. She started to mount when Windy said, "Could you put my hair back first?" Wincing, she was clearly in distress over her annoyingly long hair sticking to her skin in that in-between stage of drying and yet no longer wet. "It felt good before it started drying. Now it's annoying me, and I can't lift my arms or my skin hurts."

"Yep, sure," said Minnow willingly and confidently, taking the pocketed hairband from Windy, who turned around and dropped low enough for Minnow to scoop her hair neatly back and wind it into a clean bun, which she secured with the hair tie.

Note to self; there's a new reason why Windy keeps her hair out of her face, besides when it's muggy.

Sunburn.

"Thanks," replied Windy with relief, turning around looking like she felt a thousand times better.

"No problem," said Minnow smiling, then she mounted as Windy unlatched the gate and held it open for her. "I think I want to buzz my hair like yours," she was saying as Minnow and Marshy rode through gate.

"I'll do it if you want," Minnow told her with a mischievous smile. A proposal which made Windy' smile spread.

Minnow liked this side of Windy, and herself. They could get along without always irritating each other, and she would be the first to admit it if she was asked. Being nice to each other was way better than bickering.

"Hey, don't forget this!"

Minnow twisted in the saddle in time to catch her ballcap that must have fallen off when she'd hugged her. Minnow tugged it on, brim set against her eyebrows, and dipped her brim with a smile in Windy' direction.

Windy saluted loosely as she grunted, "It's a pirate's life for me," and hung onto the gate as though it were a rope to the sail as Minnow turned and spurred Marshy into a light canter across the bright green grass growing brighter with every new shade of first light.

The moon hung silver and heavy on the horizon to her back when Minnow and Marshy met Matt down the road where he'd picked her up last time. Together they loaded Marshy next to Ish, who she hadn't seen in almost a month. They'd have a lot to talk about on the drive to Assateague.

During the trip, Minnow explained her plan to Matt, who agreed the gamble was worth a try. As it happened, Bumble and Sailor Man Sharp were the first to inquire about the missing lady Olive, and Matt explained. They both figured there would be less questions if the story came from Matt, and after all, Maximus wasn't supposed to know Minnow that well. So, the favor was to Matt, not his cousin from Rhode Island.

Everyone caught ear of it, and didn't question the reason. Not even the old-timer Russ, who didn't really pay much attention, as he was fixed on doublechecking his horse Boy Scout, focused on the task upon them. Chowder listened next to Russ as he also doublechecked his horse's halter and saddle cinch.

Minnow stroked Marshy' forelock and kissed her plain brown marsh mud forehead to reassure her, but she wasn't trembling out of fear. She trembled with excitement.

Assateague, a herd of ponies, and the horses underneath the saltwater ponyboys', thrilled Marshy, who had been cooped up at home while Minnow was out adventuring and participating in the roundup. Minnow was reminded in this moment, that while Marshy' sweet grass sweet nature left her open to nippers the way their small size left them both open to being overcrowded and overwhelmed, Marshy was also adventurous like Minnow.

Matt would see that today.

She had a toughness in her sweet and joyful nature like Minnow, who can get a bruise without blinking and actually strived to see if she can still get more grass stains than Matt, a competition they'd probably never outgrow, or want to outgrow. A game that comes with bruises and scrapes and knots and soreness.

Marshy and Minnow were small and sweet and friendly and fun-loving; tough, adventurous, and brave. Like the marsh grass, marsh mud, the seagulls and the crabgrass. They belonged here.

When the saltwater ponyboys turned their horses to the fence, Minnow and Matt exchanged grins that bespoke just what she was feeling inside. She was still, and just, another one of the boys.

Chapter Thirty-eight

Bumble offered Minnow the honors of unlatching the gate. When she looked up and glanced at the expressions of the saltwater ponyboys astride their horses, it appeared that this had been discussed and everyone agreed.

Smiling, Minnow nodded her head one big time, and handing her reins up to Matt, who sat nearby atop Ish, she approached the gate.

Ears pricked forward in curiosity, while a small band pinned themselves in a defensive position on the far side of the penning. They were smart, and probably convincing themselves it was not hot enough to go for that swim Minnow was about to invite them to.

"Don't be like that," she told them, "if I could swim today in this heat, I'd be right in the water with you. You've got the fun part."

Minnow unlatched the gate and put her back into pushing it open as wide as it would go. Instantly a number of saltwater ponyboys trotted through to herd the wild ponies out of the penning.

Marshy lifted her head and whinnied sharply. She didn't know what was going on right away and the sudden sea of horses and ponyboys flooding past her startled her at first.

Minnow met Matt's look but told him with her eyes that she was confident in Marshy still.

Next to Ish, the white grey mellowed her almost just as soon as she'd startled.

Minnow took the reins, knotted as always at the tips, and soothed Marshy by stroking her neck and letting her hear her actual voice, which she kept low enough to blend into the noise of popping whips, hollers, and disgruntled ponies. But next to Marshy, she heard Minnow and felt her breath on her hide.

Marshy arched her neck, pointing her ears straight up with a wide-eyed expression as though insisting, I'm fine, what's wrong with you?

"Good girl Marshy," Minnow told her, moving to stand in front of her. She gripped her halter with both hands and kissed her forelock, then still gripping her halter held Marshy while the herd plodded and pushed as they flooded from the penning. "We've got this girl," reassured Minnow, attracting half of Marshy' attention, and her eye-contact every time she spoke.

The sticky air was muggy hot and the apprehension and foreknowledge vibrating from the herd felt like those buzzing bugs in the marsh and her backyard on a restless night that's too hot to sleep. The anticipation stuck to her and the saltwater ponyboys like the mugginess was doing.

Once the last of the wild ponies were being herded up the road, Minnow mounted Marshy, patting her shoulder with reassurance. Marshy didn't need it now, and let Minnow know by the decisive squeak neigh she gave. Minnow answered by giving Marshy her head and sank her seat into the saddle, gripping rein and clumps of mane as Marshy galloped to catch them up to the rest.

Marshy was bursting with curiosity and excitement at seeing new and old faces, as well as to be riding in the pony swim. Sweet-natured Marshy always did have a social side as well as a knack and eagerness for adventure.

Eagerness like when she smelled Mom's homemade waffles fluffing up and crisping in the iron smasher. *That's what it did,* Minnow told herself; *smashed batter into waffles.* If Minnow was atop Marshy she'd still bolt to the kitchen window and beg for takeout, or if she was penned in the paddock press her neck to the top railing and pace while continuously making a ruckus until her throat could only moan and she eventually got her waffles.

Bearing this in mind, Minnow reined Marshy in when they reached the rear flank of the herd because she wanted to trot over and introduce herself.

Marshy obeyed, but Minnow watched her closely. She had perhaps encouraged this with their midnight rides or when she and Windy were littler and they'd sneak into the Tall Grass and woods behind the house exploring and playing pretend. Windy always wanted to play the Search for El Dorado pretend-game, and Marshy was their trusty conveyer.

Again, Minnow rubbed Marshy' thick neck to settle her a tad. They brought up the rear flank with Miles, cousin Freddy, Bumble and Matt.

Right where lazy Bumble and bruised Maximus belong, Minnow thought smiling. She'd share her joke with Marshy when they were home and well out of earshot of the saltwater ponyboys.

Being the first muggy day they'd sweltered since pony penning week started, these five in the back with Minnow and Marshy agreed that they were lucky to have skimmed through the roundup portion with their biggest annoyance being direct, glaring heat and biting monster greenhead flies. To contend with mosquitoes now at this stage was doable.

Ballcap tugged low on her beaded forehead as usual, Minnow stole a risky glance away from the herd to scan the shimmering water. It held the appearance of moving but underneath was calmer than Minnow's pulse. She panned the nearby shore for Dad's pony penning group. Minnow didn't spot them at once, and after adjusting Marshy to quarter off a mare testing her boundaries, Minnow looked again. This time she spotted the group. Serious Dad. Mindful Summer. Steady Coby. Like Marshy and Minnow, they flanked the group of thirty-plus people taking in the experience from their kayaks by snapping photos and conversing, corralling them up nearest the marsh as any experienced kayaker or kayak guide would do.

Minnow had been on those trips and knew them well. The water was so shallow where they anchored for the wait, she'd stick her hand in the cool water and touch her palm to the silt and almost gooey mud. She even watched minnows swimming underneath her kayak and nibbling her hand. Windy played with the mud snails and saw how many she could find, until Summer scolded her to put them back in the water before they expired. So naturally next year she'd brought an empty jam jar with her.

Minnow had held a paddle last year, and pressed her hand into the marsh mud. She gripped Marshy mane and reins in her hands this year, and traversed the mud.

She smiled, and to keep doing it by going unnoticed she repositioned Marshy on the opposite side of the anxious herd, bringing up the front left shoulder.

Marshy as it turned out was a natural at this. It had to do with when Marshy was still a wobbly-legged, big-knee filly, and Minnow, Summer, Windy, and Matt, would play freeze-tag with her in the backyard.

She'd caught on quickly to the game, and squeaked and crossed her legs in the sudden changes of directions, trotting after Minnow every time.

They were a team, and today, part of a larger team, were doing what they were each born to do. Pony Swim.

Minnow, Matt, Bumble, Spencer, and Hammer, in concert with the rest, flanked and gathered at the rear in a half ring, whips snapping extra incentives as they drove the ponies from the marsh.

Clear that this was the only direction, the herd followed and few defied or tried to sprint. Minnow guessed that at the sight of water they were ready to cool off and plunged into the slack water.

Splashing, the crackle of whips snapping muggy salt air. Horses grunting, complaining, and calling to one another, flaring muzzles huffing sweet air, with heads protruding bowsprits to the water they sloshed through. In the water, it was no different than on land for the herd. They bumped each other and a stallion nipped at another stallion when he got too close.

Some saltwater ponyboys entered up to their mounts' chests. The snap of their whips on the water, encouraging the herd to keep moving, lost their sharpness and sounded like dull claps, shooting sparkling water droplets in the muggy air. It was nothing short of breathtaking, and being mesmerized.

Bumble, Sailor Man Sharp, Matt, Cheddar, and Russ.

Minnow had to rein in Marshy when she plunged into the water, wanting to swim with them as well and splash in the cool rejuvenation of the saltwater.

"No, Marshy," Minnow almost gasped, reining her in just a few feet in the water. She backed her disappointed friend up and turned her around.

Matt nodded approval and Minnow returned likewise. Marshy was tempted to socialize and play but she wasn't behaving unruly. Minnow had told Matt they could count on her.

Otherwise these few tense moments, the breathtaking scene was peaceful. Inspiring.

Marshy whinnied, then snorted, shifting her weight in the gnat and mosquito dotted bogginess. Minnow gently reeled her right rein right, nudging Marshy' belly with her right blunt heel for encouragement. Marshy veered right towards the red railing, flat bottom barge with sturdier, un-sinking ground. Once onboard, Minnow tethered Marshy comfortably to a lower railing.

Minnow and Marshy watched the majestic scene of the ponies swimming from through the railing as the barge rocked with more riders loading. She was a rider, smack dab in the middle of the swim with Marshy. Minnow contained her thrill between her and Marshy. The barge started moving, affording seconds to find their sea-legs. Minnow and Marshy were smaller than anyone, but it was still crowded. Minnow lifted her arm under Marshy' neck and stroked the other side in case she got nervous. Her eyes glued to the nicely progressing herd. People in boats hollered and clapped to keep them herded and moving in the right direction.

Minnow grinned when the applause of the audiences ahead, knee-deep in mosquitoes and mud, as well as those aboard boats, snapped every horse ear to attention, including Marshy'.

They'd made it safely across.

The saltwater ponyboys and Minnow rested the recuperating herd before parading them down the street at a gradual pace up to the carnival grounds. The crowd was quarantined from the road by easy in the saddle saltwater ponyboys, encompassing the ponies in their center. Happily, there were no incidents that occurred besides one overenthusiastic photographer who stepped on someone's foot. Parents were holding twice as tightly to their little girls' hands.

Minnow waved at them, and was touched when the shy ones smiled and happy when the other little girls waved heartily back.

Did they recognize another girl when they saw her? Minnow couldn't help wondering, and it made her feel special that a little girl may have really seen "her" ...and that she shared this secret with them.

Heading up the clamshell road beside the carnival fencing was the homestretch. Veering right, through the fence opening, strings of red, white, and blue triangles created a line for some of the crowds and a sort of broad funnel for the ponies in the fairgrounds. Minnow and Marshy were part of the group driving and yet leading them up this grassy part and through the double-gated fencing.

Troughs of water and mounds of hay awaited the exhausted wild ponies. Marshy and Minnow didn't feel a bit tired enough to slack off now. While Marshy joined the big horses by their own trough and piles of hay, finally getting the social time she'd eagerly been waiting for, Minnow helped Matt where ever he needed it. Unloading the pregnant mares from the trailers that had trucked them across the bridge so they wouldn't have to swim, was the main thing.

Unloading the precious newborns from the other trailers was her favorite thing she'd done the entire pony penning!

They were tiny, spunky, one or two so gentle that they let Hammer and Bumble pick them right up.

"That one's Queen Neptune," Matt said and pointed out to her.

Minnow had stood alone at the fence admiring the herd. Marshy and the other horses were in their own pen feasting hay, oats, and troughs of fresh water.

Minnow now stood on her tiptoes to see around its mama. She'd been focused on the herd and letting Marshy know she was there with her the voyage across the water. She'd missed which foal had landed first.

Had it been a colt, he'd be crowned King Neptune. Every year, the King or Queen Neptune foal was raffled off as a buyback. Anyone can enter and in a way, everyone wins. Including the foal!

Just at that moment the little filly wobbled from behind her mother and halted, unsteady on her legs, probably still remembering swimming through the water for the first time. Chestnut, with a white stripe up her forelock and splattered in the top and lower part of her fuzzy mane, she looked interested in everything. Which reminded her of Marshy when she first laid eyes on her.

"She so cute! Queen Neptune. Doesn't she remind you of Marshy when she was a baby?" asked Minnow, breaking her gaze of enthrallment only long enough to check Matt had heard her and see him nod.

"I'm goanna name her Minnow though," Matt said, crossing his arms.

"Why? Because she's Chincoteaguer small?" asked Minnow.

"She's not the only Queen Neptune this summer," he said, and looked her way with one of his subtle, knowing smiles that held more depth than the channel.

Minnow took his words to heart. And today indeed, of all days, she felt royal. Royally good; and right where she wanted to be.

The food area had opened up for the volunteers and saltwater ponyboys. It was one of the first things Minnow noticed when they rode in; it'd wafted right up her and Marshy' nose. Minnow remembered thinking how thankful she was that there weren't waffles cooking! She could just see herself trying to rein in Marshy and hold on as she stampeded up to the counter and whinnied an order of fluffy breakfast!

As morning waned into noon they partook of the buffet of carnival hotdogs, hamburgers, and sparkling cold water and chilling fountain soda with ice cubes!

Minnow didn't hold back her smile. Why couldn't Maximus grin?

Minnow was beaming. She felt a kinship with her ancestors. But mostly friendship, with Bumble and Hammer and Cheddar. Regardless that neither they, nor Sailor Man Sharp, didn't know he'd been riding alongside the little girl he'd watched grow up on East Side. She admired and had newfound respect from riding in the swim, for these Teagures. And for herself. She'd done it. This was where she belonged.

Chapter Thirty-nine

How did Minnow let this happen?

Since they were guppies, two people have been each other's left and right arm. Closer than most siblings. Matt was never a brother in any sense, or the one who cautions adventuring, but someone who cautioned her on the best ways how. Matt felt like – Matt *was*, another member of her family; with his own name, his own special place, in her heart.

Like one of her special places was that groove in his shoulder and collarbone area when she took naps with him – and sometimes drooled.

So, how did Minnow let this happen between them?

Perhaps the better question was, why did not more friends find themselves in Minnow's shoes?

When Minnow thought about it in that way, they were perfect for each other. They could tease one another too far and spring back from it without fail.

Had they been inching in this direction for some time? When did the first inkling spark?

Minnow could go back years to when her grudge over Matt's time shared with Tarantella Girl intensified. Were they twelve? Tarantella Girl's shallowness was never a surprise to Minnow, and for the longest time Minnow believed Matt was blind to her self-serving trait; but according to what he'd told her on the beach and then from what she'd overheard that day from the balcony, he was well aware. And at last Minnow had seen in Tarantella Girl, what Minnow had always a missed or refused to acknowledge possible. That there was a little more to Tarantella Girl than snobbery and shallowness. Or spiders.

Minnow thought back, trying to pinpoint when she started being jealous of Carly instead of just disliking?

Little moments she took for normal, as friendship, and indeed they were this as well. They now stood out like road signs, as big indicators.

Minnow's continuous and intense aggravation at Matt for choosing Carly over and over to date; her nausea and the violent desire to fill her bilge-pump with water and pump it over Carly when Minnow saw her tickle her finger down his nose like she did whenever she wanted her way or thought it was romantic – when what it really looked like was the spider seducing its prey!

Minnow tickled Matt and Matt tickled Minnow; Carly didn't even know where he was ticklish, did she!

If she was trying to tickle him, Matt wasn't ticklish anywhere but his right side and his right foot.

That's when. Minnow had felt the shift, she realized, noticing this change for what it really was, in hindsight. It started with the tickle the nose gesture. In eighth grade?

Then, when it came to kissing – Minnow just couldn't look. She left it at that. The feelings were mixed and too strong then, and they still were now.

Her heart plummeted in the cotton candy booth when she'd spotted Carly bounce up to Matt and link herself to him. Actually, physically, plummeted. *Kerplunk!*

The same as and more heavily than the shark tooth Matt startled her into dropping in the swell of a wave.

Minnow loved Matt Evers. She'd loved him like a girl loves a boy for some time.

They were still, and would ever be each other's wingman, and partners in crime.

Would they ever be those two who fall in love, partners in crime?

Could Matt love her back the way she now knew she loved him?

Would Minnow be right to chance maybe not for maybe yes, by confiding in him, as she'd done all their lives?

Minnow was now faced with maybe winning his heart, if she spoke up, or maybe losing their special friendship and that place in the groove of his shoulder if she did, as well?

It felt like a month not half of a week, when Minnow was dressing in her room following her nice cool freshening shower. She was sore, sleepy, and wanted to just collapse in her bed right now. So, inviting. So, soft...

But she'd promised Matt and he'd helped her get through the pony swim this far. She had to give her side of the bargain her best shot. Not to mention the chance to turn her arch enemy green with envy was a once in a lifetime chance. Yet that had somehow lost its taste; knowing that in the end she would have lost Matt.

Tonight, that meant attending the meteor shower watch on Assateague. Summer and Windy were going, and so at least Minnow would have someone to roast marshmallows with when Tarantella Girl cornered Matt somewhere quieter and declared she loved him still; who was Harry Macroscope?

Minnow knew she was using humor to blunt the edge and sting of giving Matt up to Tarantella Girl. But what could she do? She was just Minnow; and Minnow didn't mean star-cross, the girl I can't breathe without, my every heartbeat, or *I choose you,* in Matt's heart.

She was Minnow. Plain, ticklish, flare prone, spelunker partner, adventure loving, best friend on the rooftop, Minnow.

The only harder part of possibly kissing Matt tonight, for the last time – not even kissing her best friend in front her sisters, or classmates they'd known all their lives – was getting the words out to tell her sisters during the drive over there. She didn't mince words, since parsed they were so hard to tie together, and whole they spared her the agony of a lengthily explanation and stumbling through her embarrassment longer than she could endure.

Chapter Forty

On the beach, finding her way through the different parties and bonfires and small fires to where Matt said he would be nearest the ocean waiting with Coby, Minnow didn't even remember clearly what she said. She'd blurted something like, "Matt and Tarantella Girl broke up so I'm pretending we're dating to make her jealous so she'll get back with him."

"*What!*" they both demanded pointedly at the same time. Then Windy had to gasp with exclaim. Sharply, loudly, shocked! It felt like a punctuation to her embarrassment and public embarrassment pending!

"Why would you do that?" Summer asked, but Windy was laughing. Minnow elbowed her, hard, but that didn't even rile her, she just squirted giggles more.

"Because he's my best friend," Minnow was explaining but surprised herself at her unrapid pace, considering the bluntness with which she'd revealed all. "He's never going to see her for what she really is unless one day he has an epiphany, and that'll never happen if he's pinning after her," Minnow went on.

"Yes, it will," Summer stated calmly but with a strictness in her tone that told Minnow she disapproved of the scheme. "Everyone has those mountain peak moments. I couldn't date all my crushes, and by senior year I was glad for some of those I did not."

"Have you *kissed* him?" Windy asked with emphasis and a smiling voice and smiling face and smiling twinkly pirate eyes bouncing twinkles from off of headlights that passed them in the night, as well as from the dashboard dials glowing neon.

Right Windy, let's ask the important question!

She was enjoying this way too much.

Minnow rolled her eyes and rested her head on her hand, elbow propped on the window sill. "It's part of the charade," she said, deciding to own it, "of course we did."

But Pirate Briny Wind saw right through it, or hoping to stir up embarrassment where it ought to be found, she exclaimed, piercing the truck cab with new laughter.

"Windy, stop it, calm down," Summer told her mildly sternly, and Windy obeyed, muffling her laughter, which was worse somehow!

"There's more to it too," Minnow said. "Matt and I made a bargain. He gets me into the carnival, and I get him and Tarantella Girl back together."

Sitting back, Summer shook her head and bent it to the side to rub her forehead, blowing air out of her mouth. "You two are playing with fire," Summer replied, glancing at Minnow with a structured look as she placed both hands on the wheel again.

"I don't like it Minnow," Summer said. "You can still back out. Matt will help you no matter what."

Minnow wished she was alone in the truck so that she could confide in Summer. She wanted to tell her about those lightning bugs and sparks that faded and vanished but then when she thought that'd been the last one, she was wrong, and the sparks, though few, came alive, and the tingling...remembering the tingling, was still with her. She wanted to tell Summer how she'd kissed her last and only three boyfriends, one was in middle, the other two high school, and yet she'd never felt this explosion that she felt when Matt kissed her off-guard. She'd never had anyone who swept her to him the way Matt had on the beach Friday, just before the kiss. But that hadn't been the shock of her life.

That Matt had awakened this inside of her, shown this side of the world to her, the way someone introduces you to a forest view or undersea world when you've never seen them before. Maybe heard about them, so she'd known about them in that way.

"Can I talk to you, *alone.*" Minnow stated that one word while glaring at Windy, shriveled in the middle of the seat with her reverie. Although she could tell that got to her a tad. Being excluded never sat well with any of them, least of all Windy.

"Yes," Summer replied without a second thought or looking or glance at Windy, who sat up in her seat, smiling in defiance and pretending to still muffle her laughter just because she didn't want Minnow to win. Right now, such childish games were too petty and inconsequential for Minnow to even respond to. Her head was spinning. She dreaded Summer's disapproval. She felt mixed over Matt. Because if she gave up the charade early, she gave him up to Tarantella Girl, and whatever she felt on the beach with him those times, she would never get to dive into again, or get the chance of discovering where all this leads.

Chapter Forty-one

Minnow stood with Summer in front of the truck, whose expression was softer than her tone had been in the truck, with an unreadableness that prompted Minnow to speak.

"How did you know that you loved Coby," asked Minnow. Summer ever didn't require an interpreter for Minnow, nor now for what she meant by asking that one single question.

Instead of answering her question directly however, Summer answered it in another way. "I never saw you and Matt as ones to shift from best friends into more; But now that you're asking me that question – something's there, isn't it?"

"I don't know if anything long lasting is there; no, that's not true," Minnow corrected herself as a flood of honesty throughout her told her the truth.

"It could be; but not unless he feels the same. And that's just it," Minnow mildly rushed to stress. "It was just one moment we shared – and then, it was just one kiss; but I've never felt like I did when I kissed my other boyfriends."

"For Coby and me, it was star-struck. Love at first sight. I don't know how to tell you to navigate these waters little sis," Summer said softly, regretful, but still focused as though she maybe could give her some heading.

While folding her arms, and leaning her hip against the hood, as she settled into what Minnow innately knew was her soft, supportive, matter of fact, big sister mode, Summer replied in answer, "There are a lot of kisses and moments out there, Minnow. I wish I could help you to tell which one that kiss, and that moment you shared with Matt, was. What this feeling your feeling inside means; but this is something you've gotten yourself into, and only you can find your way out. You know how you feel, even if you don't really understand it clearly. You've got to find out how Matt feels," she answered.

Super. The girl who spends her life swimming into one minnow trap after another has to find her way out. That's never been her strongest suit, and when she did, it's usually a mess getting out.

"Try not to overthink it," Summer said in sisterly advice, and while Minnow didn't ask, she also pictured from experience. "Sometimes just letting yourself feel your feelings is the right path to see you clear. Listen you your heart."

"What if my heart's mistaken," said Minnow.

"If you're wrong, you're wrong," Summer said. "But you've got to see; how else will you ever know?"

"But I don't want to be wrong," insisted Minnow softly, shifting her weight.

Noticeable to her big sister, Summer calmed her racing heart by cupping her shoulder caps with tender strength. "But what if you're right?" she said.

"If this is something – and I tell him – I could lose him," said Minnow, her true fear and reason for hesitance, unspoken up till now.

"You can't think like that. You can't live that way," Summer said. "In life, you can't let being afraid bog you down or stop you from venturing. Feel it Minnow," she told her. "Let yourself feel it all."

"Whatever it is going on inside of you or regardless of whatever it is or isn't. Feel it; don't be timid."

"Remember your dream of riding in the pony swim?" Summer said in fresh approach.

At the sound of her saying the words *riding in the pony swim,* Minnow's eyes widened a diameter and her ears perked up. She nodded. "Yes."

"After all the no's of summers past, you haven't given up, have you?" asked Summer.

Minnow shook her head, and swallowed. "No." Summer had no idea how much she indeed had not given up, and how far she had reached and taken herself to make her dream come true. She wished she could tell her. She was tempted to when she got out of the truck, but hearing the words *rider* and *pony swim* from Summer's mouth was like spraying a fire extinguisher on that confession in her throat.

"Even when what doesn't pan out knocks us down; if it hurts, if it makes you cry, when someone rejects you – you keep being you. Keep chasing dreams. Use that rejection, that hurt as coal for strength. Do you see what I mean?" asked Summer.

Minnow nodded her head as the sea breeze lightly tugged her hem to grab her attention and coasted Summer's long hair across her back and to the left side of her face. It was silky tonight, but the salty air would soon return the curl and wavy to her brown golden streaked crown.

"Tarantella Girl said the other night at the carnival that we're mixed up. That I've convinced myself that I feel something real for Matt; and that he feels something real for me," Minnow said quietly, letting her quietly wondered worry come to the surface just enough to peek out.

"What does anyone know," she said, "to tell you, you haven't got this. Or can't because she said she doesn't think so. It's just you; you're the discoverer for you," Summer told her in closing. "There are too many sunrises to search; starts and finishes to explore. Human depths and heartfelt feelings no one's scraped the surface of – or worse – there are those who do not dare to."

Summer squeezed Minnow's shoulders in her grip with a sigh.

"I'll say this one last thing," Summer told Minnow for beginning. "You don't have to be right or wrong to follow your heart, or to go where you've never gone before."

"What do you have to be?" asked Minnow.

"Be? No. Feel," Summer said. "That's all the right you need to get you to your answers. Push forward and the gate will open for you. I don't know what will happen or present itself. You've gotta be brave enough to find out. *Your right.* That's the only right that matters."

Minnow was thankful for the cool gust off the tangy ocean. She inhaled.

"If you need me, I'm here," Summer replied softly, sturdily, kindly, and she didn't mean just tonight. She meant, as always, anytime, anywhere.

Minnow smiled a closed smile, and nodded. Summer pulled her in a tight and swaying embrace that had Minnow closing her eyes and pressing her cheek into her kayak-toned shoulder. She absorbed her sister's warmth and comforting smell. Clean, salty, sun-kissed, and slightly marshy.

"Is that all you wanted to talk to be about?" asked Summer on a lilt.

Minnow picked up on the teasing humor behind her simple question. She snorted a bolt of laughter, tickled by her phrasing and meaning. "Yep," she said. "No other world tilting, life altering, core deep realizations or questions for now."

"Okay," said Summer. Part of her voice sounded pleased, and the other layer, sisterly acceptance. Minnow wondered at it for only a moment. She'd honestly left nothing out about her confliction. She was thinking about that confliction right now. Soon, she'd come face to face with Matt; toe to toe with Tarantella Girl; and heart to heart with herself.

Chapter Forty-two

The meteor shower hadn't waited for Minnow or Summer, but she liked to think her star wasn't leaving without her. She'd chased her dream to ride in the pony swim. Buzzed her hair, pretended to be a boy, virtually lied to her parents – she admitted it, lied – and left Summer out of the secret. How much harder could it be to look her best friend in the eyes and tell him she'd fallen for him?

Minnow made her way through mazes of dispersed campfires with parties of recognizable classmates and locals stargazing from their backs or sitting cross-legged with their heads tilted upward.

Minnow found her campfire, which undoubtedly her pyro pirate sister Windy had lit and fed half a box of matches to.

Coby sat cross-legged gazing upward, and received Summer into the fold of his arm when she tapped his shoulder and dropped down next to him. Minnow admired their closeness. She'd been close like that with Matt all of her life. But it'd taken on new meaning since she got these lightning bugs and realized what they might mean.

What they feel to be – so, what they must be.

Windy laid on her back pointing out with exclamation each massive shooting star she spotted.

Minnow spotted Matt. She smiled like she always did when she saw him, somehow her nervousness melting away in the gaze of his familiar, at home regard.

Guitar played and ocean roared softly as Minnow mildly sprinted to a spot next to Matt. She felt like these Celtic sounds had been following them since a small band toured the island this week. Either he was a member of the band, or he'd picked up the tune as well. Just as Summer had, and then Minnow from Summer, and then Matt from Minnow, and Dad from Windy, who picked it up from Mom while she was painting, who heard it in the grocery store?

"Did I miss anything?" Minnow asked, leaning forward draping her arms relaxingly over her legs and tilting her chin up so she spotted the next ones.

"Just started fifteen minutes ago," replied Matt.

Just when Minnow was losing herself in stargazing and forgetting about her lightning bug confliction shrinking on the beach with campfire, ocean, music, and stars, Matt said in aside, "Tarantella Girl's seven fires behind you on your right. She and Harry Macroscope had a small discord earlier."

Minnow looked down from the sky just as a shooting star glanced the corner of her vision and met Matt's eyes. How could she compete, with this girl who had Matt wrapped up in her tender, sticky webbing?

Minnow didn't think she could control her heart. She tried, and it got worse, until it felt like it was going to cannonball out of her chest. So she stopped fighting it. She dug her hands in the mane and she leaned forward to ride this galloping wild horse wherever it was going to take her.

Heartbreak? Heartfelt? Maybe she was galloping so fast and too far not to crash. But she had to feel it. Minnow was already tangled in the ocean and sand if she did anything else but galloping.

Minnow smiled and stood, confidently handing down her hand, inviting Matt to dance to this tune traveling the island across the water and under their bare feet. With the smile, he could never refuse. Not that he was prepared to decline. It was Matt. Her best friend. Her adventuring partner.

Minnow's hand warmed with his wrapping around hers in a firm grip and she gripped back and pulled to help him up but he didn't need her skinny arms for aid.

Minnow should feel sad, but the last of this destructive cold sinking feeling diminished and obliterated altogether when Matt gave her a tug to bring her closer into his gently swaying embrace. And she remembered. *Galloping.*

The frozen expression of stun on Coby's face, mouth parted, was priceless. Their shadow had fallen across Coby and Summer, drawing his attention.

As the circle was completing Minnow saw Windy with her head tilted all the way back, peering with a knowing pirate smile up at her. Windy glared skullduggery before Summer snapped her fingers, which snapped her attention back to stargazing.

Minnow felt the teasing Windy wasn't expressing oozing from Windy to where Minnow stood barefoot, churning cool sand. But at least she wasn't looking. Everyone else was. Minnow started to feel self-conscious. She wanted to end this charade. Tell everyone to jump into the bay and tell Matt how she really felt!

Then Matt whispered, "Spider on the wind," and all Minnow wanted to do was hold onto tight to Matt and never let him go back to Tarantella Girl. That's just what she did, encircling her arms around him and stuffing her face flat onto his chest. Matt felt a little surprised, but gently adjusted his relaxed arms around her...now more enclosing.

Minnow said she'd surprise him sometime. So, that's what she would do. She'd tell him everything; in the unspoken that has been their friendship for always. Minnow pulled back just until she met Matt's eyes. He was pleased their plan was working – he didn't see it coming. She wouldn't have kissed him any other way in this moment; or she'd never be able to tell him everything her heart held and her voice was too frozen and cowardly and out of sand to speak.

Minnow kissed Matt. Not a playful kiss. Not a deep or timid one.

Minnow wound her grip around small handfuls of his hoody front and pulled and held on as she lifted onto her tiptoes and brought her mouth to his. She melted into Matt like a torch held up to snow. The lightning bugs exploded and cried inside of her. An ocean of protest, calling his name, saying choose me? And, I choose you. *I'm for you.*

Minnow shrank back onto her feet, peering with furrows of question and honesty up into Matt's eyes. He was looking at her with an expression of befuddlement – she wanted to say, *that's what it feels like.* The lightning bugs. The question. Matt felt what he hadn't picked up on her feeling exploded with the other day on the beach. There was no crab to help him to cover – and he was openly wondering, making her believe he wouldn't have pretended this feeling even if there had been a crab to blame his reaction on like she had.

Seconds, heartbeats, wild racing throbbing ones, a crashing wave, altogether, was all the time she had, or there was, kissing Matt and looking in his eyes.

She felt Tarantella Girl stop behind her. Her barefoot approach in the sand had been quiet; but Minnow had felt every intense wave permeating off of her. She kept her focus, and her heart's desire that Matt would see her heart and know the truth – and feel it too.

The expression on his eyebrow furrowed face under the brim of his frayed ballcap gave her a glimpse, a glimmer of hope, and also told her that his heart was too uninformed for there to be anything returned.

"Just another grass stain," Minnow said so quietly, as she moved away and down the beach, folding her arms, that she wondered if she'd said it loud enough to hear.

She thought she heard Summer tell Windy "No", which meant she'd started to spring up after her. Minnow could picture Windy' confusion and worry – her real worry – *this is all fun and games, right?* That kind of concerned, confused look.

"What's up with her?" asked Carly. "Did you two break up?" So casual. So spider-eye hungry.

Matt's voice made Minnow think he was watching her leave, and she heard the confusion and wonder in his voice when he replied a little absently, "Why?"

Minnow found a place on the sand to sit where the surf splashed her feet and she gazed at the star shower. It had sped up, meaning it was nearly over. Minnow's feelings had sped up, her patience ended, and Minnow run ashore. She'd not quite crashed. But her gallop had slowed to a blunt halt; tired, flaring nostrils, exertion and sweat soaked mane stringy and hide lathered...she took in the stillness...ocean and seagull sound above...flaring, breathing, heavily, charged heart...arched head...holding on...just holding steady and waiting for what comes next.

She'd told Matt. Whether or not he knew the entire back and front yard that came with those lightning bugs was more and inside her, whether or not those lightning bugs were watered down or small wattage compared to his passion and sharp keenness for Carly, or they were just infant and yet to bloom like they'd bloomed in her over the last several days...

Minnow had been true to her feelings. Minnow had discovered that there was an entire habitat inside of her that had gathered around those lightning bugs; a marsh and creeks and trees and grass and galloping horses. Trampled flowers and injured honeybees and broken dragonfly wing.

Summer had been right.

She'd had to follow her heart. She pushed, and the gate opened for her.

Where did she go from here?

Meandering, Minnow found a deserted campfire. The irresponsibility of leaving it irked her, so she sat down next to it until she felt like going back to rejoin her sisters and Coby.

Matt would be with Tarantella Girl. Had she excluded Harry from her campfire, or had she dropped him like a bottle of pesticides like Matt had said she would, if they went along with this charade?

Minnow wasn't sure. She told herself she wasn't giving up yet – just for right now. She laid on her back and watched the waning star shower. It'd grown gusty and Minnow was glad that she'd slid on her light blue hoody before she left home.

She startled when something soft and sudden hit her leg. Minnow yelped, curling her legs up as she righted herself and rubbed the tickling away. The wind gust started carrying the shadow that had the shape of a ballcap. She chased it fast to catch it before it delved too far from the firelight. She picked it up and didn't need the clear silver moonlight or bright firelight to recognize it as Matt's.

Minnow didn't stifle her laughter as she carried it back to her sitting spot turning it over in her hand. Yep. It was Matt's alright. That black smudge that never washed out – those grass stains there forever – the teeth marks that had torn the first threads were hers from when they were little and roughhousing silly and out of control.

"What, did she finally really eat him?" Minnow asked herself. She looked at the hat. "You're real slow on the uptake for a guy as smart with horses and people as you, you know that?" she said to Matt's hat, since it was the closest she had to him right now. "I told you she'd roll you up so tight one day in her web she'd swallow you whole. Just like a crispy spring roll."

Minnow stuffed it in her hoody pouch with huffed-out sigh. "Bless your heart," she said with a little twang, and laid back down on her back.

Chapter Forty-three

At last Matt found Minnow. Finding her gave him that warm easy smile he wore around her most. He was also relieved. He'd felt a gaping hurting hole in his chest and core when she'd walked away after she kissed him, and not looked back. That wasn't like her. Not at all.

When he saw the small curled-up ball she'd shaped herself into, fast asleep on the rippled sand, he breathed much easier. He'd been looking for her since he left Tarantella Girl after she took his hat to be playful and it blew away in the wind. They'd searched for his favorite ballcap he'd written his childhood by but it had disappeared, either in the ocean, or into someone's campfire. Carly had been sincerely apologetic, but that really didn't feel good enough to cut it. Unable to enjoy stargazing, and unable to reboot his good humor around Carly, which he didn't want to barbecue his chances of getting back together with her by moping, he left her soon after, making an excuse that he'd promised to drive Minnow home and he had to find her.

He wasn't lying. He would drive her home. And he *had* to find her.

Minnow was plum exhausted from the long week that had been plum thrilling for her.

Matt lowered his own plum sore self next to her and gently pulled her to him, tucking himself under her side and so that her head rested on his chest instead of the dense sand. Near enough to the small burning marshmallow roaster fire, Matt's sleep heavy eyes sank into a gentle gaze and study of her face. By dwarfed flame, ember glow and moonbeam, he made out the contours of her small nose and perky chin. It dimpled when she smiled, but dimpled the cutest with her happiest smile, which he preferred more as well as her dimple did. Thinking of her dimple deepened and with her happiest smile beaming over her face the other day in his backyard when she'd laughed, also brought to mind when he'd tickled her. He'd never met anyone who could be ticklish everywhere like Minnow was. Matt considered seeing if she could feel it in her sleep after all these years. She'd been a led weight when he scooped her up on his chest off the dense sand. Would it work?

Matt scooped sand in his hand, drained it and then pinched a little and sprinkled it slowly over the top of her hand.

Minnow moaned, tucking her hand under her chin with her palm flattened onto his chest. But she didn't wake up.

Matt was too tired to produce more than a semblance of the laughter he would have were he not half awake. She'd tickled and warmed these threads of humor in his weary bones, too weary for anything save the soft smile that sprung to his face with warmth. Minnow had missed having tickled him without even meaning too. He'd have to tease her about that sometime.

Matt decided he'd just lay there for a little while as the beach parties thinned out up the shore and let her sleep some more. Then he'd softly shake her awake on the shoulder and get them both home.

Matt gently stroked her peach fuzzy head he'd taken to. Her pluck, love of horses and riding – the gumption to buzz her hair – all to chase her dream. Filled Matt with heartwarming, admiration, pride, and new, deeper respect. If that was even possible for him to feel even more of these feelings and bond for his best friend.

Minnow was small. But that was the only way she was small.

Chapter Forty-four

Minnow stirred and felt curled around someone. She knew it was Matt long before she took in his steady breathing and clean, salty, piney smell, tinged with campfire, or the feeling of his form. She wanted to stay like this and just feel Matt beside her and cling this close to him. She did for full length moments, and just enjoyed the lolling.

She allowed her eyes to open as her ramble of thoughts woke her up more, along with her heart that for some reason was loud *pounding* – was it because of the tangy fresh and soft and free sea breeze she inhaled, or being so close to her Matt?

Her Matt might be Tarantella Girl's too – but she clung to Matt right now. And she had the best of him always with her, and her always with him. Minnow knew Matt inside and out in the way Carly couldn't and didn't.

Carly would never get that; or win that closeness with him. She didn't know what there was missing about her knowing Matt to win. She didn't have their years together like she had with Matt. She used Matt; Minnow cared and loved Matt. She *loved,* loved him; too.

Carly didn't know what that or what really love was like. She studied people and manipulate them; that was her gift.

Minnow had just pulled her eyes open when she sneezed, and made Matt stir.

Minnow shut her eyes, pretending to be asleep. But the feeling of his eyes looking at her was penetrating, the way one gets that adrenaline rush knowing someone knows where she's hiding. And after all, regarding a violent sneeze like that, who could still be asleep?

Plus, he would notice the difference in her breathing pattern and know she was faking sleeping, as they'd camped and napped together enough throughout the years to be able to discern her breathing patterns. How many times had they tried to fake each other out and pretend that they were still asleep when they really weren't?

How many times were there tides in a day, times fifteen years?

Too little with all their rambunctiousness for an accurate comparison.

So she feigned stirring, softly moaning for believability, and after a second gently tilted her chin against his side and peered sleepily up at him. It wasn't hard because her eyes were slightly heavy, though the nerve-endings in her touch and senses were functioning like un-mowed grass blade tips sensing the breeze, wide awake.

A look of unexpectedness from him softly framed his face. As though she'd grown mermaid fins and he was just seeing this side of her for the first time?

Were her morning face features altered by her cute fuzzy head too? Maybe a seagull had left a good morning gift on her head and she didn't know about it yet?

Morning time...

"Oh no," Minnow said, and it registered with Matt as well. Scrambling up they ran and stumbled finding their footing in the dragging sand folding over their feet one minute and without give the next. It was a challenge, as they staggered, feeling like led weight and rubbing the sleepies out of their eyes.

Urging one another on, Minnow squealed here and Matt growled into focus there, as the truck they're low on gas with wouldn't rev.

Matt leapt out and lifted the hood, holding it with one hand and fighting heavy eyes and forcing honed focus as he concentrated on locating the problem. Meanwhile Minnow slid into the driver's seat in preparation and when Matt moved this, jiggled that, and something else, and said, "Rev it!" she turned the key and pumped the gas to give it its morning orange juice. It sputtered and revved and Matt slammed the hood while Minnow agilely relocated herself and they hooted and raced bouncing in the bumpy truck to reach the fairgrounds before sunup.

Helpful, the jostling had woken them up by bridge crossing time, and it slammed into Minnow with an inhaled gasp that she lacked her disguise.

She pulled the other day's dirty jeans and shirt from behind the seat, as well as the boots she'd started leaving in Matt's truck. That reminded her. "Might need this," she said. Minnow drew his hat out of her pouch pocket and Matt's eyes widened. He took it and tugged it on. Matt's grin spread miles wide, looking like someone returned from a long way away. Stronger and with a wittier, undimmable sense of humor.

With a glance at Matt she stated, "Avert the eyes." Minnow tried to time her shirt change when they weren't riding by anyone but the roads felt as slow and all but rudimentarily deserted as they were in wintertime.

Everyone not sleeping in on their vacation or up before the crack of dawn for the grindstone was at the fairgrounds for the pony auction. Which they were majorly late for.

"My hat!" Minnow grabbed her head. "It's in Dad's truck! Do you have a spare?"

"Use mine." Matt offered her his, even though they'd just been reunited after thinking he'd lost it forever, but when she went to take it and her eyes were drawn to the middle of the seat, she spotted hers, and lifted it up.

Matt only took his eyes off the road a second as they rounded the sleepy Chicken City stoplight, with a puzzled look.

"I left it in Dad's last night; Summer drove," Minnow said, perplexed as well. But only for a blink.

Because she thought she had an answer, but it would mean Summer knew she'd fallen asleep with Matt on the beach, and left her in Matt's arms on the beach, all night; to figure out all that they had talked about.

She must have popped her hat through Matt's elbow window when she took Windy home. Wow – that wasn't only a grownup decision on her part – what did she tell Mom and Dad? Windy must have been arms crossed and eyes drooping all the way home.

Her hat – why would she leave her hat? Unless she knew she needed it?

Matt and Minnow exchanged looks with the same conclusion – did she know?

"How?" insisted Minnow.

"No time – we're here," he said, pulling in a park that swung them forward just when Minnow took heed and tugged her ballcap on and down close, snug.

The grass was dewy and short and glistening with morning glare shifting through trees and over buildings, casting car shadows that would be cool for another space of time. By the time the auction was over they might be able to cook an egg on a car hood in the shade.

"Nice of you to join us," Bumble said smiling, but the expression on Hammer and Chowder and Russ's dry faces wasn't out of good humor.

"Sorry," explained Matt, chest heaving from the jog as he stood straight, hands on hips. "We got waylaid," Matt said with a gesture back from where they'd come. Chowder and Russ didn't care, and Bumble held the gate open for them as they and Spencer, who just bounded up from around the auction platform, wrestled a yearling from the designated corral-stalls.

Minnow and Matt moved with the habit of a lifetime of familiarity and innate instinct, and they were ready when the bidding ended thirty seconds later.

Minnow was about to go into the pen to select the next numbered foal, who the auctioneer was announcing the details of, when Matt spoke up suddenly and said, "There's something I need to talk to you about after the auction."

Minnow sat paused on top of the stall railing, and while she was confused she also had an inkling of what he meant but wasn't saying. "Okay," said Minnow, and with a discernable nod from Matt, Minnow continued and Matt was back in focus, onboard.

Minnow couldn't wear her sunglasses in the corral area because it made everything too dark to see. Her only option was to rub her hands on one of the foals but they kept moving, a sea of skinny, big-eyed, squeaking little colts and fillies that made her smile. So, each and every one helped musky-up her hands and disguise her. She gave herself a rub like it was soap, to which Matt looked down and all she saw was the top of his grass stained ballcap as he shook his head.

Minnow felt like she held a bolt of lightning, as she and Matt secured the filly between them and brought her into the center of the circle. Minnow soothed the filly by speaking coaxingly to her, while Matt risked freeing one hand to gently smooth strokes down her throat. She remained pert and wide-eyed with fright, and Minnow could feel her little heart thumping, but Matt's gentle touch with feeling and confidence calmed her enough to stop rearing and she stood pertly taking in the audience.

The was a light chestnut brown and white filly, with pink that extended inside her nostrils. Her baby breath puffed in a cloud that reached Minnow.

A little girl around Minnow's age when she bought Marshy won the bidding, and that made Minnow smile more than anything else. Hammer had been mistaken when he'd made the remark that cotton candy was the stuff dreams were made of at the carnival. This was what dreams were made of at the carnival. That is, the Chincoteague carnival. Little girls and boys bidding on a wild little pony who would become their best friend forever and ever.

Chapter Forty-five

Windy waved from the crowd, jumping up and down to be seen. Wow, her sunburn was recovering quickly. Minnow couldn't wave but she smiled to let Windy know she'd seen her. Then she saw Summer in the crowd next to Coby, who was talking to someone further inside the crowd.

Minnow's expression dropped a little.

Summer wore a keen-eyed, knowing expression, and aimed two fingers at her eyes and then Minnow in a sequence that told Minnow she had her eyes on her. And she knew.

But she hadn't told.

Minnow didn't know whether to smile or shrink so she focused on helping Matt hold this black colt with one white nostril and blue eyes. The bidding just ended, and it was a good thing because he had power in his chest and reared lunging like a tidal wave.

Matt and Minnow took a break, even though it was only their third foal and there were still dozens more to go out. They guzzled from some bottles of water out of a cooler.

AJ, young Miles, Sailor Man Sharp, and several other volunteers and ponyboys kept position at points of the low kennel fencing, roving the bidding crowd. They clarified a bid, spotted raised hands and caught the smaller ones the auctioneer might not see from his bird's eye view or that tend to get swallowed in a big and loud space.

A little boy about nine years old held one side of a newborn filly, stroking her neck with his soft touch, while his father held the foal secured by his strong arm, with one hand under her neck and the other gripping her tail. She was small, like the little boy, but if she had the mind she might sidestep and knock him over; so his father held her gently but securely, and his son beamed with helping his father keep her calm and walk her around the grassy arena.

Minnow smiled at the sight and when they returned the filly to her friends in the stall that was filling up with foals now bound for new homes, Minnow couldn't help beaming with understanding at him. She nodded to him. The toothy boy beamed twice more back.

Minutes later Matt and Minnow were readying to reenter the stall when a familiar although unexpected voice echoed her frustration and challenge down the alley between stalls and small three-person auction deck with the open carnival stuffed with hopeful bidders and thrilled onlookers.

"So! Boyfriend stealer!" shouted Tizzy. Walking with an edgy timidity in her stride, out of a nervousness for her smelly, filthy outdoor surroundings that weren't like any she'd ever ventured into or around, willingly, which that on its own was jaw dropping. It was clear from the conviction in her stride, Tizzy had a driving purpose, for which she was squelching her outdoor apprehensions and normal fears.

Matt and Minnow were surprised and while he stepped back from the stall gate Minnow stayed near it.

Hammer saw her coming from nearby the auctioneer deck with auctioneer on the small deck above. He was approaching non-too happy but he was too late to stop Tizzy-fit. She tiny shoved Minnow so she didn't have to get too filthy from her shirt and Minnow slipped on manure and banged back into the stall gate, but not pushing Tizzy off her was a mistake.

Tizzy grabbed what she wanted and threw it down in the dirt and manure, stomping on Dad's hat when Minnow scrunched down and tried to grab it.

Matt hooked his hat on Minnow's head and yanked her up and pushed her behind him. Changing gears, he tried to gentle her with an outstretched hand in halting like he would try to settle a startled horse, asking her in a cautious yet normal tone, "Tizzy?" Matt drew her name out with inquiry. "What's the trouble?"

"The trouble with me?" she asked him surprised and defensive. She pointed. "She's, Minnow!"

"You shouldn't pick on short people!" Matt raised his voice a little in answer to cover much of what she'd just said.

"Don't try to hide her!" Tizzy ordered, drawing her pointing finger up close to her in a stern warning. She must have caught a whiff from her finger or seen a speck because she quickly squirted hand sanitizer in her hands from the pocket version and stuffed it back in her short's pocket, rubbing the alcohol cleanser dry all over her hands. "She's been lying to everyone, and now everyone will know the truth," she said with generality to the area.

"This is because Windy sprayed her with water from her bilge-pump when she was kayaking the other day," Minnow whispered hoarsely up to Matt, who didn't take his eyes off the Tizzy, but like a horse cupping his ear backwards strained slightly and heard every word. "She must have seen Summer and Windy wave to me, in the audience, and put two and two together."

Minnow felt understanding registered with Matt in the form of his back rising in taking in a long breath. Going to school together all their lives and growing up on a seven and half mile long three-mile-wide island, they got to know people very well. Even the twins.

It was well known on the island, and well aware to Matt and Minnow, how much Tizzy despaired unpleasant smells, grass, pets, trees, a coffee cup that'd been secondhand bought at the Op Shop instead of newly purchased. Just to list a few.

Being majorly squirted in her kayak with the murky creek?

On top of her already seething jealousy over Summer and Coby?

Tizzy was bound to find a way to pay Minnow and her sister back for that; even though it hadn't been Minnow's fault, she was guilty by association, and perhaps she thought by hurting Minnow she'd get her revenge on Windy. As well as Summer. She was right; only she should know her pirate sister better than to bring one or any of her family into any disagreement.

Minnow might have to physically restrain her skullduggery sister from all-out sea battle.

Hammer slipped midway between her and Matt, pointing his finger sternly in Tizzy's face with the warning, "You'd better skedaddle before Russ gets here. He won't be as understanding as me."

Tizzy had already backed up a meter at Hammer's presence – or sweaty horsy smell – but she was undeterred.

"But she lied," insisted Tizzy. "I'm being a good Teague. A *true* Teaguer," she said around Hammer and Matt as well as she could around them, to Minnow.

"If you think that than you aint no Teaguer," Hammer said low and grimly. "From one Teaguer to another – Out." The roofer didn't need to raise his voice. He commanded men from neck-breaking heights. He'd picked up on her disposition to sweaty horsy smell, and just had to step a few steps closer for her to back up instantly.

Tizzy squeezed her fists and looked tightlipped like she had more to say, but forced herself to turn around and stiffly fast walk away.

Tarantella Girl had shaken Izzy from her bored stationary spot and rustled her along to the part of the fence Tizzy had been brave in touching to cling to and move her legs over the short fencing. Wearing her black cropped tee and distressed shorts, Tarantella Girl looked confused and was asking Tizzy concerned and perplexed what was going on, as she and Izzy helped her back over the fencing that was giving her pause now.

Hammer might have let Minnow slide – he wore a stern look that for him was a sign of empathy.

But the other saltwater ponyboys had seen. Instead of staring at Minnow though, they all turned questioning looks on Russ. He was the oldest saltwater ponyboy. Having a girl sneak into the swim, and worse than that, she'd already ridden through more than half already? The damage was done. And his soured look was unforgiving. Towards her.

No, her sunken heart managed to scream as she looked at Matt. Matt turned his head sternly to meet her eyes but there wasn't an ounce of regret in his tight jaw.

"It's not Matt's fault," Minnow spoke up. It was at this time that she realized the whole auction had stopped.

The perky month old wobbly-knee foal secured between Spencer and Bumble whinnied with curious question.

"I talked him into helping," Minnow spoke up.

"Minnow wait," Matt tried to stop her, but Minnow talked over him.

"Matt's not to blame," Minnow insisted.

Russ's expression was hard. Maybe he expected a better explanation than that. Minnow only had one. "Since I was little, I've always dreamed of riding in pony penning. You know that – I've tried, every summer since I was eight," she said, looking at Matt. "But girls aren't allowed. Its tradition. I broke it. It's on me. I'm sorry."

Minnow was turning to Matt when she caught Hammer's hammer gaze; but found glistening in his stern eyes and lines, not an ounce of betrayal.

Minnow decided what she'd said wasn't enough. She had one more thing to say. Feeling a stoking in her gut, she stood a little

420

straighter, and said, "These ponies – are the stuff dreams are made of, here, at this carnival. They're what their dreams are made of."

Minnow pointed towards the direction of the at a distance and yet nearby crowd barely blocked by the miniature auction decking and murmuring with questions.

"They're what my dreams are made of," she said softer, a steady calm settling on her or defeat relaxing her. Maybe both. She felt defeat. Crushed. But also, strong. Okay. Her only regret was that she'd ruined Matt's standing with the saltwater ponyboys and the Teagures.

"I've had the time of my life riding with you," Minnow finished.

"Matt, I'm sorry," Minnow turned to Matt and told him, but the tears were stinging her eyes and she couldn't stay any longer. She wasn't welcome. Minnow swiped up her hat, swiftly handing Matt's back to him, and fighting back the tears walked in the opposite direction Tizzy had. Minnow had to find Summer and Windy and go home before she embarrassed the Teaguers more, or made matters worse for Matt.

It turns out Summer and Windy found Minnow, with Coby striding into the alley to see what on earth was going on.

Minnow slowed but walked right on, saying to her sisters as they gathered beside her and threw glances over their shoulders behind where she'd come from, "They know now. I'm not a saltwater ponygirl anymore."

Chapter Forty-six

Minnow's parents had a stern sit-down talk with her in the living room. Fighting back her tears, guilt lanced through her. She didn't think this day could get any worse. She'd ruined Matt's standing in Chincoteague – everyone would sour-eye him now, as he'd called it. The come-here who helped a girl get into the pony swim. The wholesome citizen and shining volunteer who helped Minnow break a nearly one-hundred-year-old Chincoteague tradition. She hoped her speech would help them not to socially exile him. Or make him unwelcome at the carnival or volunteering events for long. But they'd definitely start referring to him as that come-here, in far less endearing tones.

Minnow couldn't process the crushed mess of her own dream of being a saltwater ponygirl right now. A dream that'd been trampled in the mud and manure like her ballcap. Borrowed by the way. She'd find a way to wash if before Dad found that out too.

Her parents must have seen the inner battle going on inside her, and beatings coming through on the outside, because they sent her to her room, where she gladly obeyed going. Readily and willingly, mouth zipped, Minnow trudged upstairs, her heart heavy, her world in collapse. But nearing her door it got harder to hold back the tide. She let the stinging tears spill down her dirty cheeks as she crumpled on her bed.

Windy peeked her head through the door – she must have snuck past Mom and Dad, because Minnow was supposed to be alone.

"Minnow?" Windy spoke softly and carefully.

"Go away," Minnow snapped through her sobbing with half the energy she usually put in, and bunched up tighter, tucking her head into her pillow crying.

Windy didn't listen, and Minnow heard the door close right before Windy curled around her on the bed.

"I don't want a hug," Minnow snapped again, and yet she didn't jerk away. In spite of herself, deep down that's all Minnow wanted. A long squeezing hug; for someone to be close to.

Even if she was a pirate.

Chapter Forty-seven

Was Shakespeare not Shakespeare because nobody knew his real identity?

Floating in thought, Minnow was feeding Marshy the carrots she'd pulled out of the garden this morning. Marshy didn't grasp exactly what had happened yesterday, but shed sensed that Minnow was unhappy, and bothered by something. Minnow didn't mean to make her nervous, and realized that she was when she ground that carrot into paste within two seconds of biting the chunk off the tip.

"It's not fair Marshy," Minnow tried to explain to her. "But we did go against the rules. It's unrealistic to think no one would get mad if they found out. But it wasn't a fair rule, or a right one. It was only wrong to keep Mom and Dad out of the loop; even if they wouldn't have approved," she admitted.

Marshy flared her nostrils. Talking was soothing her, so Minnow kept explaining. "We're grounded now; until my graduation probably," she said, gently running the back of her fingers along Marshy' forelock.

"We might not have finished the swim," she started again. "But we're still Teaguers. I'm a saltwater ponygirl; and you're a saltwater pony."

Minnow took Marshy' noise as an agreement, even though she sounded like she'd asked a question.

It was sunrise. Minnow couldn't help thinking that the saltwater ponyboys were readying to drive the wild ponies from the carnival to the Chincoteague shoreline, where they'd swim back at this morning's slack tide.

The return swim.

She'd be gathering herself and Marshy to meet Matt up the road way before now.

If Tizzy hadn't blown Minnow's cover.

"Minnow!"

Minnow was surprised to hear Matt's voice and look to see him running across the backyard. He'd taken the shortcut through the barrier of trees and bayberry and bulrushes and was halting next to her now, and smelling fresh of woods and the thicket, he gripped both hands around the top railing, panting. Marshy lifted her head and turned it to the side to ascertain what all the fuss was about.

"You didn't meet me on the roof," Matt said, his breathing normalizing. He scrubbed Marshy' chin, causing her to relax her lower lip and drool carrot juice.

Minnow avoided meeting Matt's eyes at first and studied the prickly, dewy grass around her wet bare feet.

"I'm grounded for life," said Minnow. She fed Marshy more carrot, and Matt wiped his hands on his jeans.

"You're on their radar too," she warned him.

Minnow stroked Marshy' neck. She needed a good brushing, and once sunrise Minnow had intended to start and not finish until her coat gleamed. Marshy' coat never gleamed, but Minnow was going to give her the thorough brush of a lifetime; as reward for all of her amazing accomplishments, and apology for them not finishing the swim. She got waylaid in her thoughts though. She'd given herself the morning to figure out what she would do next.

Her pony penning days were over; she was grounded; tours, kayak shop counter duty, grocery shopping to help Mom, and doing the laundry until they thought it was time to stop punishing her, was pretty much what her future looked like for the rest of the summer. She wasn't even allowed to ride Marshy.

No more bonfires for her in the sand with the roar of the ocean next to her, for a long while. By the time her parents start considering time off on good behavior school will have started. Then she had to wait all winter until summer again to go to the beach in her bare feet.

Minnow learned her lesson alright. Deceiving Mom and Dad was something she'd not been comfortable with; however, she hadn't hesitated, and she'd done it anyway. To lie and keep them out of the loop was not how their family worked.

Our Happy Happy Happy! meant they shared everything; well. That they eventually did. That was what big families were about too.

But yet she didn't regret pretending to be Maximus to ride in the swim. How did that make sense, when she regretted keeping her parents out of the loop?

"You thought you had it hard, doing laundry for yourself. See that over there," Minnow gestured and said lazily to Matt. Dainties and towels and shorts and tees drifting lightly when the air stirred. "That's part of my punishment. And the first load of two more I'll do today. No more turns doing laundry until Mom and Dad decide."

She looked down at Marshy' mouth, then looked up to meet Matt's eyes but he was grimacing with an unenvious look at the laundry line.

"I'm sorry Matt," Minnow said quietly, but clearly, which drew his attention back. "I let you down." Minnow knew she owed him eye contact but she couldn't help glancing at her feet with a heavy heart of disappointment and shaking her head.

"Minnow stop saying that, I have news for you," Matt said, and his slightly urgent and excited voice made her head snap up. "First stop apologizing. You didn't let me down. I knew what I was getting into – but I'm not quite sure you did."

"What does that mean?" asked Minnow, sounding more like herself, which was slightly un-tempered.

"They knew you were in the swim," Matt confessed.

Minnow's jaw dropped and her eyes popped as big as pinecones.

"What!" she stated.

"Everyone knew but a few of the old-timers," Matt explained. "When you told me your idea I had a talk with all the guys, and they didn't see any harm in letting you, or any girl ride in the swim. But you know how set in his ways that Russ is," Matt said. "So we decided to keep it under our caps."

Minnow didn't know which to feel or express first! Excitement because Matt was no longer the eyesore she thought she'd made him? Anger because Matt didn't tell her?

This gave her a little taste of what her parents were feeling and where they were coming from. And Minnow felt closer to having learned her lesson.

Laughter because all this time she'd been acting like a boy, they all knew it was Minnow under the dirt smears she put on her face in the morning, filled the morning blue sky – and she'd buzzed her hair!

"You mean, all this time, all the jokes, about my tailbone that was never bruised, and calling me Maximus for it, Bumble thinking that my voice was changing and giving me advice, and everything else, everyone knew except me?!" said Minnow, and all of her emotions bubbled out and erupted forth at once. She'd moved away from Marshy and paced feet one way and then the other in her speech as she put the pieces of the puzzle together.

"And Russ," Matt said. "Don't forget him."

"I'd clobber you if I didn't love you so much right now!" Minnow shouted, leaping forward and pouncing on Matt like a marsh grass frog who made him stagger, legs wound around his waist and arms squeezing his neck.

"Yeah, yeah," he said, and then, "thank the boys when you see them."

That made Minnow climb down. "What do you mean?"

"I told you I have news," he said.

"I thought that was your news," said Minnow.

"It's the last day of pony penning," Matt told her. "You're riding in the return swim."

"But my parents? Russ?" Minnow protested.

"Russ took some convincing. Chowder was surprised to learn Maximus was you – but oddly enough, he took your side. Also. Some of the guys spun by your Dad's kayak shop and talked with both your parents," explained Matt.

"Who?" Minnow wanted to know.

"Bumble, Sailor Man Sharp, Hammer, even AJ – he was concise and particular in listing your virtues and assets as a member of the swim, as well things you could work on. And a formula in which to best help you along," he added, with a stymied motion of his hand as though giving her a boost in what AJ thought was the right direction.

Minnow smiled and almost laughed. That sounded like AJ the accountant.

"Come on – I can fill you in later," Matt urged, "bottom line is they convinced your parents to let you finish the pony swim week, and then you can wash clothes until your hands wrinkle up."

Minnow started to run to the tack room on the other side of the paddock which was inside the paddock but Matt stopped her. "I'll saddle and halter Marshy while you change into jeans and boots," Matt told her.

Minnow nodded once and was flying across the yard, heedless of slipping in the dew. She didn't need to be told to hurry twice.

Minnow changed and charged back outside again, but when she rejoined Matt who was leading Marshy up the yard she remembered something. "Hold on," she said, dashing back into the house. She knew she needed to grab just one thing.

Minnow swiped up her straw ponygirl hat that curled at the sides from off her bedpost, where it'd been hanging since Friday night. She sat it on her head with a smile.

Matt loaded Marshy into the trailer beside Ish while Minnow dashed through the them-made trails, across the yard to the kayak shop, where she burst in on Mom and Dad having a private talk over coffee mugs. In most likelihood about her.

Breathing swiftly, her heart tight with emotion, Minnow didn't know how to not gush with gratitude. "Thank you, guys," she expressed, gluing herself to Mom in a hug, and when she let go smashed herself against the middle of Dad's chest where her head came up to.

Her hat nearly fell off and she caught it when Minnow stepped back, insisting, "I won't ever keep you out of the loop or let you down again!"

"Honey. You should know that you can tell us anything," Mom told her gently, taking her wrist in her cool hand.

"We all make mistakes sweetie," Dad added in. "As long as we learn from them, and do our best not to repeat them?"

"Yes," Minnow said nodding eagerly.

Matt honked the horn.

"I've got to go," Minnow said, squeezing each parent in a hug one more time.

"Wait for us," Dad said, just as Minnow caught the jingle of car keys.

"You're coming?" she asked in bright surprise.

"Of course," Mom answered, looking briefly at Dad. "We wouldn't miss this for the world."

"What about the tour?" asked Minnow suddenly worried and frowning. "You didn't cancel it because of me, did you?"

"No, but we would have – not because we were angry with you, but because we can get caught up in work sometimes, and not spend enough time together. Family time is important," Dad said, looping his arm lovingly around Mom's shoulders. She smiled at Dad, then looked back to Minnow.

"Summer and Windy and Coby are taking the lead this morning," Mom revealed.

Minnow wasn't expecting to hear that, but pleased that she was, and happy for Summer. Summer hadn't taken a swim tour out as lead kayak guide yet.

"She's been wanting to take the reins – *paddle* – and do some tours on her own," Dad went on. "The return swim is the perfect chance. Everyone's gone home pretty much, and the boat traffic is almost zero."

"Besides," Mom added, "if Summer and Coby are going to run the place one day, why not give them more paddle now?" remarked Mom, to play off Dad's phrase just then.

Minnow smiled as she watched the loving look flow between her parents and them kiss. This would be the opportunity to allow them to spend more free time together as well. Minnow was reminded about Matt's parents, who'd left for pony penning week for time alone and to get away from the overwhelming crowds during the pony craze.

Minnow was all for it.

And the pony craze.

Chapter Forty-eight

The return swim went like a charm.

The ponies plowed through the placid water, and the air was warmer, with a breeze that spared them.

Minnow sat on Marshy and they stood on the tip of the green shoreline and watched them swim across and safely make landing to trudge up the marsh. The applause was weaker than the first swim morning, as there were hardly any onlookers. But Minnow heard Windy' clapping and her cheers. She saw her thrusting her paddle into the air for Minnow in a sign of victory – which Minnow took to heart in all the three good ways Windy meant it.

Minnow's dream had come true.

The ponies were safely across.

All, was right with their world.

Summer joined her and together they threw their paddles twirling up over their heads, water droplets spraying and glistening Windy' liquid gold, catching them easily upon their return.

Windy was right after all – there was gold in these here waters. From these here waters. They were holding paddles, holding hands with the onlookers, swimming across the water, and every one of these beating in her heart.

Minnow sat there with Marshy until every single pony had trudged safely ashore. As they moved up the marsh for sturdier ground, small bands breaking loose and galloping for the trees, Summer moved the tour group at a safe distance around the marsh, following the herd so that they could still gaze on the ponies.

Minnow decided not to distract them from the tour group anymore and waved one last time before turning Marshy back around to walk home. When she did Russ sat astride in his saddle to her right, one hand relaxed on his hip.

Minnow thought it was better if she kept her mouth closed. But she also felt like she should say something. She didn't know what was going to come out, but just as she was mustering the courage to speak, Russ spoke first.

"When a person's young, the world is their oyster," Russ started.

435

Now Minnow really did keep her mouth shut. She didn't dare speak.

The peculiar thing was, he didn't sound mad either? Minnow thought she might be seeing what she wanted to see, but as Minnow listened to the old Teague go on, she couldn't find the austere Russ who'd been this foreboding giant obscuring her participation in the swim the way the toad hole always found a way to pull the ground out from under the toads.

"As you get older you set in your ways. Then, pretty soon all you've known and grown up with either starts faden or changen," said Russ, glancing down at a point in the marsh. "It's good to have things stay the same sometimes. But change can be a new adventure; and I'd forgotten about that," remarked Russ, and then he nudged his pony Boy Scout so that he came to stand alongside Minnow. "I aint felt so shook up in a long while. Finden out, that you were a girl out there, and thinkin back to all the jokes the boys made – about your voice, your bruised tailbone–" Russ stopped there, enough said.

Minnow was quietly and happily surprised – she hadn't thought he'd paid her or anyone much mind. But he'd paid attention to it all.

"And recalling how you and your little pony here put your heart into the roundup," Russ mentioned, adding, "I'm a skinny short man myself. So, I can appreciate more than these Hercules around here, going after something twice your size."

Russ held out his bony hand.

Minnow didn't know what to say, so she shook his weathered and warm and ironclad hand, smiling softly and with appreciative summer warmth.

"Sometimes a person can get wrought up over nothen," said Russ in closing. "Thank you for reminding me that there's adventure with change."

"You think having me was an adventure?" asked Minnow, feeling a playful current of butterflies coming in from slack tide.

"This is only the beginning." Russ's horse Boy Scout shifted weight, sensing that they were about to be on the move. There was something secretive, knowing, wise, and interesting in what Russ said and how he said it, that made Minnow wonder about all that he could possibly be referring too.

"Besides. It's like you said." Russ glanced over his shoulder at the drenched and gleaming ponies meandering in bands towards the forest, while other's rested and grazed on mixed grass. Turning back, Russ finished, and looked Minnow in the eyes. "This is all what dreams are made of; here."

Russ gave a curt, respectful nod to Minnow, as he gathered his reins.

Minnow returned it, and held Marshy' reins tightly so that as Russ and Boy Scout walked onward she didn't try to trot after them with the gregarious intent of starting up a *how ya doen*?

"Well kiddo," said Bumble, halting the mirror image horse version of himself alongside Minnow.

Minnow had to look up to see them and Sailor Man Sharp gathered on her other side with a big smile. Spencer and Matt gathered too, and Hammer, along with AJ, who he gave a grim side-glance to when his horse bumped into his.

"Ready for next year?" asked AJ.

Minnow hadn't even realized that next year was possible!

She stopped holding her breath and blurted, "Yes!" and they all laughed heartily.

"Wish you were still thinking we didn't know," remarked Bumble, "I was having fun teasing you at every corner."

"I'm sure we'll find more ways," Matt replied, and she knew that look – and squinted suspiciously at him.

"Come on," Bumble said to his horse, "see ya around," he said to Minnow, and the others. They all mumbled their partings and dispersed; only Matt lingered.

"A mutiny with a happy ending," Matt commented.

Minnow smiled, giving him a knowing look. "It wasn't even a mutiny – they all knew but Russ, Chowder, *and* in part, me."

"You just aint cut out for your little sister's lifestyle," answered Matt.

"You aint either," she told him. "How did you know they'd agree?"

"Because they know what it's like," answered Matt.

Marshy stomped her hoof and snorted. Minnow patted Marshy' neck to reassure her that they'd be moving soon.

"What it's like?" said Minnow.

"To love horses," said Matt.

Chapter Forty-nine

That night at the carnival the crowds were thinner, which Minnow preferred for her last night at the carnival. Mom and Dad had agreed that she finish out her volunteer pledge but were clear about coming straight home. She was still on restriction, and Minnow wasn't going to misuse their trust ever again.

The spinning color of lights blending into each other on the faster rides – laughter – young children and adults screaming with the thrill and exhilaration of the rides along with them – the aroma of food frying, baking, and sweet pine shats, mixed with the indelible smell of horses. Minnow couldn't be happier on her last night of helping out at the cotton candy stand, where she leaned on the counter with her forearms together and pointing straight. She'd had a few customers, but as she'd observed, the crowds were light.

The night was pleasantly cooler too. It'd been so all day, a welcomed reprieve from the oven hot, and muggy stickiness of the mixed week.

When Minnow spun her last cotton candy batch she knew it might be the last one that she spun until next summer, but it still came as a surprise. She'd enjoyed her time in the booth, and when she'd closed it up, hugged Tonya bye, wished the sugar fairies a happy winter – wherever they were playing right now – and walked out, she had a skip in her step.

She went to scrounge Matt up. The crew were going to let her and Matt go on the Ferris Wheel one more time before they closed. It was part of all of the volunteers giving themselves final rides for the night, as it was also the last days of the carnival being open until next summer.

It was nearing last chance time, and Minnow couldn't find Matt. She was just about to call his name and whip out her phone to txt him when she spotted him over by the Merry Go Round.

Minnow's chest felt heavy and tight. A Merry Go Round indeed.

They looked close in intimate conversation.

Minnow shouldn't feel stung and attacked. All along she knew he'd still choose Tarantella Girl. But in her heart of hearts, she guessed he'd choose her, his best friend, instead.

Minnow turned around and was surprised at how her legs moved so easily.

Like a playful wave that catches you by surprise. "He's the adventure that steals my breath. The kind that you come back for," Minnow told to Marshy. She couldn't admit this to anyone else right now. Not Mom or Dad. Not even Summer.

Or Windy.

She'd become closer with Windy than she'd ever felt. There was a level of understanding between them now that she believed would bridge their bad moods quicker and stave off or diffuse their tempers when they irritated one another, more often.

Minnow wasn't ready though to talk to anyone and let this out of her. Anyone that is, except Marshy. Her aching secret was safe with her curious friend.

Minnow fed her carrots she plucked from the veggie garden on her way up to the paddock.

"He's the stars that fill my night skies. How plain they seem with only moonbeam," Minnow trailed off.

Grass stains would be meaningless. Without the cause for distress to her jeans. Their adventures; and traipses. Scrapes and bruise would hurt more. Unless he had them as well to share in the glory of those ouches. The scare and thrill that painted the glory. It's only half as fun when you're alone as it is when you're together and it's happening with someone you're close to. Which is as half as important as having someone to run to and tell when they're not part of it, who will appreciate the bruise and takes enjoyment in hearing about how she crashed her bike and flipped and twisted her arm almost too far, or in Marshy stepping on her foot and then sneezing on her in one day!

Memories; good times etched on their skins, stained in their clothes, Matt's ballcap and Minnow's jeans; imprinted in their hearts to stay.

There wasn't a laundry machine or detergent powerful enough to wash these importance's away.

But Carly had found a way to send *her* down the drain.

"He chose Tarantella Girl, Marshy," Minnow said, slumped in feelings. "Again."

"Minnow," Matt called as he approached. "Hey; been looking for ya," he said, coming beside Marshy on the other side of her head and rubbing her mane. "Didn't you get my message to meet me in our spot?"

"I left my phone on the couch," Minnow replied.

Matt took in her mood. "What's the matter," he said.

This was one of those split-second decision times when she could either keep her mouth shut, or open her mouth and probably put her foot in it. One of those minnow traps she swum into going with her feelings and gut that often came with her temper following, and a big mess all the way around.

Minnow stepped back from Marshy and faced Matt. "I've always been straight with you, and you asked, so here," she said, as Marshy extended her neck and lipped at her wrist. It tickled but she held back with more restraint than she'd ever known possible, bearing up to the tickle and remaining serious.

"You're wrapped up in all I know, and I can't imagine my life without you. However, I feel more for you; feelings I've never felt with anyone or for anyone else, because there's only one you. You're my best friend; and I also love you like a girl loves a boy," Minnow held up a hand and said, "don't ask me how it happened. The thing is it did. But I'll suffer through since you want to keep it as always," she said, "and I'll be alright. I'll get over it, maybe," Minnow trailed off, staring Matt squarely in the eyes. She still kept her voice steady. "I just need you." Minnow stared at Matt, staring the stronger emotions that were a tight raspy rope in her chest, like one of those from Windy' pretend pirate ships in their plays. "I love you; deeper than you'll know. And honestly, it's exhausting," she complained, tilting her head back.

She brought her head back to center. "And I won't take it back. I'd never ask for it gone. Not even if mermaid wishes were real," Minnow said, serious. "Just don't let what I've told you ruin our friendship. I know you're back together and Tarantella Girl has your heart. Just still be my best friend or I'll flare and it'll never go down."

"There's something you aint figured," said Matt, and Minnow kept her eyes in his as he moved around Marshy, who now lipped at the only other person who had been giving her attention. "Where would I be without you; my best friend, from the spit of an island, to the wide, wide world."

Matt gently pressed his forehead to hers.

Minnow smiled, because she understood his meaning; and sunshine felt like it'd returned and sunset yellow and tawny splintered through the trees and vines of the woods behind the paddock.

She didn't ask what about Tarantella Girl yet. She didn't ask what transpired between them when they'd been breaking up by the Merry Go Round, as she now surmised from Matt they were.

She just soaked up this, and Matt, and standing close to him. Just as in his backyard when they shared that one intense moment, this one too felt binding; and more. Happy.

Not unsure, intense, and perplexing.

Real. happy. Strong. And *right*.

Then Matt kissed Minnow tenderly, the way sunrise opens the day, and spills over undeniably. There was no return to the singularity of formers. Her best friend was her best everything, who meant everything to her. The world to her. They always had. They'd both just realized it this pony week. From one small spit of island, to the wide, wide world.

Minnow kissed Matt back. Once she did the lightning bugs in Minnow illuminated twice their capacity, and all she felt was happy and cool white blue glows inside, and warm sunrise sun outside. Together, she felt twice alive. Sun warm face and sun warm skin; tickling with the moving puffs of their warm mixed breaths. Matt's hands that felt slightly scratchy from being the tried and true that they were, of course, being Matt's hands, cupping her face. Minnow didn't realize she'd folded her arms around his sturdy, sunburn neck until just then.

Matt drifted back. Minnow opened her eyes into Matt's blue ones. "No more crabs?" he asked softly.

Minnow smiled, and answered, "No." In light of how they'd opened their hearts to each other, Matt had been thinking back. He'd been suspicious besides about her excuse; now there was little to hide about the real reason she'd behaved like someone had just zapped her.

"I didn't think you'd felt it," Minnow confided. She didn't need to extrapolate; he knew she meant the lightning bugs to begin with, and how she felt when she kissed him on the beach by the campfire. "I didn't think you saw it in me either."

"When I woke up on the beach with you the other morning," Matt explained, "I don't know how it happened, or *what* exactly happened. But I just saw everything so clearly. I knew what I felt – and I realized that I'd been feeling this before this pony week; long since we've been friends."

This ironic twist came as a little of a surprise to Minnow, however since she hadn't known herself that she'd been feeling the same a long time before this pony week, she understood. Her indicators upon reflection was her jealously over sharing him with Tarantella Girl; she and Matt's joking and banter seemed like playful foreplay, not just their usual fun and games.

"I thought about how you'd kissed me all day; I couldn't stop; and I started thinking about all the time we spent together pretending to be a couple. It gripped me. I don't want it to end; us like this, or how we've always been, ever to end."

Matt touched his forehead to Minnows again, curling one of her hands in his to his warm shoulder as he was.

"Your name is Evers after all," Minnow said, reminding him of what he'd said earlier in the week when he'd promised her no more schemes or colluding to get Tarantella Girl back, to convince her to help him this one last time.

"I guess we're both not too quick on our own uptakes," she added, making Matt's smile spread.

A moment of companionable pause lingered between them, where Marshy stretched her neck out so far and fish-mouthed her lips out, and the excitable birds twittered and hopped and danced from one twig to the next.

"A book walks into a café," Minnow started, her mouth twisting with a smile.

Matt snorted softly.

"And the barista asked, *what do you do?* And the book replied *do I have to spell it out!?*"

Minnow and Matt were laughing and swaying leaning on each other now.

"Come here you," Matt said, tugging her and she tugged away, tugging him to her.

"No! Come-here, you," she answered, with soft enunciation on the right words in the right way.

Smiling with her joke that she felt Matt receive and respond to the meaning of, she pulled him to her for a small, tender kiss, but bolted back bending inward when she felt Matt's squid hands tickle her stomach in retaliation for her calling him a come-here.

Matt had that set, wordless, *you were warned* look under the brim of his hat, and she knew he was going to chase her. But he'd have to catch her first.

Minnow was bare foot too, and with a squeal Marshy answered to, bolted across the soft, sweet, prickly grass, leading

Matt on a rigorous and confusing chase that'd shrink others in comparison.

There would be grass stains, bruises, and maybe more knots. She'd cherish every single one.

Marshy cheered from the paddock and pressed her chest against the railing, whinnying in her squeaky noise voice. Then she trotted up to the gate and pressing her hoof on the lower railing exerted her stocky round weight. Lifting her hoof and backing up, the latch popped open with a clean clip of metal pinging metal and the gate moved open an inch. Just as Olive promised it would when they conversed the last time she went for a midnight stroll!

Marshy nosed her way the rest of the way out and swung her head at the newfound freedom of escaping, and chased after her family herd of people!

The veggie garden however, drew her prompt attention.

That evening.

"Last chance," Minnow told Windy.

She sat on a stool they'd hauled together from Mom's shop with a mint-teal towel wrapping her shoulders.

Windy gave a decisive nod.

Minnow turned on the buzzer and brought it close to Windy' neck so she could feel the tickle of the buzzing, simultaneously lifting a handful of her hair. She shrank a little at the sensation, chuckling small.

"Minnow! Windy! What are doing?" Mom called wondering, from the back door.

"You didn't tell her!" shrieked Minnow.

Windy grimace-smiled, making an innocent noise.

Minnow was already in enough trouble as it was! At this rate, she'd be grounded for life!

"Nothing Mom!" shouted Windy, who sat in front of Minnow, blocked by Marshy, who stood alongside them both, ears pricked in interest at the buzzer sound. So, Mom didn't really have a clear view. But she had to be wondering what the electrical cord was doing plugged into the house and trailing outside.

Hence, her question?

Windy' suggestion to buzz her hair outdoors, where it was open and nice appealed to Minnow. It was the cooler part of the day, when the temperature dropped a degree, and two; the first gentle gust of the night whispered cool and caressing, alive in the trees, on her arms, around her legs, tickling her fuzzy head, and conversing with the marsh.

Now Minnow knew the real reason why the little skullduggery pirate mutineer she had for a little sister had wanted to go outside!

Minnow was grinding her teeth, controlling the impulse to give Windy the fuzzy look she was going for, but her hands were starting to feel like the more desirable tool.

"I can't watch this!" Mom told them. "I'm sure you'll look sweet my dear!" she said. "Din-din in half an hour!" With that, she closed the loud, rickety screen door.

Minnow froze, stunned.

Windy was chuckling and giggling bending forward and back.

Relief washed over her like cooling surf, and she gripped Windy' shoulder to still her firmly. "I'm going to give you a mohawk," Minnow told her sister.

Windy' green eyes bulged. "That's even better!"

Minnow rolled her eyes at the pale blue sky, and tilted her head at Marshy. "What are we going to do with her Marshy?" she asked smiling, and Marshy nickered over her shoulder with a mouthful of grass.

Minnow draped herself over Windy from behind in a close, warm hug. "I guess we'll have to keep her."

Epilogue

Tarantella Girl wound up in science class with Harry Macroscope again. Apparently, there was a magnetism there that couldn't be ignored, or shredded up for good after the breakup. One so gravitational that they shortly transcended the hurt of Carly breaking up with him to be back together with Matt, and Carly's bird-shot-down emotions over Matt choosing Minnow. She never thought it'd happen, but it had. Her own self-examination came as a surprise, mixed with much more confusing and conflicting ones about Minnow, Matt, and reflections of hers in the mirror.

She could only say she felt like and was a different person. Matt and Minnow's real relationship and pretend one that became real had taught her about the ramifications of playing with one's heart backfiring. And Harry, who had learned the downside and ruthless consequence of cockiness through all of this, was the one who started making her a better person. As she was the one who was making him one who was a better person as well. Harry picked her up, didn't mind the ruffled or singed arachnid hair, and she found she didn't want to be anywhere else but in his macro arms, good opinion, and listening to him describe science definitions. Both of which the descriptions and the sound of his voice pronouncing them made her melt and want to leap over the school library table or her tanks and kiss him passionately.

It was three days after Tizzy's tizzy-fit that revealed Minnow to the saltwater ponyboys when Minnow found a white shell on her front step. Inside were the sharpie words, *I'm sorry.*

Despite how Tizzy had wronged Minnow, and everything Tizzy had done in the past, Minnow smiled; and she hoped for the best for the girl who was apprehensive about getting a single grass stain or two day cold from pollen.

When school started at the beginning of September, Minnow had two classes with the twins. Izzy sat in the back as usual. Minnow sat in the row beside Tizzy two seats up. She passed another white seashell back to her via a kid, who almost bypassed Klepto Kevin. Kevin passed it to Tizzy though, who took it shyly, then studied it closely. On the outside, Minnow had painted the Empire State Building. When Tizzy looked up, Minnow smiled hoping it had reminded her of the city life. From the small smile of appreciation, and intrepid calm that fell over her with nodding understanding, it had, and she appreciated it. It became a normal thing for them to pass shells that they'd painted places or things or phrases on. Minnow did a joke once, like the book walks into a café jokes she and Matt did and have done since they were little kids. Tizzy painted a horse once, and a ponygirl's hat that resembled hers as best as Tizzy could wield the brush to imitate.

Izzy stopped going through the day with her eyes half closed, thanks to Tizzy's new interest, as Izzy had also found an interest as well in types of shells and the marine life that lived in them. It was the first thing that the twins discovered they enjoyed doing together, and their likeness suddenly expanded beyond their identical birthdate.

The slimy sea creatures that lived inside didn't gross Tizzy out either or send her into a Tizzy.

Also thanks to Tizzy, who had also discovered the peeking of a beginner's interest in the outdoors through this – or at least this part of it – and brought her quiet sister into the fold of her newfound passion – Mr. and Mrs. Plenty were finally happy, and couldn't feel more proud of their twin daughters!

Before, fear of outdoors and stemming deeper to fear of change, had been Tizzy's complete focus. Now? She breathed the sea air freely and with enjoyment, but still refilled her air purifier when she got home. There might be a green wave of tree pollen – you never know. Best to be prepared.

As Minnow mentioned, a work in progress.

She and Kleptomaniac Kevin were getting closer. Izzy was so interested in the world outside of her eyelids that she's absorbing life right now, and not love interests. But Minnow had a good feeling about all aspects of both their futures.

Summer and Coby were planning on throwing their wedding in March. Way before the season for kayaking started back up again.

As Minnow learned from Summer that night after the return swim, it was Marshy' squeaky whinny that had drawn her attention to Minnow. She recognized Marshy as she started to plunge in the water to encourage the herd on, or swim with them, or both. And then, apparently, there was no mistaking her little sister – atop Marshy, or any other horse. Summer had kept Minnow and Marshy' secret.

Mom and Dad were taking more time to spend with each other, handing more of the paddle over to Summer and Coby, as well as Windy, under their supervision, more and more every day. Windy had improved vastly, though she still threw out there a *walk the plank, Polly want a cracker,* every now and then. Her tooth still had that mysterious glint that mystified Minnow and made her blink twice. She'd never lose or surrender that pirate smile or her skullduggery heart. Minnow found, and knew always, she'd never want her to.

Family night was now three nights a week. Saturday, Monday, and Wednesday. Minnow was allowed to go to the beach again in the autumn, but she was still doing the laundry.

Soon it was a frozen wonderland of tree and roof icicles, frost glistening marsh, hard bootstep-hurt ground, and cold gusty wind snatching at you outside. Winter was another adventure. One that Marshy, Minnow, Matt, and everyone in and connected with *Our Happy Happy Happy!* tugged their toboggans on for, and dug out the bulky sweaters. Or if you were Matt, earmuffs – he preferred his favorite ballcap.

Olive's foal was born in the winter and Matt named him Firefly. After the lightning bugs that he and Minnow had first felt for each other; and counted, as the best of friends they were, in the backyards, the marsh, down the lane at night, and on spelunkers all their lives. They helped Olive through the birthing and watched Firefly take his first steps.

These were their roots. The island; the islanders – the saltwater – and the ponies. The come-here' and the ones born here. How Chincoteaguers pull together, without fail, every time there is hard pressure or need, is the whole reason the pony swim started, and why there is a pony swim to this day. As well as a Chincoteague.

Some people are defined by the island. Some people define it. In their own similar sense, they are both. They are island. Island, is them.

A Note to the Reader

This is Minnow and Marshy' story; first and foremost. There is an annual Pony Swim. Details have however been changed, left out, or invented to create Minnow and Marshy' adventure.

However, the kayak shop was real. And even though sold and torn down since awhile now; Adventure never ends – it is an ever-racing ocean, always beginning again, always there, ever in motion.

Our Happy Happy Happy! is wherever we make it.

Embrace the day!

About the Author

Starlight L. Cherrix grew up on Chincoteague Island. She was a kayak guide in her artist/poet father's kayak shop, who is also known on the island as "Captain Kayak".

Made in the USA
Columbia, SC
19 August 2018